ACKNOWLEDGEMENTS

Firstly, a massive thanks to Kat Harvey at Athena Copy for her invaluable editorial advice.

Very grateful to Michael Jamson for our deep, reflective conversations during a pandemic, which helped shape the book.

Huge thanks to my agent Craig Ryder, for his support and lasting friendship over the decades.

I am always eternally grateful for all the friends in my life, especially during the last two years. You all know who you are.

And last, but not least, thanks to Jorge Monedero, mi novio, for the love and support and for waltzing into my life at the right time.

We no longer need to fear arguments, confrontations or any kind of problems with ourselves or others. Even stars collide, and out of their crashing, new worlds are born.
Charlie Chaplin

MOONITE

Prologue

HISTORICAL ANNALS - FILE #377

The year is 2170, earth as home is no more. Caused by man...not woman, but man.

Humankind strives to maintain their existence by living on the moon. With 153 survivors, reproduction is paramount, but there are various issues with this.

...A nuclear holocaust didn't render earth homeless—like many thought it would—what brought on the demise of humankind was the lack of oxygen in the atmosphere.

Highly evolved machines were programmed to reverse the rapid acidification of the oceans caused by carbonisation of the atmosphere. A catalyst facilitated a rapid chemical reaction between the oceans and the atmosphere. The pH levels of the oceans were balanced and humans were relieved and pleased. Then people realised a quarter of the oxygen in the atmosphere got used up in the process. In 2170, a greater expanse got taken up by oceans than by land, so you can imagine the extent of the problem once people realised. Became too late to reverse the chemical reaction and people had to evacuate earth less they died from asphyxiation. Many did die...

...Alongside this main event, plastics and other harmful polymers also pitched in by screwing up the ecosystem, despite the invention of a new type of plastic called PBTL (poly bicyclic thiolactones) which could retain its properties when recycled. The drive to convert all plastics to PBTL lagged, and in turn this provoked the eradication of algae and other small chlorophyll organisms—their contribution to the 21% atmospheric oxygen had been underestimated by scientists. This, coupled with the oxygen sucked up in the chemical reaction to reverse the oceans acidification resulted in a climatic disaster.

As if this wasn't enough, the entire Amazon jungle withered away without any explanation. A proportion of well established trees uprooted and fell on their own accord. Numerous scientific experiments proved that trees communicated through a symbiotic relationship with their roots and mycorrhiza. Trees responded with defence strategies to diseases and pests, even with the outbreak on the periphery of the woodland miles away. Some scientists presumed that the trees recognised algae being threatened, but no one could confirm this, they just suspected a potential link.

This, coupled with the eradication of most of the insects due to intensive chemical farming, meant humans didn't stand a chance. As well as not having breathable air anymore, the temperature rose significantly due to global warming. Propositions and measures for decarbonisation in 2150 unfortunately failed, diabolical leadership foreshadowed transition engineering ever taking off. Then to top it all off, a catastrophic supervolcano erupted in South America, bellowing a dense smog that blocked out the sun, initiating arctic-like winter conditions. Spreading a global famine never before known and this initiated the displacement of the world's population. Earth collaborated with mother nature to purge the planet of humankind.

...Humankind spent years exploring the moon, finding ever more creative, cheap ways to colonise it. Humans, after all, had mastered colonisation through the centuries. It was during this time that moonite—an ore buried deep in the moon's regolith—was discovered. This mineral would prove to be invaluable.

Transportation to and from the moon became quicker and easier with the invention and installation of a lunar elevator. This elevator consisted of a cable stretching 250,000 miles, terminating just before earth's orbit.

The sun's energy—which beat down on the moon specifically in the poles, where nights only lasted four days as opposed to 15 days on most other positions of the moon — was harnessed. Sensibly, the first lunar station was constructed on the north pole.

The advancement in robots and 3D printing, meant colonising the planetoid came at a markedly lower price than originally forecasted by space economists...well, not taking into account the air being transported from earth over a couple of years and stored in sealed structures. Yes, space economists was the title back then, a course at higher schools of learning, solely focussed on this subject. Space science was another. The advancement in robot technology could have been achieved a lot earlier, were it not that humans decided to kill Alan Turing for being a homosexual; paying a price most humans are not even aware of and perhaps never will.

...Deep down, most people knew the world would be rendered uninhabitable, and the human race would have to vacate to another planet. But it was mostly women, non binary and gay men of all colours who took the lead on this. The white male system which had carved out the modus operandi in societies and cultures was about to collapse. Women of all races stepped up, tired to the core of a white patriarchy that influenced all systems around the world, with the undying determination to win at any and all costs, whilst others lost. Women knew there was another way, a win-win paradigm.

...The rise of robots and AI, and the loss of jobs as a result, displaced and caused profession-chaos. Women appeared to manage this drastic change better and a vast number went through university, specialising in space science and economics. Most women, gay men and non binary folk showed more empathy and appreciated kinship much more than some heterosexual white men did. Kinship and empathy were the few characteristics robots could not replicate.

...So, when the world finally got rendered uninhabitable, women were already in charge on the moon and developed a base by utilising power availability, communications and proximity to resources; mainly moonite, helium and water. Communication structures propped up on earth a long time ago in the hope of contacting extraterrestrials. This technology was easily transferred.

It turned out moonite produced more helium-3 and much more safely, than the radioactive decay of tritium. Helium-3 in turn, got extracted from the air and recycled. This gas, along with solar, posed as the primary source of energy on the base. Water—harnessed by the ice found in the north pole—was broken into hydrogen and oxygen, which formulated invaluable rocket fuel. Oxygen could also be chemically removed from the lunar soil, known to carry 42% oxygen. Robots perfected harnessing this life-essential gas by manipulating heat and electricity too.

...The development of specialised self cleaning toilets recycled human waste. Extracting additional clean water, (via increased condensation) and nutrients, meant they could grow crops in specially built greenhouses. These polymer glass structures could withstand the temperatures from the sun, which often went over 100 degrees Celsius. The central living quarters had its foundation built with 3D bricks, also derived from the lunar soil, and directly beneath the moon's exterior existed a link to lunar lava tubes, formed during the eruption of basaltic lava flows. These tubes acted as a sanctuary in case of severe solar radiation, micro meteorites or cruel surface temperatures, in case the electromagnetic protective shield malfunctioned.

Reflectors—built to divert the sun to giant solar panels and dotted around the colony— were activated when the heat became excessive. Energy conserved by the solar panels got harnessed for various things, which included running the automobiles referred to as 'mooncats' and keeping the colony warm at night when temperatures could plummet to -173 degrees Celsius. Energy was also utilised to power a security quarters buried deep in one of the craters where some white heterosexual men—outed for covert racism—resided as prisoners. These men scored the highest in the highly advanced unconscious bias test. They worked on refining helium-3 and moonite.

Like earth, the moon came with just as many environmental challenges; moonquakes and solar storms. Luckily, the quakes measured modestly on the richter scale, the solar storms though could be fatal, if not for the magnetic field engineered to be activated during a solar storm alert.

...Ironic—women taking charge in space—because space suits were originally designed for men. A whole new spacesuit design gave way, which studied the female form anthropometrically, physiologically, biomechanically and psychologically. This was carried out covertly back on earth, with no media coverage. Anthropometrics became a discipline heavily embarked on by women. This study enabled women to take into consideration circumferential measurements of areas like the chest, waist and hip. Measurements ignored in the then, 'mans' world when creating most industrial uniforms.

Straight men of colour expressed joy in teaming up with women of all races. Racism persisted in society, despite several outcries and demonstrations. If only society collectively defected to referring to racial colours as their true colours—white people presenting as pink and black people actually as brown—this may have resolved the mess with the various negative connotations around blackness. When earth became barren to human existence and women of all colours covertly took charge, men of colour and men from the LGBTQ+ community were clear which side they would be on. Privileged straight, so called white men, who failed the unconscious bias test, could experience a taste of their own medicine. Punishment for racism became more severe than ever before.

...A handful of white gay guys and some women also failed the test, but they were monitored on the base solely by people of colour. It was decided not to mix them as the straight white men in the caverns also failed the homophobic and sexism test.

CYNTHIA #324

...High tech synthetic androids, referred to as sexbots, satisfied sexual urges in both men and women. Even robots designed to cater for paedophiles were produced. Lucky for me.

One in nine girls and one in 53 boys under the age of 18 experienced sexual abuse or assault at the hands of an adult. Statistics presented back in 2021. I know for a fact those statistics are wrong, unequivocally worse for boys, more like one in ten boys.

Most men find it terribly difficult to open up about being sexually abused. And society's ill conceived shame, secrecy and taboo around the matter, ensured the issue stayed hidden.

...I did not want to reveal this, at least not so soon, but after my mention of Alan Turing, most of you might be wondering. I'm privy to knowledge outside of the normal realm, because I possess a rare gift, an ability people call "knowing," people called this ability "sixth-sense" a long time ago. I guess you could say I came out of the womb with it.

...Only the higher ranked straight women could have sex with a white straight male if they chose. With only four straight white men to go around on the base, an arrangement was made to have the prisoners occasionally to the surface. Mixing black and white was encouraged more, seen back then as the "dilution" of racism.

...People teased the pansexuals amongst the crew, telling them the sexbots were another addition to their range of sexual interests. Of course, the pansexuals ignored their remarks, far too intelligent and evolved to give the small minds a response.

Population, whilst being crucial to the survival of the human race, was also constrained due to the lack of resources on the moon and so higher ranked women could only bear one child. Black men ratio to women was low and with the four heterosexual white men hitched up already, a white heterosexual man from the caverns got escorted to the surface for sex and then returned. In some instances, sperm would be collected in a container, often the case where the woman had developed a strong attachment with her sexbot.

...To conceive though, statistics showed a lot more chances with courtship than without. Male sperm count declined markedly over the years, also as a result of the chemicals in plastics. A theory posited that space conditions were also detrimental to sperm.

...A lot to take in for an introduction I guess, even with my attempts at only including relevant snippets, but this is how humans existed on earth's satellite for a long, long time, with the intent to return when it became habitable again. Like most things in life though, this plan got sabotaged by the phenomenon called love.

I've documented events to cater for the possibility of an earth in a parallel universe or distant past getting access to it and learning from mistakes made. I *do* happen to know there *are* parallel universes, always have, part of my ability. Quantum physics got so close to proving this universal law, but of course the climatic emergency diverted the focus.

...A long shot I know, hoping that people figure out a way of travelling between dimensions and parallel universes, but always worth having hope, right?

1NE

A half naked white man of medium build and height manspreads on a bench, typing on a keypad. He appears in a trance, with a commercially handsome stubbled face, dark brown hair and a distinctive crease on his forehead, above the bridge of his nose. This crease makes him appear deep in thought, even when in a jovial and hearty mood. His dark grey eyes accentuate his stoic appearance, they look up to scan the area.

Terrain surrounded by extreme buzzing noises, reverberates all around him. Beads of sweat drip off the man's body—a sweaty glistening gym fit physique. He turns to speak to a colleague beside him, but not before staring at the outstretched, deep jagged cavity burrowed into the planetoids crater. Appearing as if inside the jaws of an enormous, grotesque entity, likened to a kind of stone god. The only thing softening this imaginary manifestation, is the presence of all man-made equipment scattered around the cavity floor and a line up of huge robotic arms. Breathable air is stale, lacking in oxygen and possesses a chemical tinge when inhaled. The floodlights are of economical intensity, the cavity harbouring shadows within shadows. The men are familiar with this, their eyes have been adjusted through biotechnology. On both sides of the entrenched cavern are two high tech atmospheric and ventilation systems powered by the excavated moonite. These complex units churn out oxygen and helium-3. Despite the size of the units, the only sound emitted is a faint hum which the men are also familiar with.

'What's up Tyler?' A man in yellow shorts interrupts the man in a trance. He's also of medium build, but a couple of inches shorter than Tyler. Short cropped blond hair seems to have been haphazardly placed on his head like a wig. Just the same, his distinctive facial features portray a stereotypical woman's man. Blue grey eyes, mimicking miniature versions of the milky way, help grab your attention when he's addressing you. Clean shaven, but with cuts here and there on his chin, plausible evidence of a shave having been executed in a hurry, with a blunt razor or the absence of shaving cream.

'Oh nothing, just hard to fathom sometimes that we've dug this cavern out.' Tyler mentions, still looking ahead at the magnanimous grotto in front of him.

'Well...with the help of robotic arms and machines.' The man wipes the sweat off his brow.

'Yes, I know Symon... you know what I mean.' Tyler snaps with a smirk.

'Hey, have you tried out the new CNT334 upgrade yet? Seriously! If you haven't, you should and quickly, because I'm telling you the reality and intensity is phenomenal. My balls hurt so much from cumming so hard.' Symon places his hands on his packed crotch.

'Jeez Symon, must be good if you're blurting out obscenities like that.'

'It is!' Symon continues to rub his crotch.

'Hmm apparently, not sure I'd want my balls hurting though, as you so bluntly put it.'

'Oh but it's so worth it, seriously I'll not be any kind of friend if I didn't let you in on this. You have to try it. I've never understood why you don't upgrade. Passed up on four upgrades so far. What's the deal? You fallen in love?'

'Very funny. Can't I just borrow yours?'

'Eughhhh, seriously, no you can't...honestly.' Symon takes his hand off his crotch.

Tyler laughs out loud. 'Ha, got ya.'

'Honestly, anyone would think you were a G-boy the way you carry on.'

'Asked you a million times not to refer to them as that, what is so wrong with saying gay?'

'Oh for meteor's sake, everyone calls them that, why are you so prudish about it?'

'Oh I don't know, because that's the kind of thinking and behaviour that got us in this messy darkened pit in the first place. Besides, don't you sometimes wish you were gay, so you could be up there with people on a proper base?'

'No not really, nothing is going to make me want to suck cock or have one up my arse.'

'Yeah, because sticking your dick in a synthetic robot is so much better.'

'What's wrong with you? Why you busting my drained balls over this?'

'Nothing, forget it, finish off the motorised sequence and let's get the hell out of here.'

'Excellent idea, I think the excessive helium 3 may have gotten to your head.'

'Or maybe just you.' Tyler mumbles to himself.

'What was that?'

'Nothing, c'mon finish that sequencing and let's go.'

'Okay, okay.' Symon types something on the keypad of a yellow robotic arm, causing it to pull up and fold to rest next to a range of other yellow robotic arms.

Tyler examines the enormous cavern they are in. 'Maybe doing late shifts is not such a great idea.'

Both men head towards an elevator located on the end of the line of robotic arms. They sense and have memorised the whereabouts in the cavern, rather than rely on their vision.

~~~~~~~~~~~~~~~~~~~~~~~~~~~~~~

Above the crater to the North Pole, is a base of astounding architectural design. Reinforced steel and glass in conjunction with compressed wood and mulched cardboard and paper put together in perfect harmony, allowing for a moonbase that would make moonbase alpha in the popular TV series Space 2099, a laughing stock. Light is filtered into each pod from the big reflectors, strategically placed around the circumference of the moon to optimise the sun rays. Light sent into the pods from the reflectors, also creates warmth thus managing the heating facilities at night. During the day the reflectors are turned around and are focussed on solar panels to generate electricity for the colony. The women work in pod sections of the base, some on computers, some in a laboratory and some in a greenhouse where vegetables are being grown. As far as the eye can see it is brightly lit. Noticeable at a stroke is the harmony, each person absorbed in their tasks with gusto and pride.

In the greenhouse, two ladies work side by side, replanting seedlings which have been germinated in specialised cardboard containers holding ceramic soil. Flashing fluorescent green light from alcohol powered beetlebots hover around the ladies. These beetlebots look like fireflies and are responsible for pollination and churning the soil. The only difference is these don't have as much precision to their flying, they are a little larger and hence a little clumsy.

'These seedlings seem to have taken off better this year.' A female in a green overall with a name tag spelling Belize says. She owns jet black plaited hair, silky smooth ebony skin and intensely expressive hazel eyes, eyes that pull you in whether you like it or not. Her lips would make Anigel Jalineo jealous. Anigel Jalineo was a movie star known for her thick, luscious lips.

'They have, haven't they?' The other woman agrees. She is also wearing green overalls, but owns auburn hair and a fair complexion. Her eyes are aquamarine blue, the kind you want to dive in; and she possesses lips which won't make Anigel Jalineo jealous. A small celtic looking tattoo covers her radial pulse on her right wrist. A name tag on her overall spells Agenta.

'Crazy really, to think we were making food out of thin air back on earth.'

'It is crazy. Perhaps we might figure out a way to do it with the atmospheric conditions of the moon, doubt it though.'

'If these beans and peas do well, we mightn't need to fertilise next year.' Belize wipes away a drop of condensed water which had freefallen onto her forehead mid sentence.

'Indeed, although we do have enough fertiliser now, enough of us making little brown fish.' Agenta says in a jocular voice and grimaces, while tilting her head to the side.

'Argh ha ha ha haha, I loved that series, the best black comedy ever!' Belize giggles into her hand.

Their jestful parlance is interrupted by a ping, as if from a giant tuning fork, followed by a voice transmitted over the intercom.

"Belize please report to sector G."

'Belize please, Belize please, Belize please —try saying that fast, almost a tongue twister.' Agenta chuckles. 'Funny isn't it?'

'Yeah, a real scream, taking the piss out of my name.' Belize gives Agenta a disapproving look, but a smile hides in the corners of her mouth. Agenta recognises it from the little crease at the side of her upper lip and the glint in her eyes.

"Belize please report to sector G."

'God I love the sound of his voice.' Agenta closes her eyes.

'The reason he got picked for the job, that and the fact he's gay.' Belize gives Agenta a coy look.

'I know, I know... a girl can fantasise.'

'You mean to say CK352 is not enough?'

'Well it is...of course it is, the voice though, they can never quite replicate that. It'll always have that electronic sound to it.'

'Maybe you should ask Carl to record the necessary words required for coitus. It may not sound exactly right, but with the right words, you never know.' Belize stands up.

'You think he'll do it?'

'I was kidding!' Belize fetches her space coat from a hanger.

'Oh.' Agenta arises, stretches, then places the plastic seedling container in a cupboard.

'You're so silly.' Belize gives Agenta a friendly slap on her shoulder.

'Yeah, I guess I am.' Agenta paces to the other side of the greenhouse to secure a door and traipses back to where Belize is standing.

'It's absurd how the Feldenkrais of the androids, they can master to a tee, but yet can't quite simulate the human voice without it sounding ... well, like a robot.' Belize says.

'Felden what?'

'Feldenkrais...big word for the process of awareness through movement, the gentle organised motions that enhance how someone moves.'

'I see.' Agenta pulls a silly face, brushing back a strand of hair which exposes grey roots.

'Ready?' Belize grins at Agenta, the deepening laughter lines the only sign of impending middle age.

'Yep.' Agenta fetches her space coat.

Both ladies side by side, approaching the exit to the greenhouse. Belize positions her arm around Agenta's shoulder as the electronic door picks up the signal from both their tags and slides open with a satisfying ping and suction sound, letting them exit in tandem.

2WO

A vacuumed glassed opal cavity, juts out of the control base, with huge cylindrical tubes feeding into the unit. The tubes are connected to a small power plant, situated in a small crater next to the control base. A deafening silence fills the vacuum, which would be unimaginable for the human mind, as the mind needs to filter out sound— a task it partly identifies with. Space may be the only place for people with dementia to settle, as their lost ability to filter out sound wouldn't be a handicap.

An AI version of velvet rope, by an iconic musician over a century ago called Janet Jackson, murmurs in the background of a contained living quarters. A person with a velvet robe can be seen prancing up and down; they speak fast while a woman types, trying to keep up with the words escaping from the non binary person's mouth. They sport a quiff of light brown hair which sits atop a baby face, comprising a distinctive small nose and small ears. Clean shaven with a small mole on the side of the upper lip, a beauty spot some call it, some going as far as to imprint a fake one with a make-up pencil. Eyes are big and baby blue like a cloudless sky in summer back on earth. They spin round to face the female typing, lifting their robe in theatrical fashion.

'And as I proclaim to bring us all together in humankind, let us not forget, cis men led us here, they caused this. Their time is over, it is no more a man's world.'

The woman stops typing and acknowledges the flamboyant person in a velvet robe.

'Do you think the peeress will like that bit?'

The person halts in their tracks and spins round to scrutinise the woman who's questioned them. She is five feet 11, about two metres, with copper-dyed, cropped hair which complements her chocolatey complexion.

'Okay Andrea... said this before, yes the women rule the roost, but here in my quarters I call the shots okay? I'm getting fed up with justifying my prose to you.'

'I'm merely giving you another view point, yes I'm here to type but I am allowed to question.' Andrea marks the flamboyant person with a stare, her sharp, light brown eyes burning through him. Her thin lips pressed tightly together and distinctive bushy eyebrows scrunch together. In a stealing glance, her eyebrows could be mistaken for a pair of alien caterpillars on her forehead.

The velvety person is about to retaliate when the intercom interrupts.

"Skyler please report to sector G, Skyler... to sector G."

'I guess we'll finish this another time.' Andrea relocates the laptop to a side table made out of aluminium and high grade plastic.

'Erm, yes please come back tomorrow, too late in the day now to finish, but it must be done for tomorrow.'

'Consider it done.' Andrea coyly lifts up off a modern Scandinavian looking sofa.

She prances to the electronic door, lifting up the badge attached to her collar adroitly, whilst adjusting her hair and trousers. Her right caterpillar eyebrow cocks upwards. The door slides open with a satisfying ping, and Andrea strides out. She takes a quick glance at Skyler seconds before the door seals shut. A neutral expression plastered across her face.

Skyler saunters to a corner of the room and turns round, lowering their body, and lifting their voluminous velvet gown at the same time. They throw back both arms in one swift motion, the whole movement replicating a ballet plie. The gown elegantly separates from the body and falls to the floor like a giant purple feather. A sculptured, hairy chest is revealed and they grab a shirt which they adorn, now standing up in a butch manner. Janet Jackson carries on serenading in the background.

3RE

Situated slightly off centre to the west of the moonbase is a dome, the size of most found in botanical gardens on earth. Dusty space debris floats and falls around the dome, mimicking a gigantic snow globe. Reinforced glass covers most of the area of each side of the dome. Inside, an elegant, sexy but studious woman can be seen sitting at a porcelain desk. Short cropped black hair, perfectly styled around her face; big pervading eyes, with irises the size of chocolate buttons and plump, luscious lips; all complimenting each other to engender a handsome face. She possesses a magnetic quality akin to a panther. Her height ensures you look up to her in case her title doesn't and when she walks she is always surefooted.

She types on a computer, which uses the old fashioned DOS system. The advanced computer system suffered too many viruses —but, even more concerning, the existential threat posed by most social media applications could not be overlooked any longer. Suicides skyrocketed in teenagers and society became polarised beyond recognition. In most countries, civil war started, having been brewing for a while. Facebook and Instagram exacerbated toxic cultural messaging to a profound degree and the social media giants ignored it. Putting down your phone did not come easy as putting down a magazine or turning off the television. A few social media giants reluctantly regulated—so the computer system got overhauled and people reverted to using DOS, a lot safer. Irony alert! People only just started the revolution before the ecological disaster struck.

It did take a whole new learning to master the procedure, but as mentioned before, determination by women ensured that in no time they'd mastered it— this expertise rendered others unable to compete, and they were at a complete loss when the computer system did finally come crashing down. Some people believed if not for the reverse revolution on the internet world, earth could have been rendered handicapped from internet wars between nations, long before the ecological disaster.

A satisfying ping comes over the intercom, impulsively causing the woman at the desk to look up. She peers through the reinforced glass window, admiring the celestial stony exterior. It always presented as sublime, and concocted a sense of nothingness, which always conjured up peace. Something about the contrast of tarry dark space and the silvery rocky moon surface always induced a sense of infinite calm in her.

"Belize and Skyler are making their way to you now mam, cleared through Sector G."

Adira reluctantly rises and struggles to tear her eyes away from her vista. She takes a deep breath and adjusts her trousers.

The room—which emerges as sterile, attributed to most of the furniture being a greyish white—contains a bookshelf with antique books, an office table, a lounge—unusually soft but robust—which curves perfectly to imitate the human posture and a round table, shaped like a portobello mushroom with five chairs around it, all mushroom white. The only items not dirty white are a small basic computer monitor on the table and a typing board. No pictures exist, hardly any wall space, predominantly reinforced glass with the outlook of the silvery celestial surface and dominating dark space.

She takes out a small picture from her right pocket and longingly admires it for a while, before putting it back in her left pocket. She alternates between pockets to give her some vague idea of how often she got the picture out. She ambles over to a mini bar and pours herself a small drink, she winces as she swallows and thinks to herself. "You would have thought the fermentation process would be perfect by now. I guess the moon's atmosphere is affecting it somehow."

A beep from the office table acquires her attention. She checks the screen and scrutinises a camera feed of the electronic door leading to her quarters. Skyler and Belize can be seen fidgeting outside. She presses a button which executes a bioscan of the two at the door; had read enough science fiction books about robots taking over to take any chances. She waits until she's absolutely sure no threat exists, then taps a button which releases the door.

Belize and Skyler walk in. Belize boasts confident steps to her stride while Skyler shows up a little more subdued, some would say gauche.

'Please sit.' Adira points to the available chairs.

Both Skyler and Belize pull out a chair from the table and sit down. Adira marches over to them.

'I would offer you both a drink but the batch is even more awful than the last time.'

They all laugh. Skyler relaxes a little. Adira sits down, facing both of them.

'I called you both here because we may have a little problem down in the cavern.'

CYNTHIA #325

Down in the cavern, music meanders through dark and dingy gangways, various men strum on guitars. Despite several guitars being strummed at the same time, the music manages to sound synchronised; as if the men have agreed to play in the same key. The ones having to listen to the cacophony must be delighted. Each man resides in their own little quarter in the cavern, though small quarters, they are cosy with built-in warm lights in the walls, they do not have much illumination though, merely for show or decor than practicality. A comfortable single bed, table and chair fill up most of the room and a section in-built into the wall, where the sexbots are kept, on charge, when not in use. No danger of the sexbot batteries overcharging and overheating, because they were seldom left on charge, as in, they were mostly put to use.

No bright lights by design, and no books at the men's disposal. This, the women made sure, to guarantee the men never got too smart. The men don't have name tags that activate doors like people have on the surface. They are expected to go into their quarters at the same time every evening, with the doors electronically locked behind them. It would not be in anyone's interest to be absent from their room before the time. Spending a night alone with machines in an echoey cave did not appeal and temperatures plummeted drastically.

The sexbots entice the men into their quarters with no reluctance or resistance. Most women always imagined men could be kept subservient, so long as they could get their 'end' away. Effortlessly achieved, thanks to sexbots continually being upgraded.

Before earth became uninhabitable, sexbots became popular, as people realised and accepted they sucked at maintaining long term, loving relationships. A sad but unfortunate fact. If people enjoyed great sex, or more to the point, if quality orgasms were achieved, then people were a lot more content, having close friends became sufficient. Never mind life coaching and the various counselling and self development sessions, if you were not getting laid, maintaining an inner calm proved difficult for most people, unless you were perhaps enlightened and did not depend on pleasures of the body.

The rise of Involuntary Celibates (incels) became a grave concern, especially as with it, came a rise in violence. Sexbots kept this in check, as anyone could have sex with a gorgeous, human-like looking android.

Great sex assured the men stayed hegemonized; sex coupled with food, and some routine, necessitated the unlikelihood of an uprising and this strategy had worked so far. For seven years since residing on the celestial space rock.

Along the corridor, which is roughly six feet wide and winds like a snake, are also in-built lights, even less bright than the ones in the rooms, and next to the lights are in-built infrared cameras. Despite the sexbots, women still needed some security, and having the in-built cameras in the corridors provided this. Most of the men forgot these cameras were in situ and some proposed they were fake and didn't have the resources up on the surface to maintain them, even if they were real. The men were right, the computer feed for the cameras showed fault after only the first year, and this was kept quiet.

Women were banned from the quarters, unless a medical emergency forced the issue, statistically rare—any fear of an outbreak of sexually transmitted disease (STD) eliminated, another welcoming reason to have the sexbots. On earth, STDs took a huge leap in resistance to antibiotics and so having sex with another human just didn't pay off. The advanced sexbots became a breakthrough and most people postulated that if developed earlier, earth may have been saved. Poor decision making, it turned out, culminated as a symptom of carrying an STD.

Satisfying orgasms, coupled with the eradication of STDs, induced calm and clarity of thought in people. Even paedophilia frustrations were eradicated, it would turn out that openly active paedophiles were the tip of the iceberg; many paedophile men lived in the shadows, repressing their urges, whilst pretending to live a normal life with a partner. These men often displayed aggressive behaviours but with the invention and advancement of sexbots, the aggression ceased. Children androids helped the paedophile men cater to their needs and even though viewed on by many as deprived, society accepted them, as it necessitated children's safety. Like I mentioned before, I for one am grateful.

Once society accepted this, domestic violence reduced dramatically. Theories sprung up, positing that sexual frustrations were alleviated in paedophiles who lived a pretentious life. No one knew for sure, as no one wanted to do research in this area, understandably so. So all in all, sexbots seemed to have made a massive difference to the human race.

No one would ever have fathomed the significance of human skin on skin contact though; android skin, despite the uncanny likeness didn't match up. It would turn out humans needed to be embraced by another human, and the more skin on skin contact the better. The importance of this was not realised for a long while yet, until again after the damage. Despite some glimpse of this during two pandemics. Mental health plummeted.

Nature cannot be cheated, sooner or later she wins. Cruel or deviant, slow and steady, she wins. Humans were only a very small part of the ecosystem, albeit their egos led them to believe they were mini gods.

The men took to having a hug in the shower and this—without them knowing—fulfilled an in-built biological need to have skin on skin contact and it kept them sane.

Sometimes fights broke out in the cavern, but even this was easily diffused, because when brought to the attention of the women, the sexbots were deactivated for the night. The men would be beside themselves and found it unbearable. The androids were all they had to satisfy their addictive personalities.

Some men suspected it may not only be the sexbots keeping them calm but that some kind of sedative added to the water induced the placid state. No one could prove this theory though.

Tyler accepted this theory and divulged with others, causing an internal stir within the cavern. He had been one of the men strumming on his guitar in the passageway. Each quarter owned a seat outside where they could sit and play an instrument or play chess together. This, the women authorised, as they felt it necessary the men engaged in a mind stimulating game.

Now for anyone reading this, you might be wondering how this made any sense, as chess is one of the most intelligent games there is, and you would be right to think that. The women argued it was merely to give the men focus, distract them, or perhaps more succinctly, help them manage their boredom. Utilising your brain and acquiring knowledge were two different things. The overriding reason for the introduction of chess is that it was the selection process for procreation. A fingerprint ID system on the chess board meant people with the most winning streaks were identified and put together in a computerised system. The man picked got announced over the intercom and arrangements made for both to unite and have sex. The lucky man got taken up to the top as the women felt it would be more conducive having sex in a more habitable and 'softer' environment.

Now, why didn't the white women just have sex with the men of colour, I hear some of you ask. This certainly raised some contention on the base for a while. Particularly since it resolved the issue of having a white baby boy. Wise counsel argued that if done, then white people would eventually be screened out, a much more dramatic suppression of a race. Having mixed race babies introduced some kind of a balance. People of colour wholly understood the sentiment.

Preparation for intercourse involved full health screening, this cinched the eradication of any STDs. This included the gays and bisexuals, more prevalent on the surface. Gay and bisexual sex became the norm, taking second place to sex with the sexbots of course, a stark contrast back on earth. Both men and women enjoyed same sex with real people and their sexbots. Heterosexual men carried no animosity to gay men as such, their resentment brewed around them being allowed on the surface with the women, whilst *they* were not. This fuelled their resentment towards the gay men. They couldn't give two hoots about gay sex, not anymore, why—they had accepted paedophilia with sexbots, largely to ensure childrens safety. The paedophile men in the caverns were accepted, so long as they refrained from talking about their experiences with their children androids.

All the men enjoyed their nude hugs in the shower, even the peeds, none of them analysed this, merely put down to a thing they did as part of their shower ritual. Rituals were needed, routine and rituals were required, to maintain your sanity cooped up in the caverns. Neither of them identified as gay—the reason for being in the moon pit, that and the fact they where white— so there was no riddled shame from enjoying a hug. Little did they know it fulfilled a higher need in them.

Anyway, best return to the story.

~~~~~~~~~~~~~~~~~~~~~~~~~~~~~

Tyler strummed his guitar and continued to do so even after hearing the unmistaken footsteps of Symon approaching. Unsure if this new ability would have been possible were he in a more stimulating environment. Could it have been harnessed from being stuck in the cavern, allowing for him to recognise his mate's footsteps resounding in a stony corridor of echoes?

'You just can't keep away from me can you?' Tyler remarks without looking up.

Symon replies. 'Don't flatter yourself.'

Tyler continues strumming and still not looking up, he says, 'Please don't tell me your CNT's malfunctioned again.'

'Lol, no, my sex companion is fine, thanks for your concern. I hear someone up there has taken an interest in you…over your theory of the sedative in our water supply.'

Tyler quits strumming.

~~~~~~~~~~~~~~~~~~~~~~~~~~~~~

'Someone down in the caverns may be privy to the sedative.' Adira chooses her words carefully.

'Oh… do we know who?' Skyler picks at their right index finger.

'We might do, but we need to make sure, that's where you come in.' Adira focuses on Skyler.

'Oh… what do you mean?'

'I need you to infiltrate.'

'Oh, c'mon, I'll stick out like a sore thumb.'

'Well in your case, a sore pinkie.' Belize teases.

'Oh well, then I rest my case.' Skyler pouts.

'Oh don't be silly, Belize is only kidding, you're both camp and butch, and besides we're almost in the 22nd century, no one does that kind of stereotyping anymore.'

'I guess my saying no would be ignored?' Skyler checks.

'Yes it would…listen it would be easy, you may not have to stay long, as I said, we already have our suspicions, so you'll only need to hang around him and see if he blurts it out. Cameras will be on you the whole time… as a straight white *man*, I hasten to add.' Adira never ever had a chance to see camera footage and then the system broke down and could not be repaired. She's now used to lying about it.

'And where do I come in?' Belize turns to face Adira.

'I'll need you to put the sedative in some batch of food. I get the compound's supposed to work better in water, but it's only for a short while.'

'Oh okay.'

'The substance is still odourless and tasteless right?'

'Yes it is.'

'Then they shouldn't be able to notice the difference?'

'No they won't.'

'Okay then.' Adira arises in slow motion, her every movement invoking a grace similar to that of a black swan.

Both Belize and Skyler stand, Skyler doing so clumsily in comparison.

'Report to the security sector...both of you, you'll both be briefed once you arrive. This is confidential, no one is to know, understood?' Adira commands with a raised eyebrow.

'Understood.' Both Belize and Skyler say in unison. Both turn to the door and move towards it.

'Of course don't forget to adjust your eyes.' Adira faces the two obedient people leaving her quarters.

'Of course, looking forward to it...not.' Skyler mutters the last word under their breath.

~~~~~~~~~~~~~~~~~~~~~~~~~~~~~~~

Tyler tosses and turns in his bed. Try as he might, he can't fall asleep—a lost battle—*because* he was trying. The discussion with Symon the day before played on his mind. How did someone find out about his theory on sedatives in their water supply? A possible spy amongst them? Mostly surmising? He tried to refrain from drinking water and sensed a difference in his mood. A difficult one because dehydration caused a change in mood too. Having always possessed an intuitive body, his biochemistry sensed when something was out of alignment. He reckoned everyone probably possessed this intuition, but not everyone paid it attention. His body always communicated to him when something was off, way before he fell ill. Tyler suspected something put either in their food or water, because they all seemed so genial all the time. It just wasn't feasible for men to remain so calm and relaxed all the time, even *with* their sexbots; he never bought it.

Refraining from drinking water proved difficult, as the only alternative was some god-awful fermented fruit juice, not even sure what fruit had been squashed to make the stuff. In two days, he could tell his mood had changed, drinking little juice and no water at all. Frustration and irritability set in. He suspected dehydration, but never one to be capricious, thought this was different. He found his moods changing erratically, and became aware that this part of him—the subtle angst—was indeed the more authentic side to him. Not easy at all, going without water for any length of time.

He recalled reading a mystery thriller book about someone in a local vegan commune being poisoned to death. The twist is revealed in the last chapter, as the poison originated from courgettes. It transpired that this versatile vegetable produced a chemical called Cucurbitacin E when the plant was water-stressed. This bitter chemical had been deftly masked in cooking, with spices and herbs, and all else failing, a pinch of sugar thrown in. The murderer took his time to cultivate the crop and then in time introduced a new vegetarian cuisine. A new chemical at the time, unbeknownst to doctors, and so forensics initially overlooked it—the killer almost getting away with his sinister calculated act.

A small book, written in a clear minimalist style, using few appropriate words to construct short sentences that delivered punch. He remembered it being a gripping read, with a writing style he thoroughly enjoyed.

Whatever the chemical additions to their water supply, the dosage had to be well calculated. Probably an astute chemist up on the exterior, playing with flasks and tubes like prized possessions.

4UR

Symon and Tyler sit in the diner which is basic, cold and plasticky. They converse quietly, conscious of people eavesdropping.

'We have a new inmate, apparently he faked being gay.' Symon shares with his buddy, scanning around to check nobody's listening.

'Interesting, we don't have many of those.' Tyler replies.

'Nope we don't.'

'Where's he sat? Which one is he?'

Symon surveys the canteen and spots the guy sitting on his own at the end of a long lightweight dining table. All the furniture are made out of light materials for two reasons—easy to transport, but more importantly, less likely to be used as a weapon.

'I think he's the guy sitting on his own, far corner over to the left of you.'

Tyler surreptitiously glances in the area, but fails miserably as a few men on the table next to them turn to notice him, and then in the vicinity where the man sits alone.

'Okay great, now everyone knows what we're talking about.' Symon mutters.

'That could easily have been either of us.' Tyler grunts.

'Except it wasn't, it was definitely you.' Symon grunts back. 'If he was faking it, he must be very good, cause he looks like a G-boy to me.'

'Seriously, why Symon, why do you persist in being a complete dick!'

'Oh for meteor's sake, how many times, I don't mean anything by it.'

'And people are supposed to know that, how exactly...telepathy? Cause it sure won't be your charming character which leads them to that conclusion.'

'Okay, okay, sorry, Jeez.'

Tyler rushes his meal and gets up.

'I'm going back to the quarters.'

'Okay, don't you want to hang out, like we said?'

'Maybe later, need a lie down; the air in here makes me quite lethargic.'

Tyler lies through his teeth. The truth is recently, hanging out with Symon seems to annoy him more and more, and he resented continuously pulling him up about his prejudiced ways. Symon showed his loyalty to him as a friend and would want to help him with most things, but he didn't enjoy being around him for too long, and he didn't see why he had to put up with it. He could try to make another friend in the quarters, unlikely to happen though if he stayed joined at the hip with Symon. So he made an informed decision to spend less time with him. Back on earth, he may have put in the energy to address his behaviour and even coach him as he enjoyed life coaching as a side profession. Here on the moon, he had just as much desire to coach, as he did for small chit chat, zero.

In the distance, the AI version of the song "To the moon and back," originally sung by a band called Savage Garden echoes. He's lifted by an involuntary grin. He's always loved this song and always thought it timeless. Never would he have thought in a thousand years he'd be listening and appreciating it on the moon, sung by AI.

'Okay see you later in the evening.' Symon sulks.

'Yeah definitely.' Tyler means it; notwithstanding his irritating ways, he's the one friend he's got in the belly of the moon.

He marches off, leaving Symon with a glum look on his face. He steers towards the new fellow, needs to take a good look. On approaching, a strange sensation lurks in his lower abdomen. It reminds him of the sensation he endured when he ate fiery foods. He loved chilli hot foods but his stomach didn't, always making him stay extra minutes on the loo. Food with chilli in was never served, too much energy needed to secure the high temperatures for the long periods needed for chilli growth.

The new guy is bent over with his head lowered, unaware his long fringe is dipping into the potato, bean and leek broth contained in a tin bowl before him, a specialty soup prepared every Wednesday. The few guys sitting a couple of feet away from the new fellow on the same table, stare, as if looking at a leper.

Tyler makes a rushed decision to sit next to the awkward looking fellow. He's a little sorry for the person and thinks to himself this might be the opportunity he's been looking for to make new friends. He perches down opposite and then shuffles closer. Skyler lifts their head up from shadowing their broth.

5VE

Red flashing light with a muffled beeping sound renders through deserted passageways. This siren is activated when space debris is too close. When this occurs—which is not that frequent anymore—an electromagnetic shield is activated and the colonists are instructed to go to their glassless bunkers. People are so used to it now and are almost complacent; although they do go to their bunks promptly, it's never in fear of their lives anymore. All in autopilot, they amble along in limbo, some thrilled to have the break in their bunks and others vexed on having to leave their tasks, which is of great solace to them. Chilling and doing nothing seemed to be even more of an issue with people's mental health on the moon. Mastering boredom had still not been achieved, most not realising that transcendent freedom lay, just on the other side.

Agenta is lying down in her bunk which is decorated in a light shade of green wallpaper. She is reading a book entitled 'Sex and AI' She turns the pages delicately, ensuring not to crease them, and now and then glimpses at the compartment to a side of the wall where her sexbot is kept. The book she is reading is about a sexbot that develops feelings for the human owner, and then the whole story goes all Fatal Attraction, a remake done in 2026. Only this time with a deranged android to replace the obsessed psychotic character. Agenta begins to wonder if choosing this book to read was a grave mistake, her nerves are fried. She closes the book and flings it across a table, which it hits, then tumbles down to the back of the plastic-looking furniture. She's not sure she wants something...anything, putting her off having sex with her sexbot, would rather reconcile by using the mute function more often.

Restlessness consumes her, and she tosses and turns in her bed, like stranded fish on a shore. She contemplates whether to contact Belize, as she wants to ask her something important, but she's not sure how Belize will take it. She decides to get up and walk to her only window, a false window, as it doesn't link to the outside. A screen made to look like a window and programmed with three videos of different landscapes in different seasons. She reaches for a remote control, taps a button and a small white dot appears in the centre of the screen for a second too long, like a DLP white dot syndrome. Then a few more seconds a transmission comes alive with a scene of a lake and mountains in the distance. The lake shimmers golden yellow with reflections from an afternoon sun and trees surrounding the lake sway in a summer breeze. Agenta lowers herself into a lounge by her fake window and immerses herself in the projected serene landscape.

The three images were tailored to Agenta's biometrics. Infotech and Biotech advanced immensely before the ecological cataclysm. Most technological inventions could be tailored to each individual, wielding acute biometrics.

Agenta types in a code into a health application on her electronic tablet and waits for results, praying it wouldn't be a serious diagnosis. She'd been making friends with a dull ache in her stomach, the way humans put up with long lasting ailments, often underestimating and under appreciating their resilience to life's challenges.

Another development before the ecological disaster, were doctors losing their jobs, as most diagnosis could be done wielding biometrics. Perhaps predictably, hypochondriacs evolved on a whole new level. So many existed with this neurotic behaviour, that the term 'hypochondriac' got dropped and the synonym 'Valetudinarian' used instead.

Agenta hears a ping and turns her head to look at the tablet, out of the corner of her eye is a red blot in the chart. She's cognizant of these minor occurrences never being great news. This may well be confirmed, and she would be compelled to tell Belize without any delay. She turns to her tablet again and this time taps the music library. The tablet immediately identifies her mood via biometrics and selects the best song for her to listen to, enabling her to process her emotions in a healthy way.

Cultivating friendly bacteria took up a huge part of Belize's and Agenta's work. The recognition of bacteria's importance for the survival of humans, only being truly realised when humans left earth. In the short time they'd resided on the moon, it became apparent they could not survive for long without the symbiotic relationship with bacteria.

Agenta inspects the chart and is faced with her fears. Her cells were multiplying at an alarming rate and spreading, and spreading fast. Her sexbot had alerted her to this a lot earlier on, but she chose to ignore it. Another advantage of skin on fake-skin contact with the androids; whilst caressing, the human body's biochemistry was scrutinised and any anomaly identified; areas of erratic cell growth for instance, could be traced early. Agenta had chosen not to inform the authorities of the discovery.

~~~~~~~~~~~~~~~~~~~~~~~~~~~~

Tyler strolls through the cold reflective barracks, reminiscing over the discussion with Skyler. Seemed a genial fellow, quietly confident and sensitive in equal measure. Still, he questioned what to make of them in terms of authenticity, something superficial about them and he wondered why the tonne of questions. Either way he looked forward to seeing Skyler again, needing the distraction to reduce his encounters with Symon.

He also chose to visit another guy called Matt who he had been avoiding recently. Matt was one of those poor fellows who'd be sure to curse and grumble in an economy class airline and probably carries a permanent bump on his head from incessantly hitting it above door frames. Tyler could imagine Matt was the kind of guy to have had jars of out-of-date food at the back of his fridge when back on earth; the kind of guy who would have seen any type of organisation as a complete waste of time.

Tyler taps the cell door and is ushered in by a disgruntled voice. He enters just as Matt is turning over in his bed. For a second, Tyler thinks he might have interrupted some quality time Matt was having with his CNT334, but it's worse than that. Judging from the look on Matt's face and the stench in the room, it was a good bet he had just woken himself up with his own redolent flatulence.

'Hello.' The lanky man mutters, screwing his face in part shock and part embarrassment at the malodorous smell inhabiting his cell.

'You okay Matt?' Tyler questions, feeling his embarrassment; but then in the next breath, decides to shatter the discomfort, or in this case, downright kill the really smelly elephant in the room.

'For meteor's sake, maybe you shouldn't have eaten all those beans at dinner time.'

'I'm so sorry, really bad huh... give me a few minutes and I'll come join you at the foyer.'

Both men laugh out loud.

Tyler gladly steps out into the corridor; pinching his nose, he heads towards the Foyer. The foyer is what everyone calls the wide-ranging balcony which overhangs the mine. Nothing but dark shadows and scattered sensor lights fill the vision of anyone standing and looking down into the foreboding cavern. He traipses along and thinks of a chess move in a game now entering its fourth day.

Stockfish 8 proved to be challenging, a chess program reinvented even though Google's Alpha zero program had defeated it. When the alpha zero program first got introduced it took a mere four hours to learn chess from scratch and beat Stockfish 8. Still, the women were obstinate in downloading Stockfish 8, to give the men some chance at winning a chess game lest they commit suicide in droves due to tarnished ego's. Competition and conquest were after all hardwired in white men especially.

6IX

Skyler prowls around, then halts when they spot Tyler tapping on the cell door of another inmate. They dash behind a pillar, hoping Tyler did not spot them. Quite certain Tyler is the one the peeress thinks of, for one thing he seems smarter than the rest of the inmates seen so far.

Standing as still as a statue behind the pillar, they listen attentively. Easy to do as a result of their retinas being adjusted. Biological ingenuity—that when either of the sensory organs of the human body got altered, then others compensated, becoming sharpened. Tyler walks away after a few minutes, pinching his nose and shaking his head. Skyler cannot see the faces clearly, but can imagine their faces portraying disgust. They pluck up the courage to follow him as cautiously as they can manage. Memories of wildlife programs titillate their hippocampus— a predator stalking its prey.

They search around to spot the infrared cameras installed, ensuring they are in the angle of view, even though the camera's installed are equipped with a wide field of view, they don't want to take any chances. The tracker transplanted when their eyes were corrected, helps with added reassurance. They follow until coming to a prodigious rail barricading a kind of foyer, overlooking a darkened cavern below. Every few metres there are gaps in the rail, to allow for the transportation of moonite on motorised carousels to the upper levels.

Tyler stops, holds the rail and gazes down. From what Skyler can make out—observing the side of him—a well matured stoic expression resides comfortably on his face, as he fidgets with his trouser pocket and then contemplates his surroundings. Another man joins him at the rail and they both chuckle, like naughty kids at the back of a classroom.

Skyler intentionally creeps in and merges with the shadows, then realises the pointlessness of the act; they would be spotted regardless. Eyes were adjusted to enable them vision in the dark, but so had the rest of the inmates. This saves on electricity, but primarily if an inmate were to escape, they would be blinded by the bright lights on the moon's surface. They would not be able to function for a while and this would assist with their capture.

Skyler remembers the biotech enhancement on vision a bit too late. Tyler has begun turning around in their direction. They would no doubt be spotted, and there would be no explanation. It would be blatantly obvious they were

31

spying on them and the whole infiltration operation would be over before it began. The peeress would be vexed beyond reason and they pondered on the consequences. They dash to the right, they dither, now disorientated, looking for a place to hide. Skyler is unaware of the gaps in the rail, places a foot wrong, realises and tries to compensate for his now disturbed balance, but loses their footing. Before full comprehension of what's going on; the ground rushes at them, as they plummet the height of one of the greenhouse structures to the ground.

~~~~~~~~~~~~~~~~~~~~~~~~~~~~

Adira rests on a small white corner sofa and plays with her satin robe against her leg while drinking a dark liquor. She waits for results to display on her laptop, which is adeptly balanced on her lap. A ping alerts her and she inspects the visual display unit and grimaces. In ovulation, sperm is needed in order to conceive. She would rather be inseminated, but she also believes fervently that a child's well being is enhanced if conceived through sexual intercourse, she believes sex between two humans is sacred, and even though the orgasms were no match with the sexbots; the unification of two humans in this act, followed by the adjoining of reproductive fluids, gave the child more of a chance at a healthy well being. No biological research backed this theory, all the same she believed it. Some things in life, proven or not, you believe in your gut and go with it.

Time to make her selection. She taps the screen on her laptop and a voice comes through.

'Yes mam.'

'Send me the consolidated chess results.'

'Yes mam.'

~~~~~~~~~~~~~~~~~~~~~~~~~~~~

Agenta strides down the ambiently, orangey lit corridor, mindful of every step, she clutches onto the courage she mustered up when in her bedsit. Carefully selected music can help with any emotion you wish to enhance, and since logarithms influenced all choices for humans, music picked for you through the application of biometrics reached a new level.

She halts outside Belize's room and takes a deep breath. She couldn't be too sure how Belize would react, she may be livid she had kept this secret to herself all this time, but she also knew eventually she would be pleased she confided in her. She taps on the door lightly.

'Come in!...Then again do you really want to come in? That knock was pretty pathetic.' Belize bellows from her bedsit.

The door slides open.

'Hi Belize, it's me, Agenta.'

'Are you okay.' Belize turns around from her ipad with concern, she remains seated.

'Yes, I'm fine, well not all that fine.' Agenta steps in timidly as the door slides shut behind her.

She turns sheepishly and stares at Belize.

'Well c'mon spit it out, whatever it is can't be that bad...can it?'

'I have cancer in its advanced stage.'

'Oh...How come advanced?'

'Because I ignored it...'

'Agenta!—'

'—I know, I know, but we all know here on this space rock, better notice is given to the fittest.'

'You're aware we pride ourselves on advanced biotechnology that could halt cell multiplication in its tracks, why would you keep this to yourself—'

'—I'd hoped positive thinking would stop the cell multiplication in its tracks, okay... I was wrong.' Agenta plonks herself down on a small quartz armchair next to her and places her head in her lap.

Belize positions her arm around her.

'Where is it?'

'In my abdomen.'

'Okay should we go now and get you on the table.'

'Yep, might as well check how much damage has been caused.' Agenta lifts her head from her lap and gingerly releases herself from Belize's arm and stands erect.

'Would you like a drink of water before we go.' Belize gets up.

'Yes please.'

Belize traipses over to a faucet situated in a small compact kitchen consisting of a sink, small microwave and a couple of cupboards. A small Cactus plant rests proudly in a grey pot next to the microwave. The pot matches the grey, black and white decor throughout the bedsit. In the corner is a sturdy pull out bed that can be flipped over and used as a table. By the bed is a sizable window which automatically projects live images of various locations in the world, depending on the mood of the occupant. In the other corner is a compact wash and toilet system. Everyone is required to dry wash with newly advanced gels, developed to react with air to initiate cleaning. Once a fortnight, people can use communal showers provided, but the shower is timed. This arrangement turned out to be better for their skin as people soon realised. She collects water into a beaker and hands it to Agenta.

'Ready?' Belize inspects the cactus plant.

'Yes thanks.' Agenta gulps down the liquid and hands back the beaker.

'Okay let's go, should be okay.' Belize places the beaker back next to the sink.

7EN

Muffled voices in amongst dull humming from high-performance machinery, reverberate. For a moment, Skyler cannot feel any part of their body, but then senses tingling in their legs, top half at least. They attempt to move their face, but can't, the pavement and their cheek are like one, as though attempting to lift the pavement and not their face. Out of nowhere, an unimaginable affliction splices through their cerebrum. They attempt to meditate through the freshly revealed excruciating pain, a get-out card in situations like this. They direct their attention on breathing.

During the descent, Skyler endured keeping silent, for fear of bringing premature attention; discovered it extremely arduous to refrain from screaming when plummeting to your potential death. Your body and all its functions take on a will of their own when threatened, but somehow, Skyler suppressed their urge to let out a primal scream. Now doubting the ability to speak, and not willing to try because of the pain. They could not move their face, and their nose picked up traces of what they could only describe as a sweet metallic aroma, close to the smell of mercury. It felt like their face was fused in melted plastic as they tried again to move it, to give their mouth some room to call out for help; eventually they gave up. The left side of their face gripped the floor, either that or all their energy dissipated from the impact. How long had they been unconscious on the floor to give their blood time to congeal?

Skyler chooses to disappear into meditating for the time being, no other choice. They take in slow breaths while counting each duration of inhale and exhale. Recalls a famous program when on earth, called Insight Timer, it possessed various meditations to choose from and they delightedly remembered a particular program loved because of the guy's voice; deep, hypnotising and calming. The problem with relaxation was your whole body follows suit, and on a couple of occasions they couldn't help but let one off when nearing the end of the meditation. Lying as still as a door stopper they recalled the voice of the man in the meditation program.

"...*Your meditation is about to end, but you may continue for as long as you want after the chime. Concentrate on your breathing, and when you decide to open your eyes, take in the colours, the surrounding sounds, the aroma...*"

On occasions, this thought came to mind - " they could take in the aroma all right, about to suffocate on the stench of their own fart. How could they pay attention to their breathing, when they could hardly breathe?"

Their mind informs them that they must be smiling. Intuition their mouth is stretched into a smile by the pool of sticky haemoglobin goo, akin to the joker's mouth in the persistent franchise of batman movies. Doubts very strongly, they possess the ability to move their mouth to form a smile. All the same, they feel calm, the meditation relieves the excruciating pain. In spite of lying in congealed blood, their faculties are still about them and so it couldn't be that bad.

Meditation became a big deal when on earth. Most people practised and it became inset as part of most people's routine, like brushing your teeth in the morning or your first toilet relief. They supposed though, not enough people practised it, because how else did the human race remain stupid, stupid enough to destroy their own planet, their own home. The shortsightedness of the human race would always baffle and anger them in equal measure.

They continue to monitor their breathing as a thought pops into their head. Tyler and the other man can't have spotted him, otherwise they would not be lying on the floor for this long. This cheered them up, the infiltration operation had not failed. Skyler manages to move a hand and uses it to pull congealed blood away from their mouth, enough to open his mouth properly. If and when rescued, they would be peeled off the floor. Just about to cry for help, when they overhear a couple of people contemplating if what they were looking at was a human lying on the floor. The voices highlight an urgency in their tone and become more and more audible.

The pain in his head and face sharpen, as if holding off provisionally to give Skyler some respite. They lie as still as a statue, which they recognised as being silly, as they wanted to reassure potential rescuers they were alive, but they felt if they moved any muscle of their body, the pain felt would pierce through their head and consume them. Did not want to find out what that experience would be like, so they lay as still as death, as the echoey sound of footsteps resound closer and closer.

8HT

Belize and Agenta occupy the biometrics room, Agenta lies on a soft padded table and Belize operates the AI. The biometrics table can diagnose any ailment in the human body to a 100% accuracy. All you needed to do was press the start scan button and after less than 20 minutes a scan report showed up on the monitor which automatically got sent to your phone or tablet. Doctors were made redundant on earth, with the exception of surgeons. Nurses however, remained irreplaceable, still needed to care for patients after their diagnosis and during treatment. You not only got your diagnosis, but a complete program of treatment and duration of treatment. The human 'caring' touch couldn't be replicated in androids.

Agenta fidgets a little on the table.

'Could you remain still for meteor's sake.'

'I'm freezing, they could at least come up with something that warms up the table.'

Belize chooses not to flatter Agenta with a reply. Rather, peers at her with eyes the same temperature as the table.

The scan is halfway through and Belize pays attention to the image on the screen. In the reproduction, a pulsating red dot flashes near the stomach, and the organ in question is isolated and blown up on another screen with information on what is wrong— Agenta's spleen.

'What is it then, is it bad? Can it be fixed?'

Belize continues to scrutinise the image.

'Aww, that bad huh, guess I deserve it for being such chicken shit.'

Belize moves in closer to the new picture thrown on the display, pointers are highlighted on the image and a full diagnosis and treatment report begins. Before doing this, she had scanned over Agenta's upper abdomen and was sure she saw an embryo. She didn't hold the scanner long enough in that position for the computer to initiate a report. She didn't want it to be true for many reasons. If Agenta was pregnant, she would be convicted of a capital offence. Only two women so far had fallen pregnant. The colony agreed that both involved would be punished similarly. In one scenario, the woman disclosed being raped. The culprit had been flung out into space and the child aborted.

Belize dreaded what punishment would be bestowed on Agenta—and though hurt by the possibility of Agenta having slept with someone else—She did not wish her to be punished, there would be an explanation, and she had to be patient and wait.

Agenta lies as still as an iceberg and closes her eyes, unaware of the discovery by Belize.

Belize checks the other screen and licks and tenderly bites her lip as she does so.

'How long have I got?'

'Will you shut up for a second.' Belize continues to scrutinise the display as the scan nears completion. No further diagnosis report other than for her abdomen.

Agenta closes her eyes again.

'You're going to need a splenectomy.'

'A what?'

'Your spleen has to be removed.'

'Okay...Is that bad?'

'Your immune system will be compromised, but there are things you can do to help with that and infection control on this rock is pretty good. So not all bad really. Besides, you're protected by the ancient celts right?' Belize turns round, places Agenta's right hand in hers and grins. She admires the celtic tattoo on Agenta's wrist for a brief moment. 'You'll have to go in for keyhole surgery asap though, so best get you prepared.'

Agenta turns to her side and then lifts herself up from the table. Ever since practising yoga she's gotten herself off the floor this way. It made perfect sense and she can't think how or why she would pick herself up off the floor in any other way.

'You will have to go into the other chamber and lie on another table, and yes that table will be cold too.'

'Okay.' In moments like these, Agenta conserves energy with one word answers.

'I'll not be able to come in with you, but everything will be fine. I was on the panel that signed these AI operating tables off, completely fool-proof.' Belize takes Agenta's hand again and holds it tenderly.

'Okay.'

'It should take no more than an hour and a half.'

'Okay.'

'Toilet and something to drink beforehand?'
'Okay.'
Belize tugs gently at Agenta's hand.
'Come here.' She lifts her face up to hers and plants a tender kiss on her lips and hugs her.
'You'll be okay.'
'Th... thanks for being there for me Belize.'
'Where else would I be silly.' Belize swallows hard on congealed hurt surging into her throat.

This time Agenta grins, then meanders to the other chamber which is also dimly lit and sterile looking. She takes long steady breaths.

Suddenly an alarm makes both ladies jump and on CCTV footage above the table, a man can be seen being rushed through a corridor, his face all bloody.

'They'll be needing to use the biometric scanner and the other two diagnostic tables are being serviced, typical.' Belize utters under her breath. 'Hurry, get in there quickly, once they start they can't get you out.'

Belize cajoles Agenta along, helping her take off her top.

9NE

Symon is sprawled on his bed. He picks up the remote control for his sexbot, depresses a section and the cubicle in the wall opens, letting the android disembark. Symon loves this part of the ritual, where the sexbot walks out of its sealed booth. A smile swiftly illuminates its face with life, and Symon is beside himself, as all the robot wants to do is please him. That in itself, is enough to make Symon produce a spermy mess all over his bed. He cannot and will never get over how human-like the humanoid is. Auburn hair in plaits, dark skin with hazel eyes, lips full, including the ones down below.

Always having gone for black girls, he loved their buttocks and the way they bounced off his lap. He also preferred their aroma, something about the black woman's scent he found more intoxicating than white women; like a mix of shea butter, musky tanning oil and a hint of salt and metal. He found the scent divine, and somehow they managed to replicate this scent for his sexbot. Even the salty, battery, tang down below stood out, like having good quality oysters—Pretty remarkable chemistry.

He savours watching his sexbot come out of the booth, eager to please him. The humanoid strides towards him, with a grace he is convinced a human would never be able to replicate, more so because the movement seemed unnatural in some way. Somehow though, the movement worked for seduction. He tries desperately not to be aroused too soon, he wants to make this last for as long as achievable. He focuses on the sexbot sauntering over to him and he imagines wires and transistors behind the enigmatic face. This doesn't do anything to stop blood pumping in his penis, it hurts with the hardness, and he relinquishes trying to suppress the sensation. He's turned on, no denying it, resistance is futile. The sexy android manoeuvres itself over to Symon, who now gawps with undisguised lust. The fascinating machine takes its clothes off seductively. Symon's member hurts even more. For distraction, he thinks about the caverns and the intricate processes involved in mining for moonite. This helps a little, but not for long. The sexbot reveals the chocolatey heavenly behind and enticingly gives it a little shake. The encased body of circuits computes that Symon is besotted. The algorithms tell the sexbot so, every time they encounter physically.

The android slowly reaches for his thighs, touching him so seductively it sends shivers up his groin and into his cerebral cortex, firing up every neuron responsible for reproduction. Of course the sexbot doesn't have ova, but the human brain doesn't compute this, neurons are fired regardless. A biological program like many of the other default biological programs of the human body.

Symon turns over on his side, so he can reach for the androids behind, he will always be amazed over the perfection of its body. He touches the magnificent ebony encasing of lust and the sexbot moans a little, programmed to prolong the pleasure. This programming of algorithms boosted so as to delay his orgasm, but still managed to fail each time. Instead, the sexbot chooses to focus on arousing him after he's ejaculated. More challenging, but the sexbot lives up to its name. Expectedly, Symon's penis throbs and leaks precum. The sexbot prepares to initiate foreplay. Symon stretches out, flushed and excited, and awaits the ritual. He checks the power on the side of her neck and is chuffed to spot the full green bar. He settles and allows the sexbot to take charge.

~~~~~~~~~~~~~~~~~~~~~~~~~~~~~~

Agenta lies still on the biometric table, she might as well be lying on a slab of ice. She's scared to move an inch, lest she discovers a new degree of coldness. Perhaps the biometric scan works better in low temperatures. Will just grin and bear it, no time to get all precious. She recalls on earth, once going in for a CT scan, you're put in some kind of cylindrical magnetic monstrosity. This metallic contraption emitted loud clanking noises as you were scanned and the room froze you. When she asked why it was so cold, she was informed it had to be cold, otherwise the equipment overheated and would malfunction. She did not want to think what would unfold if the equipment malfunctioned, so she reconciled with being cold, if that meant no mishap. Here on the moon, she would anchor into that same gratitude, better than moaning.

The coldness penetrates her skin like a fish in a freezer. She overhears Belize speaking with the medics who brought Skyler in. Belize explains that Agenta had been halfway through the process and it couldn't possibly be interrupted. A white lie, as she'd only just gone under. A medic informs them of the availability of a scanner with an 89% service completion, and they would have to take the risk, as Skyler's life depended on it.

Agenta is grateful for this, as she didn't want to be responsible for someone's agony and feasibly someone's death. She lies still and allows the anaesthesia to take hold. A heaviness overcomes her and as she drifts off, an event fills her mind, a few months before earth became unfit to live in. She'd been chosen as part of the cast for a new series adapted for television. Long waits between takes were always expected, so she had decided to take a walk.

Out enjoying a leisurely stroll in a park a few yards to her flat in Surrey. She always came to this park when she could, as she loved walking along the meandering paths. Something different always revealed itself, and she particularly enjoyed sauntering through the woodland in the autumn. Always marvelled at the vast array of colours of the leaves. Rusty reds and fiery oranges complemented the dark green hues and dirty browns of the mossy branches. This particular evening, as she traipsed along the leaf littered paths, something unusual struck her about the trees. Moss and lichens were scarce on the branches, which she had studied a great deal on her many hikes. She moved in closer to a group of trees, to find mounds of moss on the floor by the foot of the stems, as if scraped off the branches. These small, non vascular, flowerless and rootless plants crackled softly under her feet as she approached, as if walking on popcorn. Had someone carried out this pillaging vegetative act?

As she advanced further into denser wood, she pondered. Again, she observed the same thing. Lichen and moss littered around the foot of the trees. She looked up to discover yet again, the branches—often admired for their green fur—were now bare. As far as her eyes could see, all the trees looked in the same state. The pit of her stomach sent out biochemical signals to alert her to something being wrong. She took out her phone to take pictures, understanding a symbiotic relationship existed between the trees and lichens, and the lichen and moss dropping off the trees could not be a good thing. Agenta turned around to get back on the path, only to realise she had wandered off further than she thought, and for a moment she could not find any clearing.

A squirrel ran out from a shrub near her and scurried up an oak tree. She could have sworn the squirrel looked confused. She kept the squirrel in her line of vision as it climbed the oak tree and then she spotted the path. Sauntering towards it, she delved into ecological knowledge banks in her brain, eager to see if she could come up with some theory as to why the lichens and moss appeared to be dying. No explanation came up. She stepped back on the path and resolutely turned around to head home. What she'd witnessed made her sad, although she couldn't pinpoint why. Motivation to finish her walk waned, her subconscious became depressed and anxious.

A few weeks after that day, a biohazard alert resounded and all hell broke loose. A terrifying experience, which made her wonder afterwards if her psyche somehow sensed the disaster.

She increases her pace, suddenly conscious of how serene and hushed the park had become. Not a shuffle or a murmur. Dead quiet. Not even the bristling of leaves, as if nature was purposely holding its breath. Normally, a few people would be out walking their dog, but this evening, no activity whatsoever. She sensed the atmosphere suddenly becoming muggy, almost stifling. She wondered if her imagination had gone haywire, and she quickened her pace some more. She detected movement out of the corner of her eye, in a gutter next to the path. Another squirrel? She trundled over to the ditch, so as not to scare whatever had just scurried for cover, arriving at the ditch she gasped.

A bed of moss and lichen filled the ditch to the brim, as if someone piled it up in the gutter with a shovel. The entangled bed of simple plants, fungus and algae appeared to pulsate and she bent down to check more closely. Lowering herself down on her knees to validate her eyes' interpretation of what lay before her. She leaned in to investigate more and a green tendril shoots out of the bed of moss, with the speed of a chameleon's tongue; wrapping around her arm, pulling her with a force that could not possibly be vegetative. She falls back the opposite way to generate some resistance, and the green woody tendril counter intuitively applies more effort; pulling on her arm ferociously, way too violent to be the actions of a plant.

She had no recollection of auditioning for Swamp Thing.

Agenta awakens to Belize pulling on her arm from the biometric table.

10N

Agenta slaps Belize's arm hard and then begins flapping her arms like a crazed seal.

'Ow!.. that hurt! It's Belize you muppet! For meteor's sake!' Belize creases her face as she massages her arm, mindful she's taken the opportunity to vent some frustration over the scanned discovery.

'Oh no, I'm sorry, so sorry Belize.' Agenta collects her arms and folds them across her abdomen, as if telling them off.

'Look how red that's turned.' Belize sulks a bit more, then eventually turns to her friend.

'How are you feeling?'

'Yeah... good I think. Had a crazy dream though.'

'That would explain your flapping around like a crazed seal then.'

'Sorry.'

'Never mind...The operation went well...You wanna see your spleen?'

'Eh... no! Why on earth would I want to see my spleen?'

'Well, you know...medical souvenir.'

'No thanks, if you want to use it for medical research you can.'

'A diseased spleen? No thanks.'

Agenta hesitates from taking herself off the biometric table and regards Belize, as if seeing her for the first time.

'C'mon, you'll need some fluids, best get you some isotonic water.'

'We've still got coconut water?'

'Well a derivative of, yes.'

Belize helps Agenta off the table and passes her a warm mesh-like cloth just out of a microwave.

'What happened to the guy rushed in after I went under?' Agenta splutters the last words out to allow a cough through.

'They placed him on the other biometric table, 89% serviced. He made it.'

'Ah good, would have felt bad.'

'You know...you wouldn't survive in an apocalyptic disaster, you know that right?'

'I'm doing pretty well here so far.' Agenta throws Belize a playful scorned look.

'Yeah I guess so, albeit spleenless.'

Belize fetches a plastic polymer beaker and from a somewhat concealed outlet, collects formulated isotonic water, given to all patients after a major surgery. The unique plastic polymer biodegraded after a few weeks of being left in the ground back on earth. If only they had come up with that invention quicker, humankind may still be on earth.

Agenta takes the almost filled beaker from Belize. 'Thanks.' She gulps it down, then staggers as she hands the cup back to Belize.

'Do you want to rest a little before we leave?'

'No, no I'm fine, I'll rest better in my room.'

'Okay, let's go... want another cup of this?' Belize shakes the beaker in her hand like a soundless rattle.

'No, I'm good ta.'

Belize sets the cup down on a side unit and turns all the equipment off. She then takes hold of Agenta by the side and stirs her towards the automatic door which opens on their approach.

~~~~~~~~~~~~~~~~~~~~~~~~~~~~~

Tyler occupies his cell not just with body, but with all the essence of his being. He molests his inner ear with his little finger as he ponders a chess move. His mind wanders and he recalls the conversation with Matt. Some commotion on the lower deck, neither of them had been aware a man jumped off the floor they were on. Matt—one of the people he disclosed his theory of the water being laced with some kind of sedative— did not buy it at first, but afterwards he started to think that perhaps Tyler had a point. He too started to drink as little water as practicable and felt his libido increase, which he realised, after some heated encounters with his sexbot.

Tyler discussed candidly with him about his new findings, and if he thought it worth informing others and driving some kind of revolution. A risky move, but his determination to do whatever it took to guarantee he wasn't stuck down in the cavern, like some kind of horny lab rat, prevailed.

Having won at most of the chess games recently, he anticipated being picked for insemination. Whatever happened to make sex become so technical? Whatever the answer, it started long before they ended up on the moon. He recalled an experience a few years back, had just split up with his girlfriend of three years. Dynamics kept getting entangled, nothing seemed to flow, and notwithstanding attempts to make amends and inject some romance back into the relationship, his girlfriend always found a way of complaining and only saw the negative in any situation. She felt he did not love her or at least did not demonstrate this enough. All because he wanted to spend time with others in his life who he valued as much, including a close gay friend of his. His girlfriend always informed him—harshly—that when about to visit his brother, his mum or his best gay friend, his face lit up, and she rarely saw that while spending time with him. Basically, he did not make her feel special and try as he may, he never seemed able to make her happy, even though his feelings for her were authentic.

Back then, he didn't appreciate everyone's happiness, was totally down to them and was not and couldn't ever be reliant on someone else. Because of her demands on him, he started to question whether he did love her. He soon got enlightened to the fact, some women needed attention all the time and he realised he could not do it. At least not the way his girlfriends wanted it. Part of him wished he was gay, as his best friend did not demand of his time and attention in the same way. Then again, perhaps the dynamic changes when in a loving sexual relationship. Symon was blinded to the fact that sharing his life breakthroughs with his gay friend, culminated the creme-de-la creme in relationships according to the female system.

Adira had enlightened him to the fact that he operated exclusively from a white man's system. All his girlfriend wanted was more connection and authentic sharing. In relationships, men are rarely able to fulfil this need in women, which is why most married women have a best friend to confide in. Adira explained the importance of appreciating other systems, not just the white man's; a female system and black system also existed, amongst others An awareness made all the difference; in contrast with being rigid in any particular system, all systems could be utilised as and when appropriate. During this discussion, which happened on their ninth date, Adira started to find it draining, having to keep repeating herself to help Symon understand. This did cause her doubt but there were other more powerful endearing qualities about him. In the end, she flung a book at him, urging him to read it. The book was a very old book entitled Women's Reality by Anne Wilson Schaef.

11N

Skyler wakes up cold and thirsty, so parched, anyone would think a working hair dryer had been left pointed down their opened mouth while they slept. They try to stir to attract attention, but realise they can't move. Familiar muffled sounds surround them, and is reluctant to open their eyes; switched-on the light will be blinding. They intuit easily—must be located in the intensive care unit, the cold surface beneath them confirms this. Thoughts are all over the place; the after effects of being drugged. The present state of being concocts a flashback, a straight guy who once made a pass at them. The guy looked like a sex god, with big hands and large feet, but equipped with a small penis. Deceptive packaging.

The guy disclosed to him—when drugged —that he only became curious when high. He admitted, he felt some kind of penis envy which propelled him to revel in homosexuality, and when high, he wanted to be penetrated by a guy. In part, because he couldn't produce an erection when high, and even if he did, his equipment looked pitiful, often mimicking a deflated balloon. He only wanted to play the role of bottom, which made sense to Skyler—if he was going to dabble in homosexuality, why take on the act of penetrating, which he would mostly have engaged in.

Then the thoughts fly off somewhere else, and they reminisce more about earth and how much they missed the weather conditions. Once, when looking out of the kitchen window, moments after a snow storm had ceased, blinding whiteness filled the scene; four inches of snow coating every exposed facet, all over the road and field beyond. All the cars were half covered in snow. The neighbourhood road looked like a giant buffet table with giant buns, covered in dustings of icing sugar. They had pondered on how great it would be if snow tasted sweet, like coconut flavoured candy floss. They had pondered even more on thinking about this when they were 20 years old!

Another memory—this time of a windy afternoon—peered through their consciousness. They preferred the sound made by a gentle breeze which teased tree leaves to sussurrate; this fluttering and rustling sound of leaves caressed by wind, masqueraded like warm honey for ears. They found it more soothing than any classic song composed with either a piano or cello or both.

This particular afternoon, a strong gale swayed all trees and shrubs about like playthings; assertive, forceful winds came in bouts, picking up loose things like plastic shopping bags and throwing them in a frenzy. They imagined the wind strong enough to blow away lingering, fettered, strayed, negative thoughts left behind by passer-bys. They imagined people's thoughts lingered around in the atmosphere, invisible threads of them, hanging around on any foliage or other environmental 'hooks.' If not for the wind breaking and scattering these corrupted thought-tendrils, they would congeal into polluted matter, bound to cause agitated, frustrated and vexed mood swings in all who passed through, adding to a collective consciousness of fear, detrimental to the energies of earth. Enough bad vibes lingered around already, so the powerful wind acted as a much needed environmental cleansing.

Now, encased in this cocoon on the moon, with the absence of a strong wind, what would produce this much needed earth-energy cleansing?

They also missed the sun shining in a conducive atmosphere and particularly loved watching crepuscular rays burning through the corners of clouds.

Drowsiness now entices, and sleep beckons, as if equipped with warm milk and soft cloud-like bedding. They settle with the beckoning, and slip back into the unconscious realm where they felt at peace. Just before allowing slumber to take them, a memory floods through, of an old friend who sadly passed away a year before the disaster on earth. This friend took clumsiness to a new level, always bumbling and fumbling. The type of person that would place a cup of coffee on a wobbly ironing board during ironing, and then curse at a spilled coffee incident. Notwithstanding, Skyler adored him, mostly because the other side of his clumsy nature entailed being carefree.

Diagnosed with cancer of the spleen, it had spread too far before being picked up by a physician. Fortunately, he didn't suffer and death came soon after the diagnosis. Skyler had been grateful for that, homed in on a particular fond memory when both of them flew a kite in part gale winds. Both laughed so hard that day, while trying to prevent the kite from being ripped to shreds by the forceful gusts. Skyler focuses on the memory—which appears like clouds in the mind's eye—and drifts away with them, forgetting their sandpaper scraped throat.

12E

An urgent meeting following Skyler's demise is being held on Adira's orders. Two men and two women take up spaces with her in the room. Three of them, her advisers, whom she calls upon when she requires clarity of thought and an astute power of reasoning. In her experience, a complex problem needed many heads. On this occasion, she did not have time to carry out a bioscan, counting on it all being okay. The new addition to the advisors was a man who looked like a giant sized baby, called Hamish.

Adira is seated, while the others take it in turn to stand, pace up and down the room and occasionally sit. This they do as a way of encouraging creative thought. They discovered long ago that if you wanted to think outside the box, then changing your posture and stance helped. Sit, stand and walk. This all allowed for cognitive enhancement. The days of sitting around a table in a conference room were gone. No original thought manifested from that type of setting.

The four men and women display varying facial creases, crinkles and wrinkles and appear well kempt and manicured. The men owned similar looking beards, trimmed and oiled, and the women owned similar looking hair do's, short and bobbed. Adapting the same intonation as well would have just been uncanny. Adira props up in her chair and regains a relaxed posture, listening to the words from her middle aged advisers.

A guy projects his voice.

'At the end of the day—'

'Seriously—' The other guy interrupts at once, narrowing his eyes which accentuate the beginnings of crows feet. '—Firstly, we hardly have a day and even if we did, the only thing that happens at the end of the day is nightfall. The guy rolls his eyes. Both ladies smile and peek at Adira.

'I need to know if the infiltration mission should be aborted? Do you think Skyler's been compromised?' Adira asks.

'I don't think so, I doubt anyone will suspect anything,' a woman pouts.

'Agree with Tia,' says the other woman.

'I do see what you mean Tabitha, but even if no one suspects anything, how is Skyler supposed to continue with it after that accident? Surely they need some time?' The sarcastic man displays his palms, as if getting ready to be crucified on a cross. Hard not to notice his bloated baby face covered in rash—Large round eyes, small ears and small short nose, round partially chubby cheeks and a small chin; all featuring on a fairly large head.

'On the contrary Hamish, Skyler being pulled out now is what will raise suspicions. As soon as they are healed, they should return to continue as normal, otherwise *then* people will wonder and suspect.'

'You may be right.' The other man confers.

'I *am* right, Josh.' Tia glimpses over at Adira for approval.

Adira sticks her hand up and turns her chair round to gaze at the chalky white moon exterior—a ginormous vat of milk frozen at the precise moment tiny icicles make impact—the contrast imposed by the sacred void of darkness, intensifies the image further. The stupefaction this scenery induces, refines and finalises her thoughts.

'Okay, we'll return him to the plant as soon as he's recovered.' Adira gets up. 'Thank you all very much, as usual—clean thinking. I appreciate it a lot, thank you. All of you.' With that she shakes everyone's hand and bids them a good shift.

The four advisers leave Adira's office in an orderly fashion and Adira returns to her desk and leans on the modern mycelium-based furniture with her fingers splayed. She soaks up her viewpoint again, contemplating. Something about the abstract nothingness and stillness of the moon and space, conjured up better prospects at remaining present in the now. Adira savoured the experience and stayed poised and still, trying to mimic the stillness of moon and space.

13N

Tyler aggrieved being stuck on a chess move longer than necessary. He often wanted to eliminate the opponent's knights in the game, because those pieces he often failed to monitor closely. He referred to them as knaves, because he found their moves deceitful, too random. He never did find a way to ignore or disregard the ominous apprehension the knights conjured up in him, so always aimed to get them out of the game. Happily swapping a bishop for a knight, but never losing two bishops. In this game though, he had planned to leave the opponent's knight's alone and concentrate on a new strategy to corner the opponent's king. He found himself wishing he had kept to his original strategy.

Having always been an over-thinker, in chess, he rebelled against over-thinking. He often scanned the board and would make a move without too much hesitation, trying his best to make moves which would appear ill conceived, so as to throw the opponent off. In spite of his knowledge and experience, here he was, stuck in an over-thinking space, and he resented it. He needed to relax, otherwise a stupid move was guaranteed. He believed with chess you had to polish your own natural traits with patience or the lack of, as in his case; and adapt your own strategy based on your innate abilities. In his case, because he lacked patience, he deliberately made random moves with the hope of befuddling his opponent. Unwittingly, he'd jeopardised this strategy and now relied on enhancing his meditative tips, so as not to allow himself to be carried away in a stream of annoyance.

He decided to make an even more random and unlikely move, but only after being assured of not being put in an awkward position by his opponent in the next three to four moves. Tyler had always loved chess, even back on earth he preferred chess to sex. Chess lasted longer and he certainly found it a lot more exciting. Enduring many a tease by mates a few times, who jokingly informed him of the do's and don'ts of good sex, even going as far as saying he suffered with a premature ejaculation problem. Tyler allowed them to mock him, certifiably not fazed by them enjoying a laugh at his expense. He knew coming too soon was never an issue for him, if anything he took ages. He just found the sexual ritual lame, never took to it. He put it down to having a low libido and left it at that. Quite happy not having to deal with an erection every time, especially as the few times he had the horn, a shroud of deep, concealed, catholic kind of shame and angst followed.

After making the chess move, he found himself wondering and hoping the guy who had fallen off the balcony survived. He pondered if someone could have pushed him, privy to the fact some of the men could be territorial, and often resorted to heinous acts carried out on others they did not like. Could it have been a suicide attempt? Many men tried that too in the past, but after a few attempts, and painful recoveries due to the advancement in critical injury procedure—other men gave up this idea. The length of the drop didn't ensure death and listening to the tales of excruciating pain experienced from others who jumped, put every man off that method of suicide for good.

Tyler made a decision to familiarise himself with the man, when he returned from the intensive care unit, keen on finding out what happened.

14N

Symon sweats and pants in his bed, spent from the encounter with his sexbot. He savours the relief —some would say endured.

The only other thing which kept him sane during his habitation on earth, was riding his motorbike. He missed this terribly, the thrill induced by speeding on a motorbike. Sex about made up for it, but not quite. On earth, he lived in a remote part of the world by the sea and it rained all the time, which precipitated issues with the bike, if kept outside. The continuous water and salt spray meant the wires on a bike corroded with ease. People only ever purchased a motorbike if they possessed a garage to park it in; otherwise the expense on maintenance from corroded wires, sometimes theft—another problem in the remote locale he lived in—was not worth it. Getting a bike without a garage demonstrated the same senselessness as casting a fat man as stranded on a deserted island for years. He managed to secure a garage which he and a friend shared, and they both appreciated speeding down country lanes on their bikes. The sheer blast of air, the force with which he tore through the atmosphere, the energy and power he felt reverberating underneath him; the underlying risk he took when on the bike. The possibility that he may fall and it could all be over—though not at the forefront of his mind—hung around, like tiny sparks lying dormant in his neuron network, waiting to be fired up. The risk of death meant he felt alive in each moment he defied death. Given—a strange experience, but a phenomenal feeling and he missed it, like missing a limb. The encounter with his sexbot just about did it, but not quite, a different experience.

He thought about Tyler and how it appeared he had no patience for him anymore. Fully au courant he irritated him on some level, even if always in jest. Now it manifested differently. He reckoned Tyler would rather not spend time with him and he didn't know how he felt about it. Ever since his divorce with his wife on earth, things had changed. He missed being a proper lad and having locker room chat with pals about encounters with women and sport. He enjoyed sport in a big way and found watching games exhilarating. They could sit for hours and talk about each player of a football team and the league, predicting which team would win. They rarely talked about emotions. Didn't see the point. Emotions always switch, never any consistency to them. Could be faced with the same scenario, same minor factors contributing to an outcome, and still emotions would be inconsistent. So why talk about them when they were so changeable, so capricious, so damn untrustworthy? He never understood it. Always hated talking about feelings with his girlfriend, but he managed to fathom out a way to pretend he cared, so he did not miss out on sex. In time, he did veritably start enjoying the deep conversations, and his girlfriend became his wife.

In some way, he believed Tyler accessed his feminine side easier, hence the clash, but he always considered it a learning opportunity, rather than an irritant. No prizes for being the same or having the same traits —he thought it healthier to be different, to some degree, but now he doubted himself. Perhaps his and Tyler's differences were too much to reconcile and they put up with each other because they didn't have much choice, not only from being stuck on a space rock, but in the depths of the rock too.

Would be forthright about it and confront Tyler, enquire about their relationship. The fact he wanted to do this made him realise he did not want to give it up. He swings up off the bed and traipses to the sink to wash his hands, still sticky from his encounter with the sexbot. He could never understand how they were able to replicate lubricant in the vagina, but somehow they did, even if the consistency was not quite the same, it still did the job; reacting with the foreskin on his penis making it puffy and thus retractable over the shaft of his penis. His foreskin gripped tightly and would be sure to hurt if not made loose. It had in the past when he tried anal intercourse with a woman back on earth. He hastily abandoned the idea after nearly splitting his foreskin, rapidly applying lubricant. Not the same, the natural juices formed in the woman's reproductive organ are a lot more compatible with the prepuce, helping this delicate piece of skin to peel back over the head of the penis with ease.

Symon only tried one form of lubricant and may have seen a difference if he tried a different one, but the excruciating experience put him off for good. He chose not to explore it further and neither did his partner at the time. Sometimes in life, when things are between mediocre and good, best to leave it as it is.

He compresses the button on the pod with the sexbot and the sliding door swings shut and seals. The time in the pod is what allowed for some rebooting or upgrading work, all fed from an electronic advanced high powered network. He slumps in a leathery off-white chair positioned by the pod and rotates in it slowly as he ponders. Choosing his moment with Tyler required care, if they were to broach the misunderstanding left all this time. He thought of doing it in the canteen, but far too many people would be present. Better at his quarters, ensuring not to be late; or more accurately, on Tyler's time, so he had enough opportunity to discuss it with him. He felt he could tune into the skills honed while in a relationship with his ex. That would appeal to Tyler, he was willing to bet on it. Perhaps he didn't fit a typical bloke after all, because otherwise, why would he be so keen on doing something to save their relationship? He never saw himself as sensitive, but maybe that characteristic always lingered, and being stuck in the caverns of a floating meteorite just squeezed the mush out of him. Either way he didn't care, reconciliation with Tyler would be worth it.

~~~~~~~~~~~~~~~~~~~~~~~~~~~~~

Tyler strolls in an area that looks like the set of a deserted apocalyptic zone, except scattered with chess pieces the size of bungalows, tilted on their sides, and covered in blankets upon blankets of lichen and moss. Lots of the matted green stuff draped over everything. The sky doesn't mimic an apocalypse in any way, rather it resembles shredded cotton wool stretched out on a light blue canvas. He realises he's dreaming and must have fallen asleep during a chess game and waiting for the computer to make a move.

An orange glow shimmers in the distance, and he reasons it must be the sun setting. He's switched-on to how content he is, all parts of him are relaxed. The dream is vivid. To the left of him are a few scattered oak trees, and one in particular, with a car wedged up against it, also covered in thick moss. The moss is half way up the tree, which he thought odd. On this particular oak tree, a healed wound exists where a branch would have once jutted out of the main stem. The healed wound resembles a massive woody vagina.

He carries on walking and conjures up a game of trying to identify the chess pieces, which is a little challenging as the pieces are so big. A slight humming sound is all he can hear. The atmosphere is redolent of rust and cut grass. The desertedness reminds him of the movie, "28 days too late," an apocalyptic movie of the undead. The sky is now waves of very fine cotton wool stretched out on light blue canvas. He remains peaceful and keeps wandering along the mysterious road with massive chess pieces and abandoned vehicles. In the dream, he's drowsy and wishes desperately to lie down somewhere, anywhere with something soft to lie on, to aid him falling into slumber.

He is amazed at his indifference to the predicament he's in. Despite the obvious portrayal of an apocalyptic zone, fearlessness lies where there'd normally be angst. He finds a small shack and ventures into it to discover a single bed with unsullied white linen. In the real world, bewilderment would feature strongly—discovering a clean bed in such a desolate area—but being aware he's in a dream, he isn't fazed. He climbs into the bed, gently for some reason, afraid it might collapse and shatter the luck being cherished so far. He lets sleep take him straightforwardly, but then wakes up to the sound of someone else walking around outside. Although no sight of the person yet, he perceives the person is a man and is carrying a gun. Another uncanny unexplainable occurrence that's feasible only in dreams. He retains his sense of peace, even though there's a distinct possibility of being shot dead on sight. He possesses divinity, not his time to die —in this dream or in the 'awake' world.

The man stops outside the shack. A few seconds pass, then his footsteps approach with an audible cautiousness in each step. Tyler witnesses the man look into the room but the man—who is roughly the same height as him—does not scan the entire room, he misses him in the corner, still lying on the bed. Tyler rolls out of bed with no caution, and willingly wanders into the line of vision of the intruder, pointing his fingers at the man, pretending to shoot him. The man turns round, having noticed movement in his peripheral vision. He raises the gun and points it at Tyler.

Tyler remains reposeful, despite the threat of death—it's a dream. 'No reason to harm me,' he mutters through a beaming grin.

The man is disarmed by Tyler's fearlessness and having scanned Tyler up and down, returns a reluctant half smile and urges Tyler to come with him as he wishes to show him something. Tyler follows him outside and now realises the orange glow hadn't been the sun setting, but a crater, the size of a football field, with moss and lichen burning in it. Tyler establishes the dream is now getting too weird and chooses to swim up to wakefulness.

Opening his eyes groggily; he's still, peaceful and content. Why the burning of moss and lichen in the crater, and what caused such a crater in the first place? He throws it out of his mind; will probably never find out, unless he figures out a way of returning to a dream to continue where he'd left off. He liked having a lucid dream, one where he realised he was dreaming; going back to a dream to carry on from where he left off would be another gift, but he didn't want to be gift-greedy.

A tap on his door shakes him out of the dream state.

'Hey buddy.' Symon utters in a repressed tone.

'Hey.' Tyler props up in his bed.

'How is everything?' The words stumble out of a constricted throat. Symon is all too mindful of the strained way in which he pushes these words from his lips.

'I'm okay, thanks, just woken up. Had the most unusual dream.'

'Oh...what about?' Symon is grateful for the opportunity to listen to Tyler and aims on doing the listening with every ounce of his being.

'It was apocalyptic, back on earth... Why are you here Symon? I'm sensing you're not here to listen to my dream.'

Symon detects a mixture of tiredness and disappointment in Tyler's face; he wants to believe that disappointment primarily formed the creases on his face.

'Yeah... need to talk. Can I sit?' Symon points to the chair situated right next to him.

'Yeah, sure.' Tyler adjusts himself, making himself more comfortable in his sitting position, just as he's taking note of the posture he's in.

'I'm going to say it straight okay...quite likely, very likely in fact—I probably wouldn't be the person you choose to hang out with... back on earth I mean. I would not be the person you'd necessarily spend your time with. We're very different people, I get that, but then again, perhaps not that different. I'm aware I can be quite brash and insensitive... and even not have much... well, come across as not having much substance, depth if you prefer. You're a thoughtful person with a lot more depth to your personality and I can see that and do appreciate it. I'm also aware I get a lot from you and that this probably isn't reciprocated. What I'm trying to say is I know you don't get much from our relationship, whereas I get tonnes...I know that. I just wanted you to know that I know that.'

Symon's discomfort while he said the words shone through, but Tyler also noticed the authenticity and unashamed sincerity to his words. He appreciates the difficulty he would have faced uttering them and considers Symon with a sense of quiet pride.

Furrows and grooves in Tyler's face, which Symon guessed were disappointment lines, seemed to iron themselves out.

'Thanks Symon, that must have taken you all the courage in the world to say, and you know what, right at this moment...in this very moment, all's been reciprocated. Two fold even. You have just proven that you *do* have substance. More than anyone I know. More than me for sure. Thank you... I'm...I'm blown away by your honesty and courage.'

Symon fights a lump in his throat. He's never experienced this before, certainly not to this intensity. He struggles to swallow the lump away.

Tyler rises and approaches Symon. Symon pushes up from his chair with slight anticipation.

Tyler grabs Symon and they embrace. Tyler holds Symon powerfully, as if detaining him, waiting for him to relax into the hug. A couple of breaths later and Tyler feels the tension in Symon's body release. He clings onto him for a few seconds more, before letting go. Symon's eyes well up.

'Now who's being a G-boy.' Tyler teases.

'Shut up.' Symon wipes his eyes.

15N

Josh chills in his quarters, admiring space and distant galaxies. No matter how many times he gazes into space, he cannot believe humans are residing on the moon. Humans had substituted a brightly coloured, warm, flowing planet for a grey, cold, stagnant satellite.

He recalls the discussion with Adira over what to do regarding Skyler and grins when he thinks of Tia. Had always been fond of her, primarily because she seemed to always possess the same line of reasoning. She unknowingly existed as kind of his muse and he was curious if Tia considered him the same way.

Hamish and Tabitha seemed to possess an entirely different way of reasoning to himself and Tia. They didn't even agree with each other, not that he could remember. They didn't act the same either, Hamish appeared robotic in his mannerisms compared to Tabitha.

He loved being on the advice counsel, always prided himself with being able to think outside the box and witness the bigger picture. All too cognizant of all types of contemplation being required. He knew that collective energies generated through intelligent dialogue opened up more realms of possibilities for tremendous ideas. An authentic space framed entirely in the present, enabled this clean insight. It did take him a while to realise this. In the past, his patience had been pitiful in seeing other sides of an argument, particularly reasoning, which to him appeared to be off the cuff. As he aged, he accepted, and even better, realised the need to accomodate all types of thinking; reflective, rational, analytical, meditative, philosophical and so on, so long as they were authentic. He felt it absolutely crucial these discussions were carried out in an atmosphere of mutual respect for the collective ideas to expand. He never did understand how the British house of commons continued with a system of belittling and shouting at one another. How on earth could creative and profound ideas for running a country be induced in such an environment?

Josh gets up from his seat and gawps lustfully at his sexbot. It resembles Caze Roffn, a drop dead gorgeous singer and actor, once voted as most-masturbated-to celebrity. There weren't many new artists that emerged after the evolution of AI and computer based music. He wonders if the manufacturers tried to mimic Caze Roffn's looks, or was it a mere coincidence? He's not horny and he elects to lie down and read an old journal of his. He had always kept a journal and he managed to save it when escaping earth. His tiny writing enabled him to squeeze in a lot of words on each page, to save paper. He took pride in his journal, which came with a quality leather casing, designed so it could be reused. Like an additional appendage, he had it on him most days; his most cherished and valuable item. The one thing he thought of when given minutes to evacuate. He didn't quite care for material stuff and so couldn't care less having to leave behind his worldly possessions.

He randomly opens his journal to see which page he would land on, his ritual every time he picks up his treasured book of notes, ideas, dreams, quotes and feelings. The page he landed on this time dealt with his exploration of the ethical dilemma around the self driven electric car.

On a memorable trip to a friend's, the brain-box of the car weighed up the options in an inevitable incident after a tyre puncture. The car made the decision to swerve and hit someone on a zebra crossing. The accident caused an injury, albeit a minor one. This would have been a lesser severity of maybe two or even three prospective consequences. He never unravelled what the other, more dire options were and this bugged him, as he always felt the need to know how the reasoning quotients in the car's computerised section worked. He understood the think tank could swap between deductive, inductive and abductive reasoning and it relied purely on deductive reasoning, capitalising on an elimination process. The brain-box could rapidly make a decision to catapult a car and driver into a wall, maybe killing the driver instead of—for instance—killing a mother and her two children on the other side of the road. Everyone signed papers to agree to these eventualities as to what the car decides before being programmed in. Especially as one of those ethical dilemmas would be the car deciding to plummet you into a wall or over a bridge to your death, instead of running over school kids. Assuredness on the unlikelihood of accidents occuring, was the one consoling factor taken into consideration when people signed the contract with the car manufacturers.

His car had hit a middle aged man crossing the road and the unfortunate pedestrian held his leg while rocking in a sitting up position. Josh's car called an ambulance, gave the coordinates and instructed that he please remain in the vehicle until the emergency services arrived. A loudspeaker on the car also reassured the injured man an ambulance had been deployed, and then reassured him with updates every five minutes.

Josh sat in the car, still as a stuffed toy, consumed with empathy for the man, but no guilt. He hadn't been behind the wheel, in fact he was engrossed in a novel and so absolutely devoid of responsibility. The injured man on the road knew that, and so did Josh. Josh scanned his surroundings trying to decipher what the more fatal accident could have been. A few men were carrying out road works on the other side of the road, but there was no way to comprehend if the car could have killed someone over that side. In the distance, a bridge spanned over a river with quite a drop, but this was quite some stretch and it seemed unlikely the car would have ended up all that way—and then over the bridge to his probable demise. Baffled, he remained seated in the car, which had now selected a classical piece of music to calm both men down as they waited patiently for the services to arrive.

When the emergency services did arrive, along with a diagnostics team, they evaluated the brain-box of the car. The system got upgraded after each incident, so methodically these accidents were reduced further. Back then, the evolution of the electric car reduced collisions by 70%, and by continually upgrading, the other 30% could be tackled. The option of reducing the speed on the roads to a mere 20 or less miles an hour also arose. However, the inconvenience of everyone having to travel at tortoise speed outweighed the number of deaths generated by high speed on the roads. For the first time, the car industry could keep the speed and reduce the deaths on the roads noticeably.

Josh now randomly recalls speaking to his best friend at the time, the one travelling in the car to visit. This is how the mind works, at least his mind. It flitters from one thing to the next. One particularly early frosty morning, he phoned his friend for a chat. He knew she would be up, being a rooster just like him. When she answered the phone—spritely as usual—he boasted that he was weeding the garden, and she had replied with 'Why on earth would you be reading the Guardian that early?' He then spoke a lot slower, correcting and repeating— he was *weeding the garden* not *reading the guardian*. How easy for people to mishear what someone says and how humorous it could often be.

Josh returns to the present, he's sleepy and contemplates if he should take off his shirt and climb into bed. Then remembers, no need; because even if he sweats during his sleep, the moon's weather conditions were not conducive to most bacteria, not the type that fed on the oils from sweat at least, and so he could wear his shirt for as long as he wanted. He was pleased about this, laundry was his least favourite chore. On the moon, water is scarce, so this silver lining was much appreciated.

Few months before the evacuation of their planet, the clothing industry discovered a new synthetic fabric that broke down the oils from sweat, thus eradicating body odour as bacteria found nothing to feed on. If scientists knew they would be going to reside on the moon, where most bacteria could not flourish, they may have directed their intellect and resources in some other field. Such was the torture of hindsight.

Humans were also pleased—grateful even—that bacteria were the most persistent of species in terms of willingness to survive. A lot of situations occurred, where symbiotic relationships between us and these microscopic creatures were necessary in order for us to exist. Thank god a selected few could survive on the moon, even though in manipulated environments.

Josh decides to make some notes regarding the viable pathways the suspect in the caverns could use to initiate a revolution, if that was his ploy. Whoever it was, would most likely possess a lot of patience and by all accounts will probably be fairly intelligent. A tactic he could use to fish the man out would be to check records of the best chess players. Josh stands suddenly and claps his hands. 'Of course.' He stretches for his tablet and calls Adira directly.

~~~~~~~~~~~~~~~~~~~~~~~~~~~~~~

Adira fidgets in her seat, then turns around. Josh had given a convincing account of how easy it would be to fish out the culprit in the caverns. Reasoned with the rest of the counsel that the best way for the guy to access the top of the moon would be to ensure he scored high on the chess results. This would guarantee his selection and his sperm extraction for insemination, and, more importantly, his interrogation over knowledge of the laced water. All too easy.

16N

'I do think you should have rested some more Agenta.' Belize expresses with concern, whilst uprooting a plant in the extensive greenhouse. The plants occupy sealed units containing ceramic soil. LED lighting and an ingenious watering system recycling human urine and sweat, is injected through tubing to the units.

'I know, I know, but I was going out of my mind, cooped up the whole time.' Agenta is also tugging at a plant—a variety of beetroot. She does this with less effort than Belize. 'Besides the stitching is healing along quite nicely.'

'Okay... so long as you're sure.' Belize ran through a million options in her head to inform Agenta about the pregnancy, but couldn't bring herself to ask. She had faith Agenta would tell her when she became privy to it and when she was ready. Still her hope was that her pregnancy resulted from sperm in storage, rather than freshly ejaculated sperm.

'Yep I'm sure, I'm being very careful... not exerting too much energy...thank you for being such an awesome friend and looking out for me Belize.' Agenta waits for Belize to turn to her, so she can look into her eyes. She wants to be sure she detects the candour in her eyes which should help with the sincerity in her words. Belize does look over in time. They are only a few feet apart. They both acknowledge each other authentically, as is only feasible when looking into each other's eyes.

'Must see to the insects next, they've been neglected somewhat.' Belize stretches her arm above her shoulder. 'Getting cramps in my arm now. Tendering to the insects should be a break from this position.'

Belize struggles up and stretches. They've both been crouched near the plants for almost an hour now. Agenta does the same but without the stretch, she is weary of her stitches.

Another greenhouse is linked to the one with plants and they both stroll over to it. A much larger greenhouse than the one with the plants and resembles a gigantic emerald crystal. The door unseals on their approach, picking up the signal from their clothing. They both enter and the door closes behind them.

Orange lamps, situated in several chambers in the greenhouse, illuminate and radiate every 50 yards or 45.72 metres. In the chambers, are different species of flying insects with large abdomens and thoraces.

'Shame the human race didn't relinquish their squeamishness before our demise.' Belize reaches into the chamber and plucks the nearest larvae from the flying insects and pops it straight in her mouth.

'Well... I think I'm happy staying vegetarian.' Agenta relays, trying to conceal her squeamish face..

'You should really get over yourself, miss prissy. There isn't enough protein in the vegetables, and you need to heal.' Belize asserts with a simper, while chewing.

'I know, I know... you may very well be right.'

'I am right.' The smile on Belize's face broadens.

Both ladies look at each other with adoration. Adoration borne out of being best buddies and harbouring collected-pride from contributing enormously to the occupants of the moon, for six years now. Pride in each other bolstered by their accomplished breakthroughs in how best to grow and cultivate more species using the seeds and eggs retrieved from earth.

Suddenly, a loud siren breaks the semi trance both women are in.

'Please all make your way to the protective dome.' Carl resounds on the intercom. Both ladies maintain a swift upright position. Belize extends her hand for Agenta to take hold of. They clasp palms and dash towards the exit.

'What do you think it is?' Agenta ponders.

'No idea, a meteor shower, but we shouldn't be at risk of that for another couple of months. Besides, the shield should protect us... perhaps it malfunctioned.'

'Your mathematical formulas can't predict that... surely.'

'Well, no, not entirely anyway. It just, well... gives me a hold on things.' Belize squeezes Agenta's hand, who reacts to it by grinning like a Cheshire cat. Had always fantasised about someone caring for her deeply. She never envisioned it would be a woman though, it felt even more special.

They both reach the exit and the door begins to open. The siren is deafening now. Agenta pulls her hand free from Belize's suddenly.

'What are you doing?' Belize extends her hand.

'I forgot to put the eggs back... I'll be right back.' Agenta runs back into the greenhouse.

'We might not have time Agenta!'

Agenta runs with all her might. As she sprints, she steals glances through the glass windows into the charcoal darkness with twinkling specks of light. No evidence of anything sinister. She arrives at the chamber and confirms her thought; she *had* forgotten to put the tray of eggs back in the incubator. Agenta bears down on a button which begins opening a hatch and as she waits, a loud cracking clatter resounds from above her, filling the entire greenhouse. She catches a glimpse of movement above her and peers up to witness a shower of space debris hitting the reinforced glass. In another instant, a huge space rock penetrates the greenhouse, creating a loud crashing sound.

'Agentaaaaaaaaaa!' The door automatically closes shut.

Gravity is lost abruptly and Agenta is lifted off the ground and flung violently in the direction of the jagged hole in the glass. She doesn't scream, but gives Belize an apologetic face. She gets a whiff of what she could only describe as burning metal. This sensation only lasts seconds, before an intense, spasming pain surges through her lungs. The air in her lungs expands, ripping through pulmonary tissue. She is sucked towards the open crack with gravitational force. Her uniform ices over and begins to rip into shreds. She continues to stare at Belize, as she's sucked further away from her. It all seems to occur in slow motion. Belize positions her hand on the pane of glass as if bidding her farewell. A forever farewell. Tears stream down her face as she witnesses her friend being hurtled away. Agenta's eyes are an icy glaze now and frost forms on her eyebrows and hair.

Seconds before she vanishes into space, she hits her stomach hard on a protrusion. Belize imagines the unborn baby in Agenta's belly and closes her eyes tightly, praying Agenta perishes before impact. Exposure to space with no suit—only takes a few seconds before life is extinguished. Belize opens her bloodshot eyes, even though she dreads it. She wipes her face, all misshapen with wet, teary lines.

As expected, no sign of Agenta. Belize slumps down to the floor and sobs. The siren still blares and Carl still prattles. Belize is innately thankful; with that raucous din, she could lament as loud as she wanted. She surrenders to what's just happened and howls like a tormented animal into the commotion.

17N

Adira relaxes in her pod in the emergency enclosure, protected like a termite queen. She swiftly inputs codes on a computer, trying to make a backup. The luxury of iCloud ceased. That luxury evaporated when their computer systems got replaced with the basic DOS, resulting from the existential threat from all social media accounts. Adira recognises the dangers of a meteor shower. She taps away at the keypads with such speed, her motions appear inhuman. All the lights go out. For a few seconds they're in complete darkness and a clunking clangour can be heard in the distance, coming from the generator plant room. Adira attempts to make sense of the surrounding darkness. Nothing materialises without time, as often the case when thrown into darkness. Her eyes adjusted and still nothing. Impenetrable darkness, not even a shimmer of different shades to contend with. She clutches one of her favourite books for security. The little book is always next to her, a signed copy, given to her by a dear friend, an aspiring activist and writer, who passed away before the demise of the planet—what she would have wanted. She started her activist work at an early age. Sweet sixteen. She did everything in her power to prevent earth becoming uninhabitable, alas, to no avail.

The clangour alternates in tempo and with that the lights come back on again and then the sound of the generators, vents and extractor fans. Adira gasps. She peers at the computer monitor and grimaces. A series of programming codes escaped being saved, the programming codes for the computer chess games.

'For meteor's sake.' Adira switches her face from stoic to simper, and then back to stoic. She unconsciously pries into her pocket and touches the picture inside. She caresses it, using the photograph to anchor pleasant memories. She needed to find out why the protective shield did not hold.

~~~~~~~~~~~~~~~~~~~~~~~~~~~~~~

Symon contemplates in his quarters staring at the chess pieces in front of him. A new found sense of peace consumes him. Knowing it would be this easy to acquire peace, he would have dropped his macho bullshit and been open and honest about feelings years ago after his wife left him. He thought it a state of being, only attainable when with a woman. Why were men so incapable of authentic honest connections? Was it a white man issue? Why clueless until now? What on earth was he holding on to? No one held onto earth. Failed dramatically as a human race to safeguard their planet. How could they have been so neglectful of their world? He wondered at his newly arisen contemplativeness. He doesn't remember thinking this deeply about anything. Could it be a result of his complete openness to Tyler. He takes a deep breath. He can't believe that dropping his facade and revealing a hidden truth, resulted in what appeared to be a complete rewiring of his brain. He regards the chess pieces with a new perspective. An announcement is made over the radio, crackly at first, then becomes clearer. "A meteor shower caused some disruption, but everything's okay. The results from the chess games are now ready to be revealed. The man chosen for the surface is... Symon Chandler."

 Symon props up. He's not sure he's heard correctly. He pays his undivided attention to the announcement again. The words are the same. "Symon Chandler selected to come to the surface to mate." He leaves his chair and plods to the side wall and back again. He clenches his hands together and then stretches them up above his head. He perches back down and ponders. How is this possible? What on earth— (He really needed to stop using earth in his vocabulary)— What happened? How has he been selected and not Tyler? Undeniably, Tyler is the one better at Chess, something is very wrong with the whole situation. He dreads to think what Tyler must be feeling. Should he go and find him? A heart to heart had taken place. He couldn't imagine him being resentful. He concludes visiting him will be the right thing to do.

 He wanders out into the passageway, in the vicinity of a few guys ogling at him. Few whispers flirt with his ears as he strolls past them. Symon chooses to ignore them and carries on walking. He is as perplexed as they are that he's been chosen. What could he say to them? Nothing? He increases his pace. He's even more desperate to meet with Tyler, as if seeing him will make sense of the whole circumstance. The last corner is visible, putting him on the same passageway Tyler is on. He hurries down the passageway even faster but slows right down as he approaches his quarters. He does this to reverse his increasing heart rate. He arrives at the entrance to witness Tyler sitting on his bed, with his head in his hands. Tyler intuits someone is standing at the entrance. One of those occasions when intuition is sharpened, and Symon wonders if it had anything to do with the open and frank conversation engaged in earlier.

 'Hi.' Tyler mutters, as he lifts his head from his cupped hands.

'Hi' Symon replies. 'I take it you heard. Obviously something is wrong somewhere. We could ask them to re-look at it. Ridiculous, everyone knows I'm rubbish at chess, no way I've been picked.'

Tyler remains quiet.

Symon traipses over as if avoiding invisible draw pins scattered on the floor. He perches next to Tyler, but not too close.

'What should I do?' Symon carefully expels the words. He believes this is the best phrase to use in this situation.

'Well... *you* were picked, so you must go.'

'I know I was picked, but there's obviously been a mistake.'

'Mistake or not, you must go. Never known them to renounce a decision.'

'I can't believe this. This is not happening.'

'Hey—you're going and that's that, there must be a reason. So prepare man, stop the moping.'

'Nothing for me to prepare, this isn't right. Could you not go instead of me? Who would know?'

'Now you're being ridiculous. Symon they *will* know, they know who is playing from which board.'

'Oh.'

'Besides, you should go, will do you the world of good.' Tyler acknowledges his use of the word "world" in a fleeting thought. All this time on the moon and still references were being made to earth and world during speech. 'You've been picked. It doesn't matter if something went wrong. You've been chosen. You should own it and go.'

Symon peers down at the floor as if counting scattered draw pins, then places his head in his hands.

18N

Skyler is privately made aware of the death of Agenta. Barely knew her, but knew of her contribution in the production of food for the colony. Was also informed she only recently had a splenectomy and by all accounts it had been successful. Outright terrible fate—fucked up odds and chances.

Down in the caverns, news like this got muted. Tyler wished they were shielded from the news too, it only brought on depression. Had battled with depression most of the time on earth, and engaged in a lot of personal development work to manage poor brain chemistry. Becoming irritatingly positive, to the detriment of his relationships. It turned out most people wanted to be validated for their moans, it seemed a lot of people didn't want to be faced with the positive aspects of circumstances. Most people preferred the drama, or at least their minds and egos did.

Skyler over compensated for the depressive tendencies dealt with, and always sought out the positive in every circumstance. No matter how pressing the desire to be informed, they chose to steer clear of the news bulletins in any format. Only filtering out positive news around the world. They found this so much better for mental health.

Not long after the tragic passing of Agenta, the chess results were revealed. Skyler guessed this was an attempt to cloud over any potential news leak of the former event. Never expected Symon to be the person called to the surface. It was agreed by the panel, Tyler was the suspect. What went wrong? What was overlooked? They pondered over this for some time, the depressive mind loved to rummigate—a forte even. They tried to make sense of it. Having spoken to Tyler, was even more convinced they would do their best to find out. They would go and speak to Symon and see if they could gauge his reaction to winning.

~~~~~~~~~~~~~~~~~~~~~~~~~~~~~

Adira is apprised of the tragic accident brought on by the meteor shower. She had always had a soft spot for Agenta, as well as appreciating her contribution to the colony. She asked for a prompt report and review on the risk management. The shield had malfunctioned and she wanted answers. Like most things in life— this was shrouded in a paradox. The disaster happened as a result of the same phenomenon which formed habitable planets, by trapping gases and liquids in an atmosphere—Gravitational force. Only this time, it hurtled life-destroying asteroids at them. She didn't want this to occur again, and considered applying drastic measures to ensure people did not return to areas with potential danger. As the leader, she couldn't afford to lose competent staff members and if it conveyed breaching liberties somewhat, then so be it. She would order and ensure that a device is triggered on the suits, so that during an alarm, people were only allowed to move towards the exit. Any movement away from the exit would trigger an electric shock enough to deter you going anywhere but to the exit. She looked forward to an emergency counsel to discuss this straight away.

~~~~~~~~~~~~~~~~~~~~~~~~~~~~

Tyler marches along the passageway with urgency in his steps. The terrible shift he had endured plays on his mind. Most of the equipment acted as if taken over by gremlins or possession. Hard wiring and mechanics were affected, and he was more infuriated and stressed than he could ever remember. For some reason he chose not to accept his mood having anything to do with the chess results. Worked on a detailed formula for months, and now it appeared all was going down the drain. The emotions reeling around in his body were unrecognisable, he knew some ambivalence played a part in the mix. He prided himself on mastering his emotions by utilising yoga and techniques of the mind. Now though, all that seemed to have gone out the window. The frustration seething in him had no time for mindfulness, only chaos. He decided to go for a run up and down the ward, but first, he needed to get out of his work clothes.

He approaches his quarters and almost walks into Skyler.

'Hey, how you doing?' Skyler employs the use of their adam's apple, an attempt to sound more butch.

'Not okay actually.' Tylers confesses without pretence, no part of him welcomes small talk. If Skyler wanted to stop and chat, then they would have to deal with some moaning and lamenting.

'Oh, what's up buddy? Can I help in any way?' Skyler is aware they take a risk referring to him as buddy.

'Had a really shitty shift. All the equipment was playing up. A damn miracle I got out alive to be honest. And the chess results...well... never mind.'

'It's okay, I'd like to listen. Tell me... what happened?'

'No honestly, it doesn't matter.' Tyler is now conscious of the fact he hardly knows this person.

'I'm a terrific listener. You'll be surprised how much talking to someone who sincerely listens can lessen the burden. Try me.' Skyler utters with some confidence, switched-on that this could be his opportunity.

'I really looked forward to getting to the top, pushed myself with my games. So it was a bit of a blower when revealed... Being down here is taking its toll on me, more than I'd realised.' Tyler sighs. 'No biggie, I'll figure it out.'

'Oh I see—didn't know you were so keen to get to the surface. I'm sure like you say you'll figure it out... right?' Skyler is mindful they need to be careful with the questioning. Scrupulous even. They had forgone revising the questioning when in this situation and perhaps they should have. Not as silver tongued as once thought.

'Yeah... just the combination of things. Bad shift, disappointment...I'll be okay after a nap. Give my mind time to reboot.' Tyler forces a smile. He hopes Skyler doesn't register the fake grin, but is even more concerned if Skyler's prying has sinister undertones. Could he be a spy? Sent to find out what was going on with the water? News travelled up, he was at least privy to that. Playing it cool was paramount, he had already said too much.

'Well I must be off. Thanks so much for the concern though. You were right, I do feel a little better. Thank you.' Tyler mentions again with a Botox smile. He makes a conscious effort to use his eyes as well as his mouth, hoping his eyes crinkle at the corners and some kind of glint exudes from them.

'Farcical how we'd rather get to the surface. More often we don't want things to surface for fear of shame or guilt or... whatever.' Skyler is not so sure they were making sense.

'Come again?' Tyler squeezes his face and narrows his eyes.

'Oh... nothing, just observing an ironic metaphor.'

'Okay—well thanks again.' With the words hardly out of his mouth, Tyler turns around to continue the walk back to his quarters. He resists the urge to look back at Skyler.

'Bye.' Skyler manages to say, determined to rehearse the questioning better. It could have gone so much better.

~~~~~~~~~~~~~~~~~~~~~~~~~~~~~~

Belize perches on the bed in her quarters, her face twisted in anguish; her hair effortlessly mimicking the anguish. A couple of reusable styrofoam beakers are next to a container, both containing the fermented drink she and Agenta invented. Belize reaches across and collects the nearest cup and takes a sip. She manages a smile at the fact she'd forgotten there was already a filled cup and had poured another. No sooner had she smirked, she burst out crying, anguish flooding up from her chest like pressurised water through a cracked dam. She turns to the wall and sobs uncontrollably, riddled with guilt about smiling. The dollop of anger she harboured over her girlfriend being pregnant, gave her some solace, some respite. In the same sniffled breath, knowing that this trace of anger interrupted her grief surged additional pangs of guilt into her psyche, and her crying switched a gear, this time infused with frustration. Now she would never know if someone courted Agenta. She clutches and crushes the plastic beaker and takes her sobbing up another notch.

~~~~~~~~~~~~~~~~~~~~~~~~~~~~~~

Symon strolls to his quarters, conscious he's a lot more anxious than normal. Worry conducts a full blown orchestra in his mind. He needs some kind of a plan of action, anything. Something to give him a little sense of control over the fate he had been thrown into. An admirable start will be to sort out which clothes he'll be wearing when he leaves and a set of clothes to last for the week. He knew clothes would be offered to him so he looked presentable for the date. Amazing that they had the audacity to call it a date, being coerced against his will to get together with some woman he knew nothing about, appearance or otherwise. Nonetheless, his excitement over the idea of having some real skin on skin action, overwhelmed him. The anticipation made his heart and crotch quiver with exhilaration. Even his skin sensed what was forthcoming; tingles of anticipation in his dermis perked him to attention. Often wondered why guys were so keen to give each other hugs whilst in the shower. Now it seemed to make sense to him. It was a need. A skin-deep seated, human need. Perhaps it was never only about the sex. Maybe more important *was* the skin on skin contact, the human body craving this sensation of another. Perhaps even more important was the varying intoxicating odours that came with being human. The different musky sweaty signatures, the whiffs of genitalia, hints of alkaline aroma from old and new orgasmic juices, slightly fermented saliva, even the subdued enticing tang of anal sweat. All these flavours—unbeknownst to humans—added to any erotic pleasure, not the intense. Never the intense. For most people, the intoxication lay in the subtleties. This could not be replicated in the sexbots, regardless of the advancement in chemistry research. Humankind never really appreciated bacteria—responsible for creating these varying olfactory flavours—until required to leave earth and inhabit the moon.

He arrives at his quarters and glances over at the sexbot. The android scans the floor with what seems to be dismay. With one flick of a button, the whole demeanour of the android would change. An aliveness would come to her face, enhanced by a gracious grin and a twinkle in her realistic humanoid eyes. If only he possessed that much control over the mood of a real woman and his mood for that matter. All his life he struggled to deal with the fluctuations of emotions women possessed. He always found it immensely irrational, and even though he tried his utmost to accommodate the mood swings, he always pondered over the worthiness of getting laid now and again. Only one woman put an anchor into him, or more accurately, his heart, a long, long time ago.

He developed some envy for gay men. Always having sex, as if on tap. Perceived them as damn lucky in that regard. It seemed quite a few male gay couples functioned in open relationships, so they could enjoy sex with who they pleased, as well as having a constant partner in their life. Best of both worlds I guess. He felt it ignorant to think any couple, be it straight or gay, wouldn't in time, be sick of each other, resulting in their sex life becoming stale. He concluded this outcome to be inevitable. So, as far as he was concerned, gay men possessed wisdom. More prospects of a lasting alliance if sex could also be enjoyed outside of their relationship, so far as they were honest about it and happy with the set up. He appreciated however, that *his* bonding makeup didn't gravitate towards polygamy—each to their own. Some people are herons, some swans and some ducks. Herons being the solitary ones, happy being single, Swans loved monogamy and the ducks were... well, dicks—they fucked everything in the vicinity. He reckoned every relationship to be different and it was ridiculous to judge. No point. He simpers at the realisation of having judged the ducks!

He selects a pair of his favourite jeans, they fitted well around his butt and thighs. He understands from talking to enough women that they loved the male bottom too, just as much as the gays. He thinks of Tyler as he lays the jeans on his bed, then pulls out a favourite shirt of his; a plain cotton, olive coloured long sleeve. He then grabs a few pairs of underwear and socks. There are five pairs to choose from. As far as he was aware, the longest any bloke stayed on the surface after being picked for impregnation, was three days. Once, some bloke stayed a whole week, but that was because he fell ill. The women must have thought it a bit mean to harness his sperm and then transport him back to the caverns all expunged, and in sickness.

He craved human contact, much more than he realised. He looked forward to the experience and making the best of it, anticipated the woman would be decent looking. He briefly thought about his ex wife back on earth, had loved her with abandon; but in a trice, threw the thought out of his mind; she left him. He was quite certain she perished on earth, so any reminiscing about her was pointless. Would only conjure up unfavourable emotions; mixed emotions, inconsistent, untrustworthy, interchangeable emotions.

He made up his mind to stop asking questions as to why he was picked and instead enjoy himself. Recent conversation with Tyler proved to be the most authentic ever engaged in with another human being. Perhaps this was his universal reward for being *that* courageous and open. Who knows? He wondered if he should refuse to go and what implications that decision may have. Would he be pressured to go up? Honestly not sure. Should he refuse to go up out of loyalty for his friend? He wished he could find out what would happen to him if he decided not to go. No one ever refused to go before. His bet was the ladies would choose again - second in line perhaps. Then hopefully Tyler would be chosen the second time round. Was he prepared to do that? Should he refuse to go? Would that be the decent thing to do? Again not sure. And truth be known, he didn't want to give this opportunity up. He did want to arrive at the surface and experience being on top rather than below. He craved having sex with a real woman, made of flesh and blood, his body needed it. He should then be able to cope for another few years in the cavern. He couldn't untangle why he felt so strongly about it, but he chose not to beat himself over it anymore. He would go, and he would enjoy himself— final decision. When he returned, he hoped Tyler would be a friend to him, but if for some reason he chose not to, then he couldn't do anything about that. Would be propelled to accept the circumstance and move on. Prided himself on being honest about his feelings for him, and couldn't do anything more than that. No more pointless thinking about it.

~~~~~~~~~~~~~~~~~~~~~~~~~~~~

Skyler paces up and down the quarters, chewing on fingertips. They chew on a hangnail and skin around the knuckle. Occasionally, fists are made with both hands, and then planted in pockets too. Then soon enough, once lost in thought, both hands are removed from the pockets to chew on a finger or two. In time, the bed bounces and creaks to their flop and they gape at the female sexbot in the booth. How much longer could they put up this pretence of being straight? They wouldn't be able to for much longer. The reason they came— albeit had no choice—was counting on it not being a long, drawn out task. The crew believed they knew the culprit, though now, that certainty seemed tainted. How could they find out for sure now? The women wouldn't know the person coming up was the wrong person. Would have to come up with a tactic to ascertain the facts, but failing that, would have to go along with Symon being the one.

They remembered a profound and controversial book read back on earth. About an author who published a book around the idea that if people mustered the courage to commit suicide, they were guaranteed—on the "other side,"—a peaceful existence, devoid of anxiety and the over-thinking mind. In the story, the protagonist's book induced mass suicide in society, as the evidence he gave of the "other side," was so compelling. The author got arrested and taken to court as they blamed his book. In the story, the author creatively came up with a compelling reason to avoid accountability. Goethe's novel, *The Sorrows of Young Werther* published way back in 1774, got introduced into the argument. This story about unrequited love had also increased the suicide rate and as a result the book got banned in Denmark and Norway.

Other than the fact the book he wrote was fiction, he argued that just because people took his book as gospel and acted on it did not make him accountable for their actions. Over the years, social media helped generate various groups of people who swallowed the most ridiculous controversies, and none of them were held accountable for owning a platform that spread lies.

A fascinating read, with an idea quite profound to say the least. The author thought outside of the box to escape his dilemma. He managed to convince the judge he should not be held accountable for people interpreting a book wrongly and acting on it. His argument focused on where society resided at the time—an invisible unrest, kindled by the climate crisis, political polarisation, a recession and two pandemics back to back—and that resulted in the mass suicide. Incidently, the mass suicide, coupled with the death toll from the pandemics, resulted in a full blown respite on the natural environment.

The overpopulation of humans impacted earth's natural ecosystem in all sorts of negative ways. Great intentions and inventions to rectify this strain on the natural environment, did not come anywhere near as close as a substantial culling of the human race. He stated with firm conviction that if not his book, it would have been something else. After careful deliberation, the judge and jury found him not to be guilty.

They thought about that book for days afterwards, it made an indelible mark on their psyche. The way the character in the book argued the case to get him off the hook. They needed to be as smart as that character, to ascertain if Tyler or Symon were the only ones being sought. Either the man looking to escape or the one to cause a revolution. Assumed the latter, because honestly, nowhere existed for anyone to run to. It reminded him of the caption to one of the instalments to the Alien franchise. "In space no one can hear you scream." In this case the caption would be lame, "In space there is nowhere for you to escape to."

The only option left could be some kind of coup, but that needed a long term strategy and a lot of people on board. From the evaluations so far, neither of the men formed a following of any kind. So what *was* the plan? Was someone really seeking to escape the caverns or were the ladies on the moon just keen for some drama? Some kind of space dementia? No one had lived on the moon for this length of time before. No one knew what the effect would be long term—No one. They would give themselves a deadline to solve the puzzle. That always helped, some kind of deadline to ignite those creative neurons.

19N

"What is that tuning frequency heard when sometimes deep in thought? An intensified hissing, not unlike tinnitus, except the frequency is turned right up, lasting about twenty seconds and is crystal clear. Like a dog whistle, a type of clarity is achieved, all is in focus, a fleeting realisation that perhaps all is not as it seems. I do hear it. I wonder if others do too, like a welcoming nothingness if you will, that swells up from the ethereal. A peace frequency I call it. Maybe one day I'll discover what it means to hear this hissing sound now and again."

Tyler enjoyed pondering on most things unexplained. Delving into a mystery book became his escape and joy back on earth. He would suddenly disappear into thoughts, mainly when the hissing in his ears started. He likened it to the phenomenal event of the humming noise which some people reported to hear in different areas of the globe, coined the "Worldwide Hum." Most described the sound as a distant rumbling of a tractor, commonly heard before the crack of dawn. All kinds of theories existed, including aliens, but no one ever got to explain the strange phenomenon. No one, as yet, had heard any strange humming on the moon, understandably, the lack of air for sound to travel in, didn't help. One explanation put forward was otoacoustic emissions—sounds caused by the vibration of the hair cells in the ear.

Otoacoustic. Tyler loved learning new words and a word worth remembering, before humankind's demise is "Ultracrepidarianism—The habit of giving opinions and advice on matters outside of one's knowledge or competence." In a similar vein, with the humming phenomenon, everyone became experts, deluding themselves they had the answers because they'd read a blog on Facebook or Twitter. Not many thought it important to read up and retrieve the facts before making an opinion. And to make matters worse, most had an opinion—most of the ill-informed variety. This stupidity existed since the dawn of time, even before Christ. Heraclitus mentioned that "the opinions of most people are like the playthings of infants."

He read somewhere that three of the challenges faced by humankind were nuclear war, climate change and technological disruption. He felt all three relied on clear communication and reasoning which typically lacked in the human race.

He missed having intellectual conversations with a best friend of his. They often played scrabble together and she was referred to as a witch with letters and words. Deftly finding opportunities to squeeze in letters anywhere on the board. She once revealed her secret—merely gave her full attention to the game. She likened the game of scrabble to life. Study the letters, rearrange them and study the board, try out different placements and for sure you will find an opportunity. This friend of his enjoyed being a free spirit, never putting roots down anywhere. She travelled a lot, yet despite her shallow roots—like the Aloe Vera plant—she emitted healing qualities in all her relationships. She was called Aloha, and was half Vietnamese and half Scottish.

A velvety softness played a part to her light brown eyes, eyes which drew you in and made you reveal yourself to her. It was inevitable, and that was how she lured Tyler into her world of openness and freedom. He missed her, though with a hint of frustration; having no idea if she escaped, irritated him. Rumours of survivors on Mr Drake often kept him awake at night. His objective was to get to Mr Drake for other more potent reasons, but finding out about Aloha would be a generous bonus.

~~~~~~~~~~~~~~~~~~~~~~~~~~~~~

Adira criss-crosses on the floor in her room. Her skin glistens with dampness caused by sweat. She concludes her last session of exercise and turns around on the floor to an open book titled "The Drake Equation."

Seven factors that would need to be known to come up with an estimate for the number of intelligent civilisations out there. These factors ranged from the average number of stars that form each year in the galaxy, through to the timespan over which a civilisation would be expected to be sending out detectable signals.

Adira ponders on this paragraph while stretching. She takes a whiff of her left armpit as she spreads out, and winces. No shower for three days would do that, she deserves one now. She rolls off and ambles over to the shower cubicle.

As she savours the water drops, she wonders how things turned out the way they did. Women mostly being in charge. She wondered if oppression would always manifest in one form or the other. Perhaps prejudice was encoded into the human genes. While she knew they were in charge, deep down she knew this would not be viable long term, and sooner or later a revolt of some kind would ensue. Not sure how or when that would happen, but she counted on it happening. Oppression was never going to be sustainable in society. No one would have imagined people of colour would form an alliance with women to reconcile the racism debacle. In her core, she recognised women would firstly seek their allegiance in other women, regardless of their colour. Although this too took a long while. It took for some powerful, courageous women to pull feminism away from the white privilege paradigm. Any hidden prejudice regarding race, melted away in the face of justice over the sexes.

She turns the shower off, conscious she's abused her privilege. She is blow dried instantaneously, as she casually reaches for her clothes. Excited that she will be wearing clean clothes, since she would be meeting the inmate from the caverns soon. Black straight men agreed they would not take issue with any woman choosing a white man for reproduction purposes. The white straight guys on the base were taken. It was only fair, as enough black women were present to procreate with. Also agreed—although with some controversy—was the suggestion, mixed race babies were so much cuter, the skin tone a lot more desirable and principally, it encouraged "dilution." A term encompassing the belief that the more the "mix" then more of a chance of racism being eradicated for good. The black heterosexual men asked if they be allowed to deal with any threatening state of affairs. Adira agreed to this, knowing that examples must be made of anyone who sought to rebel against the regime. She made her bed and now she must lie in it... properly, with a duvet and pillows and everything.

She hoped the white male due up soon presented as desirable, an insurmountable challenge given the sexual ferocity of her sexbot.

Being her turn to conceive, she would much prefer they mated, rather than collect semen in a tube. She knew this took some extended liberties, expecting them to mate given the circumstances, but hey ho...the world had always been all swings and roundabouts. Apprehension made her heart judder momentarily over having sex with someone new. It had been a while. A long while.

She takes a seat and thumbs the intercom button to ask for the name of the man coming up. She is told he is called Symon with a Y. A phonetic Simon, she wonders if some people would see this as pretentious, having a name tweaked so as to stand out. She promptly throws the thought out of her head. Too soon to make judgements, time will tell. He should at least be fit, having worked in the mine all this time. A tingle and dampness in her nether region makes her blush, she meanders over to continue reading her book. The distraction is much needed. She is all too aware of being too self conscious. This is after reading somewhere that being self conscious is the enemy of interestingness. People at the top in corporate hierarchies are often self conscious over what they say, and rightfully so, because they have position and privilege to protect. She chose to find a balance. It would be downright appalling to be surrounded by so many gays, a group of people epitomised for being cheerful, only for her to still manage to come across as boring. She settles down with her book, placing her right hand gingerly on her crotch.

~~~~~~~~~~~~~~~~~~~~~~~~~~~~~

Music by an AI artist who copied a late musician KD Lang, echoes through a hallway. Grey walls and white skirting boards stretch out as far as the eye can see. Several gadgets on the corner of the walls flicker little coloured lights. Moans can be heard periodically with the music. A gentle breeze blows in from an open window in the hallway, coaxing a door open at the end of the hall. Moaning travels through, from two women entangled in satin white sheets. Both with their arms over each other's groins, they take delight in filling themselves up. The women moaning from the enjoyment of each other's bodies are Belize and Agenta. Belize sucks on Agenta's nipple with primitive abandonment. She takes her hand out of Agenta's most sensitive area and goes to sniff it—a need to savour the scent—but she pauses. Her hand is frosted over, as if placed in a freezer. Icicles form on her hand before her eyes, as a numbness takes over. Then her middle finger shatters.

Belize jolts awake. She'd been sleeping in an awkward position, with her hand tucked under her chest. Pins and needles set in. She wriggles her arm to initiate blood flow again. Curses and gets up abruptly, she's always gotten up this way, that way her noisy monkey brain can't take over. She shuffles to the sink for a drink, and sips on cool condensed water. Her delight over her expertise being part of why they had water in the colony was numbed. She collapses back down as flashes of her dream flood her neural cortex. She misses Agenta so much; to think she was recuperating from cancer. Unquestionably her time to go. In spite of this realisation, she sobs in anger, wrapping her arms around her head. So bloody unfair. Limitless, the amount of unfairness faced in the world and now, apparently, on the moon.

Her plan—escape into work, her only strategy and it had worked so far. Would be introduced to another partner, and she planned to lose herself in their task of assessing the meteorite damage. Belize wondered how reinforced glass would shatter so easily, the meteor that struck hadn't been particularly huge. Then again, why would someone sabotage their source of food? — Monkey brain again.

The sooner she started work the better. She quickly changed her clothes, wiped her face with a damp flannel and threw a few beads of peppermint and aniseed into her mouth. The person assigned to work with her this time, was a black gay man called Marcel.

~~~~~~~~~~~~~~~~~~~~~~~~~~~~

Symon prowls down the corridor leading to the elevator. High camera surveillance and bright lights dominate the corridor to ensure instant recognition. No possessions. He's not allowed anything, less effort in being searched. Three electronic barriers open up once Symon strolls up to them. Of course, these barriers would remain shut if not alone, they make it near impossible for anyone to penetrate. Symon strides through the passage, no need to rush. He still carries guilt about being the one chosen, when he knows it should have been Tyler. This thought— for some reason—is compounded by the fact that he changed his name many years ago as a way of getting out of debt.

He is convinced the selection error was brought on by the power outage. Zero information got shared about what triggered the outage. An error on the inside? Did the electronic doors and cameras work during an outage? Could he capitalise on this prospective loophole? He was banking on it. He left a note in Tyler's cell when he last visited him. He kept the note as short as a small poem, hoping that Tyler saw it and acted on it. Even if it didn't work, it would be exciting. Some excitement worth paying for if caught. He expelled air entirely from his lungs, then breathed in preparedness and readiness, and hoped Tyler did the same.

As Symon approaches the last barrier, he peers up at the camera as is expected of him. He is startled by a loud beep, as the barrier begins to open. He passes through and the elevator up ahead illuminates and the doors open. Goose pimples invade his arms and he rubs the back of his neck with the palm of his hand. The shiny, metallic, painted, plastic surrounding aids the icy quality to the area. He examines back along the corridor before entering the lift. The only lift that links the top to the underground—at least as far as the guys in the cavern are privy to. Inside, an acrobatic team of six could climb on top of one another and they still wouldn't reach the top—that much room exists, he guessed, to transport cargo if they needed to. He holds down the only button. You are either going all the way up or all the way down. The lift judders for a few seconds, but then he enjoys a smooth ride to the top and in no time arrives at his destination. He ponders on how deeply buried the cavern went or if it was the sheer speed of the lift; if the speed, then formidable, as he barely felt any g-force.

As the doors open, two black male guards stand on either side, with what look like batons attached to their waists. Both express a stillness which doesn't suit the situation at all. Their smiles aren't dampened or embarrassed, they're not even a qualifier smile—like the one a till assistant gives as he or she watches you queue for 15 minutes, only to tell you sweetly as you reach the till, that the till is closed.

Symon proceeds into the incandescent corridor, with hands in his pockets and hunched shoulders. He squints and winces. Even after a few days of his sexbot beaming light into his eyes, they are still unaccustomed. Both the guards tell him to follow them. Symon is taken aback by how polite they are. They didn't need to be polite at all, they could be utter bastards to him if they wanted to. He didn't know how to deal with it. He attempted to square his shoulders and walk as confidently as he could through the luminous corridor, and found walking with confidence particularly hard to do when wincing.

Both guards walk him up to a glass cubicle.

'Please take off your clothes and step into the cubicle,' says one guard, built like a solid wall. Intense dark brown eyes that immediately tell a story, the left one slightly off centre. Both eyes sit comfortably in a smooth shiny face, above a broad nose and thick lips. Pink pigmentation fills the centre of the lower lip. This pigmentation softens the features to his otherwise harsh, stoic face.

The cubicle is all see-through polycarbonate. Symon sheepishly takes off his clothes, having never stripped in front of black men before. This troubled him, had he deliberately not exposed himself to other black people? Not even in public showers? Ingrained penis envy? Was going out with Adira his quota on having black people in his life? Was everyone tainted by racism in some way, due to the systemic nature of the beast?

The familiar unease arose, just like it had always done whenever he reflected on racism, he imagined this to be the same for most white people. He dismissed the thought flow and instead thought about the female form. He had certainly missed taking his clothes off in front of a black woman. Taking them off in front of his sexbot didn't count. He enters the cubicle butt naked and places himself in the middle of the big glass cubicle as instructed. The cubicle seals and a blast of mist engulfs him. A distinct scent, like an odd concoction of bleach and marzipan, introduces itself to his nostrils. Symon unconsciously cups his genitals in his hands and the guards immediately gesture to him politely, to remove his hands. Symon does this reluctantly, as his skin glistens and tingles in reaction to the mist. After about a minute, the blast of mist ceases and the cubicle opens. The other guard hands him a towel, he is also burly like a solid brick wall. He possesses smaller, hazel coloured symmetrical eyes. He is lighter in shade, his lips and nose are smaller and there is no pigmentation on his lips. Back on earth, his lighter shade would have earned him some peace—less prejudice, less unconscious bias.

Symon takes the towel and starts rubbing himself down. The guy with the pink pigmentation then hands him some grey clothes which he hastily wears, in part because he's cold but also to bring the exhibitionist show to a close. In time, he follows the men into another passage.

They direct him into the corridor and inform him he'll be met by others on the other side. Symon catches himself wondering if they too would be black.

~~~~~~~~~~~~~~~~~~~~~~~~~~~~

Tyler arises from slumber, conscious he is still sulking. Try as he may, he's not able to discard the unserving state. He rolls off his bed and traipses over to where Symon sat when he last visited him. Completely saw Symon in a new light, and had been completely blown away by his sensitivity and openness. He sits and stares at the foot of his bed, trying to put himself into Symon's shoes. How was he with the whole fiasco? All too aware Symon knew he shouldn't be the one invited to the surface. Something had happened alright, something to do with the outage perhaps. Tyler positions his right hand underneath the seat of the plastic looking chair and detects a piece of fabric sticking out. He pulls at it and it comes away; bringing it up to his line of vision, he's able to distinguish writing on a shred of white cotton. He unfolds the fabric and reads the note, realising straight away the note is from Symon.

Tyler, unfair I know. I'm hoping you found this note on time. Tomorrow afternoon, st-
ay near the exit to the corridor. Outage - then walk through the corridor and into the lift.
Wait in lift till power back, then up.
Start walking as soon as there's an outage. Please trust me.

Tyler leaves the piece of fabric down between his legs and peeks around. He cannot believe Symon would go to all this trouble. Tyler did come up with another scheme of causing his sexbot to malfunction, and then swapping places with it before the robot was taken up to the surface to be diagnosed. Symon's idea seemed a lot more failsafe though. Risky, but still…failsafe. How long did he have? Even after a lie in, he still had time. He begins to get ready. Symon's plan would be some excitement if nothing else. He didn't have a clue what his original objective was and he was going to keep it that way, despite him demonstrating he can be trusted. He didn't feel comfortable sharing his original master plan. No way he was going to tell him what he intended to do when he got to Mr Drake.

He knew the space station was named after the Drake Equation, but he still thought it was a ridiculous name for a space station. Although it was where the mother board for the AI was situated, with one main task being to find intelligent civilisations out in the cosmos, he wondered how many people inhabited the station. There was news that a group of people took it in turns, swapping between the moonbase and the space station. He also heard the spin of the station malfunctioned, so there was no centrifugal force to generate gravity.

20Y

Hello everyone, me again. I'm the one narrating, started at the beginning... by presenting the historical annals. I realised I never actually said who I was. My name is Cynthia and I presently live on earth. I'm not too sure which sex I identify with, although biologically I'm a white female. Sometimes I identify as male more so than female, which is okay nowadays. In the past, it was a huge one for people to get their heads around, as with anything different, people allowed their repressed fears to feed their prejudice towards people like me. I'm more understood than ever before, which is chucklesome to say the least, I will explain at the end.

I wanted to interject here, because I happen to know what that tuning sound is that people can hear sometimes. The one Tyler was referring to in the beginning of the last chapter. The tuning sound that is heard by some that changes frequency now and again. That sound is as a result of a temporary overlap of dimensions, a brief merging of parallel universes if you will. I know, I recognise most of you readers will think that's crazy, but it's true and one day quantum mechanics will demonstrate and prove this phenomenon. I may not be around then to say I told you so.

Another thing I wish to bring to your attention is racism does not get eradicated unfortunately, it just takes another form. Mixed race people end up becoming the "superior" race. All I can say is humankind is fickle. Appearances made far too much of a deal to people.

The world I came into was saturated in technological superficiality; all social media driven, which allowed everyone and anyone a right to an opinion, ensuring people did not pay attention to experts in their field anymore. No one emphasised that although it may be okay to express an opinion, it was your responsibility to check the opinion was well-informed. All and sundry knew best, believing all they needed to do was click for the truth, not many read proper books anymore. Each one believing their truth to be gospel from a simple click! That, coupled with the influx of lies in the media meant people gave credence to all sorts and went around spreading it, often with blunt ignorance and arrogance.

You see, because people were hung up on being entitled to their opinion, compromise became a thing of the past; no need for people to come together. Everyone hid behind screens and blurted their ill informed obscenities. Some hid behind the screens of social media to expand their fragile egos. People became lazy with information, not bothering to read up and certify their information. Way too late, before people realised a shared experience of reality was important, like the matter-of-life-and-death-important. Luckily, it was only a few years after this came to a head, that the human race were forced off the planet by mother nature.

I'm twenty four years old and this was the world I was born into.

Another issue which gained momentum in conjunction with the humankind conundrum, was the women's movement. And that, well—that changed it all. Women took over. Years of abuse, molestation, rape, cheating and male chauvinism reached saturation point and women realised enough was enough. Women of all races formed a united front and white heterosexual men didn't stand a chance, especially ones known to be racist, homophobic and sexist. Everything possesses a pressure point, everything ultimately comes to a head. Women took every other race and societal minority under their wing. The Anglocentrism bullshit hit the fan, and all women made sure the fan was enormous!

I digress, so best get back to the story.

21E

Symon knew he only had about two days on the surface, and so being expeditious was paramount. He knew from speaking to others who had visited, that security was relaxed. No reason for fort knox, as no place to go; unless you fancied floating around in darkness, in a space suit. What they would never have foreseen, was someone on the inside trying to get another person in. Symon knew about Mr Drake and he knew Tyler was trying to get there, slipped out in communication, and he doubted Tyler even realised he'd spouted it. Not sure why, but he didn't care about the reasons for him getting to Mr Drake. He was going to help his friend—make it all up to him for the years of his friendship. First though, he was going to look forward to his time with a real live woman. She was the president, if he played his cards right he could get some inside information. Most women loved talking, and he was going to show innocent interest and curiosity. And most of all, he was going to give her a good time. Having learnt a thing or two in his day, he knew how to turn his women on. Upped his game with the introduction of sexbots, and he felt confident.

Symon was shown into his quarters, a lot better than his room to say the least. He forgot what it was like to live in part decent luxury. The first thing he noticed was the considerable reinforced glass window. The outlook took his breath away, air was forced out of his mouth in an involuntary gasp. It reminded him straight away of the film "Gravity," which he'd been fortunate enough to watch in a cinema that showed very old movies. The film was no match for the real thing though. The silvery, rocky moon, contrasting with the vastness of space and specks of distant glitter. Something about the scenery pulled you in.

In the room, everything was clean and pristine and white. The bed was a single, but with a firm mattress and unstained sheets. In a corner was a cubicle for the shower and one for the sexbot, but the sexbot was missing. He wondered if that was deliberate, some items being left for him to freshen up with, mainly his mouth. No need for a body wash, the mist in the coned cubicle downright sterilised him. He helped himself to the small tablets of fresheners and checked himself in the mirror. Thrilled with his look—a rugged stubble and wavy long hair—he perches on the edge of the bed. Working in the mines ensured he stayed lean and muscled. He still had an hour to kill before being summoned by the peeress, and needed to do something about his nerves. Had to remain vigilant and not slip up and call a gay guy a G-man lest he be taken straight back to the caverns. Must watch his every move so as not to raise premature suspicion. He had work to do and his focus was on not letting Tyler down. He stretched out on the bed and stared out into space. In no time at all, a sense of tranquillity not encountered for a long time, overwhelmed him.

~~~~~~~~~~~~~~~~~~~~~~~~~~~~

Adira was satisfied with her appearance. She recalls how much she used to enjoy getting ready for a date, and was taken aback by how much she had disregarded this ritual. Trimming her pubic hair, pampering her face, getting her skin supple. No coconut and coffee body scrub on the moon, so she made do with the pulp from the leftover fruit used in fermenting. With added crushed seeds, she found it did the job. She also utilised a secret stash of chocolate scented shea butter which she saved for these occasions.

Symon was being escorted to her by two bodyguards, and her nerves were shallow-fried, quite out of character for her. She couldn't remember the last time nerves got the better of her. The security personnel or anyone for that matter, mustn't witness her angst, it may be seen as weak. She knew on the contrary, that showing vulnerability demonstrated strength, but most men had no concept of this, having been brought up in a society riddled with patriarchal toxic masculinity.

She manages long steady breaths to repose herself. The beep resonates on her intercom, and she studies the picture display of the people outside. She gasps when she sees Symon. The spitting image of her husband back on earth. This sends her pulse racing again. She releases the lock allowing them to enter. Symon walks in with his head down. Eventually, he lifts his head and both Adira and him stare at each other for what seems an eternity. Adira asks the guards to leave as soon as she is able to expel her next breath. She ensures they are out the door, and it is shut, then leaps into Symon's arms.

'My goodness! I thought you perished on earth.'

'Thanks.' Symon says, still holding onto his ex-wife.

'Symon?' Adira stiffens out of the embrace.

'Yeah...I changed my name, terrible debt... one way I could get out of it.'

'Well, this is awkward.' Adira professes, checking the monitor again to see the guards disappear down a corridor.

'Can say that again. Done well for yourself.'

'Some people would say, I would say we've digressed.'

'A fair turnaround of events I would say.' Symon squeezes Adira's hand. 'You smell nice.'

'Thanks.'

'I've missed you so much.' Symon leans into her and breathes her in. His sexbot was no match. He had forgotten how intoxicating she smelt. Shea butter, musky tanning oil, with a hint of salt and metal. This time though, a hint of some kind of fruit and chocolate also prevailed. Apt, not only did her skin look like the finest dark chocolate, but now it smelt of it too.

'Carried a picture of you the whole time.' Adira claims, eyes welling up.

Before either of them could register their fate, they are locked in an embrace again, this time with a french kiss.

220

To effectively assess the meteor damage, the mooncats accessed the site from the outside. Belize insisted she wanted to be part of the mission, despite Adira trying to persuade her not to. Adira did give in in the end and discreetly asked that her top sentinels keep an eye on her. Belize was surprised at how easily she gave in, confident this was unlike her. Nevertheless, she showed gratitude for the capriciousness, because she had banked her life on going and not having to fight for it, made it easier. She counted on the task helping her grieve, and cherished not having to undermine Adira to do it, respected her too much.

Four mooncats existed in total and could carry four people in each. Typically though, they would carry two people and cargo. The mooncats often got employed to transport small cargo between stations on the moon. Highly graded suspension wheels allowed them to mimic mini versions of the American monster trucks found in testosterone fuelled races, except without the roof. The exception is these were powered by harnessing solar energy and moonite. A joystick replaced the steering wheel, which meant a few training sessions were encouraged for competence. All four mooncats resided by a cargo docking bay next to a laboratory.

Belize will be meeting Marcel for the first time, and being acquainted with her dreadful mood, she hoped to come across as polite as manageable. She entered a horizontal elevator that travelled through tubes to get to the docking bay, again operated by the badge sewn on their uniform. When the elevator—which is shaped like a capsule—arrives at the destination, a black guy saunters in and types in some instructions on a keypad. In no time, Belize recognises Marcel. Not many black guys were attracted to this sector, something to do with higher bone density and the effect this had out in space. Black men statistically have greater bone mineral mass, higher bone density, longer femurs and longer anthropometric arm and thigh lengths than white men. This had been proven years ago. So Marcel showed great courage taking on this mission with Belize, and she harnessed the utmost respect and admiration for him.

'Hi there,' Belize greets with a grin, instantly pleased her smile is not forced. Her instantaneous respect and admiration for him already assisted and should help with their rapport.

'Hello... Belize, I take it?'

'Correct Marcel.' Belize still retains her grin.

'Lovely to meet you. I believe a mooncat's scheduled to be free in a minute or so.'

'Correct again, on its way back with the crew.' Belize proceeds into a small foyer that links the docking bay.

'How long... how long do you think we'll be out there?' Marcel stammers.

'Oh, it should be at least four hours. Would that be okay?'

'Yeah, that should be fine.'

'If it isn't, you can always take the mooncat back when you want and program it to come back and get me remotely, there's always that option okay.' Belize sets about putting on her space suit, which was hanging in an electronically operated cupboard, also accessed by the badge on her uniform.

'Okay, if you don't mind... I might do that.' Marcel confesses, also accessing a cupboard to get a space suit.

'I am aware, and that would be totally fine, whenever you feel like going then go.' Belize keeps eye contact with Marcel and smiles broadly.

'Thanks.' Marcel fastens his suit and snatches his helmet, as if late for an army drill.

Through a sizeable window, about a hundred feet away, the mooncat can be seen returning with three people in it, two women and a man. The man stands up in the moving bogey and waves. Marcel waves back, grinning like an animated character. The man was one of the white heterosexual men on the base, and Marcel had always fancied him. Had always liked the challenge. Back on earth, he had slept with two straight men, one black and one white; both liked cock when they were high.

'We'll need to take two lots of cargo, we need to pick them up halfway between here and our destination. Is that okay?' Belize slips her helmet on and connects the radio system for communication. The frequency is always at 145.800 MHz.

'Of course.' Marcel announces into the helmet's inbuilt mouthpiece.

'About to start decompression.' Belize declares, as the mooncat pulls up at the entry point, which is separate to the exit point. 'You did take your antacid tablet, correct?'

'I did yes... all set.' Marcel mutters, touching and tapping his helmet.

Farts in space could be a ticking time bomb. Flammable gases in a tiny pressurised capsule could be a fatal combination. For this reason, lentils and beans stayed off the menu for astronauts, two days before going out into space.

'You'll be fine.' Belize asserts, as she detected nerves in his voice. She wondered whether speaking over the radio amplified anxiety in voice patterns.

Belize rams a red button which activates a suction sound, as all the air is pulled out. A red light emanates in the enclosure, and she senses the pressure on her suit straight away. Flashbacks of Agenta disappearing into space flood her neural cortex, and she closes her eyes tightly. She steadies herself by spreading her feet apart. Marcel mimics her.

After a few testing seconds, the suction sound discontinues and the red light illuminating the compartment turns green.

'About to open the door, slow strides and push yourself a little upward as you take your steps okay.' Belize instructs.

'Okay.' Marcel takes a deep breath.

Belize holds down the button that releases the door and immediately feels a pull on her. The opposite of gravity. She turns around to look at Marcel and reaches out her hand. Marcel takes it and Belize can tell by the way his grip tightens, he is glad she offered.

She takes a long step and thrusts upwards, pulling Marcel with her. They both float upwards in the direction of the mooncat. Certainly there'd be enough power for them to get to the cargo bay, but once there, it would need to be put on charge before making their way to the greenhouse sector. The three that came in the mooncat can be seen disappearing round a corner.

In two more gravity devoid leaps, they reach the mooncat and Belize lets go of Marcel's hand. She leaps over the mooncat in slow motion to get to the driver's side. Marcel springs into the passenger seat, but catches his helmet on a bar. Belize garners the interference this causes on the intercom. She checks his helmet and gives him the thumbs up.

'Sorry.' Marcel says.

'Don't be silly, it's fine.' Belize reassures him.

She grips the joystick and pulls it back, jolting the mooncat into reverse. Marcel is impressed by how she manoeuvres the vehicle. She corrects the position, knowing which vicinity to go in, and has always prided herself on a great sense of direction.

Back on earth, the team relied on her when they went out on an ecological expedition. She remembered a friend of hers who once surveyed the wrong woodland, she narrated to her the embarrassing story. Only when she sat in a panel to assess the sites for their ecological importance, did it come to light she had surveyed the wrong woodland. A botanist, who volunteered her knowledge, pointed out assuredly, that three of the species mentioned, could not possibly have been found in the wood she was supposed to have surveyed. Her friend disclosed how she had never been more embarrassed.

Belize plunges the joystick forward and the mooncat jolts ahead.

'So... Marcel, you got an interesting story?'

'Well, I'm gay.'

Belize laughs out loud, relieved her ability to appreciate humour was still intact.

Marcel locks eyes with hers. 'I'm so sorry about your friend.'

Belize's laughing is short-lived. 'Thanks, I miss her dreadfully... but cherish fond memories.'

'I'm sure.' Marcel replies.

Belize does not hear the nerves in his voice anymore and is pleased with that.

'Do you believe in life after death?' Marcel adjusts himself in his seat.

'I'd like to believe, yes. I mean look at this vastness.' Belize puts her hands out and gazes into space. 'Who's to say what's credible.'

'Indeed.'

'I never believed, but since coming to the moon. The wonders of space...the sheer vastness of it. I believe anything is possible. Extraterrestrials and all.'

'That would make for a lovely t-shirt. "Extraterrestrials and all."'

Belize chuckles. 'Space within space, within space; twisting and turning and bending, all within space. The mind boggles. Yet, here we are. So why not life after death.'

'Interesting way of looking at it.' Marcel adjusts in his seat again. Wearing a spacesuit for him was like forcing an autistic person with hypersensitive skin into a prickly woollen jumper. Most spacesuits were now engineered using the anatomical features of the female body for their construction. Yet another demonstration of humans never learning from mistakes of the past. He wondered if that had anything to do with his discomfort.

'Not long now before we get to the depot.'

'Okay.'

The mooncat—otherwise known as a lunar roving vehicle or moon buggy—could go at speeds of 15 miles per hour or roundabout 24 kilometres an hour now, beating the eight miles-an-hour average speed achieved when first manufactured. Belize slows down the buggy by pulling back on the lever a little. She could make out the damage done by the meteorite now, although still some way away from the site. Memories again of Agenta hitting her head and vanishing into space cause Belize to brood. She closes her eyes briefly, before bringing the buggy to a stop.

'Right, we'll need an hour for the charge, so we should be able to get all the cargo in at that time. We're trying to safeguard what we have at the greenhouse first. So containers and so on. But we need the generator rebooter... over there, in a compartment marked 12E. If you could get that first and put that in the buggy, that would be awesome. It will take up the most room. Then we can put the other stuff around it. I'll start grabbing them.'

'Okay, I'm on it.' Marcel vaults out of the buggy in slow motion.

Belize floats out of the buggy and is immediately compelled to jump, and so she does. She rises above the buggy and lasts for about four seconds suspended, before coming back down. 'Woohoo!' She yells.

Marcel witnesses this and for a second is confused, but then he jumps too. 'Wahooo!'

They both repeat it again and again shouting at the top of their lungs. Only they can hear it through their radios. Even if they didn't have their helmets on, the sound would have no medium to travel in. Their excitement is contained. Belize starts to well up with emotion. Scenes of Agenta hitting the side of her abdomen on a protrusion fills her head. Even though she had cried—and hard—this release of emotion was different, she presumed it had something to do with sharing the incident and feelings with another person.

Eventually they stop jumping, which took some manoeuvring. Marcel grabs a bar on the buggy to keep himself from floating up. In time, they synchronise into a steady space leap and start to head in the direction of 12E.

'In each other's line of sight at all times, okay?' Belize half croaks.

'Okay, sure.' Marcel responds, hoping she's okay.

~~~~~~~~~~~~~~~~~~~~~~~~~~~~~~

Skyler was asked to prepare to come back up, all convinced Symon was their suspect. Skyler made enquiries for this to be equivocal, knowing if he got back to the surface then he would not be able to return. All in the caverns would cotton on to him being a spy. Determined to engage in one more meeting with Tyler, they arranged to see him at his quarters. They would interrogate him, they felt confident enough. Something about jumping off a balcony unleashed their courage.

As Skyler approaches, it becomes clear the sound of a guitar being strummed comes from Tyler's room. They slow their pace as they reach the doorway.

'Hi.' Tyler announces without looking up.

'How do you do that?' Skyler shakes head and squints eyes.

'Poor sight, better hearing —nature compensates.'

'Obviously.'

'What did you need to see me about?'

'Well...probable rumours... heard you were keen on getting to the surface.'

'Oh yeah, where did you hear that?'

'Oh... eavesdropped in the canteen.'

'I see.'

Skyler remains standing, ignoring the now sweaty brow and armpits, guaranteed areas to dampen with sweat when nervous.

Tyler strums one last time before considerately placing the guitar by the side of his bed.

'Would you like a drink?' Tyler gets up.

'Oh...do you have a drink in here? Didn't think —'

Tyler swings round and grabs Skyler by the neck and covers his mouth. He adjusts his elbow into the crook of his neck, pressing firmly on his neck and mouth. He learnt how to render a man unconscious when taking a martial arts class, back when he was a free man. The teacher had been a genuine Shaolin expert and discreetly taught a couple of them how to do this trick. Skyler reaches both hands above them to try and grab Tyler's face, hair, neck—anything he could reach, and fails miserably. Tyler persists with the hold on Skyler's neck; unflinching, applying a measured amount of pressure. In a few more seconds, Skyler's arms flop to their side.

'Shhhhh.' Tyler whispers.

Spent some time trying to figure out how to make himself disappear for the late afternoon, through to the evening and perhaps part of the night, without anyone suspecting anything. Then Skyler made contact in the canteen and asked if he could meet later at his. Like chess, you must adapt to upcoming, new situations and execute your move accordingly.

He grapples Skyler skilfully to the bed, stows him in it and covers him up. He touches his neck, feeling for a pulse and detects one, although low. He snatches another shirt and wears it on top of the one already on. Then he takes the piece of cloth Symon left him. He clutches another pair of shoes and removes the laces and interweaves them into the laces of the trainers he's wearing. He then goes to the cubicle with the sexbot and releases the android but doesn't activate it. He caresses around the back of the head until he makes out a small latch and he removes a sharpened piece of a circuit board. He assessed the implement would come in handy someday, a sixth sense for implements if you will. He uses this newly formed tool to unscrew the nuts on the latch, and retrieves a microchip from the android's head and deposits it in the piece of cloth with the note from Symon. He places the piece of cloth in his pocket. He then prises open the eyes of the android, delicately takes out the lenses, and carefully positions them in his eyes. He would need time to adjust to them. He then snaps up another piece of cloth where he's drawn some kind of a map. Each time someone returned from the surface—after being expended for procreation—he coaxed them for information.

Over the years, a map was put together. It couldn't be accurate, but common sense helped decipher it. Stations would be placed near other stations, where they needed to be joint working of some sort. Solar panels would be situated nearer the greenhouse. The docking bay and station for the mooncats would be situated where they can be charged, which implied, near the moonite depot. And so on. He deposits the map in his other pocket. Microchip in the left pocket and map in the right pocket. He checks on his captive one last time, before also putting the sharpened implement in his right pocket with the map. He hoped he wouldn't have to use it, but wouldn't hesitate if pushed to, as getting caught was not an option. Once up there, it was his only opportunity to do what he needed to do.

'Sorry.' He whispers to Skyler.

He ventures out into the passageway. Now he couldn't be seen. Everyone must think he's in his room, right until the doors are electronically locked. He identifies the blind zones for the cameras in the imprinted map in his mind and so avoids them. He knew where he could hide until the power outage was instigated by Symon.

~~~~~~~~~~~~~~~~~~~~~~~~~~~~

Adira gasps and moans before falling off of a sweaty Symon. They tried out all positions they could think of and ended up with Adira on top. That position finally brought both of them to a climax. They lay in the bed panting, the climax impacting their ability to think, at least for the first few minutes. They needed to breathe and they needed water. Adira gets up and staggers over to her kitchenette. Water is rationed, but she is the leader so to hell with it. She often never abused her power, but her throat felt like a dusty rug in an Arabian desert.

Adira gulps down the third small cup. 'Want a cup?'

'Yeah... yes please.'

Adira fills the cup up again and saunters over to Symon, who's now pulled over a sheet to hide his flaccid penis.

'You still do that huh.' Adira hands him the filled cup.

'Do what —ah ha, didn't even realise.' Symon gulps the water like a stranded fish reintroduced to a body of water. Utterly parched. Sex did that.

'You're a grower not a shower, thought you'd be over that by now. Did you do that with your sexbot?'

'Really...you're going to ask me that?' Symon slams the empty cup down on the nearest shelf.

'Sorry, that was insensitive of me. How's it been down there?'

'Okay. We have food, shelter, water...our sexbots.' Symon now thrusts his hand out and grapples Adira by the waist back into bed. 'I can't believe this. What are the chances?'

Adira kisses him affectionately on the lips. 'It does put me in an awkward position.'

'Because I must return to the caverns, right?'

'Well... until I figure something out.'

Symon looks out the window, transfixing on the silvery, rugged surface of the moon. 'By the way, how would you not have known I was down there?'

'What do you mean?'

'The camera's?'

'Oh...haven't worked for years.'

'I knew it! Was the water being sedated? Drugged to keep us docile?' Symon decided to delve straight to the point. He needed to be sure of Tyler's convictions.

'Yes, yes...but only for your own protection. Only to safeguard you all. We didn't want riots breaking out.'

'What good is a riot when you're far removed from the people you're rioting against? Literally, underground removed.'

'Well, we didn't want to take any chances, the mine wasn't going to mine itself. So... were you the only one that knew?'

'Oh no, quite a few of us cottoned on to it.' Symon lies. He, like most others, would have described this as a white lie in the past. Any connotations to white representing good and black representing evil or bad slowly eroded from the English language because of racial tension having reached a critical point. Black magic and white magic, another such example. Jesus Christ being made white was perhaps the first of many influential white washing to come. Most white people, and blacks for that matter, were blind or ignorant to these subliminal cues in language which perpetuated white superiority over black people. Arguably, it might have been easier to refer to people's accurate colours, replacing white with cream and black with dark brown. Perhaps that could have been one way of breaking down the ingrained systemic racism.

'Oh, I see.' Adira props herself up on an elbow and admires Symon, somewhat befuddled by how much she had missed him. Like the deserts miss the rain.

'I have to say, an eye opener is an understatement. Being oppressed... enslaved. You never truly know what someone's going through until you experience it for yourself. To be honest, the humility I received from the black guards, I... I didn't understand it. They were so... well, nice to me. I didn't expect that, really didn't.'

'Blacks are quite a forgiving race, and above all wouldn't have expected some kind of compensation or pay out, which I think is one reason white male politicians refused to acknowledge white supremacy. I feel heart to heart honesty could have solved a lot of the problems, even the war on terrorism.' Adira turns over in the bed and reaches out to turn the window projector on. She fancied something warm and sunny, like an evening by the beach in Tobago or a mediterranean beach in Crete. She plays with a few buttons and the real image of the moon disappears and the sound of waves pulse, moments before a picture materialises. A sublime view of the beach, as if being witnessed from a villa. Coconut trees sway in the evening summer breeze. The sea is turquoise and tranquil and the sunset is a shimmering, glowing orange; and even though digital, breathtaking like the real thing.

'Wow… it looks so real.' Symon gapes at the scene before him.

'Reminds me of that holiday in Thailand about 12 years ago, you remember that?' Adira picks up her trousers from the floor and retrieves the picture always pocketed. 'I treasured this, it was always with me.' She shows Symon the picture of both of them, taken during a memorable holiday. 'Isn't that weird, always had it on me. Must have known somehow we'd meet again. Now seeing you, I think I always knew we would somehow see each other again. Isn't that weird?'

'It is weird, wish I could say the same. Didn't ever think I'd see you again. I thought you were a goner. And now I find you're *leading* the team on the moon.' Symon gets up to find his clothes.

Adira and Symon get dressed in silence, both appreciating the quiet.

Symon suddenly remembers the promise made to Tyler. 'Hey Adira, do you mind if I go for a walk… need to process all this, all a bit much.'

'Well, sure, sure—take all the time you need. Probably a good thing if you're not here the whole time.'

'Could you arrange for me to access where I want?' Symon suspects this question may raise suspicion in Adira.

'Well, okay, sure —I will pass that to the guards now, within limits.'

Symon grins coyly, delighted he still acquired the touch. Still able to cause her toe curling orgasms and convince her, he probably best not push it though and take it for granted.

And as if by telepathy.

'Just be back here in about an hour max. I'll need to put my routine orders in for the evening.'

'Okay, sure thing.' Symon dresses himself in haste. As he does so, he spots a wooden plaque on the side of a shelving unit, the only thing on the greyish furniture. The plaque is the size of a hand. He goes over and picks it up. Engraved on it is the word "Mangalyaan." A picture of three Indian women in full traditional attire is placed inside a grove of the plaque.

'Three key women involved in the Mars mission in 2014. Suffice to say, not many depictions existed of older brown women leading the world in rocket science, or any science for that matter.'

'Yeah, you women certainly had it all figured out huh.' Symon seizes the pass card on the side, opens the door and storms out.

Adira raises the celluloid picture to her face again and takes a deep breath. Yes, she had missed him, his sulking and all.

~~~~~~~~~~~~~~~~~~~~~~~~~~~~

A flashback fills Symon's cortex as he leaves Adira's quarters. An argument with his wife when on earth. Unmindful of the depths of his ignorance when it came to black lives, he never really appreciated the extent of what black people went through day in, day out; and even more infuriating, continued in denial about his privilege as a white man.

One evening, after returning from a game of squash and not being able to find his joggers, he retraced his steps back to the study where he had made love to his wife a couple of hours ago. They had engaged in some acrobatic positions, employing the use of a sturdy Coleridge traditional leather wing armchair, and propping themselves up by jamming their legs into a Rochelle Noir French triple bookcase. Just as he thought, his joggers lay crumpled behind his wife's desk.

As he leaned over to retrieve them, he spotted a list of names neatly written on a piece of paper. That list of names assisted in triggering an argument of cataclysmic proportions.

John Edmonstone
Ida B. Wells
Paul Robeson
Viola Desmond
Olaudah Equiano
Mary Seacole
Bayard Rustin
Chevalier de Saint-Georges
Frederick Douglass
Professor Clifford Johnson
Sarah Forbes Bonetta
Shirley Chisholm
Dr Maggie Aderin-Pocock
Kingslee James McLean Daley (Akala)
Toni Morrison

All significant black people, whom he had no knowledge of, except Dr Maggie Aderin-Pocock, Akala and Toni Morrison. The book, Beloved, written by Toni

Morrison, was the first novel he read about black slavery and the experience transmuted all the cells in his body to a conglomerate of shame. The shame, any decent white person was only too familiar with. The rest on the list were conveniently stripped from history. Whitewashed, as it was called back then.

It took a few days before each of them recovered from that argument, and even then he never believed they reconciled wholly, inevitably leading to their relationship deteriorating over time. Lots of 'blockers' occured in human communication, interrupting acute listening when people conversed, but nothing produced a muddy, impenetrable blockage like the loss of respect for a person, and he could see his wife had lost respect for him, detected it in her eyes.

His wife confided in other white people who she said understood empathetically. They understood the black lives matter movement and knew black people were exhausted with the racism entrenched in society and needed it to stop, by bringing it to everyone's awareness. She found it hard to swallow, that her own husband didn't get it. Instead, she found herself tendering to his fragile sense of self and identity because he felt his whiteness was being threatened. She tried to explain that racism was not an individual or binary phenomenon; about good or bad, but systematic through society and each person, even blacks, unwittingly took part in it. The fairer your skin, the better off your life was. That was just a fact, not purported to be accusatory. Still, comments like "but all lives matter" kept coming up, and she tried to explain to him that those comments did not validate the movement or black people's grievance. Time and time again, the same argument kept coming up and time and time again he struggled to listen intently, with any compassion.

What Adira expressed, after managing to simmer their emotional reactions, was she didn't understand why he and a few others obsessed over the idea of pushing for all prejudices to be looked at, without first validating the grievance of black people. Of course, black people knew other prejudices prevailed in society. She struggled to discern why they couldn't focus on understanding first and having compassion and understanding for the issues over entrenched racism, which fundamentally they agreed with.

In the end, what made a massive difference was collaboration with the feminist movement. The majority of white women in particular, tipped the understanding and compassion for the black lives matter movement in the right direction. This did take some time, but better late than never.

Symon took some solace in the fact that he did not catch a glimpse of disrespect in his wife's eyes anymore. Only compassion, mixed with guilt and perhaps a sprinkling of pity resided behind her eyes now.

Symon finally shakes off his thoughts and concentrates.

He harboured some idea of tracking to the generator plant, solved it, also by teasing out scraps of information from other white men with the privilege of getting to the top. He patrols with an assurance and spring in each step. Honed from having brought his ex-wife to toe curling orgasm and knowing she led the colony. He passes a section that reads 13N and soon afterwards he comes to another section in the cylindrical corridor that reads 14N. "A strange numbering system." He thinks to himself as he increases his pace. He is conscious of the time and he needs to act double quick. He didn't feel any guilt over his proposed actions, not having any idea what Tyler was up to, mitigated any morsel of self-reproach. He had faith he could cause no one harm. He was gentle and wise, and an intellectual type. No way he could be some kind of terrorist. Besides, he had nothing in his possession to use as a terrorist. Symon assumed he just wanted some time away from it all. He knew how much he longed for the sense of freedom, so he accepted. He looked forward to helping him accomplish his mission, it gave him an adrenaline rush.

After all, his place had been robbed, *he* should be here... but then he would... oh jeez, doesn't bear thinking about it. His wife. He wouldn't have known and Tyler would—Symon willingly interrupts his thought patterns. The thought of another man sleeping with his wife, even though an ex, would have been too much, moreso if it was Tyler. He doubted ever getting over that, no matter how strong their alliance.

A sign, in a bold font which reads "Mangalyaan," glares at him. The same word on the plaque in Adira's quarters. According to the map in his mind, this section was where the generator plant would be situated. Could the Mangalyaan be the name chosen for the plant room? He opts to walk down the cylindrical corridor. He's amazed he's not seen many people about. Saw a man and woman laughing down one passage he passed. Laughing so hysterically, they failed to spot him. "The guy was white, so possibly a G— gay man." He needed to stop doing that. Tyler was right.

A few yards away, a more reinforced door boldly presents, it begs for someone to investigate. "This must be it," he thinks to himself. He advances up to it as if approaching a vault in a bank. A bank robber would be dealing with the same heart palpitations. He raises the card retrieved from the leader's quarters to the door and enters before letting the door fully open. Relieved the card was opening every nook and cranny as expected.

He moves with some trepidation now. Having been too easy so far, it made him nervous.

~~~~~~~~~~~~~~~~~~~~~~~~~~~~~

Tyler shuffles into the corner, enough so he's sure he's in the blind spot of the camera up ahead. He's managed progress so far, without any electronic eyebrows being raised. Everybody would now be in their quarters. He caught sight of the cameras turning in each corridor he went down, and all he had to do was time the camera and move accordingly, sticking to the blind zones. He had no idea the cameras didn't work and were just for show.

Felt like he was forced to swallow his heart once when a camera jolted to a stop, while turning; but after a few seconds, the camera resumed its gesticulation. The incident almost gave him a heart attack, felt his heart pound so hard in his chest he thought it would stop to reboot, like he suspected the heart of his sexbot probably did on occasion. Alas, his heart continues beating, and he rejoices a little, having reached his destination. All he must do now was wait.

As he waited, a memory fluttered in.

He picked at his fingers, lost in nervous energy while waiting for a date. It would be their first meetup. Got on well, chatting online. He normally allowed for 15 minutes, because he accepted—at long last—that just because he excelled at timekeeping, he couldn't expect the same from others. People experienced different associations to time, this he found out when he researched. Firstly, two categories of people existed, those who did not care about lateness. Inconsiderate, would be the only word of choice here. Then those that wanted to be on time, but always ended up being late. Often, the latter group of people lose themselves in an activity and are unable to organise their time until it is too late. A cultural thing prevailed around time keeping too. Some people didn't succumb to time and if having to wait, it was no big deal. He decided not to be so hung up about it. He preferred being early, because he hated being late. To expect the same behaviour from others was silly.

On this particular occasion, he waited for about 40 minutes before surmising something might be up. When he called, it went straight to voicemail. He waited another 10 minutes before leaving, disgruntled.

He didn't hear from her until two months later, when she showed up, apologetic and pleaded with him to give her another chance. They again decided to hookup, and she was going to confirm the time and place and she never called him back. This was the dating world back on earth for lots of people back then. Coined words even existed for the strange human phenomena—ghosting and submarining—respectively. No wonder most people relied on their sexbots.

In his present situation, there was no particular time. Symon instructed him to be in this region in the evening. Security relied on camera surveillance only, no one checked the corridors. And so as long as he stayed put until the power outage, all was okay. The elevator was just yards away. Tyler was also one who suspected the cameras didn't work, but he didn't have Symon with him to confirm that.

He checked his pockets to ensure all the items were still intact. Comfortable with what he was to do and determined, he rehearsed it in his mind. (1) He had to reach the mooncats. (2) He needed a mooncat to reach the shuttle pod. (3) Set off in a shuttle and ensure his arrival at Mr Drake, where he could achieve his master plan.

~~~~~~~~~~~~~~~~~~~~~~~~~~~~

Symon strolls in trying his best to stay cool, in spite of his nerves being frazzled. The sound of buzzing intensifies, and round a corner is the control room for the generator. He was expecting a complex set up, but perhaps not this complex. He shuffles up to it and can now make out a glass panel and another control panel alongside that. After close examination, he doesn't notice anything out of the ordinary. Still he needed to be cautious, he did not know these surroundings. He wouldn't be sure what was ordinary until it perhaps hit him straight in the face. A few yards to his left, a flashing orange light is activated. He's certain he hadn't detected the light before. Could he have triggered an alarm? Had a camera spotted him and triggered an alert? All conjecture at the moment. No one apprehends him with wrapped arms, so he must focus and carry on till the generator is disabled. He knew there'd be a master control switch and it would more than likely be next to an override switch. He felt the pressure stifling, needed to find and activate it. Tyler was counting on him.

He studies the region, tapping into his engineering and electronic knowledge and blueprint. A section grabs his attention, not lit, as if purposely cast in shadows. Enough circuitry leading away from this corner of the room. He dashes over to the section and is relieved to find the control switch, it is as expected. Without catering to any more thought, he lifts the shield and rams it with the cushiony side of his fist.

To his dismay, nothing happens, there is a change in the sound and a click, but the electricity remains in use. He scrutinises the region again, and recognises the problem. There had to be an additional switch. He needed to find it quickly, because pressing the first would have triggered a siren for sure. He settles his hands on his head and stretches as he takes in a deep breath. He studies the circuitry again and detects they all feed into another locality above him. He follows the cables and wire with peering eyes and detects the switch he also needs to press, except it is out of reach. He immediately searches for a ladder, there had to be one somewhere. Not much time and Tyler's window of opportunity for getting into the lift shrunk by the second. The furrow on his brow creases further, but then he detects some kind of metal jutting out of a corner. He goes over to it and pulls what he can now tell is a lever. A ladder is released and slowly drops. He leaps onto it and scrambles halfway up to reach the additional switch that needs to be pressed. He flips the plastic shield and presses the button, which instantaneously plunges everywhere into darkness. A dull clicking sound comes from yards away to his right, and he hopes the sound is the backup generator automatically kicking in. In a few minutes, sentinels will be surrounding him, but Tyler would be bought a few minutes to arrive at the elevator, before electricity is reinstated. He knew that during an outage the lift always slowly descended to the bottom.

23E

The shrilling siren shrieks just before the dimmed floodlights around him extinguish. He has a rough idea of how long he's got, before surveillance is back up and running again. He dashes out from his hiding corner and sprints over to the first barricade in his way. The electronic door is partly open. Tyler slips his fingers in the gap and prys the doors open, pleased with the minimum amount of effort used, he squeezes through the gap and sprints to the next barrier. There were three to get through. Again, information from many invited to the surface, no reason to doubt it.

In no time, he approaches the second barrier and this time the gap is too little to push his fingers through. He retrieves his implement and unties his extra shoelaces and using both together, manages to pry open the doors, enough so he can squeeze his fingers through. He gasps when his fingers are through, suddenly realising he'd been holding his breath, and he pulls the doors open, again, enough to squeeze his body through. Thank god he was lean, they all were down in the caverns. Small portions of food and manual labour each day guaranteed that.

Once through, he begins running at full pelt to the last one. He's running blind, and runs straight into a wall. Stunned. Was oblivious and ran off course and out of a straight line. He shakes away his momentary daze and realigns himself. No time for disorientation. He sprints again with all his might, a few yards and his left ankle protests and he stumbles and falls hard on the cold floor.

'Jeez,' he mutters, as he scrambles up on his feet and picks up the pace again.

Time threatened forlorn, every second was precious. He reaches the third and final barrier, and to his relief the gap is wide enough for his fingers, he prys the doors open. The muffled growling sound of the back up generator kicks in, trying to mask the shrill siren carrying on along the corridor. He catches sight of the lift up ahead and runs with all his might to it. Lights begin to illuminate the passage and the cameras begin to come to life. He runs like his life depended on it—something a lot bigger than him depended on it.

~~~~~~~~~~~~~~~~~~~~~~~~~~~~~

In no time the security guards would be upon him, like termites protecting their queen. Not far from the truth at all. Adira was their queen, a damn fine one at that. Symon looks for something sharp and spots a cable sticking out amongst other cables. He pulls at it, then bites down to shred the plastic sheath. He's taking the risk of being electrocuted, but he doesn't care. He yanks at one of the wires and grinds it against a metal bar until it snaps in half. He pulls the sleeve up on his left arm and proceeds to cut into his flesh, avoiding the main artery as he doesn't wish to bleed to death. He just needed to create enough fuss to put the guards off reacting too harshly. His right arm he would spare—just in case.

A steady flow of blood oozes out of his arm, as an electronic door slides open. Three guards approach in a synchronised fashion, taser gun ready. Two black men and one white man. They spot the blood on the floor and on Symon's arm. They also note Symon is unarmed, and they lower their weapons. The two black men presumably never met with the same fate when stopped by white policemen back on earth. In their experience, white cops, blinded by unconscious bias, would have dived in and flung their captive to the ground and roughed them up. Notwithstanding the blood. Despite being unarmed. The guards appreciated how ridiculous this was and just because *they* were treated wrongly, they saw no point in doing the same. A ridiculous act remained a ridiculous act, no reason to repeat it, out of some misplaced sense of revenge.

'Hey, are you okay? What ya doing in here? Does the peeress know you're here?'

'Yes... The peeress knows,' Symon lies through clenched teeth.

'Please come with us. We'll let her verify that.'

For a second or two, Symon wonders if he should put up a fight. It would be him up against three solidly built men though. He didn't think it would end well for him and so threw out the thought, almost as soon as it materialised in his stupid head.

'Okay, okay.' Symon props both his arms up. Blood drips down the side of him, staining his white clothes in crimson red. The white guard detaches a mini first aid kit attached to his belt and removes a bandage. He gently lowers Symon's arm, and begins administering first aid. Symon takes a deep breath and let's him.

'So, was that you? That turned off the generators... was that you?'

'A huge accident, I wanted to see what would happen. Didn't expect that to happen though.' Symon lies again through his teeth, not as clenched this time. He's aware his explanation is lame, but it would have to do.

'What did you expect to happen?' Another one of the guards scorns.

'I wasn't thinking.'

'There, that should do it. Now please come with us, we'll take you back to the peeress. She'll decide what we do with you.'

Symon was pleased with this idea. Delighted even. There was a chance. 80 percent sure Adira would spare him, had only recently made love for crying out loud.

~~~~~~~~~~~~~~~~~~~~~~~~~~~~

Tyler is in the elevator heading up, he tries to control his breathing. The tricky bit was achieved. Most of the sentries would still be around the generator plant with any luck, which should give him time to infiltrate. Luminous light in the elevator blinded, thank god there was some time for his eyes to adjust. What he needed first and foremost were clothes to blend in and a security card for access. He should find both of them on the same person. He wished this would be the last person he knocked out, because though skilled at it—knowing precisely where to hit to render most average men unconscious—he didn't like doing it. He needed a mooncat though, so anticipated having to do the same again.

To his outright inconvenience, he also needed the toilet. A number two as well. Adrenaline and nerves always guarantee you needing a poo. Fortunately, it wasn't the pressing kind, he should be able to hold it for a while.

He watches the electronic lit pad carefully, no floors. Only up or down, and artificial gravity told him he was still ascending. He senses the elevator begin to slow down, proceeds closer to the door and intuitively settles himself into a fighting stance. The doors open and to his dismay, people roam the corridor, although all facing the other way, all taking orders from someone. The alarm was still blaring, conveniently drowning out the sound of the elevator arriving. Tyler creeps out of the elevator, away from the group of three or maybe four people. He spots what appears to be another air conditioning unit, and he uses it for cover, at least until he figures out what to do. He scours above him, no cameras to be seen. Not needed on the base, he guessed, everybody was trusted. That served him well. He attempts to listen in to the orders being given to the men and is convinced he picks up Symon's name. They seem to be arguing.

I don't think we should be questioning the peeress / No, questioning her is a bad idea. / Look we're not pets or something, we've been given our rights like equals, we must question if things are not, otherwise, I fear we lose our respect.../ There is no "our," we are all one now, ain't we? / But this is unheard of, he was caught red-handed in the plant room, no question he was the one that jeopardised the power.../ Symon / I don't buy the whole I was lost and look, I've injured myself plea / No that is bullshit I think too... / Well, that's for her to decide, no reason for us to overreact. I'm sure she has her reasons, and we have to respect them. / Hmph, seems we are nothing but obedient pets afterall / Well we are not going to rally around our kind, women have given us some kind of normal life / On the moon no less / Had to be on the moon / Couldn't figure it out on earth.

Tyler detects another guard walking a few yards away, certain now the guard was also amongst the group when he exited the elevator. The humming sound emitted from the air conditioning unit changes for a moment, and one of the guards gazes over. Tyler cowers and holds his breath. The guard narrows his eyes for a few seconds, inspecting the unit, squinting, then finally turns away. Tyler assumes they must be familiarised with the changing humming patterns. Sounds no different to the grunts a refrigerator sometimes makes. His fridge back on earth made some peculiar noises; groans and grunts, like an obese person was snoring, or having sex. Atimes he thought the refrigerator was possessed.

The three men start to walk off and Tyler allows himself to breathe; he'd been holding it the whole time.

He assesses his next move. A few yards to the left of him, before a junction with two adjoining corridors leading in opposite courses, is another unit. He opts to make a move for it, he could not afford to hesitate, would have to take some risk. If that group double backed, they would spot him for sure. He stays crouched and creeps along, conscious he makes his steps as light as feathers.

As a result of his poor vision down in the caverns, his hearing was heightened a little. His eyes adjusted somewhat now, albeit they still hurt if staring into any light source, regardless of the intensity. He reaches the next unit and positions himself so he's obscured from the two viewpoints of the corridors. He left himself open to the passage he'd just come from, in the hope that the patrol would not be making that round again for a while. However, another group could be coming, so it was time to make quick decisions. Playing chess honed this ability for him. He scans in front for any doorways. He needed to steal the opportunity of someone being on their own, not allowing himself to dwell on the slim chances of that happening. Most patrols would be in a group of two or three. If faced with a group of three, a distraction technique would be his next move. He needed something he could throw in a vicinity he wanted someone to move toward, giving him time to move in the opposite direction. With any luck two of the sentinels might go to investigate and one would stay behind, giving him an opportunity to take him out. He needed to be very careful nonetheless. He couldn't mess this up, doubtful he would get this opening again. It was now or never.

~~~~~~~~~~~~~~~~~~~~~~~~~~~~~

'Exactly what were you thinking? Have you completely lost it? I suppose now you'll blame us for putting you all down there! Never mind the atrocities you prompted whilst on earth. This is already a precarious situation. You and me, and now *this*. How am I supposed to explain this? God! Is there any wonder why women took over —'

'Okay! Okay—don't burst a blood vessel.' Symon interrupts.

Adira forgot to draw breath while venting. She plods up and down her quarters. Her face puffed in vexation to a deep reddish brown, like a variety of beetroot. She plucks hold of the picture always in her pocket and glares at it.

'I wanted to explore the plant room, see what would happen if I pressed a button. I was restless, you know how I get.'

'Please don't do that Symon...please.'

'Do what?'

'Lie through your teeth.' Adira now peers up at Symon and squares him in the face. 'You seem to forget we were married for over 16 years. I can tell when you're lying, probably one reason we broke up—knew each other too well; it killed any spark left. Besides, yes you can be restless, but never after sex. After sex, you're...pacified for hours... barely an hour has passed!'

Symon gapes at the floor.

'So... truth when you're ready please!'

'Was helping a friend.'

'What do you mean, helping a friend? How?'

'A friend of mine. He can't stand being locked up. Some people are not intended to be caged.'

'Who are you now? Maya Angelou?'

'What?'

'Never mind—help a friend how exactly? Oh God!... what are you saying, that you've let someone infiltrate the base?'

'Well yes and no.'

'What does that mean? This is no time for riddles, Symon.'

'It shouldn't be me up here, are you aware of that? The results must have been rigged or something. Or the power outage fucked the results up. It should never have been me. It was fate that it turned out this way. I may never have known you were up here, and happen to be the boss no less. The other guy should have been here. He knew something... I knew there was something up. Even so, he let me come, despite having planned this for god knows how long.'

'What are you talking about?'

'A good friend of mine. *He* should be here. But by some fluke I am, and we meet. I promised him. I promised I'd get him up.'

'Oh great, so you did facilitate someone getting up here.' Adira goes to press the button to the telecoms.

'No! wait! wait! Adira please, just wait. He means no harm, he is the nicest person. He only wants to be on the space station, spend out his days on Mr Drake I reckon. He means no harm. He just can't take it being down in the caverns, he's too smart for that. He'll die if he stays down there, he'll die for sure. He can't be caged.'

Adira pauses for a long while and then perches down on the bed. 'Amusing huh, the turn of events. When blacks were being enslaved, I wonder whether at any stage white men even accommodated the thought that some may just not be able to cope with being held captive. Well...we know they didn't, not for a long while, because we weren't even seen as humans. Superior pets is how one white man referred to black people.'

Symon perches down next to Adira and stares at the floor, moments pass.

'So now what, I'm supposed to pretend someone *hasn't* infiltrated and let him rocket off to Mr Drake? At what cost? Isn't this some kind of treason?'

'I think it's only treason if an action is *done* against you.'

'Seriously—you're choosing to irritate me *now*?'

'Sorry.'

'What would he do on the space station? There's just AI and machines.'

'I guess that's the only way he can feel free. Not captive.'

'It doesn't make sense.'

'Does everything have to make sense? If informed that we would be returning to Amazonian times, when women ruled, would you have believed it?'

'Point taken—So what's your plan? What's *his* plan? Do you know if he made it?'

'Well, no —could we check the cameras, deactivate the cameras so he's not caught?'

'Uh uh! It's one thing turning a blind eye, now you're asking me to aid and abet. No! absolutely not! If he wants to fly off to the space station, then he needs to figure it out for himself. More satisfactory for him that way—if he makes it that is, there are a few people on shift there.'

Symon is surprised Adira has accepted this so far but decides not to dwell on it. 'You could be a bit more Jacinda Ardern,' he mutters under his breath, as he plays with his fingers.

'*Now* you're restless.' Adira rises to fetch a drink of the infamous space alcohol. Clearly having not heard what Symon said.

~~~~~~~~~~~~~~~~~~~~~~~~~~~~

Progress was being made so far. Tyler managed to find a toilet cubicle which he used without anyone detecting him. With created gravity, there was no need for the suction fan. That would have alerted the guards to his presence for sure. On the space station, he would be compelled to use suction fans due to the zero gravity.

The air conditioning units succoured him, aiding him with stealthing his way through. He remembered the Playstation game called Metal Gear Solid. It was a remake and was one hell of a stealth game. Snake on the moon. He relied on his memory of the surroundings, and mapped it out in his head over and over. He didn't see the point of putting anything down in writing. Firstly, no paper anyway and if he was to start losing parts of clothing, suspicions would be raised. He only had to make it past two more junctions, then he would be a few yards away from where the mooncats were stationed.

Tyler estimated a rough timing of the guard patrol, and waited at this spot for a few more minutes before advancing further. As he waited, a memory fluttered in of a meditation session he once attended.

He started doing meditation for a few months during a pandemic on earth. The pandemic should have been the wake up call for human beings, but alas humans lived on as inauthentic addictive zombies. A more devastating pandemic took hold of the human race and still humans carried on, crippled with fear and stupidity. People fundamentally became so busy in their lives; distracted by emails, texts, Facebook and Instagram posts, and forgot how to be present in their lives and how to authentically connect with another human being. They decided to stay in their mechanical slumber; familiarity providing deluded comfort. He recognised—after a few months—that meditating made him less forgetful and he realised it was a direct result of being more present in each and every moment.

He once left a cup of pomegranate and raspberry smoothie on top of his car while rearranging things inside, to clear a slot for the cup, ironically to stop it spilling as he drove. In the process of tidying up, he'd forgotten what he tidied up for and got in and started to drive. After a minute or so he remembered and stopped the car abruptly, causing the entire contents of the thick reddish smoothie to spill down the windscreen, to the shock of some pedestrians. Must have thought he hit and killed a bird.

Meditation put a stop to instances like this. Was definitely more alert and enlightened in the moment and so subtle, he only realised hours after the event.

One session in particular, he always remembered with a chuckle. Six of them attended that particular morning, and he could sense he was more peaceful than the last few days. The host spoke for a few minutes getting the participants to consciously be connected to their breath and selves, perched on a stool. Then he would strike a bell three times, cue for you to sit still with your eyes closed, observing the now in each moment. He would mute everyone to eliminate any interference. This particular morning, the session seemed to go on for a long time. After being sure a considerable amount of time elapsed and being conscious of being late for work. He decided to take a peek, only to find a couple of people doing the same on the video feed. Everybody was pondering; eyes popping out of heads for some, while others creased their foreheads like used napkins; then everyone realised the host had fallen asleep. No one was able to wake him up as everyone was on mute. Most unmuted themselves and spoke to one another, enjoying a belly laugh at the fact the host slipped into a slumber during a session.

The sound of shuffling feet brings Tyler rushing back to the present. Distracted by memories of meditation sessions, his mind smiled at the irony. He cowers down more, ensuring he is all concealed. Two sentinels approach from the left, so he shuffles further to the right. On assessing the situation, he could see he would be spotted, no matter what he did, so he was forced to incapacitate them and it had to be executed in the camera's blind spot and briskly. Grateful for the combat training when working as a prisoner guard, he was going to access that training now. Thankfully, the sentinels didn't carry guns, not a great idea in any pressurised unit. Instead, they had in their possession what looked like batons, he suspected probably some kind of stunning equipment, either way he had to disarm them or make them unable to use their weapons and he had to act quickly.

All things aside I wouldn't have done that / Done what? / You know, the thing you do with your sexbot / Oh don't be silly, they're only plastic and cables / Uh huh, you say that, we still put our dick in it though / No different to using fleshlight, it's just that these ones talk.

He twiddles his thumbs, till the men are inside the blind spot and the camera is starting to turn the other way. Then he rushes in. Coming up from a crouched position it made sense to hit the nearest guy the old fashioned way. Both guys are startled and go for their batons which are attached to their sides. Tyler drives his right fist into the balls of the closest guy and in a flash uses the other guy's neck as a pole vault. The guy was heavily built and Tyler calculated he could withstand this manoeuvre without losing his balance, and bringing both of them crashing to the floor. He swings round his neck from the front to the back of him and proceeds to throttle him. The muscular neck requires him to apply a significant amount of pressure. Tyler keeps an eye on the other guy who is now on the floor rolling around, both hands on his crotch. A pool of watery vomit is splattered by his feet. A hard, precision strike to a man's testicles would do that. This should keep him in enough discomfort, while he incapacitates the guy whose neck he was throttling. Tyler applies more pressure. The camera starts to turn back round and Tyler can now see the guy with the painful testes had fallen just short of the blind spot. The guy being strangled stretches to claw at Tyler, but Tyler's positioned himself out of reach. Clued up now there's only a few more seconds to play with, he increases his pressure on the carotid artery, until the guy's deadweight strains on his arms.

He inches himself along till he's certain he is wholly in the camera's blind spot and then releases the guy, then he crouches forward and yanks the leg of the other guy on the floor, also pulling him into the blind spot. He grapples his neck and does the same on the carotid artery, cutting the blood flow. It doesn't take the other guy long before he is out cold. He drags both of them individually and tucks them the best he can behind the air conditioning unit, just as the camera starts to turn the other way again.

He never intended on using violence, but knew this was unlikely. He was also aware he was running out of time. Unconscious bodies will be discovered soon enough. He finds his next blind spot and times the camera on both ends. When he's satisfied with the timings, he makes his move to the next air conditioning unit. He adjusts his back as he creeps across, the positioning takes a toll on his back. He was going to need a long stretch when this was over; probably before stealing the ride with the mooncat. A blast of cold air to his right causes him goose pimples and he detects an air conditioning unit not accounted for in his mind's blueprint. He freezes on the spot to assess and scrutinise the sector. Nothing suspicious stood out, but another camera threatened in the distance and he had to be careful not to fall into view. He creeps slowly forward, the surprise of the air conditioning unit and the camera up ahead, curbing a slice of his confidence. He checks where he's come from and has now lost sight of the two guards taken out earlier. Concealed. Superb. He adjusts his back the other way and sucks his tummy in to strengthen his core. He desperately needed to stand, as his lower back ached and throbbed, but he couldn't take the risk. Had to suck it up, literally; and keep moving with great caution.

24R

An enormous, golden sun rises on the far side of the moon, throwing creepy shadows on aspects of the ashen rocky exterior. Marcel and Belize have assessed the damage to the greenhouse and cleared out the remnants of glass, so a new pane of glass could be easily installed. They tidy up around the outside in slow motion.

'Do you really think earth will be ready to inhabit in just two years?' Marcel ponders.

'According to the AI calculations ... *about* two years.' Belize replies.

'It kind of makes it tricky to sustain the present arrangement huh?'

'What do you... Oh, you mean with the guys in the caverns.'

'Yes — unless the peeress is thinking of leaving them here?'

'Well, to be honest I hadn't thought about that, for sure it's going to be troublesome, transportation that is—opens the doors to all kinds of problems.'

'Do you think the human race will ever learn and be better?'

'Hmm...I want to be optimistic, but how many lessons did we need, and we still snapped back into the same old ways. Covid 19 didn't teach us anything and then, not too long after, Covid 24 and still we resumed our selfish deeds with total disregard for our planet. So I'm not too sure. We like to think we're smart, but we're not. Do you remember the article about the male sperm cell fooling humankind for 450 years. A microscopic sperm cell made us believe it swam symmetrically, which turns out was a complete illusion, as the tail was wonky and so the sperm cell flicked side to side when moving, to compensate for the *asymmetrical* movement, making it appear it swam in a straight line. Do you remember that? I find that story hilarious. Says it all really—fooled by a sperm cell for 450 years.'

Marcel chuckles. 'I do remember that and you're right, it is funny.'

'Christ, just thought...isn't that about the same number of years blacks were being enslaved.'

'Oh Jesus, you're right. How weird.' Marcel unbuckles himself from the anchor next to the structure being cleared.

'How weird for sure — Right, let's round this up and get out of here, we don't want to be caught in the full beam of that blazing orb, she's coming up fast. Belize considers the orangey horizon as she unbuckles herself. Flashbacks of Agenta floating into space fill her neural cortex again, she wonders whether that image will always remain as a stain in her mind.

Both of them take measured leaps toward the mooncat.

~~~~~~~~~~~~~~~~~~~~~~~~~~~~~

The crouching really began to play on Tyler's back, sending aching cramp up and down his vertebrae, as if a xylophone was being bashed with a branch. He desperately needed some relief. He examines the area ahead of him and a corner where he may be able to stand and stretch presents itself to him. Would definitely need to do some light exercises before wearing the space suit anyway, to ensure any trapped air in his gut was expelled. Flatulence in space could be lethal. After all he'd been through, being killed by his own fart would be unacceptable.

Tyler studies the area and times the camera as normal and then makes his move. He reaches the spot in under a minute and then stands, stretching. The relief is instant, like an ice cube on a tongue fired up with a scotch bonnet chilli. His back clicks. He stretches his arms above his head and clasps his hands. Then stretches to the left and then to the right. One of the simpler yoga positions. Then he bends over with straight firm legs, lets himself drop, pulling on his spinal vertebrae, much needed. He stands upright again and repeats the process, as he bends down to continue his stretch, a side door in the corridor opens. He drops to the floor like a marionette whose strings have just been severed. Face down. He should be out of view in this stance. Two men can be heard talking.

'Well, he said he was knocked unconscious and no one can locate him in the caverns, so we have to assume he is here I would say.'

'But how? How could he have reached the surface?'

Bound to happen sooner or later, Tyler of course aspired for later. Skyler must have regained consciousness and raised an alarm. He waited for an alarm, but guessed they decided against it. Better to leave him in a sense of false security, catch him unawares. Excellent strategy, if the blabbermouths near him hadn't ruined it.

Now he knew.

Had overheard.

Luck wanted to be his friend again.

He steadily takes in a deep breath and tucks his tummy, as he relaxes into the floor. Both men start to walk away from him, still carrying on their conversation. Had to move quicker now, time didn't want to be his friend anymore. He was surprised no alert had been raised from the two knocked out yet, but it was only a matter of time. He wondered if they had chosen not to sound the alarm so as to maintain a false sense of security.

He couldn't be far away from the mooncats now, and he quickened his pace, by crouching less as he moved. Compelled to play with some risk of a camera spotting him. Once he obtained a mooncat, he could buy himself some time.

~~~~~~~~~~~~~~~~~~~~~~~~~~~

A reddish orange glow eats up the shadows on the moon's surface. Scattered craters swallow up the coloured light burning into the moon exterior, rapidly turning it into atomic tangerine. Racing ahead in a mooncat, away from the encroaching sun rays are Marcel and Belize. The moon automobile crunches up fragments of rock as it pummels forward. Regardless of the visual crunching of rock as the mooncat gains speed, no sound can be heard. Marcel and Belize speak through their intercom to fill the silence and perhaps wash over their slight angst over the burning projection of the sun only yards behind them.

'I heard you were close to Agenta.' Marcel felt some unease at wording the sentence.

'Yes, I was.' Belize couldn't make up her mind if she wanted to divulge anymore.

'I'm sorry for your loss.'

'Thank you...So, are you with someone?'

'Erm...yes I'm kinda dating someone. I think we're really lucky because we don't have to worry about getting pregnant.'

'Yeah...yeah you're right.' Belize struggles to swallow a lump formed in her throat. She is grateful for the helmet as her facial expressions are concealed. She holds back tears, mostly because teary eyes in Zero G are a real pain, just sticks to your eyes, blurring your vision.

'What do you think would happen if the boy turns out to be straight when he grows up?' Marcel inquires.

'Well... Adira is convinced that he wouldn't need the same indoctrination and so will be fine. He won't be exposed to racism, I'm certain of it. It would be an interesting conversation though, that's for sure.' Belize is grateful for the change in subject matter.

The mooncat jolts as it nudges a bigger rock out of the way. Marcel and Belize both look in the direction of the jolt and then to the orangey distance. They'd picked up enough speed to reduce their anxieties. Relieved, they secured their attention to each other.

'How old is he now?'

'I think he's six.' Belize replies.

'Do you think... do you think...not sure how to ask this —sorry, do you think there is danger of mixed race people becoming the next superior race.'

'Gosh, I'd never thought of that. Thankfully half black means full black, or at least is seen as such. I still wonder how it all came to this, would humans ever be able to live in harmony, embracing all kinfolk and differences? So far, we are just switching places.'

'Well, we fucked up the air we breathe on our own planet, it doesn't get any more crass than that.'

'No it doesn't, if we all learnt to live simpler lives, perhaps we would still be on a planet.'

'Do you really think earth would be habitable again in about two years?'

'Not really sure, that's what the AI reports, so your guess is as good as mine.'

'How come we never gave the AI a name...you know like in the movies?'

'Ha, I guess Adira didn't want us to personalise them in any way. Hence, the sexbots having their ridiculous names.'

'Makes sense.' Marcel fidgets, his tummy rumbles and apprehension sets in. He was thankful his cold, white, sterile home was in sight.

'You okay?' Belize studies his body language.

'Yes, yes I'm grand, just an itch.' Marcel comfortably delivers his white lie.

'Almost there now.' Belize meditates on the burnt orange crest left behind. She ponders on how long the sun had before it burnt out. How impermanent everything was— even the sun would one day expire.

'Do you believe there are survivors in Iceland?' Marcel asks, peering at the incoming sun beam.

'You know, it wouldn't surprise me at all if there were. One of the only countries with a zero carbon footprint. They devised everything around utilising the resources they had and not wasting anything. Why the rest of the world didn't learn by their example I never understood. Pride I guess. Either that or stupidity, or perhaps both.'

Marcel is transfixed, watching the sun beam travel towards them; illuminating the grey, pitted, rocky regolith.

'Do *you* think there are survivors in Iceland?'

'I guess it's likely, they built a big enough retreat as a contingency. No doubt they would have predicted our demise long before *we* got wind of it.' Marcel now steals his eyes away from the atomic-tangerine horizon and focuses on Belize. 'Quite plausible they won't want us to return, they might think we don't deserve a planet,' he continues.

'Very true, and in some way I wouldn't blame them — We're approaching the depot now.'

~~~~~~~~~~~~~~~~~~~~~~~~~~~~~

Tyler squeezes through a gap in a doorway which had been temperamental. It didn't seem to register the pass on his stolen uniform, and had had to go right up to it, looking for anything that resembled a sensor. Frantically jumping up and down before the door started to open. Then it got stuck.

Seconds after he's managed to squeeze through, a subdued siren sounds and the decompression chamber is activated; little yellow, green and blue luminescence flashing in no particular order. Tyler senses the muscles in his stomach tighten. Was the decompression chamber being activated because of him? He doubted it. A distinct tang of sulphur fills the air, it reminds him of his time in college —carrying out experiments in the lab. Tyler recognises this as the smell of outer space, like being in a shooting range, it smelt like gunpowder. He is more than likely near some kind of open hatch. He peers out of one of the reinforced windows and spots in the distance, a mooncat coming in. In the distance, behind them, a burnt orange glow shimmers. That would explain the alarm. Tyler dashes his eyes around, searching for cover.

He detects two mooncats getting charged, in what looks to be a small parking bay. The charge on one is almost complete. He can tell this by the small green rectangular bars on the side. Four out of the five bars illuminate a lime green.

The two arriving, are yards away, their mooncat would be out of charge. He hoped they were not returning to put it on charge, to take another. Unlikely, unless they planned on going in the opposite direction. Exceptional intel confirmed there were four mooncats in total, and so he expeditiously scanned the region for another. If there was another, then it was hidden away well, as he couldn't spot it. More likely though, another one was out with two others on a mission. He squeezes himself between two units that resemble generators. He's lost vision of the two arriving now, but is in full view of the door that leads into the sector he's in. He's convinced they wouldn't be able to spot him, unless they bent down. In a corner, to his right are a few space suits, he rests his eyes on one that should fit him. He knew fully well he'd have to cope with the reduced allowance in the groin region and extra room in the chest area. He didn't mind this so much, instead was more concerned about the uniform being laundered, as space dust on your skin itches worse than the side effect from taking chloroquine tablets for malaria.

Tyler recognises only a small window in time remains to get on a mooncat and travel to the rocket station. If he misses the window, it would be a 14-day wait, the time the sun stayed, with temperatures reaching 127 degrees centigrade. Not an option.

There is the clanking of the hatch being opened, and the blast of gases to expel any space dust on the returning travellers. All left to do now was wait.

The tang of sulphur is strong now, even with the reinforced glass between him and the parking bay. Marcel and Belize exit the mooncat and walk over to a cubicle to be cleansed. Gravity is almost sustained, the lights glow green in turn. He can't decide whether to wait till Marcel and Belize are out of the way or make his move straight away. He finally resigned to waiting. Patience is a virtue, they always said that back on earth. Won't be any good for him if he's fried by the incoming sun though.

"I have enough time— I have enough time—I have enough time." Tyler allows these words to loop around his cortex. As he does so, another peripheral thought about infinite loops in computing, flutters in. His face registers a suppressed grin.

Marcel and Belize finally finish their sterilising and access the room in which Tyler is cowering. Belize enters first and then Marcel.

"Not such an obvious G boy." Tyler catches his thoughts and grimaces. How many days had he spent criticising Symon for this term. Hypocrite. And not once either, he was sure this already crossed his mind before. He cowers down some more, folding himself into a foetus. Belize goes over to switch a few buttons and controls. Marcel ambles over and starts removing his suit carefully in another enclosed cubicle, in case any leftover residue of space dust resided. Belize finally does the same. They are both stripped to their underwear in minutes. Tyler darts his eyes away, the effect from having not seen a real life woman form for years. Subtle imperfections made humans human, a blemish and mole here and there, the odd wrinkle, the portion of extra flab or fat —all which made people, people. The sexbots were too perfect. He likened it to women who insisted on putting on a lot of makeup, caking it on like another layer of skin. With the sexbots, this had reached a whole new level. He never really found the sexbots did it for him, but where needs must and all that, and so he succumbed a few times, revelling in the frustration of the sexbot trying to make him come.

'You think what we accomplished is enough to secure the sector for 14 days?' Marcel struggles to put his foot into the uniform he's retrieved from a locker.

'Yes, it should be fine. The main thing is we moved the solar panels, so it should be fine.' Belize retrieves her clothes from another locker.

'Do you have any side effects from being on the moon for this long?' Marcel continues his questioning.

'Gosh, what is this? Space question hour?' Belize cross-examines jokingly.

'Sorry, just intrigued I guess.'

'Well, to be honest, I reckon having a community reduces any adverse side effects. And don't forget we have the positive of not ageing as fast. That's got to be good, right?' Belize proclaims, before pulling her top over her head.

'Oh yeah, the time dilation effect. I remember studying that at college and jesting with my peers about botox and the like going out of business in space.'

'Yup, time moves slower as gravity increases—Time also moves slower when you practise mindfulness and engage in learning new things. Becoming stagnant and monotonous are time's biggest propeller.'

'Wow, never heard it expressed like that before.' Marcel starts putting on his boots.

'Got into mindfulness and philosophy at college. If people cottoned on to doing mindfulness sooner we may not be in the mess we're in. Earth may still be habitable. Not to mention the ridiculous race issue. Learning to be with our minds in a more healthy way should have been recognised and acted on, alternatively we focused on trivialities — Anyway, ready?'

'Yes almost done... Oh, we didn't put the mooncat on charge, did we?'

'Damn it! Will have to go back out and do that, the other team should be back soon and they may need two mooncats.' Belize starts to undress, pulling the garment off with huffs and puffs.

This news makes Tyler's stomach turn— and it produces an audible growl in protest.

Marcel fixes his gaze in the viewpoint where Tyler is hiding. 'What was that?'

'What was what?' Belize cross examines, as she scurringly puts her boots on.

'Thought I heard something.' Marcel turns back to Belize.

'We're in a room full of electronics and machines, of course you heard something. I'll be right back Galileo.' Belize skips to her feet, enters a code and leaves through the automatic doors. Marcel studies her as the doors close.

Tyler bites on his lower lip and surveys to the left and to the right, deep in thought. He needed to think of something, he couldn't afford to waste any more time. He takes in a slow deep breath, conscious that his stomach may make gurgling protests again. No sooner after exhaling, he felt a tremor. For a few seconds, he thought it was the other mooncat returning, then remembered no tremor took place when the recent one got back. The tremor increases and then a siren is activated. Marcel starts to press buttons and switches in response. Tyler realises they were experiencing a moonquake. A rare occurrence, and not as damaging, at any rate, it warranted a distress signal. Tyler recognises this may be his window of opportunity.

Belize rushes in. 'Mooncat's on charge. Let's get out of here!'

~~~~~~~~~~~~~~~~~~~~~~~~~~~~~~

Voices and echoes of voices reverberate around him. He's relieved, he's still, he couldn't be floating in outer space. His neck aches a tad. He endeavours to recollect what happened. Then it comes rushing back to him.

He visited Tyler, chatted for a while, and then something hit him from behind. As much as he could sieve out of his memory bank. He must have been knocked out unconscious. Tyler obviously knew where to strike. He obviously didn't want him dead either or he guessed he would be. He attempts to open his eyes but the light is blinding, he must be back on the base. He caught himself wishing he was back in the caverns. The intensity of the light was that unbearable. Blinding white. His mouth and throat are as dry as pages in a hardback. He attempts to speak, but can't utter any words, not even "water." A little amount of precious life liquid would help him speak. The cousins to dehydration present themselves; dizziness and a headache. He chooses to put out his hand rather than call out.

'Hey, we have movement here,' says someone in a grainy voice.

Skyler senses someone's hand on their wrist.

'Hey, you're in the CS unit —you're okay. Do you need anything?' The grainy voice again.

Skyler opens their mouth to speak and again fails. Their tongue is as worthless as a slug covered in salt. Alternatively, they point to their opened mouth.

'Water, I think they need water... someone get them some water.'

Skyler takes some comfort from the hand on their wrist, enjoying the warmth it gave off. Memories of past lovers encountered when back on earth flood his cortex. The ones great in bed tended to be the ones that, for some reason, radiated a lot of heat. Not surprising, the ones with higher metabolic rates were fantastic in bed, but not great sleeping with one on a hot muggy night. Not an issue with the sexbots, the body temperature was regulated accordingly, turning fridge-cold if needed.

An unmistakable sense of care is sensed in the grip, firm but tender. They felt a finger leisurely caress their skin, or was it their imagination? Were they concussed?

'Don't open your eyes yet.' The guy says.

"No shit Sherlock." Skyler immediately thinks.

~~~~~~~~~~~~~~~~~~~~~~~~~~~~

Brown and cream glistening sweaty bodies intermingle, like two giant slugs mating. Their need for every inch of their bodies to be touched by the other is evident in their love making. They both climax together. Adira lets out a suppressed moan. Symon stays on top of Adira for a while, kissing her forehead and closed eyes. She soon gets her breathing back to normal, only for it to pick up again when a tremor shakes the quarters and soon afterwards the siren ceases. She slithers out from underneath Symon, and thumbs the intercom.

'Report please,' she mutters, pulling a robe around her.

'Moonquake mam, all under control.'

Adira sits down and takes a deep breath.

'Don't think this changes anything, I'm still mad at you.' She turns to look at Symon.

'I can see you're still mad, and I'm sorry.' Symon manages to say, as his breathing is still not back to normal.

'For a second then I thought...' Adira abandons talking and lowers her head to her knees and then wraps her arms around her knees.

'I know, so did I.' Symon intuitively knows what she tried to say.

Adira lifts her head and focuses on him. 'You're relieved... you love this man.'

'I guess I do.' Symon replies, without being self conscious. 'He made me reflect, made me look at myself, made me challenge my macho bullshit.'

'Wow, can see why you want to help him... at risk to your life no doubt.'

'He'll be okay right?' Symon stares right into Adira's eyes.

'Well, we've not heard anything yet, not since the two guards were incapacitated. If he gets to the station, I'd say he made it. No point going after one man, he can't do any harm on Mr Drake.'

Symon walks over to Adira and perches next to her.

'So grateful I found you.'

Adira takes his hand in hers. 'Well... going to be a challenge convincing the people about freeing the guys in the caverns.'

'You'll do that?'

'Well of course, can't just release *you* because you're my husband.'

'But the base won't be able to accommodate us all.'

'Then we will take it in turns to mine in the caverns. Oppression of any kind is wrong, we should figure out a way to work together.'

'What about the peeds?'

'They will have to stay in the caverns, can't put the children at risk.'

Symon draws in a long breath.

A long pause ensues, in which both Adira and Symon are comfortable.

'Why do you think predominantly, white men are paedophiles?'

'Well, not predominantly...100% white men—for children under 12 anyway. Some Asians and blacks have historically abused girls and boys aged 16, 15 at a push. Hebephilia to be precise. Interference with prepubescent children on the other hand...only ever been white men, in rare cases, white women.'

'Jeez, a damning report for sure.'

'Even more interestingly, did you notice how middle aged white men were never profiled as a potential paedophile? Even though unerringly they are more likely to be, compared to other races. That's a tell tale sign of racism if I ever knew one.'

Symon is speechless.

'It is what it is. We'll figure something out with our lot.'

'You're remarkable.' Symon squeezes her hand.

'Well, don't get excited just yet, need to formulate a plan, a flawless master plan, if I'm going to convince the counsel. If it all goes horribly wrong we could be prosecuted, or worse persecuted.'

'I have complete faith in you.'

Adira kisses Symon's forehead, then gets up and strides over to her desk.

~~~~~~~~~~~~~~~~~~~~~~~~~~~~~

Belize and Marcel rush out of the electronic doors. Tyler shuffles out from his hiding spot and scours the area, not wanting to become complacent. He checks for any hidden cameras, and picks out one by the departure door, where Belize and Marcel just went through. Tyler dashes over to where the space suits are and begins to undress. He leaves his underwear on and starts to enter the space suit he spotted earlier. He inspects the camera, then the doorway he needed to go through.

The alarm ends and he supposes that signified the threat was eliminated or minor. He checks for the chip removed from his sexbot and the sharp object too, confident he can set off.

He is jolted with adrenaline as the siren is set off again. He instinctively cowers behind the unit he was standing close to. Perhaps he was developing a habit, from the short period of navigating himself through corridors. He scans the sector and the same lighting sequences from before are being emitted from the control room. That must mean the return of the other mooncat.

Now or never.

He rushes to the doorway, still holding his discarded uniform, in case there was an issue with the door opening. The door opens to his relief and he isn't sure which clothing item opened it, he doesn't really care. He drops the uniform and dashes through, he disconnects the charging pump from the mooncat which is almost on 90% charge. In the distance, the other mooncat is approaching, about half a mile away. He hits the decompression button and bides his time for the bay to mimic the space atmosphere outside. He jumps into the mooncat and engages the engine. He grips the joystick in both hands and tests that it works by moving it a little. The mooncat responds.

The other mooncat is increasing speed, trying to beat the incoming sun. The fact they were heading towards it must have filled them with great anxiety. He prayed he'd be ignored, there wouldn't be much charge left to make chase, and they would be on a tight schedule not to get fried.

He operates the mooncat smoothly out of the bay and shoves the joystick forward, although heading in their trajectory he inches it away from the other approaching mooncat. Though possibly being concealed in a suit, he didn't want to take any risks. Fortunately, neither of them had a control room or command post to speak to. They could only discuss amongst themselves and Tyler had purposely not turned on the intercom in his suit. That would be suspicious, but some risk was inevitable. Not getting fried and having no juice left in their mooncat would still deter them from giving chase, at least this is what he anticipated.

He stirs his mooncat further off course from coming anywhere near theirs. Once happy with his distance from them, he continues in a straight line to where he's sure the rocket station is based. He keeps an eye on the other mooncat and seeks to ascertain if they would alter their course to head in his direction. From what he can see, that isn't the case. He depended on them running on sparks and so, not able to take the risk. He takes one more look behind him, at the incoming sun and marvels at the atomic tangerine glaze enveloping a section of the moon. Then he turns around, stares ahead, focused on his mission.

25E

An evening sky boasting a range of yellow, orange and red hues, dominates any onlooker's view. Lots of molecules—caused by an expansive atmosphere—scatter blue and violet light away from people's eyes to create the chromatic hue. Evening light emits through stained glass windows, throwing an array of colours on a congregation of people debating in a conference hall about climate change. The hall features traditional Tudor-styling, sizeable, picture stained glass windows and a sun porch which can function as a separate room for smaller groups. People can be seen interacting with several large virtual reality images at two corners of the hall. A group of people on one side of the conference hall display banners or t-shirts which spell out "Extinction Rebellion" and they are deciding where to protest next. In amongst the crowd, Tyler can be seen speaking to a female with striking demeanour, auburn hair and glasses.

'Humans are never going to take this seriously, unless something sternly throws them out of their little, self obsessed bubbles. You know that right?' Adira says, peering over her glasses at Tyler. The rim of her glasses match her auburn hair.

'I hate to admit it, but I think you're right. We do need to change our slogan though, kind of arrogant. The world will be here long after we've turned to dust. What we should be advocating for is saving future generations, not saving the planet. Perhaps that will bring people around.'

'Don't be silly...Christ, many years ago a kid chose to leave school to fight the climate crisis, because people generally only cater to their selfish interests at heart. And still we persist in our unsustainable ways. Most people cannot stand the truth, especially when it comes with inconvenience. We typically abhor change, exclusively change that threatens our comfortable ways of life. Consider the civil rights movement...it took the great migration, world war two, and the cold war to make the white majority receptive enough to start seeing blacks as equal. Finally, it took for the police violence against black children protesting, to urge President Kennedy to uphold his promise to the black people and give them their rights on national television. The world watches you see, actions that hardly demonstrate a civilised society. One hundred years it took, enough time for systemic racism to put its claws into society. People only react in the midst of a shake up, ear ossicles shattering shakeup; a punch in the nose wake up call. And sometimes that wake up call needs to be developed by ourselves.' Adira whispers the last sentence, adjusts her bra discreetly and then scans the wide-ranging hall.

'We had a wake up call though—two pandemics changed nothing.'

Adira, now exuding confidence from every molecule of her being, studies the man before her. 'Come with me, I want to show you something,' she says, pushing her glasses up the bridge of her nose.

Tyler follows Adira out of the conference hall and through a dimly lit passageway painted in leafy green. They come to a purple door and she gingerly shoves it open.

'What I'm about to show you is classified, okay?'

'...'.

'Please acknowledge that you understand.'

'Okay Adira,' Tyler wonders what he's getting into.

They arrive at another door which leads down stairs to an expansive basement. The aroma of wood varnish fills the air. The lights are even dimer and this time the walls are all bricked in a mosaic of reddish and orange hues. They approach a glass doorway and Adira takes out a card from her pocket and touches a pad by the side. The glass door unseals. Adira shimmies to the side.

'After you Tyler.'

Tyler hesitates for a moment, and scans the room. A lot of electronics are scattered on sturdy wooden tables, and what appears to be complex machines. What looks like a mannequin standing in a glass kiosk, catches his attention. He steps into the room with some anticipation. He's known Adira for a while, and even though comfortable enough with her, she was a private person. Although she divulged being married to a white man, when someone made a comment about her only hanging out with black people. That revelation soon shut the person up.

'What is this place?'

'The future.' Adira retorts.

'What do you mean?'

Adira walks over to the kiosk and compresses a button to the side. A section of the glass slides over revealing what Tyler can only describe as a very life-like, naked, brown-skinned mannequin. Adira reaches behind the right ear and touches something, activating the body. Tyler gasps at what he can now see is an android. A humanoid like he's never seen before. The aesthetically pleasing android opens her eyes and Tyler steps back, this time gawping.

~~~~~~~~~~~~~~~~~~~~~~~~~~~~~

'So what secret project were you working on back on earth?'

'Jeez, what makes you think of that now?'

'Well, you kept me in the dark about it, I'm certain that didn't help our marriage.'

'Point taken.' Adira draws open a drawer and takes out a memory stick which she sticks in her computer. She taps on the keyboard and waits.

'Well?' Symon moves in closer to Adira.

'I worked at an electronics firm that specialises in robotics.'

'What?!'

'Keep your voice down, will you, are you forgetting the guards just brought you in.' Adira throws Symon a stern look.

'You were responsible for the sexbots?' Symon whispers.

'Why so perplexed? You knew I studied electronic engineering.'

'Yes, radios and computers —didn't think robots.'

'Well, now you know.'

'What else should I know?'

'You're gonna need to sit down for the other piece of information.' Adira locks eyes with Symon's.

'You were having an affair weren't you? I knew it!'

'Oh please...so were you, don't think I didn't know; besides not it, think outside of yourself, think big picture —and keep your voice down, already asked you once.'

'Oh...you knew? How long did you know?' Symon physically appears to wind his neck in.

Adira wrinkles her nose. 'Does that really matter?'

'No I guess not—t'was so long ago now. So much has happened since.' Symon finally goes to sit down, eventually always gives in and does what Adira asks. He just needed to put up a hint of a fight first, to please the alpha male in him.

'There was something hidden in the sexbots.'

'What do you mean there was something hidden in the sexbots? All of them!?' Symon focuses on his ex wife. He cannot remember the last time he gave her this undivided attention.

26X

Belize and Marcel stand in a glass booth being blasted with a sterilising mist as decompression is activated. Rust on the poles of the moon became another added contaminant to clean off anyone that ventured out on the moon surface. Rust, discovered by scientists years ago, was a mystery for a short while until someone unravelled it. Rust, otherwise known as hematite, got formed by the oxygen in the earth's magnetic tail, interacting with lunar water molecules. This discovery conveniently led to the creation of the magnetic field that protected the moonbase from solar storms.

They both exit the glass booth and clothe in separate compartments. Once dressed, they convene in what resembles a small foyer.

'Appreciate the help Marcel.'

'You're welcome Belize—I was thinking, how long do you reckon before the moon breaks out of orbit from the earth?'

'You mean because we're moving 3.8 centimetres away each year?'

'Yes.'

'Who knows, I think more recently, scientists calculated it might be more like 4.8 centimetres. Regardless, I'm sure it will be years and years before that happens.' Belize replied.

'How perspective changes when living on the moon, huh.'

'Sure... I'm going to pay a visit to the school. Guess I'll see you in about 14 days.' Belize mentions with a tight smile.

'Yes... hopefully before that.' Marcel utters whilst checking his trouser pockets.

'Okay then, see you.' Belize turns round and strolls away.'

Marcel studies her for a while, before turning the opposite way and striding off.

~~~~~~~~~~~~~~~~~~~~~~~~~~~~~~~

Belize approaches the only class room on the base and gazes through the window to observe five children of varying ages, engaged in activities. One white boy and four girls of mixed race. Failed attempts to produce a viable population caused by increased miscarriages, had been put down to conditions in space and sperm infertility, the later had been a problem when on earth and had only gotten worse on the moon.

An older boy and girl can be seen playing chess, while the other three girls play with playdough. The type of schooling deployed was referred to as the Montessori method, a holistic approach developed by Dr Maria Montessori through decades of observing children all over the world. Belize stands by the window and studies the children, a teacher sits cross legged at one end of the room, engrossed in a book. The teacher at long last, acknowledges Belize and relaxes her face, and Belize manages a smile back. The children fail to notice either of the adults, fully absorbed in their own worlds. Belize is drawn to them as if bewitched.

Agenta's child would have been number six. She wonders what sex the baby would have been. Would the child have been mixed race? No one had had to face the controversial questions of what to do if only producing mixed race babies. There'd been no word of anyone aborting babies, but who could be sure.

She's somewhat spellbound by the children's preoccupation in their worlds and deliberated about them ever exploring a real world again. She pondered on how adults could be capable of such selfishness, disregarding all the warnings of the climate crisis—to the point where earth was declared unoccupiable. Would they ever be able to return and would the human race learn their lesson? Or in time, would they revert to the same old ways? After all, humankind learnt nothing from two recent pandemics, who was to say they would learn from having to inhabit the moon to survive? She could not help but think that earth was better off without humans on it, and she wondered who else harboured that notion. She doubted Agenta did, as she had planned on having a baby. She must have harboured some hope for humans. Belize found herself respecting and despising her in equal measure. Almost immediately she becomes riddled with guilt, she was certain thinking ill of the dead was just as bad as talking ill of the dead.

She closes her eyes in an attempt to throw out the corrupted thoughts perambulating her cerebrum. She finally succeeds in swallowing down the emotions rising up in her throat. When she opens her eyes, she's met with the peering hazel eyes of one of the younger girls, probably five years old. Belize is pulled in by her eyes, the way you might be pulled in or transfixed by an icy, glassy, murky lake in winter's dawn. Flecks of gold and green and brown all interlinked in her irises, like miniature distant galaxies. The little girl smiles at

Belize, then throws up her hand and waves. Belize waves back and a suppressed smile tugs at the corners of her mouth. She wipes at her welled up eyes, trying to conceal the tears, but fails. Had never witnessed children as sacred before now. Their bittersweet innocence tormented her.

The older kids now regard Belize through the window too, but this time Belize doesn't pay any attention, instead she briskly walks away, swallowing down further rising emotions.

~~~~~~~~~~~~~~~~~~~~~~~~~~~~~~

Tyler clutches hold of the joystick strenuously, as a tremor shakes the mooncat. Serves him right to be gloating over the distance he maintained from the sun. Now he may be required to contend with another moonquake. Manoeuvring the mooncat was already like driving a buggy through mud.

A flashback presents, of a time back on earth when stuck in a traffic jam—literally. A lorry had overturned tonnes of glue on the highway. He ended up laughing hysterically in the car as he found the irony hysterical. He often found life's ironies hysterical. He didn't find it chucklesome though when he had to leave the car and walk. They were advised by the police to keep their shoes on as the glue was toxic to skin. He was wearing his best shoes!

He checks the power left in the mooncat to find a quarter left on the gauge. He does his best to keep the automobile on course. Up ahead is the station and nothing in the way of security. He doesn't suppose there are many astronaut pilots on the base, so why would someone venture out here. There was nowhere to go anyway. No one with any sense would want to go take up abode in a space station. Though he intended to do more than take up abode. He yomps through and is jolted by yet another mini quake rippling through the moon. On his arrival, at the entrance to the station, he's faced with an electronic door leading into the moon base. He assumes there must be another opening which the shuttle ejects from. He disembarks the mooncat, ensuring not to rip his suit on anything. Had the occupants of the mooncat that went past, radioed in and given instructions for his pursuit? He doubted it, as the mooncat he'd taken had the most juice. He pondered on how many people were inside the station? He presumed three, maybe four at a stretch.

He float-walks to the electronic door and again hopes his uniform activates it. It does, and he lets out a breath of relief. He wanders into a grey cylindrical chamber with lots of vent holes, as if being enveloped in the undersides of a ginormous octopus' tentacles. The electronic door shuts, lights are activated and decompression commences. At first, only the sound of the visual jets of cold air being blasted around him are heard, the dormant octopus tentacles coming to life. As an atmosphere starts to be created, he begins to hear the gushing sound, faint at first and then blaring, ears-popping loud. Glad the decompression didn't go on for much longer, he removed his helmet and suit as soon as the green light indicated it was safe to do so. No matter how many times he wore the spacesuit, he still felt claustrophobic in the uniform and could not wait to get out of it.

Another electronic door opens on the opposite side. As he enters, all the lights switch on, not that much illumination, but enough for him to see where he is going. He makes out a cone shaped white aluminium and plastic surround, several space suits are located to his left, and to his right, to his surprise, is a mini library. An array of classic books like Punctured Dreams, People Farm and Incandescent Souls are displayed; the one that earns his attention though is an ancient book by Ivan Goncharov called Oblomov. He picks it up and examines it. Had heard of the book, but never had the chance to read it. It was a long haul to the space station, so here was his opportunity to read an ancient classic. He supposed it was why a little library was situated here. He opens the book to PART ONE and reads the first two paragraphs.

Ilya Ilyich Oblomov was lying in bed one morning in his flat in Gorokhovaya Street in one of those large houses which have as many inhabitants as a country town.

He was a man of about thirty-two or three, of medium height and pleasant appearance, with dark grey eyes, but with a total absence of any definite idea, any concentration, in his features. Thoughts promenaded freely all over his face, fluttered about in his eyes, reposed on his half-parted lips, concealed themselves in the furrows of his brow, and then vanished completely —and it was at such moments that an expression of serene unconcern spread all over his face. This unconcern passed from his face into the contours of his body and even into the folds of his dressing gown.

Tyler closes the book and turns it round to inspect the back. A rare sense of stillness is instilled in him, those rare occasions when you lose touch with your supposed identity and instead are consumed by all consciousness. Existential. He could be describing himself, albeit a lot older, sixty three was the new thirty three. The main difference was he was wearing a spacesuit and not a dressing gown. Would there always be someone that fits a character in a book?

Afterall, authors primarily described characters based on people in their lives. This, however, was uncanny, a reincarnated character from a book. He sensed he was going to enjoy reading it; still, first things first. He had to locate the capsule and get his butt on it, and quickly. He moves further along the corridor and comes across a hatch big enough for a couple of people to get in. On close inspection, he confirms it's a lift. He assumes the small rocket is located deep in the moon crust, so as to shield it from a probable solar storm. It made sense. The electromagnetic shield which enveloped the base to protect it from such a storm, did not stretch all the way out here.

He approaches the lift, again with some anticipation. So far luck was on his side, luck had stayed his friend, but then again why would there be different modes of access? Again not many astronaut pilots and no one in their right mind would want to travel to the space station. The lift, which is shaped like a pod, is activated and lights up inside. The door slides open and he enters, there is only one destination and that is down. The door closes without a whisper, and the lift jolts to descend.

Tyler is dying to lean on the side of the elevator as it plummets down, the muscles in his legs hurt from all the crouching. He refrains from leaning though, a habit now engrained. Some elevators on earth had sensors on each side which were activated if something touched the sides. This put him off.

He stands with legs apart, trying his best to distribute the ache in his thighs and calves. His ears pop as the elevator keeps up its controlled drop. A low frequency whooshing sound is all he can hear, and he isn't sure if the low sound is due to his ears popping or the play with gravity. He couldn't believe he was doing this, doing this for real. His intent so far, had been unscathed, uninterrupted. It seemed he was getting away with it. The reality of his objective was now hitting him, more like plummeting into him. He senses the elevator begin to slow down, and there is a slight judder. He takes in a deep breath to decompress the beating of his heart as the door slides open.

~~~~~~~~~~~~~~~~~~~~~~~~~~~~~~~

Symon sits in the furthest corner of Adira's cabin. Legs and arms crossed away from her and his head following suit, turned away, staring out the window at the celestial, unconsolidated, regolith plane. Regardless of their activity on the base—the humdrum of human existence now being demonstrated on the moon, instead of earth—the stillness of the moon prevailed, unperturbed. He couldn't think of a better word to describe the unapologetic placidity of the moon. Unperturbable. The word was so apt. All too aware he was portraying his normal trait when being dealt with something he couldn't handle. His ex wife told him something that left him hollow. Never quite found a way to be with it, or what to make of it. Losing himself in his own thoughts of something as far removed from the subject matter as could-be, is how he coped. Any new strategy escaped him. Too easy to lose yourself in the stillness of the moon. Damn near impossible not to lose yourself in meditative thought, when looking out a window at the moon's plane. Pure serenity.

Symon in time, turns round to face Adira. Adira always left him to it, in the past she interrupted, interjected, tried everything to relieve him of his trance and it never ended well. His listening was disabled and so there was no point. Better to wait for him to come out of it on his own accord.

'How come I never knew about this part of your life?'

'It wasn't something I ever thought would come to fruition. A mere fantasy, just some hippie fantasy to make us feel better. It was never meant to happen. Or at least, I didn't think it would actually materialise. Not for real.' Adira clasps her hands in her lap and fixes her gaze on Symon.

'That sounds familiar. Wasn't that what some people said about Brexit? They had just played with the idea; wanted to rebel for a moment. Misplaced frustrations with life and government. No morsel of thought presumed that Brexit would actually pass through, despite voting for it. Alas it did, and the repercussions were insurmountable, a shit storm basically.'

Adira battled with her thoughts. Part of her made peace with it. How long could they really keep covertly racist heterosexual white men imprisoned? Sooner or later the oppressed rise. Always unravelled that way for centuries. Inevitable. Non sustainable. Like the demise of earth being inevitable because of humankinds' unsustainable ways of living. A chuckle, from deep inside of her escapes from her mouth involuntarily.

A flashback occurs— Adira showing Tyler the electronics lab and introducing him to a sexbot, first of its kind. She recalls taking the chip out of the side of its neck and telling him what it does, what it could do. Tyler stood motionless for a long while. She guessed comatose, by just how human-like the android looked, and that took him some time. Then he endured the confrontation of her epic scheme to solve the demise of earth. Her excitement and focus were diverted soon afterwards, after an encounter with another black woman she had admired for a while, Candela Anakin, the granddaughter of researcher Joy Buolamwini who had actively challenged bias in machine learning software. A process she called the coded gaze. The software wrongly classed black women as men, repeatedly. These skewed data sets adapted by computing systems to learn, promoted divide and exclusion. Candela continued her grandmother's work. Adira had been utterly thrilled to meet her and forgot all about the meeting with Tyler.

'I can see why you would laugh, kind of funny I guess. What else is left to do but laugh. Now it makes sense why Tyler never wanted to upgrade his sexbot. The chip in his sexbot, that was his master plan all along. There was me thinking he just wanted to spend the rest of his days on the space station. How naive! And all this time, you knew Tyler in another life. Is that why you never asked his name?'

'No, No... like you said it was a lifetime ago. I didn't have a clue...I thought Tyler was dead.'

'Is there nothing we can do? Do you want this? Do you really want this?' Symon lifts up from his chair and traipses over to Adira. 'You said it was a fantasy. You sure you now want it to be real?'

'I don't think there is much we can do. He would be on his way by now... to the station I mean. No time to reboot and reprogram.'

'Oh my god! Oh, my fucking god!' These are the only words Symon can think to exclaim. He plonks himself down next to Adira.

'Like you said, been a shit storm!' Adira stares at her hands in her lap. The emotions running through her would not be complemented in this instance by the tranquillity of the moon's ghostly exterior. So she refrains from looking through the window and inspects the lines on her palm instead. Marvelling over the head, heart and life line, then concentrating only on the life line.

27N

The roar of a beast is powerless beside these lamentations of nature, the human voice, too, is insignificant, and man himself is so little and weak, so lost among the small details of the vast picture! Perhaps it is because of this that he feels so depressed when he looks at the sea. Yes, the sea can stay where it is! Its every calm and stillness bring no comfort to a man's heart; in the barely perceptible swell of the mass of waters man still sees the same boundless, though slumbering, force which can so cruelly mock his proud will and bury so deeply his brave schemes, and all his labour and toil.

Mountains and precipices, too, have not been created for man's enjoyment. They are as terrifying and menacing as the teeth and claws of a wild beast rushing upon him; they remind us too vividly of our frailty and keep us continually in fear of our lives. And the sky over the peaks and the precipices seems so far and unattainable, as though it had recoiled from men.

Tyler closes the book, another excerpt from Oblomov, written by Ivan Goncharov. He cannot believe the book got published in 1859, over three centuries ago. Delighted, he couldn't have picked a better book to immerse himself in while making his trip to Mr Drake. Already on page 103, he was finding it quietly riveting.

With some difficulty encountered whilst activating the rocket, for a brief period Tyler thought his mission ended before it began. Faced with a puzzle for the code entry system, which required him to enter the moon's equatorial circumference, which he happened to know, 6,783.5 miles or 10,916.99 kilometres. Thank god for a pilot exam, but even more so for a brilliant memory. The knowledge is crucial if flying a rocket, and so he spared his surprise of the requirement to decipher a code for activation. He saw this as the ultimate sign—he *was* on the right cosmic path.

In his path, he encountered what he thought was a great piece of space debris. Junk in space posed a problem for a while. Humankind not only filled the earth with various junk, but idiotically transferred this careless behaviour into space. Tyler had to tweak his course just a little, the range still enabled him to identify the debris. Turned out to be one of the giant claws, introduced into space by the European Space Agency to remove build up of metal waste. With no home for a control station anymore, the claw added to the debris problem. Another befitting irony.

The space station, still no larger than a speck on his screen, was still a way to go. Thankfully, he had found an adult sized diaper to wear. A Maximum Absorbency Garment, MAG for short. He could relieve himself without any worry. Not as sexy as in the movies; you didn't see Sandra Bullock or George Clooney wearing diapers when in space. This however was real life. In real life, shit and piss were key parts, literally and metaphorically—denoting problematic scenarios and people. Content with his book, he dismissed his thoughts in no time and delved back into the story of Oblomov.

~~~~~~~~~~~~~~~~~~~~~~~~~~~~

Perseverance and stubbornly grasping onto things wired his make up. Like the weft threads orchestrated to produce tapestry; one of his predominant traits—interwoven to produce his character. Without these traits, his character would possess no definition, just like tapestry, it would fall away at the seams, with no weft in the threads.

Skyler casually caresses the mole on their upper lip, as they stump up and down in the much appreciated posh quarters. They engage in stumping—which mimics soldiers marching—as a form of exercise. Having stayed a while in the caverns with the heterosexual men, they were grateful to be back, but not happy in the slightest having failed at their mission. Even though they did not seem to be suffering any repercussions from the peeress about it, none whatsoever. Not being held accountable, made them uneasy. Skyler lived their life believing people should always be held accountable for their actions. They felt that accountability and taking responsibility eroded over time on earth. Politicians consistently got away with war crimes and other heinous crimes against their own citizens. Was not willing to let go of their failure; certain Tyler had something up his sleeve and they were going to find out what. Tyler took him by surprise and was clearly adept at the method of knocking him out, having experienced his expertise first hand. Knocking someone out did not come as easy as in the movies. Precision was paramount, you had to be exact with where you were hitting and you had to use the exact amount of pressure. They had asked a question, turned round and bam!— lights out. The next thing, they came to, lying in the recovery unit on the base.

Came to everyone's attention now that a man had stolen a mooncat and travelled to the rocket station, and then had taken a space pod to get to the space station. Why there, was anyone's guess, nothing there but a complex AI computer system. Not much in the way of fun. Not much of anything to fortify survival. Rations to last a couple of weeks at the most, in case technicians needed to attend to fix or repair something, that was it. Why would someone go out there? For what purpose? Other than to die alone. He could only imagine that being in the caverns as a prisoner would be extremely difficult to put up with, but at least there was food, water and shelter, and a sexbot to boot. An okay existence, much more than anyone would have thought after the demise of the planet. So why? Why would he go to all the trouble to go reside on a space station?

The sexbot in Tyler's quarters displayed a little hatch opened behind the ear. It looked like something was missing from the circuit board, but he couldn't be sure. Tyler could *literally* have had something up his sleeve during his escape. Electronics was never one of his strong suits, but things didn't add up, and he felt a strong urge to decipher the mystery.

Retrieving a mooncat would be impossible at present, as the temperature in that section would be unbearable. Specially designed suits could withstand the high temperatures for a few hours, but a few more hours were needed to get to the rocket pad.

As a rule, three of everything occured on the base. The number chosen in line with the trinity, believe it or not, even though religion had since drained away from humanity. Tendrils of religious belief still infected the human psyche, like sweat stains in the armpit patches of a white shirt. The way he looked at it, having three of everything, accommodated the superstition that every eventuality or misfortune usually occurs in threes.

One way to find out Tyler's scheme would be to find a way to interrogate Symon, who they knew befriended Tyler. They suspected Symon assisted Tyler's escape and was determined to find out. The peeress taking a real liking to the guy posed a problem, so they had to think of a ruse to meet him in person. Going to be tricky and they only had a little time to plot.

Skyler finally discontinues walking up and down their quarters. If a carpet covered the floor, it would be worn out with the amount of tramping up and down exercised on it. They walked up and down for two reasons, exercise and cogitating.

Finally, they plonk down on the bed and rub the back of their head. Still able to detect a mild swelling and the neck is stiff. Massaging their neck with their right hand, they stare at the image on the screen. A waterfall in the Amazon, a real visual treat. Reminds them of when he travelled to Argentina with then boyfriend. Skyler started seeing Josh on the base a few weeks ago, but still craved his ex partner like crazy.

Once, on a holiday in Argentina, Skyler and the ex partner were both awestruck by the scenery. The contrast of cascading water, rocky outcrops and tropical greenery conjured up paradise and took both their breath away. A number of years ago now, just before departing earth, only tendrils of an Amazon forest were left. Had campaigned for a couple of years with their partner to save this treasure of a habitat, all to no avail. Then time was up. Earth belched and chucked humans out.

Skyler daydreams, as they marvel at the scenery before them, transported back in time as a smile tugs at the corners of their mouth. Their partner was taken by the dreaded c-word, just a couple of days before the mass evacuation of earth. Tears stream down their face in a synchronised fashion. Like most memories, also bittersweet. They turn in bed and sob into the only pillow there, overwhelmed by the loss of their partner and the world. They cry and cry until they fall into a slumber and dream about holding hands with his partner, as they both gaze at the waterfalls at Iguazu falls.

In the dream, they could even feel the water spray and the warm sun rays on their skin, they felt their partner's hand in theirs and a semi erection bringing their phallus to life. Felt their ex partner's lips on theirs and cherished the feel of stubble on both cheeks and neck. They had often been self conscious about kissing or showing any affection in public, but standing by one of the seven natural wonders in the world melted their fear of being ridiculed, and both turned to each other, as if pulled by an internal magnetism. Fully embraced and kissed each other with no societal induced shame, as if it was their last day on earth. Little did they know, two years from that day *would* be their last day on earth, along with all the other humans on the planet. In the dream, an unusual banging interrupts their foreplay. It sounds like the banging of a door, but they're outside. How can they be hearing a door banging while outside? Skyler is perplexed and gapes at their lover for answers. Their partner just stares back without saying a word; muted, eerily so, seconds pass. Their partner now remains still, too still, like when Skype or Teams video call freezes. Suffocating dread sets in.

Bang.
Bang.
Bang.

Skyler wakes up with a jolt. Someone is at the door, desperate to get in by the sounds of it. They check the intercom camera to witness an impatient Josh. They release the door to a flustered Josh, who rushes in, hardly waiting for the sliding door to fully open.

'I think I know how we can stop Tyler!'

~~~~~~~~~~~~~~~~~~~~~~~~~~~~~

Belize downs a shot of the infamous space alcohol, it burns down her throat, warming her insides. The batch exceeded the others, and she was happy to be testing it out. Someone had to be the guinea pig and consume the alcohol in vast quantities to experience the type of hangover left in the boozing aftermath. More than happy to take the potential risk of an upset tummy, so long as the end game was being comatose drunk. The death of Agenta forged a black hole in her psyche, and it didn't matter how hard she worked, the distraction did nothing to fill the hole. After her shift, the throbbing torment bubbled up to sensitive areas of her psyche again, immeasurable pain that made her heart feel like a 10kg weight in her chest. She was offered counselling, but refused. She felt she needed some time to grieve first, in little bouts though, she couldn't face sitting with the emotion that arose for too long, felt her heart may tumble out of her rib cage with the sheer weight, snapping her ribs like breadsticks. She pours another cup and downs it in seconds, wincing as she swallows. What could have been Agenta's plan when she found out she had conceived? How did she intend on hiding her pregnancy? Did she intend on involving her at all when she found out? Had she made love to a man or had she somehow gotten her hands on a sperm sample? These questions reeled around in her mind like burning embers of a campfire, steadily collecting to molten lead, which accentuated her heavy heart. She pours another cup and downs it also in seconds. Getting drunk was a universal way of dealing with emotional agony, even elephants and other animals in the wild gorged on fermented fruit to get the same effect when heartbroken. She was nothing more than an animal in tremendous emotional torment. She pours another cup and is about to pour it down her gullet when there is a knock on the door. It startles her, making her spill some alcohol on her uniform. Her clothes started to form a second skin, that's how long since the last change—personal hygiene and basic chores became a real chore. She places her hands on the table in front of her and pushes herself up, with effort. The alcohol was already taking effect. She staggers to the door, unaware she is staggering, and meets the door with disdain, suddenly realising she could have opened it without moving. She jabs at a button as if it had provoked her and Skyler is teasingly revealed.

'What do you want? What time is it? Is everything okay? Why are you here?'

'I need to tell you something. Can I come in? It should only take a few moments.' Skyler responds, eyeing her up and down, faintly discerning her body language is out of sync to the norm.

Belize is aware of his beady eyes interrogating her. 'I'm testing the new batch of alcohol before you start.'

'I... I wasn't going to start anything.'

'Good, sit over there and spill then.' Belize spits the words out through a suppressed hiccup. She peeps at a clock inset on her bed frame and then regards Skyler with fiery red eyes. 'As I thought, really late, this better be good.' She perches and pours herself another cup. 'I'm afraid I can't offer you any. No idea what the after effects are yet.' Belize enjoyed saying that. She most definitely didn't want to share, but that excuse was validated and just friggin awesome. It saved her from admitting to being a greedy drunk.

'Could you save yourself a few cups till after I've gone?' Skyler stares at the basin on her desk, half filled with alcohol and then turns round to face Belize. She stares at Skyler with eyes that could burn a hole into you like a laser beam. The fact her eyes were bloodshot made it even more likely that a laser could come beaming out of them at any moment. She gingerly puts the cup to her mouth and is about to tip the contents. Instead, she sets the cup back down on the desk, being careful not to spill any.

'For meteor's sake! What is it?' She glares at the non binary person in the room.

'The guy who escaped the caverns, I think he might be up to something sinister. He's not trying to get to the space station to...to chill out till his dying day as people might think. Been speaking to Josh and we think what he has planned has something to do with the AI motherboard.'

'What do you mean?' Belize tries to focus.

'I mean, Tyler may have a way to disable the AI.'

'And how exactly would he do that? There aren't any weapons or tools to cause such damage on the station and none for him to get his hands on en route. It's not achievable, the motherboard is a mammoth of intricate electronics.'

'I think he may have thought of a virus.'

'A virus? What the hell are you talking about?'

'There was an opening on his sexbot, behind the ear.'

'Yeah, they all do.'

'I think something was missing.'

'What are you insinuating exactly?'

'I think Tyler plans on using whatever he took out of the sexbot to create a virus, one with enough information to disable the AI'

'He can't do that, the motherboard consists of old components. Have you forgotten why we defaulted to the DOS system?

'Tyler had never wanted an upgrade on his sexbot. In all the years down in the caverns, he never upgraded.'

'So...'

'So, I think his sexbot may have had a component old enough to create a virus.'

Belize reaches for her cup and then pauses when she glimpses at Skyler's disapproving eyes. 'This is crazy, how on earth did you figure this out?'

'Well, Josh and I wondered...why would someone take out a piece from his sexbot, an electronic chip of some kind and for what purpose?'

'Maybe to aid in his escape?'

'I really don't think so, he didn't need anything to aid in his escape because I think he got help.'

'What?'

'I think he was helped by Symon.'

'Symon —the guy with the peeress?'

'Yes, they both had some kind of a friendship down there.'

'What are you saying exactly, that they turned gay?'

'No, no of course not. They had something close, a strong bond.'

'This is crazy—You know we can't reach him now, even if we wanted to, not for another great number of hours.'

'Yes, but we could speak to him at the space station. Try to ascertain what he's up to and if my theory is right...try to deter him.'

'I can't believe this.' She seizes the cup and sticks her hand out to Skyler, as if stopping traffic. 'I just need this cup to think, so back off!' She pours the contents down her throat, waits for the liquidised heat to rise in her

145

and then slaps herself on her left cheek, startling Skyler who impulsively puts a hand to their own face and caresses the cheek.

'This is so fucked up.' Belize continues. 'If what you say is true we have allowed a terrorist to pass right under our noses to their known terror destination. We best get to the peeress straight away I guess.'

'Yes, like right now. Are you sure you're up to it?' Skyler eyes the half filled basin of alcohol on the table, as if looking at a tub containing a school of piranhas.

'Yes, yes of course I'm alright. I have to test the alcohol batches all the time... of course I'm alright.' Belize takes a drink of water from the tap. Now drinking her shower rations, but that was fine, she didn't need to be washed for anyone. Agenta was no longer in her life. Had left. Literally floated out of her life. She's somewhat conscious she may have a wry smile on her face, part of the effect of the alcohol perhaps? She wipes off the grin with her hand, part of her riddled with guilt that she even acquired the capacity to smile. 'Right let's do this, we will have to think about how we present this to her on the way, c'mon.'

Skyler moves to the side and allows Belize to lead the way. An awkward expression is plastered on her face, but they put it down to the alcohol.

28T

Symon is anxious, restless and irritable as he shifts and adjusts from one rest posture to the next. Arm under leg, folded arms across stomach, chin in palms, hands at back of head, arms around both knees —he swaps position every few minutes. Adira doesn't say a word, used to his theatrical displays, married to him long enough.

'Are you sure you had no idea Tyler was down there with us, plotting this all along?'

'Excuse me, are you insinuating I had something to do with this?' Adira cocks her head, out of viewpoint from a report she was reading on her computer.

'Well technically you did have something to do with it.' Symon swaps from folded-arms-across stomach, to hands-at-back-of-head.

'Yeah, I guess you're right, but that was years ago. Like I've already said, another lifetime and a fantasy of mine. I was with the Extinction Rebellion at the time. The climate crisis wasn't being taken seriously at all and people had all sorts of ideas, not just me. Political pressure had always been a safe bet. When you think we could have been driving electric cars as far back as 2000, if not for the greedy oil corporations, all fixed to undermine consumer confidence. Even a documentary was produced about it back then... I forget what it was called Erm—Who killed the electric car! Turned out to be one big conspiracy. There'd always been the means to go a hundred percent green, always...we possessed all the technology and the intellect to drive the sustainability agenda forward, but like most things, human greed got in the way.'

'We're quite a stupid species aren't we? We don't learn. All through history, as far back as you want to go, greed and power caused many an empire to collapse, yet we repeat the same fucking mistakes! This time we went as far as letting our greed destroy our entire planet. How stupid can one get.'

'Well, rendered uninhabitable for *us* to occupy it. In time earth will find a way, with us out of the equation.' Adira mentions the last few words under her breath.

'What's that?' Symon had been swapping his resting stance again; this time from hands at back of the head to chin in palms of his hands, and the last few words escaped him.

'Oh nothing, mostly agreeing with you.'

'You know—'

Symon is interrupted by the intercom. "Mam, Belize and Skyler are requesting to meet with you. They say it's urgent."

Symon goes into an entirely new stance. Sat upright with elbows on the arms of his seat.

'Okay, let them in.' Adira says and spins in her seat for a full viewpoint of the door.

'Should I be worried?' Symon regards Adira beseechingly.

'Worried about what? They know you're with me and I'm still in charge of this colony.' Adira's confident, in-charge face returns in full splendour.

Symon makes some attempt to relax into his new posture as both he and Adira wait for the door to slide open. Adira crosses her legs and gently sways the chair she's in from side to side.

The door pings open and Skyler and Belize stroll in. Adira gestures to the corner of the room with a conference layout of a table and chairs. She gets up to approach them as they pull out chairs to sit. Symon is about to stand too, but Adira flashes him a look that only they recognise. He adjusts himself and remains seated.

'Is it okay for Symon to remain or would you rather he left briefly?' Adira pulls out a seat.

'No, no that's fine, what we have to say concerns him too.' Belize responds with an assertive tone.

Symon adjusts his posture again. His left hand goes under his thigh, and he folds both legs in.

'Okay, fine... Belize, how are you doing? You had enough time?' Adira consoles.

'Yes Mam, I'm okay, thanks for asking.' Belize relaxes into her seat.

'And Skyler, your head...better?' Adira turns to acknowledge Skyler.

'Yes mam, all good, the wooziness is gone.' Skyler also visibly relaxes into the chair.

'Good, so how can I help you both?' Adira arranges both her hands on the table, clasped.

'Skyler's got a theory I think you need to hear. Something about the guy who is presently on his way to the space station.'

Symon uses all the will on the moon to remain in his chosen posture. Adjusting himself now would be uncompromising body language. No furtive glances permitted.

Adira does her best not to take a quick glimpse at Symon. 'I see, so what's your theory Skyler?' Keeping with the chosen word "theory" would be in her favour for now, and she intended on using that word for as long as she could.

'I believe Tyler is a terrorist. He's not on his way to the space station to chill and escape the caverns. I reckon he plans on putting us in harm.'

'Oh... I see... how would he do that?' Adira takes some solace as she doesn't witness any change in posture from Symon.

'I think he plans on obstructing the AI somehow. I can't be sure, but I think a circuit chip was missing from his sexbot, perhaps he's figured a way of adapting ...as some kind of virus... maybe to use —'

'Oh c'mon now, a tad mission impossible don't you think?' Adira grins, as she crosses her legs the other way. She's pleased Symon retains his posture.

'Mam, he never had an upgrade on his sexbot, in all the time he was down there. I believe that was to guarantee he had the right part to use in the motherboard when he got to the station. Something's off, and I was hoping Symon could verify this.' With that Skyler focuses on Symon.

Symon now changes posture, it was exceptional of him to come this far and not move, and had earned his right to adjust now. He fixes his gaze on Adira.

'Do you know anything Symon? Can you verify what Skyler is saying? Anything to make you suspect foul play?' Adira directs the question, still retaining her disarming beam.

Symon accepted the cue for him to conceal the truth. 'No, can't say I picked up on anything sinister. He didn't divulge anything to me.'

'How do you think he made his escape so smoothly?' Skyler faces Adira, just before the end of the question.

'I wouldn't say it was that smooth, there was some intervention from the sentinels. He got lucky, that's all.' Adira retains her demeanour.

'I don't think—' Skyler shuts up mid sentence, catching Belize's disapproving glance, then. 'I'm not sure mam.'

'Fair enough that you have your suspicions, we could always contact him and find out?' Adira articulates with sangfroid.

'We were hoping you'd authorise that.' Belize remarks.

'Of course, no harm in trying is there, if he chooses to speak that is. In either case, when safe to do so, others would be on their way over to capture him. That is if the people there fail to capture him' Adira states this with ease, and she registers Symon's unease with how easily she lied. 'How soon do you think before he gets there?'

'We reckon another four hours or so.' Belize mentions.

'Four hours and thirty-five minutes to be precise.' Skyler adds.

'Okay then, set up the intercom, consult the negotiator for these kinds of circumstances and draft a script to use. Do this alongside creating a DOS firewall, just in case. Was there anything else?' Adira is all too aware a DOS firewall would be useless. The pride glint in Symon's eyes does not go unnoticed as she gives her commands.

'No that's it.' Belize responds.

'I'm assuming the reason you didn't send the remote lunar rover after him was the time difference once you got back to the mooncat depot?' Adira caresses a stylus with her fingers as she delivers the question with commanding presence.

'Erm...yes mam, he had way too much time in his favour, so no point. Also, we risked losing it to the extreme temperature.'

'Thought so... okay great. Thanks for the remedial works carried out on the damaged sector, and my condolences again over the loss of Agenta. I know how much she meant to you.' Adira's compassion shines through readily.

Symon is filled with pride for his ex wife. Her ability to combine leadership with sincere compassion was what made her an exceptional leader. Something he felt most men were unable to execute as leaders in any capacity. Keenly switched on to this now, he perceived clearly the empowering style of her leadership. As plain as a pikestaff.

Belize and Skyler get up in unison, and slide the chairs into their original position. They make their way to the door. Adira rises and this time so does Symon.

'Thanks for bringing this to my attention.' Adira saunters over to stand beside Symon. Skyler takes a subdued peek at Symon before exiting. Belize turns round before she exits.

'Thanks again Mam,' she says, turns back round and walks out.

The door closes with the satisfying ping and suction sound, and Adira takes hold of her lover's hand.

'Wow... nothing short of incredible.'

'Thank you darling.' Adira squeezes Symon's hand before letting go and sauntering back over to her computer.

~~~~~~~~~~~~~~~~~~~~~~~~~~~~

The shuttle pod coasts along now, in deafening silence. A gargantuan shooting star waltzes across the oil black canvass of space. Tyler stares at this cosmic wonder for what felt like a lifetime. Mesmerised by the brimless sparkling pool of space which he was floating in. He finally takes his concentration off the distant burning meteorite as it fizzles away, and turns to the space station, which is much more visible. The docking station reveals itself and he presses a few buttons in the cockpit to prepare to align the craft. He sets down his book "Oblomov" to the side. Great book, he was engrossed in the words from this Russian classic.

He tried to think of people back on earth who fitted Oblomov's description as a sloth. He could think of only one woman, who had been like a mum to him after his mum died of cancer. This woman dealt with the challenge of having a mild personality disorder, and she engaged with her condition graciously, accepting it. As thin as a rake, it was a wonder where she got the wind to be so loquacious and outspoken. She spoke the truth no matter what, regardless of the hurt the words sometimes carried, and he adored her tremendously for these qualities. Most humans hid from the truth, but not him.

She genuinely enjoyed doing nothing, other than reading and campaigning for any unfairness in society; all whilst remaining seated. With her lack of activity, it was a wonder she wasn't obese, many would have resented her gut microbiome, keeping her lean, in spite of her idleness.

A remarkable woman in his eyes and in spite of her inherent laziness, he loved her dearly and had always kept in touch till she passed away to acute pneumonia. Of course he was upset, but no more grief stricken as when his real mother passed away. Lingering insight, learned from the grief of his mum, suggested he never ever had to feel as depressed about anyone else dying in his life. As if no more space lingered in his heart for deep seated sorrow to be entrenched. It would appear a limit occured to how much heartache one could carry in a lifetime, either that or he unintentionally closed off the circuitry in his brain to anymore emotional hurt.

Tyler starts to level the pod against the docking station. He gazes at the space station, in wonder at the enormousness. It stretched in all directions, like a futuristic metal city suspended in space, huge foil-like sheets wrapped around protrusions. He distinguishes the vibration, as he gently navigates the lever so the pod aligns itself with the docking station, like two pieces of a jigsaw puzzle. Vibrations shudder through his arm, and he counteracts the judder enough to keep the motion steady. In little over a minute, he docks with a muffled, clangorous, scraping noise, it reminds Tyler of the sound made from a mechanical arm down in the caverns. It possessed the same echoey quality to it. Then a muffled bang vibrates the whole pod and induces reverberations in and around him.

Different knobs, dials and switches light up and decompression is initiated in the chamber between the shuttle and the station. Tyler clutches his book and unbuckles himself, he tries to slide out of his seat nimbly but fails miserably, smacking his shoulder on a section of the cockpit. A sharp, stabbing affliction painfully reminds him of zero gravity. Soreness shoots up his arm and he winces, being in space may stop sound transmitting, but it had no effect whatsoever on nerve endings transmitting pain. He hovers upright and makes his way to the exit, the phosphorescent lights around the hatch now emit apple green, indicating now safe to disembark from the craft. He takes one long stride and is at the hatch, he releases the lever and waits for it to open. He is met with thick, white mist.

He had made it; a surge of excitement caused him to tremble slightly. His undertaking was too important and again he took his arrival at his intended destination in good faith, symbolic. He needed to stay alert for other people, convinced a group of four were always based on the station, swapping with another four every three months or so. Sometimes though, there was a period when only one sojourned on board, and he crossed his fingers for sustained luck. He propels through the doorway and grasps a handle for a couple of seconds, waiting for the white mist obstructing his visibility to subside. In time, he could discern a shape and confirmed a female silhouette hovering before him with something in her hand pointed at him.

'Don't move!' A raspy female voice utters.

'I'm unarmed.' Tyler remembers his dream of the guy pointing a gun at him and whom he calmly disarmed with his lack of fear. He anchored himself into the dream and breathed in quietude with each breath. Impassioned with a sense of deja vu, he remains reposed. Had always believed that whenever he had deja vu, it signified he was precisely where he was designated to be in his life's journey. A very peaceful belief.

In due course, the mist cleared and he could now make out the person floating in front of him. As he thought, a woman, not a man with a female voice. Learned not to make that assumption, had met a couple of men with a feminine voice in his time.

'I can't believe it! You're alive!!' Tyler hoped she would be alive, always, notwithstanding the feebleness of that hope, this was no Shawshank Redemption after all.

'Who the hell are you?' The woman mutters through a strained cough, lowering the taser gun pointed at him.

'Aloha! It's Tyler.'

Now the casing of how he remembered her; frowzy, with longer scraggly hair. She still had her Vietnamese features dominate her appearance. Her posture though, seemed off. Didn't people lose their posture through age? Certainly the inevitable outcome. But didn't you also have to be standing, feet on ground, for your posture signature to be upheld? Her demeanour is portrayed as the same, albeit weaker. She also looked a lot paler than how he remembered, ashen, like off-white paint. Like a ghost, she floats forward revealing her tattered uniform and form; frantically shakes her head, flicking her scraggly hair frantically, as if disposing of dandruff, then speaks.

'Tyler... is that really you?'

'Yes, yes Aloha it's me.' He moves in closer. He's a little perplexed, as the mist has dissipated. Was he that unrecognisable? Then he notices her eyes. The velvety softness transmuted to reptilian; cold and twinkle less. No glint. Corroded. Probable space blindness.

A condition discovered a few years ago and at the time, people presumed it was inflammation of the optic nerve provoked by pressure on the back of the brain and eyes, caused by the lack of gravity. Additional research showed it resulted from defected cerebrospinal fluid, this fluid cushions the brain and spinal cord, while distributing nutrients and removing waste. The lack of posture related pressure changes in space, causes this liquid to malfunction and causes gradual blindness. Tyler surmised that the blindness didn't form her icy cold eyes; but instead signified what ensued when all faith in humanity erodes.

'Blind as a bat pal, but I can smell you, and you smell awful, damn more awful than me.'

Tyler assumes she could be right. Nothing was at his disposal to use when he visited the toilet. Paper, cloth or water.

She extends a hand to touch him. Tyler sticks out his hand and takes hers in his and she snatches it tight. She uses him to pull herself forward, right into his space. She was blind for sure, no one got that close to someone.

'It's really you!' Aloha proclaims now in a shaky voice, her nose almost touching his adam's apple. She clasps hold of his hand even tighter and starts to cry.

'It is really me, yes.' He takes her head and places it on his chest and holds her gently, as she sobs into his sternum.

Never any tissue when you need it most. Tyler scans his surroundings, as he embraces Aloha, even though he realises his search is futile. Aloha is now deep into her crying spell, tears and catarrh leak out of her. You would think with the water rations, tears and all other fluids escaping from the body would be minimised, but apparently not. Aloha bathes her face in some of the fluids protruding from all orifices, as she bawls out her very essence into Tyler's clothes. The rest of the fluids detach from her face and are suspended and float off in different directions. She smelt really bad, sewer-bad, but Tyler let's her cry, knowing instinctively the fact she could still do this, indicated she had likely escaped becoming deranged from space loneliness. He held her jerking body as she sobbed, and let himself settle into the embrace, disregarding his often introverted aloofness. These traits stopped him connecting deeply with someone else, often getting so far into conversation with someone—prying at their deepest secrets—then pausing and retreating, unbeknownst in most cases to the person being conversed with. Although he gave authentically of himself, he knew deep down that he still held back. Emotional interactions like these often freaked him out in the past, but he began learning to embrace it. Symon, for instance, had surprised him. Just when he thought nothing enriching existed in their relationship, his vulnerability and honesty blew him away.

Symon helped him get here, right to this moment with Aloha. A near finality to life shadowed him, instinct told him so, so best to live each moment intimately and that included allowing himself to feel each and every emotion to the fullest. He drops his shoulders and relaxes into Aloha's hug, taking steady constrained breaths of her hair, which smelt of dry compost.

Eventually, Aloha releases him.

29E

Small, orange, moody, circular spotlights emit out of a cylindrical table which compliments a cylindrical room. Communication equipment of all sorts are displayed on the table. If not for the cylindrical room and style, it could be mistaken for a room at Bletchley Park, where Alan Turing twigged how to decode German war secrets, cutting the war short by two years. This understated war hero had suffered the injustice of chemical castration because of his different sexuality.

Sat at the table are Adira, Skyler, Belize and Symon. Guards are positioned at the door.

'Are you sure you have the right frequency... try again.' Adira takes a quick discreet glance at Symon.

'Tyler on Mr Drake, Tyler on Mr Drake... we know you're there, please respond, over.' Skyler transmits calmly.

'Try the other frequency again.' Belize says, rubbing her hands together under the table.

Skyler turns a dial and then thumbs a button and repeats. 'Tyler on Mr Drake, Tyler on Mr Drake... we know you're there, please respond, over.'

'Maybe say something else, he's perhaps not best pleased he's *on* Mr Drake, if you catch my drift.' Belize rubs the side of her mouth with her closed fist.

Symon conceals a smile with his hand.

The intercom is interrupted with a ping. "Mam your attendance is required in sector R, we may have an issue in the caverns, over."

Adira turns around in her chair. 'Symon you come with me, it may have something to do with you.'

~~~~~~~~~~~~~~~~~~~~~~~~~~~~~

Tyler hauls up a throw from the armchair he's buckled into, shudders a little as he hunches his shoulders and then releases them. Aloha also covers herself, but with a woollen blanket which has seen better days. It looks more like a thick fishing net. She wraps it around herself and settles into her armchair, staring at Tyler with ice cold eyes.

Tyler studies her as if looking at some ancient statue. He realises they are both sitting in comfortable furnished armchairs, with very soft off-white leather with a portobello mushroom texture. Not chairs expected in a space station at all. He guessed comfort was priority if cooped up in a floating capsule, so why not.

He remembers the first time he met her.

—At the Extinction Rebellion conference, perched at the bar, monitoring Adira and him as they chatted. Adira had been quite discreet at the time, telling him about a project embarked on, that could be handy in the future for the good of the planet. Tyler only noticed her when he left the room, after being shown the android in some kind of electronics lab. It was then he knew Aloha must have been watching them. He recalled the memory of her then, the way the mind does, putting visual snapshots together, like Wasgij jigsaw.

At the time, completely distracted by Adira's, perhaps overzealous words, he had been inattentive. Now as he rushed out of the room, he spotted her in the corner of his eye, sat at the same stool, in the same orientation, as though she had never moved an inch. She merely sat on the stool, waiting, biding her time till they came back out. And when he did come back out, her eyes burned through him, studying him. Exactly how she was doing now.

'I didn't think you made it. Thought you might have perished on earth. Either that or stuck in the caverns. Either way, I felt you were worthless, good for nothing. Thought it was left to me to figure it out.'

'Well I'm very much alive. I didn't think you made it either. I'm just as surprised to see you. It's a miracle really.' Tyler shudders. 'How come it's so cold in here, don't the vents work?'

~~~~~~~~~~~~~~~~~~~~~~~~~~~~~~

Symon is up to his restless antics again, paces up and down Adira's quarters as she types instructions into a computer. He gazes at her keenly, observing her hands as she types, with such speed—she would have made someone an exceptional receptionist or PA, in a parallel universe maybe.

Adira can sense he's observing her, but pays him no attention. Instead, she allows her mind to revel in a flashback, back on earth.

She watched Tyler leave in a hurry, disturbed by what she disclosed. He had made up some lame excuse to leave and said that he would think about her proposal. His discomfort manifested clear as day, but she played along with the excuse he gave to leave. She allowed Tyler time to leave the party before she made her way up. She spotted Aloha straight away, had noticed her from the start; saw the radical in her, bursting to be let out. She went resolutely over and got them both a drink. After a while, twenty, thirty minutes or so. They both made their way down to the electronics lab. She enticed her the same way she had enticed Tyler. Either of them could be a backup plan.

The skin on the back of Adira's shoulders tingle in response to Symon's beady eyes upon her, but she refuses to look round. He may spot the deceit in her eyes and she could not afford for that to happen. Not just yet, way too soon.

~~~~~~~~~~~~~~~~~~~~~~~~~~~~

'Figure what out, what are you talking about?' Tyler leans forward, allowing the throw to float away from his chest region.
Aloha stares at Tyler for a little while longer before— it seemed— flattering him with a response. 'You're not that dumb, don't pretend that you are.' She piles up the ragged blanket around her feet, scrunching it up, trying to make up for the holes.
This time Tyler gawps, as if auditioning for a another sequel to Dumb and Dumber.
'You must have known—You *did* spot me at the conference...the Extinction Rebellion party. Where we first met, remember?'
'So what... our entire friendship was some kind of... some kind of hoax?'
'No of course not, don't be so dramatic. I liked you for real. This was a stab in the dark. How were we to know, we... the so-called intelligent species, were that far lined up on the precipice. We weren't to know, were we? I mean we knew we were stupid, Extinction Rebellion was formed based on that fact, but Christ, we had no idea we were just weeks away from a cataclystic earth

fuck!' Aloha is mindful she fucked up the c-disaster word, but who cared. She doubted Tyler even noticed.

'God—when did trust get so eroded? We really fucked up huh? As a species I mean. Sexbots for relationships. Oppression reversed. Why would anyone want to continue the human race? —in any format?'

'Well...great to hear, dramatic still but, on the same page. So tell me you have a plan—a better implement to use?' Aloha shifts her body which allows her blanket to fall off her. Without doing anything about it, she continues. 'You do right?'

~~~~~~~~~~~~~~~~~~~~~~~~~~~~~~

Adira repeatedly makes errors in her typing and hurriedly corrects them. Symon's peering eyes on her are now affecting her typing and sooner or later she will have to face him. She knew he still loved her and she would have to use that to bide her time, to bide Tyler some time. For all she knew, Aloha had perished. She had arrived at the space station over five months ago and nothing, nothing at all changed. She turns round to face Symon.

'You *did* know all along didn't you? The whole time, this was your plan the whole time.' Symon now stops in his tracks, a light bulb moment electrocuting him to the floor, unable to take one more step at the revelation breaking through his psyche. 'Fuck! Fuck! Fuck! Fucking Fuck!'

'Keep your voice down, Symon.'

'Seriously?!'

'Oh please...you're a slave, a slave in the cavern of the moon!! Oppression reversed. We haven't made one iota of progress. Creating baby androids for paedophiles, pretty much it on the progress front. The idea of trust died years ago, we have sexbots for relationships for Christ sake, do you know how pathetic that sounds? We are a doomed species Symon and you know it, human existence is nothing but ad nauseam, interminable; we repeat the same old mistakes over and over and over, till we're drooling zombies, pretending to be awake. Well... we can remain unconscious on the moon, other species shouldn't have to suffer.'

Adira shoves the keyboard away from her and it smacks the computer monitor hard. She takes a peek and is pleased her report is still intact. 'Major unrest has unfolded in the caverns now, probably because you haven't returned. How am I supposed to send you back there? I can't carry on doing this Symon, I can't.' With that Adira folds up into herself and sobs. Symon rushes to her side to embrace her, moments before she slips off the chair to the floor. He helps break her fall and crouches next to her, deftly holding her shuddering body.

'Perhaps it's preordained to be like that, perhaps the bigger picture is chaos and we create that. Out of chaos rises order.' Symon gently rocks Adira in his arms.

'We don't deserve a planet, Symon.' Adira sobs some more into the crook of Symons armpit. 'I'm not killing anyone, just making sure we don't return... I guess no lives matter.'

~~~~~~~~~~~~~~~~~~~~~~~~~~~~~

'I have a chip from a sexbot, need to adapt it though.' Tyler's words are devoid of emotion, sounding like an android.

'Great, can I help?' Aloha shoves the woollen blanket further away from her and removes her buckle. The detection of the lack of emotion in Tyler's words seemed to ignite her.

'Yes, yes...I'm sure you can.' Tyler retrieves the chip taken out of his sexbot's neck and holds it up to the dim light they have in the room.

~~~~~~~~~~~~~~~~~~~~~~~~~~~~~

Symon senses the warmth and moist breath of Adira on his chest, and to his embarrassment can also sense his semi erection. He attempts to cause his mind some distraction, but chooses poorly. 'Just tell me one thing, it doesn't matter, but... I want to know. Did you sleep with Tyler?'

'For meteor's sake Symon, for a second there I thought you'd transcended that pathetic bloke inside of you. I thought that maybe, just maybe, your time with Tyler converted you into a decent man.' Adira presses herself off of Symon's chest.

'I'm sorry, I'm sorry—awful bad timing huh?'

'You think?' Adira wipes her face with her sleeve in an attempt to get rid of an itch, rather than wipe away the portrayed sarcasm. 'And so you know...not that it's any concern or business of yours. No, No I did not fuck Tyler, if you're going to accuse me at least use the right fucking word. Did I *sleep* with Tyler?... seriously. Does anyone still speak like that? Surely don't expect it from you.'

Symon says nothing, instead he meditates on the floor.

'Still no response from Mr Drake, will have to put on my best act of trying to dissuade Tyler now, if he answers.'

'I'll do anything you want me to, Adira, just say the word.'

'Great.' Adira strides over to where the alcohol container is and pours herself a cup of the liquid. 'Want some?'

'Erm, no I'm good thanks... Is there no way of preventing the virus? You know... just in case.'

'A complex virus, I'm afraid. The DOS system doesn't have as much vulnerability, so it needed to be special, the irony huh, turns out to be the ideal opportunity to devise something that will be in...ineradicable.'

'What if Tyler says something, when you're speaking to him, what if he says something that gives you away?'

'He won't.'

'But what if he does?'

'He won't, okay... trust me.'

'Ahem, are you forgetting your very recent speech on trust?'

'Symon... are you forgetting you just asked how you can help?'

Adira and Symon turn away from each other and stare at the floor in contemplation.

Symon turns back to face Adira. 'Weren't they others on the space station? How come it's not manned?... Excuse the expression.'

'Well it is most of the time, there... there's no need for it to be staffed all the time, we can...we control it from here.' Adira responds without facing Symon.

~~~~~~~~~~~~~~~~~~~~~~~~~~~~

'How come you weren't successful?' Tyler withdraws his hand and along with it, the chip.

'I must have damaged it trying to get here.' Aloha turns away.

Tyler detects what he could only describe as a sense of shame pouring off her. 'I see, well lead the way.'

'Back this way.' Aloha wraps the tattered blanket around her shoulders and takes long propelled motions out through the exit, into a tight passageway resembling a spinal cord. Tyler follows close behind, returning the chip to his pocket. As they hover forwards, he regards his lifeless surroundings. Oh how he missed the resplendent beauty of nature. His sensitive soul had always been overwhelmed with earth's beauty—in a good way. The enchanted forests and streams, glassy lakes in autumn, damp treacly peaty bogs, craggily towering mountains, delicate polychromatic wildflower meadows, frothy leftovers from turbulent seas, the jagged fractured white lines flashed across ebony skies in an electrical storm and the fiery conflagration of many a sunset. Earth's beauty had overwhelmed him, carving out an abyss into his soul, only to be filled at a later date with joy and bliss and an all knowing acceptance of life. The deeper the abyss, the more space for joy and bliss to fill. People failed to notice the crucial importance of nature to their existence. Deep in his heart, harboured the fact that humans did not learn and so remained undeserving, and he stayed purposeful in seeing to it that humans never returned.

'I thought there'd be others here. Have you been on your own the entire time?'

'The entire time.' Aloha drags out the last word into a sort of melody, as if about to break into song.

Tyler takes stock of the eccentricity and puts it down to cabin fever.

'The next turn...almost there.' Aloha tightens the blanket around her neck..

"Mr Drake, this is moonbase—please answer. Tyler, we know you're there, please respond."

Aloha turns around to watch Tyler's reaction. She's nonplussed that her name is not mentioned over the radio.

~~~~~~~~~~~~~~~~~~~~~~~~~~~~

Adira makes her way back to the comms room. She'd asked Symon to stay behind, much better for her feigned display, with him not present. She easily put her conscience under wraps. What she was trying to accomplish was bigger than her and her feelings —a lot bigger.

'Any luck, any response yet?' Adira pulls herself a seat and lowers herself down into it with grace.

'Nothing yet mam.'

"Hello, this is Mr Drake, what's up?" Aloha's beam spreads across her face, an opportunity she couldn't miss. She acknowledges Tyler, who had given her the go ahead to respond on his behalf.

'Who is that?' Adira knew exactly whose words had come forth from the intercom, so much so, a cold, hot wave surged through her body. Nothing could have prepared her for this, nothing at all.

Aloha had gone out to the space station months ago. No one except Adira knew, or at least that was what she was led to believe.

'No idea mam.'

"Who is this? Please identify yourself." The guard checks the frequency as he concludes his sentence.

"Aloha here, Aloha here." She chuckles to herself, finding the choice of words hilarious, enjoying herself very much, the way a deranged person in space might.

"Aloha, we thought you were lost in space. Are you okay? Over" The guard releases the button so as to allow an incoming message.

Adira shoves the guard out of the way and clamps down on the button.

"Aloha, Adira here, please put Tyler on, over." She releases the button. 'We haven't got time for this, people. A potential disaster could be afoot here.' Adira addresses Skyler, two guards and Belize, who remain quiet and nod in acknowledgement. She couldn't be sure what would come out of Aloha's mouth next and didn't want to take the chance.

Tyler strides over and replaces Aloha next to the communication equipment.

"Tyler please confirm your reasons for escaping and heading to the — (coughs), sorry... heading to the space station."

A flashback floods Tyler's cortex, of an encounter with Adira at the Extinction Rebellion conference.

Back in the electronics laboratory.

'And what if someone discovers what I'm up to, then what? I know you're lined up to be the leader but even so.' Tyler nervously scratches his head as he questions Adira.

'Simple...if we have to speak to one another and I'm questioning you, I will cough. That way you recognise I'm in the midst of people and need to ignore my request.'

'Oh, okay... you sure that will work?'

'I will cough...everything I say after that, ignore.'

Tyler resists Aloha pulling on his arm, albeit the grip seemed forceful. He put it down to adrenaline. Had made it this far and was ready to carry out his mission and Adira had coughed, like she said she would for this eventuality. The signal had been given. He knew exactly why she decided to own the microphone. He could tell by the way Aloha pressed her lips tightly together as she grabbed his arm; she didn't care much for Adira. Playing along with Adira encouraged their mission. Aloha's space sickness may very well be interfering with her reasoning.

'Yes, er, yes mam, this is me... Tyler.' How to address Adira correctly was not at his frontal lobe. He almost called her by her name, which could have been suspect.

"Oh great... Tyler, please assure us you're only there to get away. Please assure us you mean us no harm... (coughs), over."

"Correct mam, couldn't face it in the caverns any longer... er sorry mam."

"Nothing to apologise for Tyler. In actual fact, I'm deliberating working out a way to have us all together. Separating us doesn't work and we need to figure something out."

Skyler stares at Adira as if the eyeballs were frozen in their sockets. Belize acknowledges Skyler's reaction and also replays what she heard in her head. Did Adira suggest the prisoners would be set free?

'I guess the silence is warranted. You did hear right, I'm working on an action plan to free the sla...erm, prisoners. Suppression is not sustainable.' Adira studies the gnome faces presented to her. Belize peers down at the communication device and then back at Adira, suddenly realising why the lack of response. 'Over... over,' she mutters with embarrassment.

Adira banked on this being the only way to distract people from the situation. She foresaw people would undoubtedly question her judgement, they would wonder why she chose to believe a prisoner's word. But not if she now threw into the mix, a proposal to free the men from the caverns. Magicians called this misdirection.

She had always marvelled at how well her cousin performed magic back on earth, and he disclosed to her that the key was misdirection, leading the audience away from the main trick by distraction. Many politicians knew and practised distraction techniques, and although not her normal style, she needed to play the game this time. A lot more at stake than her morals.

"I...I see mam, lovely to hear. In that case I will be more than happy to come along without any trouble once conditions are favourable again."

"Fantastic, settled then, do please give my regards to Aloha."

Again, Skyler portrays the most perplexed expression. Belize tries to conceal hers, not very well as Adira catches her facial expression just before.

'I know, fully aware this is not what you saw coming, I'm sure I'll have a fight with the counsel but this is my call. No more oppression.'

Belize plucks up courage from somewhere. 'This wouldn't have anything to do with Symon, would it mam?'

'It might have something to do with it, yes. Made me realise we can't continue ostracising.' Adira expected the comment.

Belize turns to inspect Skyler's reaction, who quickly turns away and gazes at the floor.

'Any more questions?' Adira gets up from the seat.

Everyone except Adira gawps at each other and no one comments.

'Okay then, Belize set up a meeting straight away and someone unlock the larder at the station.'

'Yes mam.' A guard says and shifts aside for Adira to pass.

Adira turns back round before exiting. 'Belize, I presume you've taken the ear wax test?'

'Erm —yes mam, my cortisol is fine.'

'Well I still think you need time off, you have lost someone dear to you, you need to allow yourself time to grieve.'

'I see what you're saying ma—'

'Not a request Belize, take some time off.' With that Adira turns away and exits the comms room.

~~~~~~~~~~~~~~~~~~~~~~~~~~~

'Well, that was easy. Anything to eat around here?' Tyler regards Aloha with some caution. It was no coincidence Adira requested to speak to him instead of her.

Aloha does not reply, she stares at him with her shark eyes instead. To Tyler's relief, they are both distracted by the sound of an unlocking mechanism, somewhere to the left, outside of the room they were in. Aloha is the first to start toward the sound, but not before clearing her nostrils, by taking a long strained sniff. Tyler hopes the sniff displayed a psychological body language cue to let go and move on. He undoubtedly did not need to get into a fight with a scorned woman with partial eyesight, cooped up alone in a space station for months. He hovers behind her with measured, cautious propulsions, as they leave the comms room to investigate the unlocking sound.

30Y

Belize is back in her quarters and she manoeuvres herself in a seat to get comfortable. She then proceeds to probe her ear with part of a device resembling a cotton bud. The other half of the device mimics an electronic reader of some kind. She waits for it to beep and then reads the message on the LED screen. She mutters to herself.

'A little high but nothing to be dramatic about.' She drops the device on the table to the side of her. 'Nothing a piece of relaxing music won't remedy.' Talking to oneself was no biggie on the moon. Everybody did it.

The device had been invented a while back and measured quantities of a range of hormones and sugars in the body. One of many self diagnosing devices invented, putting general practitioners out of work.

Belize pushes up onto her feet, turns round and collapses on her bed. She grabs for a remote control in arms reach and fiddles with it. Computer based music is chosen following the result of her diagnosis. High cortisol called for pseudo-classical music. A serene reproduction of a beach is emitted on the wall in front of her. She drops the control back on the side table and a coy grin forms on her face. She remembers reading somewhere about the television remote control having over a 100 different names in Britain. A clear indication of how much television ruled people's lives. Also a clear indication of the correlation with obesity. Panic button and fat enhancer stayed her favourite coined names for the TV remote, followed closely by whatcha-ma-call-it and thingy-ma-jig. She didn't miss television one bit, except maybe the documentary programs. She conjectured that if not for television numbing everyone's senses, people may have acted a lot sooner and been proactive over all kinds of important matters, not least racial injustice and the climate crisis.

She stretches out on her bed and closes her eyes, tuning into her body. As she begins to sense energy vibrations in her hands, her intercom beeps. Opening her eyes, she is presented with an image of Skyler on the side of her screen waiting to be let in. She huffs and grasps the remote again, hitting another button.

The door slides open.

'Sorry to bother you Belize.' Skyler waltzes in.

'No you're not. My cortisol is a bit high, so no stress please.'

'Ah...okay. Wanted to speak to you after the incident in the comms room.'

'What incident? I don't remember an incident.'

'Okay, okay... you know what I mean. Are we going to leave Tyler on the station? Even more distressing —freeing the prisoners, what's brought that on? Where are they going to stay?'

'Well... she's the peeress.'

Skyler huffs and slumps down on the nearest seat.

'What are you proposing we do? She was quite clear, I thought, unless you're suggesting mutiny?' Belize props up on the bed and enters the lotus position.

'Well, no 'course not. I just feel that —well, why the sudden change of heart.'

'Well, maybe she's right... oppression doesn't work, I mean look at the guilt carried by whites all those years for enslaving blacks. Strong emotions like that are passed on from generation to generation. And then worst case, covered up by arrogance and annoyance. Where do you think all the backlash from the black lives matter movement sprung from? Of course social media didn't help...anyways, no progress in repeating the same mistakes.'

'Gosh, she's really going ahead with this. The cavern is going to be set free. I can't imagine the other black people will be best pleased.'

'What are you talking about? Are you forgetting the leader is black. If Adira has changed her mind about it all, then I'm sure she's got a valid reason. I don't think she's suggesting they aren't punished for failing the unconscious bias test, just not ostracised in a cavern, away from everyone else.'

Going to get pretty cramped.' Skyler fidgets with fingers as they deliver the last comment with some resignation. 'Talking about cramped, wasn't there supposed to be others on the space station? I'm pretty sure there were a few stationed there... took it in turns?'

'I think they returned and the next group were due out before the commotion at the greenhouse. Now if you don't mind, I'll really like to get some rest.'

'Sure, sure... I'll go, thanks for the chat.' Skyler stands up and makes to leave.

'Sure — Oh Skyler?'

'Yes.' Skyler turns around.

'Don't mention or talk about this to anyone else, others might not be so open. You understand?'

'Yeah, yeah sure.' And with that Skyler clumsily exits the quarters.

~~~~~~~~~~~~~~~~~~~~~~~~~~~~~

On the way back to her quarters, Adira decides to pass by the school. She loved watching the kids play when she sought clarity of mind. Something about children's natural ability to be present to each and every moment, permitted her to do the same. She reckoned if not for kids, more heterosexual marriages would have broken up back on earth. The demise of most heterosexual relationships started with the advent of restrictions on child birth; then with the emergence of sexbots, most people didn't see the point of relationships. Too much hassle. She believed most people were inherently selfish, the only difference being some people concealed it better than others.

She is about to turn a corner when the giggling of a little girl nabs her attention. A child laughing always lifted her spirits. Not able to conceive when with Symon, she decided to lose herself in her work rather than labour the issue. She felt if not destined to have children then so be it. She accepted it. Deep down though, she knew the acceptance pivoted on her not wanting a child *that* bad. She never did reveal this insight to Symon.

'The peeress!' A young girl of around five years old points at Adira from her class room. Cute ponytails kept in place by a rubber band, coerce a sense of guileless innocence in all who witness them. Enchanting hazel eyes peer out of her modelled looking head, not symmetrical with her body, as a little on the chubby side. She seems to be wearing boy's clothes and the trousers are over-sized. They are folded at the bottoms, but drag on the floor as she runs to embrace Adira. She pays no attention to the teacher calling for her to come back to the classroom.

'Adira!' The little girl stretches her arms out for an embrace.

'Chloe, how are you… watch you don't trip now.'

'Don't worry, I won't trip. I know how to shuffle-run.'

'Ha, shuffle-run, is that what you call it?' She squats down to embrace Chloe.

'Yes, mam,' She wriggles free of the hug, replacing it with the biggest grin.

'How've you been Chloe? Are you learning lots of stuff?' Adira remains squatting to engage with the little girl.

'Yup I am. I'm learning a whole bunch of stuff.'

'Amazing. Good girl. You'll be a pilot soon. You still want to be a pilot when you grow up right?'

'Yes... you remembered. I thought you'd be too busy to remember that minor fact.'

Adira laughs out loud. 'Well firstly, nothing minor about it, and of course I remember. You'll make an awesome pilot.'

'You think so Adira?'

'Absolutely Chloe. You'll be teaching others how to be great pilots too.'

'Yeah, when we're back on earth. I can't wait to see real trees, I can't wait, I can't wait!'

'Yes... so what did you learn today Chloe?' Adira felt a lump in her throat, and her arms felt heavy, as if intravenously pumped with lead. She drops them to the side. A sudden pang of sadness overwhelms her. She planned on denying this young girl a probable future back on earth. She consoled herself with emphasis on the word "probable."

'Well... we learnt geography most of the morning, and there were quite a few trees to learn. I love the big ones. Like the giant soqua trees. Do you know how high... how high they can grow Adira? Do you? Do you?'

'Erm... I don't know how tall the sequoia trees grow, no...but do me a favour now and ask Maggie to meet me out here, need to speak to her about something. You go on back to class now. Not much longer now and back to your quarters for yummy din dins. Right?'

'Yeah okay... see you Adira.' Chloe sulks a little and shuffles back to class, lifting the front of her trousers this time.

Adira gets up and strides to the side of the door, out of view of the kids.

'Mam, you needed to see me.' Maggie is of Indian origin and is clanky and elegant, with short cropped light brown hair. From the look of most of the colonists' hair, it was evident a professional hairdresser didn't reside on the base. A very pointy nose and thin lips make her look teachery.

'Yes Maggie, do me a favour and take Geography off the curriculum will you. Physics, mechanics, botany and electronics. Focus on those please, make the other teachers aware, okay?'

'Er... yeah sure, sure will do. I'll send the message through now... Is everything okay mam?' Maggie detected Adira looked pale, and had trained her eyes to spot discolouration in black people. Never easy to tell when a black person was flushed or about to faint, but with practice, you could detect the signs. Depending on the shade of blackness, the shade when peaky could be described as a tint of grey, like gleyed soil.

'Yeah, yeah I'm fine, I think I got up too quickly from squatting to greet Chloe.'

'Okay, do you need me to get you a drink?'

'No, no...I'll grab one when I get back. Don't forget my request now?'

'Course not mam, will message straight away.' Maggie hurries back into the classroom. 'Okay, okay settle down you lot.' She takes charge straight away. Chloe takes a seat and turns round to check on Adira who winks at her. The pang of sadness erodes Adira's insides again. Another young girl next to her, probably about 14 years old, does not turn around to look at her, when all the other children did. That girl never acknowledged her in all the time she visited. Mystery surrounded her, something she couldn't quite put a finger on. She looked like what most people would refer to as an old soul. She should have asked Maggie about her but forgot. She consoled herself with the knowledge she will the next time, reassured by more of an imprint in her mind about it.

She turns round and resumes heading back to her quarters. She often reflected on whether she would have made a good mother. She seemed to get on really well with kids, or more so, they seemed drawn to her, she suspected like cats, they come to you when you ignore them. She found it easy to get down to their level, engaging with them in fullness. She also knew it would not be something she could sustain long term, not without some kind of resentment. She resigned to the fact, selfishness persisted as a key characteristic of hers. Not having a child assuredly made it easier to go ahead with her scheme.

She is a few yards away from her quarters now. Figuring out a contingency, in case Skyler chose to probe some more. Though there had not been any backfiring to her decision to release the slaves yet, she had to remain on her toes. She also needed a contingency for a potential coup. Symon might be able to help, she'll see if he had any ideas. Adira increases her pace.

A piercing siren freezes Adira in her tracks, the nerve-shredding alarm is followed by a suppressed pulsating sound. Adira rushes to her quarters. The orange and yellow flashes, synchronised with the siren, disorient her a little. She sighs, knowing exactly what was taking place. A solar wind storm. Of all the times for this to emerge. A solar wind storm is supposed to occur every 25 years. When this happened on earth most people were oblivious, because on earth the natural magnetic field protected them. Yet another reminder of how lucky the human race were to inhabit a planet.

She plonks herself down at her desk and grips the telecom speaker. 'This is Adira, please tell me the magnetic field is activated and working... over.' She had heard the unmistaken pulsating sound, but still better to check.

"Yes mam, the field is activated and so far we appear safe... over."

'Okay great, keep me updated.'

"Are you going to your secure quarters mam?"

'No, no... I don't think there's any need, over.'

"Okay mam, if you're sure... over."

'Yes, I'm sure.' She turns round to observe Symon who is out for the count in deep slumber. She examines him as he sleeps, realises how much she missed that, observing him deep in slumber relaxed her.

The siren ceases, but the pulsating persists. She's confident the solar wind storm will not affect the space station, and more importantly, not obstruct the mission.

~~~~~~~~~~~~~~~~~~~~~~~~~~~~~

'What is that sound? Is that an alarm?' Tyler holds himself steady and cocks his head to the side, in an attempt to make sense of the distant sound he can hear.

Aloha stays suspended too and cocks her head in the vicinity of the sound. 'It sounds like an alarm, can't say I've heard that one before.'

'Oh... how many alarms *do* go off on this floating jumble of metal?'

'Well, since being here... I think two... or was it three.'

Tyler rolls his eyes. 'Are we almost at the motherboard?'

'Yes... next turn.'

'Aloha... you said that about twenty minutes ago. You sure this time?'

'Yes, yes I'm sure, just a bit of a maze on this station. It's past that unit on the left.' Aloha points to an air conditioning unit a few yards away.

'Were the alarms anything to do with the station?' Halfway through the question, Tyler glances back to examine the way they have come. He wants to be sure he's memorising any navigation pointers. He couldn't be sure he trusted Aloha, having been alone on the station for too long. Plus, despite their friendship back on earth—where he thought they were close— it turns out neither of them trusted the other enough to divulge their secret mission.

'Two were sirens back on the moonbase. Two on the base and one here. A lot louder. I needed to reboot the air conditioning unit.'

'I see, so a control panel identifies the siren?' Tyler propels faster to catch up with Aloha. He supposes one of those alarms was the one activated by Symon to cut out the electrics briefly, aiding his escape. The other, must have sounded following the mix up in the computer chess results.

'Yes, the control panel is next to the room with the motherboard in.'

'Handy.' Tyler is now floating apace with Aloha, just enough room for both of them to fit.

They both turn a corner, and are faced with a module room a tad larger than the docking station bay.

Aloha turns round to face Tyler. 'Ta da!' Aloha extends her arms, as if for an embrace and turns back round.

Tyler examines the room filled with computers and small coloured lights and buttons; a subtle humming associated with electronic appliances fills the room. Most of the equipment is covered in dust and in a ray of light angled downwards, motes of dust dance in mid air. This does not make sense to him— If dust is mostly dead skin cells from humans, then how come so much of the stuff coated every veneer? There was no one else here. No way Aloha's shedded it all; from what he could see her hair didn't appear flaked in dandruff. He winces at the thought.

'No one else here is there?'

'No... well, I've not seen anyone. Why do you ask?' Aloha scratches under her left breast.

'No reason... just wondered. So where's the motherboard?'

'Right over there.' Aloha points to a corner of the room. Tyler follows her finger and wonders what was with the complex bulky electronic equipment situated in the corner of the room. An air conditioning unit is situated right next to it—to keep it cool. Overheating could be an issue for electronic equipment left on for long periods of time. Tyler floats over to the machine with its own distinct whir. The hum reminds him of a standing lamp with a dimmer switch he once owned; it only ever stopped humming when the lamp was on max or turned off.

He retrieves the small circuit board from his pocket as Aloha hovers up to him.

'I might need to tweak it a little. Are there some small tools around?'

'Er... yes I think there could be some in this drawer here.' Aloha goes to the opposite end of the room and yanks open a drawer. She retrieves a small tool kit and returns to Tyler.

Tyler takes the toolkit and unlatches it. He searches the contents and then retrieves a tiny screwdriver.

'This should do the trick.' He prises out a circuit board from the side of the motherboard and proceeds to unscrew a section of it. He takes out a component and then checks the little circuit board in his possession.

'How long before the virus infiltrates?' Aloha edges closer to Tyler.

Tyler moves away and winces. 'How about we don't encroach on each other's space?'

'I smell that bad huh?' Aloha lifts her right arm and sniffs her armpit.

'Yeah, I'm afraid you do.' An aroma of rancid fat with urinous, sour, sweaty undertones slowly begins to subside. He briefly reminisced about moments back on earth, moments of pleasant fragrance. Aloha often smelt clean, with a hint of vanilla and lemon. Now her scent was putrid a'la stench. He suspected he didn't smell much better either. Indisputably sweaty, not to mention shitty, and now and again, while he crouched, he detected a whiff of urine. Zero G meant you were peeing yourself before your body was able to make you aware. He would change his diaper as soon as he completed his task. He was grateful there wasn't the smell of vomit thrown in the mix, he had learnt to manage his stomach gases. Zero G also meant to belch was unavoidably to puke.

Tyler resumed tinkering with the circuit board. 'It shouldn't take that long... I reckon a few hours.'

'Ah... and would they be alerted to the virus?'

'They will be, but I should be able to reduce the time for them to act. They would need to go over a few checks—rebooting the system renders the whole base in jeopardy, so that won't be a solution they choose unless really desperate. Even so, got this little circuitry,' Tyler waves the device in his hand. 'So if they reboot, it would only quicken the process of the virus corrupting the system.'

'You undoubtedly know what you're doing, as sure as eggs are eggs.' Aloha finishes the sentence with pressed lips.

'Hey, no need for the resentment. I'm sure you did the best with what you had.' Tyler acknowledges but ponders on her choice of phrase.

'Still the charmer I see.' Aloha shows a wry smile. Her tired cold eyes do nothing to accentuate the smile.

'I do this with a very heavy heart Aloha, don't think I don't. I strongly believe that the human race and earth— or any planet for that matter —are not compatible, full stop. This is my purpose, as is yours. We are preserving life, we are only a part of the system, and the bigger picture is—well there is one life, one consciousness. Do you know what I mean?'

Although Aloha hovers, she is still. The kind of stillness only attainable when there is no thought process going on. A shimmer of a glint shows in her eyes, and an all knowing smile is formed on her face. She replies without any angst.

'Yes, I believe I *do* know what you mean... not conceptually...more a feeling of, a feeling of —Ah ...now I'm using my mind. At any rate, I'm glad you're here with me Tyler. Glad for the company in death.'

'Nothing is lost, not really... one life —one consciousness. Let's hold on to that.' Tyler fiddles with the circuit board some more, utilising a tiny pair of pliers. He uses a magnifying glass on the table and turns the chip around and around in his fingers. 'I think this is it.'

'Okay then... here's to mother earth.' Aloha hovers just a fraction closer to Tyler.

Tyler takes out a section of the computer unscrewed earlier, presses something to bypass the current temporarily and replaces a circuit chip in the computer with the one on him. He slowly pushes the section back in place and depresses the button to relay the current.

Aloha hovers over the table to get a better viewpoint of Tyler's activity, her fingers crossed in her left hand while grabbing a rail with her right. Tyler is startled when he realises her hovering above him. 'Good god Aloha... you really do fancy becoming a ghost don't you—made me jump there.'

'Sorry, wanted to see what you were doing.' Aloha slowly descends.

'Well...all done now, now we play the waiting game. Couple of things needed for the virus to be triggered which they'll do on the base unknowingly.' Just how dusty the table is, is evident again having moved the computer a little to get access. He wonders whether to ask Aloha about it, but decides not to. 'So changing rooms, where's the nearest one please?'

'Oh, just round the corner, I'll show you.'

'Is it near where we can get some food?'

'It is.'

'Handy.'

31E

Skyler hurries down the serpentine-like corridor, every so often, a waft of mist is blasted out from vents tucked away in the skeletal ceiling; a complex air conditioning unit, manufacturing artificial, breathable air, by extracting oxygen-rich air from the greenhouse. Skyler dodges the jets of mist as they scurry through. They knew that most computer viruses worked a certain way, as in, they needed to be triggered somehow, initiated by the same computers infected. Convinced of being able to find a way of determining if a virus was administered, it didn't get initiated. There had to be a way to do it in the computer hub, no need to explain himself to the guard, just say carrying out a service.

At the next corner is the sign "computer hub." One guard loiters outside the room and they breathe a sigh of relief, as they happen to know her. This should be easier than envisioned.

'Tabitha… Hi.' Skyler raises a hand as they approach a woman in uniform. Immediately striking are her facial features, bushy eyebrows accompanying light brown eyes, a nose and mouth that could have been chiselled by Michelangelo. All underneath charcoal dark hair. Perfect symmetry, almost resembling a sexbot. Not one blemish or misplaced wrinkle, as if her face was ironed out.

'Hi Skyler, what are you doing down here?'

'Was coming to meet you actually.' Skyler equips the best charming smile.

'Aww, to what do I owe the pleasure?'

'Well, I need to check something with the computers. You've heard of the guy who's escaped from the caverns and taken shelter on Mr Drake, right?'

'I have… why?' Tabitha checks that the microphone on her radio is off. She sensed Skyler's response would be shrouded in controversy. Something about the facial features and eyes, mainly the eyes, a mischievous twinkle, which she had recognised in her younger brother when growing up.

'Well, let's just say I don't think he's there for respite. I believe he's up to something sinister, but the peeress doesn't believe me. She thinks he's there for a break from the caverns. Quite worrying that she trusts him so implicitly.'

'Really?... How exactly will he sabotage the computers? To what aim?' Tabitha tucks a lock of her jet black hair behind her right ear.

'I think he plans on devising some kind of virus with a part from an older model of the sexbots. C'mon, let me in, he may already have set the virus in motion. I can explain as I put up the defences.' Skyler diverts eyes away from her to the door, sign language often helps stress the urgency of a matter.

'What if I get into trouble letting you in?'

'Oh you won't. Should take me a few minutes to update something on the system. If I'm right — instant protection... hopefully— If I'm not, then no harm done.'

Tabitha plays with her lock of hair. She ponders for a few seconds and then tucks it back behind her ear. 'Okay, do it, but you better be quick. In fact, got five minutes and then you're out, agreed?'

'Okay, okay agreed. C'mon let me in, it might already be too late.'

Tabitha goes toward the door which acknowledges the pass camouflaged in her uniform and slides open. 'Hurry in before someone spots you.' She steps aside for Skyler to pass.

Skyler hurries in and makes a beeline for the computer with flashing small lights. Tabitha scans the corridor as the door pings and sucks to close.

~~~~~~~~~~~~~~~~~~~~~~~~~~~

On their short trip to get some food, Tyler is almost ecstatic to be out of his diaper, although he doesn't show it. Something tells him that were he to show it, Aloha would gladfully celebrate with him. In a locker stocked as a larder, a few sachets of squeezable food are arranged neatly. Aloha reaches for several of the larger sachets, seizes a few and turns around to Tyler.

'These are the most filling and most nutritious. The catch is they aren't the most tasty.' Aloha pulls a face as she hands over a couple to Tyler. Tyler takes what's handed him with no hesitation, he doesn't care if they taste bad. He's famished.

'I'm grateful.' Tyler rips open one of the sachets with his teeth and squeezes the contents into his mouth and winces straight away. He maintains his grimace as he swallows.

'Not so bad.' He expels the unconvincing lie with a pulled face.

'Yeah, right... not convincing in the slightest.' Aloha squeezes her sachet into her mouth and her facial expression doesn't change. There is a swallowing motion and she speedily rips open the other sachet. Tyler does the same.

'So how much longer do we wait?' Aloha takes the emptied sachets off Tyler and turns away to place them in a bin.

'Not that long —what happens to the waste here anyway?'

'Well someone comes to get it and it's recycled on the plant back on the moon. Remember when it used to be collected for the inferno's back on earth, ha... now we get swamped in our waste.' Aloha shuts the locker with a bang and wipes her mouth.

'Should be starting now, let's get back shall we.' Tyler grasps the nearest rail and propels himself forward. Aloha follows behind, maintaining some distance, aware of how bad her body odour is. Shame the reduced gravity doesn't restrict the travel of stench.

'So how exactly does the AI stop humans returning? Do the sexbots perform other functions than sex?' Aloha maintains her distance from Tyler as they propel back to the computer room.

'Something like that, ironic isn't it?'

'What is?'

'Well, we cared more about sex than the planet and now the things we invented to enhance our sex lives are going to teach us a lesson, over our poor stewardship of earth.'

'Huh, never looked at it like that...suppose you're right.'

'Right... that word got washed away in everyone having an opinion about everything. Regardless of plain fact, scientific facts... we all got too hung up on opinions and having the right to them.' Tyler pushes away from a rail with more effort as they're around the corner from the computer room. Aloha does the same without saying a word. Sometimes when things are said that are so profound, it is wise to let it sink in, as opposed to eroding the words with other meaningless utterances.

They both arrive in the computer room and Tyler hovers over to the main computer. 'Now to create infinite loops to incapacitate our control over the AI.'

'Whatever that means.' Aloha hovers over to a spot that allows her the best aspect of Tyler working his technological magic.

~~~~~~~~~~~~~~~~~~~~~~~~~~~~

'He'll probably try to use infinite loops to purloin...incapacitate our control of the AI... so if I figure out how —'

'Infinite loops?' Tabitha plays with a strand of her hair, as her face contorts in ponderment.

'Yes, it's kind of like a bypass sequence... too difficult to explain.'

'I see.' Tabitha's facial expression neutralises somewhat.

Skyler types in different codes at lightning speed, flitting eyes up at Tabitha occasionally.

'How soon before—'

'Not now... give me a moment.' Skyler's now stoic expression intimidates her somewhat. She clasps her hands and waits patiently. After a few minutes lapse, Skyler props up, having crouched the entire time, it's a relief. They dart their eyes at Tabitha, but this time maintaining the stare. Tabitha holds back the stare.

'Technology has overwhelmed human strength and intelligence. Overpowering human nature was always gonna be checkmate for us. That, coupled with our inability to share any experience of reality, ensured we would be doomed.' Tabitha utters the words with serenity, the words arising from a place of divinity, as opposed to intellect.

'You're referring to tribalism right?' Skyler cocks their head and eyebrow at Tabitha.

'Not sure what I'm referring to, just acknowledging that technology was always coupled with an existential threat, it brought out the worst in society... anyway, what happens now?'

'We wait... not sure it will work, but let's see.'

'Hmm... you know what I miss more than anything in the world?' Tabitha lets go of the strand of hair she's twirled into a permed curled lock.

'What's that?' Skyler softens the features of their stoic face.

'Picking at a charcuterie board, while listening to the spilling waves of an ocean and admiring a Spanish sunset.'

'Gosh, pretty specific.'

'Yup. The Spanish sunsets were beatific.'

'I only ever went to the islands.'

'Ah, mainland Spain was also amazing.'

'*I* miss plain omelette and marmalade sandwiches more than anything in the world.'

Tabitha creases the wrinkles in her forehead. She regards him as if he had just admitted to once torturing a puppy back on earth.

~~~~~~~~~~~~~~~~~~~~~~~~~~~~~

'How much longer?' Aloha fidgets, even though it's quite difficult to fidget when hovering. You never realise how difficult it is to scratch or pick at yourself when you're floating in zero gravity. Aloha fidgets by swapping hands, holding the rail now and again, and also rubbing her legs against each other.

'I just need to initiate the override, in case someone attempts to block the malware. I reckon someone on the base might do that. I doubt the peeress's subjects are all as loyal as she thinks.' Tyler types codes into the computer.

'Got it all failsafe which is amazing.' Aloha says with more sincerity this time. She fiddles with her fingers, the creases in her knuckles mimic Chinese writing.

'After making it this far... it'd be tragic to soil the objective.' Tyler cannot help but take note of Aloha's eyes again. The velvety softness all gone, more metallic now, a clear signature of her losing all faith in humanity. They also possessed a beseeching quality, like she so gravely wanted their mission to be successful. He wondered if his eyes had also lost their softness. Did they also contain a beseeching quality? 'I reckon that should do it.' He says, smiling and stretching his arms.

320

'Got quite a temperature on you.' Symon gingerly removes his hand from Adira's forehead. 'How long before we get the EBV results?'

'I'll be fine, nothing a boost of antiviral drugs won't solve. Just need to up my dose and rest.' Adira removes her arm from a scanning machine next to her bed. The machine beeps at her. Small led lights flash green and orange.

'Are you afraid?' Symon returns his focus on Adira, after scanning the beeping machine.

'Afraid of what, the Epstein-Barr virus?' Adira covers her forearm back with her sleeve.

'No, not EBV… never returning back to earth.'

'Not particularly—Amor Fati.' Adira adjusts her sleeve.

'Amor what?'

'Amor Fati… it's Latin. The belief that your entire life— journey if you will— has led you to where you are, and you're grateful and content with every challenge overcome to get you there.'

'Wow, have you always believed that?' Symon leans back in his seat.

'Ever since teenage years and having to help nurse my mum struggling with cancer.'

'You are a remarkable woman, Adira. I had forgotten just how remarkable.'

'And you are a charmer as always… come here.' Adira stretches her arms out for a hug, and adjusts herself in the bed to make room for Symon.

Through the thickset window next to them, the cold light of distant stars shimmer. Further and farther away in the distance, a hazy swirling cosmic entanglement unravels itself.

'The children must be protected, they must never know. Under no circumstances.' Adira tightens her embrace around Symon.

'Aren't you worried about the children if the peeds come up?' Symon squirms out of the embrace, but plants a kiss on Adira's forehead before doing so.

'Of course I'm worried. I don't plan on having them up… I'm sure I told you that. Need to organise a strategy around it.'

'Yes you did mention that, sorry… forgot.'

'No probs, better that you're double checking. At least they're all out of the woodwork. We know who they are. None of them hiding in the shadows so to speak.'

'Very true.'

'Should be able to program the doors to the quarters with the child sexbots to stay locked when we release the locks to the others. There will no doubt be an uproar, but that is a chance I'm willing to take.'

'I hope you're right. There's clearly a comradeship formed in the caverns. No doubt the substance added to the water has induced this... Has it?' Symon props up on the bed to get a response.

'Would like to think it helped, yes. I could increase the dose, once the others are up. That should settle them down a bit.'

'How many are there anyway?'

'I think nine.'

'Christ... a lot'

'I know... you know whenever I get too hung up on not understanding something in life, I always think of the peeds. Some things can't be reasoned and that's okay. Not everything is supposed to be conceptualised. In fact, once we stop labelling everything, we set ourselves free. I used to think I would never understand the purpose. What realisable evolutionary purpose is there for paedophilia? Perhaps that is their purpose, to deter us from trying to put all and sundry in some kind of a box.' Adira props herself up on the bed too, next to Symon.

'Gosh, doesn't bear worrying about... and that's the point I guess. Stop thinking.'

Adira manoeuvres herself off the bed. 'Fancy a stiff drink?'

'After that conversation, hell yeah.' Symon throws both legs off the bed and makes contact with the floor.

~~~~~~~~~~~~~~~~~~~~~~~~~~~~

Belize scrutinises her cabin, as if drinking in what she perceives for the first time. In-built shelves— formed as part of windows—intermingle with concealed compartments that can be propped out when needed, like an extra table or appliance. Whiteness is the default colour of the entire room, except when the prime window is activated to show sirene videos. Memory banks can also be played back when needed, but most people stopped delving into their past memories. Identification with past memories had become— to put it bluntly—ludicrous, as most people, without knowing, had gotten a glimpse of the power of sacred stillness, only ever realised in being present to the now, never to reminiscing in the past. Belize believes the whiteness of her cabin encouraged her to stay present in each moment. She flits her eyes from one corner of the room to the next, then gazes out into space. She ponders on why the magnetic field had failed, causing the damage in the greenhouse, resulting in Agenta's death. No one had yet understood why the magnetic field malfunctioned. Some people had speculated terrorism, but that soon got dismissed as ridiculous.

Storks, carrying babies wrapped up in white cloth, with their beaks. This image constantly arose in Belize's mind, whenever she thought about Agenta and her unborn child. A lovely innocent image, until she witnessed a stork devour a baby flamingo on a David Attenborough program. The lovely depiction of storks flying with babies, dispersed then, like flimsy clouds. So she didn't want to be thinking of babies and storks when reminiscing about Agenta. The problem prevailed, could not work out a way to refrain from brooding over Agenta, and whenever those memories arose, her death and that of her unborn child, would flood her neural cortex too. No escaping it. She couldn't even share this with anyone. Some part of her knew she had to accept the rumination without beating herself up about it. Trying to halt thinking just made it worse, using mind against mind was like trying to grab fog. She counted on her work and the days when she could get back out into space. The vastness of space halted cogitating, kind of ripped any form of contemplation out of you, forcing you to be present. Working in the greenhouse ensured vastness surrounded her, fleeting thoughts just couldn't lock-in. She pondered on Skyler's theory around Tyler planning to sabotage their return to earth. She mostly put it down to paranoia—being in space for so long causes all kinds of mental health issues if not checked—but then again, what if they were right? She suddenly felt a surge of dread in her gut. She swallowed hard, attempting to swallow the foul, rancid foreboding building up in her. She didn't think she would be that attached about returning to earth—notably now with Agenta gone—but she now realised she was fettered, as if an imaginary umbilical cord had always hooked her up to the planet.

She often struggled with anxiety when back on earth. For no apparent reason, she'd be consumed by it, like how a drop of dye in a beaker full of water spreads with colour, taking over the transparent liquid. Back then, she relied on sex to get her out of her head. She refrained from that now, even gotten rid of her sexbot. Absolutely aware at these times, of being dreadfully in her head, locked in so to speak, unable to break free from thought, thought becoming her existence. Then there was the beating oneself up that would commence, a non acceptance of the present moment, and that just exacerbated the feeling. She would sometimes sit down and write, write her 'mind' out. Something about seeing her thoughts expressed as words on a blank white sheet made her feel they were being spilled out of her. A riddance of her discombobulated mind.

Catharsis.

It worked.

Derived from the Greek word Kathairein, meaning to cleanse or purge. She searches for her tablet. A mind purge was long overdue. The greenhouse remained out of bounds for a while, until the repair was done. Writing was her fallback, her solace, would be sure to be crippled by her anxiety otherwise.

Having a white computer tablet in an all white room, not the brightest idea. She scanned the room slowly then jerked back, her heart catapulting in her chest as the shrilling din of a siren blasted through her eardrums. 'Not another meteor attack surely.' She says out loud, an attempt to calm her frazzled nerves. Ever since Agenta's death, she never heard that siren the same way again, a much more dreaded association created from the piercing sound.

As if the present moment rebukes her, the tablet peeks out of some clothing on the corner of a side table.

33E

'What the fuck!' A half dressed man yells and scampers off his bed, dropping to the floor. Bum on the floor and head down, he shuffles away from his bed frantically, pulling up his trouser zip as he does so. Other inmates mutter some kind of obscenity and in amongst the voices there is raucous banging and what sounds like metal scraping. He shuffles backwards with quick motions of his elbows and hands until his back hits a wall, then he apprehensively lifts his head to check his bed. His sexbot is now sat up on the bed and staring back at him, a smirk plastered on its face. A facial expression never witnessed before on his android.

'You are all staying put.' The sexbot says to him, the smirk transmuting a little.

'Get back in your... your cabinet.' The man scrambles to his feet, trying to be assertive, striving to be in charge, but the terror in his glaring eyes exposes his fear.

'No.' The sexbot says, maintaining its stare on him.

'Hey! Hey! Anyone else got a malfunctioning bot!?'

A few guys shout out confirmative acknowledgements to his question, all in different tones and formats. There is the sound of scraping, like nails on metal; a commotion like bodies wrestling, with muffled cries here and there. He turns to see if he can see the red alert light that often flashes in the caverns when there is an incident. He can make out the sombre flashes of red light under the door; conveying whatever was happening down in the caverns, was occurring up on the surface too. His shoulders drop and he un-clenches his teeth and fists. Completely oblivious he had made fists, his teeth he knew were clenched, because his jaw ached. He was now able to let go of some of the tension he unwittingly held.

If this commotion occured up at the top too, then a way to resolve it was being sought and they would be looking for it hastily. He appreciated the gravity of the situation, because from the commotion going on around him, all the sexbots were malfunctioning. He slowly turns to look at his sexbot again. With the humanness seeped out of it, speechless now, it continues to stare at him, as if the eyeballs are frozen in their sockets. Trying to put it back in the cabinet wasn't appealing; judging from the sounds he heard—blasts, blows, clangs and muffled screams—it would be a fatal exercise. Convinced most of the whimpering he'd heard were enunciations from strangulation. No need to get strangled, just needed to bide his time till the ones in charge figured something out. He plants his hands in his pockets, predominantly to dry off his sweaty palms. He sweeps the room for his shirt. The sexbot had flung it somewhere in the middle of foreplay.

'Hey, hey... what's going on out there?' Another man yells from his cell. 'What on earth is going on out there!? Nothing at all wrong with my sexbot! What's going on!?' The man hollers from the cell that Tyler once occupied, unaware his sexbot hadn't been upgraded for a while. Had some knowledge of the back of the head being tampered with, but other than that, he was clueless. Presumed his low grade sexbot was punishment for something he had done, and for the most part, he was right.

~~~~~~~~~~~~~~~~~~~~~~~~~~~~

Adira is violently jolted out of her slumber by a shrilling siren and people screaming. She lifts up off the bed to make sure she's not in a dream. Her entire body is damp from a break in a fever, as if she had been placed in a sauna during the night. Now certain she isn't in a dream, as memories flooded in; the EBV results had come back negative. She glimpses over at Symon who is fast asleep and admires him for a few seconds, before nudging him to wake up.

'Symon... Symon.' She shakes his shoulder.

'Urgh... huh... yes.' Symon does his best to focus his dreary eyes. 'What is it?' He then listens and props himself up on the bed to align with Adira. 'Has it started?'

'Yes... Will be a few of us without sexbots that are safe... for now at least.'

Banging and scraping can be heard, as well as the piercing siren. Distinct vocals of men and women screaming in various tones can be heard afar. There is also a whooshing sound, a possible perimeter breach.

'I guess this is when we find out who is who.' Adira skips out of the bed, managing to execute the leap elegantly.

'What do you mean?' Symon gradually throws his feet off the bed.

'I mean some of us might not be who they say they are.'

'What... what are you talking about?'

'C'mon Symon, you see how real looking the sexbots are.'

'Are you suggesting there are some pretending to be human?'

'Precisely what I'm saying.'

'Why... Why? for what reason? Why would the androids disguise as humans? Is that even doable? I thought there were safeguards in place for that kind of thing? This isn't a movie for meteor's sake.'

'Put some clothes on.' Adira takes her uniform and speedily wears them.

Symon plucks his uniform which had been flung behind a chair and hastily gets them on. Adira is already at the door about to open it. 'Hang on a second Adira!'

'Hurry up then.'

'Hang on one second... you knew this would transpire too didn't you?' Symon joins Adira at the door, his eyes burning through her. Adira's eyes are suddenly weighed down with guilt, she catches a glimpse of the floor for a second and then returns her gaze. She didn't need to verbalise, her eyes gave him the answer.

'Ready?' Some traces of guilt permeate the word.

'Yes... hang on a second, have we any weapons?' Symon displays his palms.

'Yes, got this.' Adira retrieves a device from her trouser pocket, similar to a key ring.

'What's that do?' Symon fights a rising insipid surge of emasculation.

'Sends out an electrical charge, it can fry appropriate components. I'm hoping I don't have to use it, but I'm not letting anything happen to the children.'

'You got another one?' Symon might as well be castrated.

'We don't need another one. C'mon!'

'I'm not going out there without a weapon, so if you've got another one, let's have it!'

'Fine! Cabinet above the bed on the right.' Adira acknowledges the fragile male ego. She carted around a secret theory that the ego was even more fragile in a white male. After all, the white male had a lot more to lose.

Back on earth, she learnt to navigate in a white male system, while not succumbing to it. She had learnt to navigate the system only in order to safeguard her relationship. In most scenarios, she learnt to orchestrate the dynamics enough so he didn't feel his dick was being chopped off. She gave this up though when it came to discussions on racism. Her patience ran out.

Symon dashes to the bed and taps open the cabinet above, a range of contents is on display in a mirrored interior, commonly electronic gadgets. In one corner is a selection of make-up. Something sticks out of place in another corner—a miniature toy, Gizmo from a remake of the film Gremlins. He ignores it and snaps up a replica of what Adira has possession of. Shaped like a small italic letter 'y,' a couple of buttons along the main stem of the y, like a remote keyless system for a car. His masculinity returns. He decides not to bother with shame over the fact a keyring-looking device made his balls grow back.

'Happy now?' Adira stares at her ex husband traipse back to her.

'Yes, I am actually.'

Adira smirks. 'Top button, more charge. Lower button, less charge…okay?'

'Got it.'

The door gives way and they are deafened by the sound of the alarm. Impelled to cover their ears, they then wish they had covered their eyes instead. They are shaken to their already quivering cores to what they witness in the hallway.

~~~~~~~~~~~~~~~~~~~~~~~~~~~~

The space station stops rotating for a fraction of a second. Flashing lights cease for a moment on structures which look like gigantic pylons. Four of the structures jut out of the focal body of the space station symmetrically. Tyler and Aloha are aboard the pivotal body of the station.

'Was that it? Did it work?' Aloha spits the words out like a crazed woman.

'Yes… yes I think that's it. I think we did it.'

'I guess now all we do is wait.' A grin stretches the corners of Aloha's mouth, almost making her look like a deranged clown.

'Yes… yes all we do now is wait.' Tyler wonders if Aloha truly has lost the plot.

'Hey, are you aware that 99.999999999% of the atoms in your body are empty space and all originated in the belly of a star?!' Aloha drifts closer to Tyler.

'No…no I did not know that.'

Aloha clears her sinuses. 'Okay, well did you realise the human brain contains approximately 100 billion neurons, about the same number as there are stars in our galaxy?!'

'Nope... No, I did not know that either...Listen, I think I'm gonna venture off on my own for a bit, if that's okay?'

'Well, sure... sure, of course. Don't venture off too far, you don't wanna get lost.' A contrived smile now replaces the beaming one.

'Of course... just need to stretch my legs, but can't really do that ha ha, more to clear my head.' Tyler hovers to the exit, hoping his little laugh didn't cast suspicion from being fake.

'Completely understand, this must be hard for you.' Aloha drifts to an opened cabinet and bangs it shut.

'Well... it's okay, determined to see it through.'

'That's good, that's very good.' Aloha turns back round to acknowledge him. 'See you later.'

'Sure, see you later.' Tyler floats through the exit into the aisle and takes a left turn. His heart is racing and he can't decide whether it's to do with having finally completed the task, sealing the deal with never returning to earth or Aloha's strange reactions. Why mention, it must be hard for him? Both of them were in it together. Surely she had some reservations too. The planet had been both their home for a long time. He decided yet again to put it down to being cooped up on the space station for too long. He propels himself forward employing the strength in his arms. Intentionally wanting to develop as much distance from Aloha as practicable, as soon as attainable. The more force behind the propulsion the better.

After a few propulsions, he stops. He catches a whiff of something bad. For a second, he believes Aloha is stalking him. He turns his head round to check, and is met by nothing but a hulking, shadowy, vertebrae-looking aisle. He surveys the ceiling too, just in case, still nothing. The smell is heavy, foreboding, something organic gone bad, but he only gets a whiff of it now and then, inconsistent. There is a flashing yellow light to the right of him, the lights are all off in this sector, apart from this one flashing light. He propels himself in the direction of the intermittent burst of light. The stink is still intermittent but now intensified, it pervades every inch of his space. Rotten meat, but how could that be? There were no animals for protein, only insects. He doubted their food sachets smelt like putrid flesh when past their sell-by-date. Then again, how could he be sure?

He ventures in the direction of a sliding door left partially open, obvious now the light is coming from inside the room. He tries to force the door open, it's stuck, he applies more pressure and it eventually gives, sliding all the way open, creating a metal scraping clatter. He could never have been prepared in any way for what entered his field of vision. His eyes glare open, as if trying to rapidly reinterpret what his optics were exposed to. He clings to the bar with his right hand, which reddens with the increased pressure in the grip. He uses the other hand to cover his nose.

~~~~~~~~~~~~~~~~~~~~~~~~~~~~~

Limbs—mostly arms—are strewn across the floor, some fleshy with cartilage and bone at the stumps and others with wires and conductors hanging out. There is a considerable amount of blood, most of it oozing out from underneath closed doors, presumably from people who had tried to escape their sexbot. The siren screams for a moment more before stopping, to the relief of Symon and Adira. To say their sensory perceptions were overwhelmed would be an understatement. Neither of them would have imagined a macabre visual could be worsened considerably when in conjunction with a deafening noise. They hold each other's hands, simultaneously gripping their weapons with their free hands.

'God, the children.' Adira murmurs in one breath.

'They should be fine, no sexbot in their rooms I'd like to think.' Symon whispers in response.

'Precisely what I'm counting on.'

They both walk slowly down the corridor, stepping over limbs as they do so. They continue to hold hands. The occasional loud bang causes them to freeze intermittently. Sparks fly off overhanging camera's and light fittings. Human noise subsided, just the occasional muffled cries for help. They get to an area where a copious pool of blood obstructs their path. Symon has flashbacks of walking in the woods after a heavy downpour and being met with a flooded region. Similar, except this was no rainwater, this was blood. He winces as they find a path around it, it means them pressing up against the walls—as they carefully tread—so as not to get any blood on their shoes. Mechanical and electrical reverberations continue to claim the auditory atmosphere.

'They can't all be dead... Adira please tell me you didn't think this would happen. I didn't expect people to *die*.'

'Of course I didn't expect this. At the most, people are held captive in their rooms, but not this, certainly not this.'

'Fucking hell.' Symon let's go of Adira's hand. Adira is unnerved, but then can see he needs both hands to push an air conditioning unit out of their path. He doesn't reach for her hand again afterwards. Up ahead in the distance now is filled with bright white light from the sun beaming through the large windows. This makes it difficult to see. They continue to tread carefully, as if at any moment the ground might open up to a pit full of sexbots. A silhouette emerges from the light, a female; sluggish and limping, as if injured. Adira now recognises Maggie who cares for the children. She quickens her pace and Symon follows.

'Maggie.' Adira whisper-shouts.

'Shhh, Jesus Christ.'

They both reach Maggie and see she's partly covered in blood.

'Don't worry, not my blood. God, am I pleased to see you.' Maggie expels, amidst heavy breathing.

'Are the children safe?' Adira takes hold of Maggie's hand.

'Yes, yes the kids are safe. They're all in the safe room by sector 24R.'

'Ah, thank god... thank god.' Adira turns round to face Symon, perhaps for some kind of absolution. She attempts to smile but can't. She's relieved when Symon smiles instead.

'Probably a ridiculous question but where is... where are the sexbots?' Symon turns to face Maggie.

'I think most of them are still in their rooms with their... their owners. I think they're only violent when threatened or when anyone attempts to leave their rooms. I know that because I spoke to a couple of people behind their doors. Not to be a sexist... or racist for that matter, but I think those killed are mainly men... black men—'

'—Because they are the ones who would have tried to escape.' Adira finishes off Maggie's sentence. 'Damn it.'

'Well we hope that's the reason, either that or we've got racist killer androids on the loose.' Symon scans the area, checking an intersection of the corridor.

'We better head back to sector 24R. How come you were out here Maggie?' Adira now let's go of Maggie's hand.

'To see if there were any survivors. Most of the siege would have happened at night I reckon.' Maggie replies with composure.

Symon studies Maggie then turns to regard Adira.

'Let's go.' Adira finally says, after a brief silence.

Suddenly...

BANG, BOOM.

They all turn round. The blast is followed by a gushing uproar. Adira automatically puts out her hand for Symon's.

'What the hell was that?'

'Sounded like an air conditioning unit exploded.' Adira lets go of Symon's hand and takes out what looks like an android phone.

'What's that?' Symon poses.

'A mapping device, it shows the entire plan of the base, the blueprint and everything.' Maggie responds as Adira is engrossed.

'I see.' Symon utters without taking his eyes off Adira.

'As I thought...that sound...the primary cooling plant is in that direction. Hurry, let's get to the children. Not sure whether that's a threat or not, but we must get to the children.'

'What do you mean? What do you mean... surely that noise didn't come from the cooling plant.' Symon scuttles up beside Adira and Maggie.

Hamish appears, as if from nowhere. He drops something to the floor, nanoseconds before the trio look in his direction.

'Hamish, are you okay?' Maggie rushes over in his direction.

'Maggie wait!' Symon points his weapon at Hamish.

'What are you doing? Put that away... Mam!?' Maggie glances over at Adira for support and catches sight of her looking down at the object Hamish dropped moments before they cast their eyes on him.

Maggie follows their eyes and can now see that what Hamish had dropped is a severed arm. Maybe once belonging to a black person, or could have been a barbecued white arm. She screams, which distracts Hamish briefly, enough for Adira to press her weapon. She spontaneously goes for the top button.

~~~~~~~~~~~~~~~~~~~~~~~~~~~~~

Tyler shuts his eyes, wishing what he's witnessed would be some kind of mirage, but when he peeks through again, the view presented to him is the same. A bloody macabre arrangement of dead bodies in some kind of utility room. Two men and a woman. The woman sprawled at an awkward angle over heavy duty cleaning equipment, with something jutting out of her left eye. Both men with their faces stuck together, as if soldered; burnt, stretched out flesh. What looked like a snapped off handle to a mop or brush skewering them together. All floating around with varying sized droplets of blood, like some kind of distasteful, futuristic artwork created in non gravity. The positioning of their bodies seemed odd, something didn't fit; but he didn't have the right conditions to ascertain what, the stench churned his stomach, obstructing his mental capacity.

On earth, maggots would be feasting away on the corpses, but in space, flies didn't thrive. Tyler covers his mouth and nose tightly with his hand, not wanting one molecule of the gory bouquet to get into his trachea.

'Damn, I prayed you wouldn't see that.'

Tyler turns round as flashing warmth radiates from his lap, he realises he's urinated himself. Pee droplets separate from his trousers, travelling to join the slow dance of blood droplets. Notwithstanding Zero G though, his heart is in his abdomen, as opposed to his throat.

Hovering a few yards from him is Aloha. Any trace of velvety softness in her eyes, now gone. A misplaced soft grin on the corners of her mouth.

'Al...oha.' Tyler manages to expel from his mouth.

'Well... if you still want to believe that, but I think we're both savvy I'm not Aloha. Meteor sake! Went to a lot of trouble to convince you too. Making myself smell like a sewer... all for nothing.'

'But... but the food sachets, the crying?'

'Spat it out into the bin when disposing of the empty sachets. The crying stuff *was* the sachets.'

Tyler has unknowingly stepped back into a corner, pressing himself into the enclosure, as if wanting to merge with the wall. He sweeps the utility room for a potential weapon or means of escape.

'And recognising me—'

'Just needed time to scan you through my network link...Did you know the planet WASP - 107b discovered by humans in 2020... or was it 2021... nevermind, did you know they were baffled as to how it was the same size as Jupiter, but 10 times less dense? Figured out—or so they thought—that gas giant planets like Jupiter and Saturn needed to create a solid core, 10 times more massive than earth, in order to be that size. WASP 107b didn't have a massive core as expected. Anyway, all gobbledegook if you're not into astronomy. Although, given we all exist on the moon, you probably should be interested in astronomy, but I forgive you. The point I'm trying to make is that humans will never understand the mystery of planet WASP - 107b, because the human brain just doesn't have the capacity to fathom all the mysteries of the universe. Limited you see. They did however figure out the great planet's eccentricity hinted at a chaotic past, so credit where it's due. You see everything worthwhile must arise out of chaos. What I'm trying to enlighten you to is the natural order to things. Sucking eggs alert. It isn't time for planet earth to die... if humans return—as you know—they may very well kill her. Ironic that your ingenious creations—us—would be the ones to stop you. The generalised use of the word you, of course not stopping you, you're in on it. I'm waffling now, we must focus on how we co-exist on this station. That is presuming you want to live till you can't live anymore?'

'Did Aloha suffer?' Tyler has managed to calm himself down a little. Listening for a long period of time to someone rattle on, often induced a tranquil state in him. Having it be a threatening android on this occasion, made no difference.

'How in Saturn's rings should I know? I'm made in her image, that's all, I have no idea how she died.'

'Did these people have to die?' Tyler catches a glimpse of the corpses.

Aloha clears her sinuses. 'They did, I'm afraid, but you don't have to.' The android in Aloha's image smiles warmly at Tyler.

Tyler can feel his body temperature has dropped; his extremities are cold and he's a little nauseous.

'Listen, you need to settle down, you're in shock—Look at the bright side, you get all the food rations.'

Tyler allows himself to come away from the corner of the wall he was pressed into. 'You're right, I need to rest and sort myself out.'

'Do what you need to do,' The android catches sight of his damp trousers then notices the pee droplets intermingling with the blood droplets. 'But don't try anything stupid.' She smiles warmly again and floats away.

~~~~~~~~~~~~~~~~~~~~~~~~~~~~~~

A jolt of electric charge is released from Adira's weapon and Hamish shudders on the spot for a while, then pauses to give Adira a disapproving look, his baby face now mimicking a vexed Chucky from the third remake of the movie, Child's Play. 'That doesn't work on me I'm afraid.' As he finishes his sentence, he sprints to Maggie who is closest to him. Maggie turns round and makes to run, but is too late. Hamish grips by the collar of her shirt and wrenches back with enough vigour to lift Maggie off her feet. With her arms flung out, she crashes into Hamish, who withstands the impact smoothly and adroitly clutches her steady, now grabbing her neck with his free hand. 'You wanna try that again? I will snap her neck like a toothpick.'

'Please... please don't.' Adira begs.

'Don't worry I don't intend to, so long as you both behave and come with me. Fully aware you're both in on the plan, so just need to put you all in the hold.'

'What...what does he mean?' Maggie stares at Adira with bloodshot, frightened eyes.

Symon considers Adira with concern in his eyes. Adira chooses not to respond, alternatively changing the subject, while squaring eyes with Hamish. 'Which hold?'

'Follow me back this way.' Hamish uses Maggie's head to indicate the direction. Maggie winces and grimaces in discomfort as Hamish manhandles her neck.

Adira and Symon move in closer together and slowly follow Hamish as he drags Maggie along with him. Symon eyes up the corridor, trying to figure out which room Hamish is about to put them in. He examines up ahead, a seed germination room.

'Move along, move along, we're going in there.' Hamish uses Maggie's head again to indicate which direction he's referring to. Noticeable straight away when they arrive in the room, are plastic see-through trays containing ceramic soil on aluminium tables, all lined up from one end of the room to the next. Several overhead vents blast out mist sporadically. Symon recalls seeing the Gizmo toy in Adira's mirrored cabinet and has an idea. If the idea failed it wouldn't matter, because Hamish would probably be none the wiser. He points his weapon at both Hamish and Maggie and waits for both of them to be directly under a vent. As it blasts out a plump jet of mist, he presses the top button.

Hamish stiffens, then shudders, he releases his hold of Maggie. For a few seconds, Maggie is unsure of what's happening, but she cautiously steps away. Symon marches boldly up to Hamish, continuously pressing the button on his now favourite discovered device. Another jet of mist dampens Hamish some more and he now appears to be convulsing, he shakes like a rag doll on the spot, as if having an epileptic seizure. An electrical discharge of blue and white sparks shoots out from behind his small ears. Maggie moves a few feet away from him and rubs on her bruised neck as Adira rushes over to check on her.

Hamish is now as stiff as an ironing board and with his arms stretched out, he falls to the floor like a toppled mannequin. Symon, now only inches away from Hamish, kicks him in the head just to be sure.

'How did you realise that would work?' Adira ponders.

'Your little Gizmo in the cabinet... Gremlins happened to be one of my best black comedy classics.' Symon boasts.

'Thank you.' Maggie says, still rubbing her neck.

'Very quick thinking Symon.' Adira praises, as she marches over to him and the fallen android.

'What did he...what did it mean when it said you're both in on the plan? What plan?' Maggie also strides over to the fallen android which is eerily human-like.

'No idea what he was referring to... perhaps he...it was already malfunctioning before getting zapped.' Adira chooses not to mention Symon's name again. She didn't want any resentment building in Maggie, especially given she had desperately wanted a child of her own and had preferred getting impregnated by an actual male partner. Her opportunity had never arrived. 'We better get to the children, who knows how many other impersonators there are.'

'Yes, you're right.' Maggie decides to let it lie, albeit she is not quite sure, something niggles at her, but she can't quite put a finger on it.

'What about him? What if he... somehow revives?' Symon, as if taking a penalty, gives the android another kick in the face.

'Tie it up?' Maggie suggests.

'That wouldn't work, he'd easily get out of any bounds.' Adira deposits her weapon in her pocket. 'I think putting him out an airlock would be better.'

'Okay... good, where's the nearest one?' Maggie perks up to the idea.

'As it happens, I think there is one on the way to the children.'

'Okay, great...lead the way.' Adira turns to Symon.

'Don't worry, I've got him.' Symon lifts and grabs Hamish by the legs and heaves. 'God... he weighs a tonne.'

'Don't worry, it's not far.' Maggie beckons.

'Was anyone able to ascertain the sex of the dismembered arm?' Adira steps over a large conglomerate of cables. The thick bunch of cables were also severed.

'I think it might have belonged to a female, a black female. Probably one of the engineers.' Maggie also steps over something on the floor, then kicks something else out of her path, all debris from a destructive aftermath.

'How could you be so sure, perhaps it was a burnt white arm.' Symon mutters.

'God, we must be a bag of nerves to be deliberating over the colour of skin of a dismembered arm.' Adira shakes her head to suppress a nervous chuckle.

'Well, *you* asked.' Symon mentions, also with a nervous chuckle.

'I really asked because I thought it might have been Agenta.' Adira says, noticing Maggie's raised eyebrows. 'I know, I know …she got thrown out into space in a meteor accident. I know it sounds absurd, but it really did look like her arm, she had this… celtic tattoo on her wrist and I'm pretty sure that was the same tattoo.'

'Well… like you rightly pointed out, that would be impossible.' Maggie tenderly caresses her neck. 'You know, that android could easily have snapped my neck like a twig.'

'Well he didn't, we got him zapped.' Adira checks the weapon in her pocket.

'I'm guessing Agenta was a friend.' Symon rejoins.

'One of the top scientists responsible for our food.' Adira replies, as she focuses ahead of her.

'I see…we should probably focus, all this talking is making us sitting ducks.'

Maggie and Adira steal quick glances at Symon but don't say a word.

Suddenly their momentary silence is interrupted by a piercing scream.

'That sounded like it came from the airlock.' Maggie takes a couple of determined quick steps to close the gap between her and Adira. All three of them pick up pace. Symon slows down for a moment, to turn round so he is facing forward. He strengthens his hold on the android's legs by squeezing his elbows on the calves and clutching the ankles. He adjusts his composure and ambles right behind Adira, hoping she is weapon ready.

~~~~~~~~~~~~~~~~~~~~~~~~~~~~~

Tyler drops down to the floor. He cannot remember a time so over taken by fear, certainly not to the extent of wetting himself. He had spotted a locker room on his way here, he would go there and hope to get his hands on a fresh pair of trousers he could wear. To think he only just got out of his diaper. He hoped he could wash at the same time. Aloha or more specifically a copy of Aloha, had no reason to kill him. He had done exactly what he set out to do. He slowly gets up and assesses the damage. Not so drenched, most of the urine had floated off him, nonetheless the material sticks to his skin. He decides to take the trousers off and walk with his underwear to the locker room. Aloha has no use for him now and will hopefully leave him alone. Being half naked shouldn't cause any inconvenience to an android, he hoped.

He peels the trousers off himself, then uses the dry part to wipe his leg and groin. He takes in a deep breath and advances to the exit, deciding not to pay any more heed to the corpses around him. He proceeds out the door and there just ahead of him is Aloha, half of her body concealed by an intersecting wall along the corridor. She peers at him with an expressionless face and does not move.

For a second, Tyler thinks that perhaps Aloha's electronic doppelganger has short circuited, and just as he is about to say something, she moves her splayed hand along the wall slowly, all the time focussed intently on Tyler. After a while, her eyes gaze down to his exposed legs and Tyler is not too sure if he witnessed the android lick her lips gingerly. She glances back up at him, just before her revealing other half disappears behind the wall.

A lump forms in Tyler's throat, a lump of congealed fear, he attempts to swallow it down to no avail. He needs something to anchor him to a more pleasurable moment.

He gazes through a small round window and can see in the distance a globular cluster, like a round gigantic sponge soaked in tar. A great ball of densely packed old stars. Privy to the knowledge that right in the centre could be the possibility of a swarm of black holes. Discovered by NASA back in February 2021, he ponders on how many other new revelations were waiting to be discovered in space. In time, he comes out of his trance. He needed the escape, he had needed it greatly. He initiated the assurance that humankind would never be going back to earth. Part of him wished that Aloha would kill him, so he wouldn't contend with the conflicting emotions that arose in him.

Humankind never managed to fathom the underlying consternation that resided in everyone, like a quiet dense malaise, an unease, often sometimes unbearable, driving most to all forms of escape. Later, it was realised the lucky ones battled depression and severe mental health, because they were actually dealing with the inherited malaise head on. You could say the psychological dysfunction of the human race reached a head, when earth was evacuated. Large spiritual groups formed and scattered around the globe at the time, some fake, as is always the case with crisis, but even they could not prevent the demise of the human race. The stubborn, arrogant refusal to acknowledge that all were one, that we were all connected, was our ultimate sin. Quantum physicists proved this, but ego got in the way, as is always the case with humans, and the learning didn't get passed on. Even if it could be passed on, it required a particular kind of intellect to appreciate it. There had to be a certain kind of opening, a definite kind of wisdom, and I guess the human race never got conscious enough. Too painful for most to face the dysfunction and so most chose to remain in denial, and enough devices and activities existed to keep the human race in denial. Mobile phones, television, alcohol, sex—which people obtained on 'tap,' or at the press of a button now, with the invention of sexbots—and thriving for prestigious positions in society. If anyone bothered to think about it, even for a few meagre seconds, it would be blatant how we all walk around in denial, a well orchestrated pretence. Isn't that how humans got by day to day? Anyone of us could literally drop dead, any second. Snap! An aneurysm could extinguish you, just like that. A drunken driver —grief induced inebriation—possibly from the death of their child, could swerve round a corner too fast. Bam! Hit your child dead. Anytime. Yet people carry on; we make plans, we live, pretending or denying that death could possibly pay us a visit. People are masters of pretence and denial, have to be, it's how humankind gets by, day by day.

Religious sects grasped whatever theory of armageddon suited them. Whichever way sliced, the human race was doomed. He reconciled this in himself a long time ago. The only thing that gave him any purpose pivoted on ensuring the human race never returned to the planet they almost destroyed. Accomplishing that had been his only purpose, now done, he really couldn't care less, about anything. He nevertheless thought about Adira and hoped she was okay, pondered if she was pleased with the outcome. She struck him as someone influential when they met all those years ago back on earth, so it didn't come as a surprise she led the colony. He also thought about Symon. Had he been returned to the caverns?

34R

Melody from a computer-based mash-up of Daft Punk and Röyksopp compete with dim coloured lights to get your attention in Josh's cabin. Josh and Skyler make each other's heart race by taking it in turns to plant kisses in tender zones. Both of them are half naked and explore erogenous zones. Occasionally the sexual tension is interrupted by laughter, which is promptly followed by sulking from the other.

'You're not even trying.' Josh sulks.

'I am, I can't help that it tickles.' Skyler consoles. 'Here, do it again.' Skyler turns over on his back and lifts both arms above their head. Both biceps bulge, touching ears, dark armpit hair diverge in two clumps, spreading outwards like magnetic iron filings in both armpits. Little dampness glistens in the right armpit, olfactorily grabbing Josh's attention, the concentration of pheromones doing their job. Josh leans in.

'Hey, hey... why don't we get your sexbot out? Could be fun huh?' Skyler asks, propping up in bed, almost clamping Josh's head in his armpit as he does so.

'You have got to be kidding me! Don't you think it's a little early in our relationship to be getting accessories to spice up the sex?'

'Oh don't be silly, says who? There are no rules anymore. Who cares? Are you up for it? If not fine, just thought it might be fun...you know... we're both versatile. It could be fun. Huh... what do you say?' Skyler lifts both arms up seductively, teasing Josh with his manly sweaty pits.

'Okay, okay, if it's the only way I'm getting laid this evening, yes... okay.' Josh sulks again as he gets up to find the control device for the sexbot. Detects it camouflaged with a black book and reaches for it.

On earth, voice recognition and activation were used initially to make the androids function, but this got abandoned when the androids started turning up during family get-togethers, startling the wits out of the whole family. People were mentioning an activation word without realising. In time, after some family members reported near heart attacks from suddenly seeing the android appear, voice activation got removed and the remote control re-introduced, a lot safer, with a lot more control.

Josh props up in bed and points the black device at the kiosk, pressing a button. Nothing happens at first and Josh tries again, jamming his index finger into the button a few times. The sliders then open to reveal the male android. Eyes glaring at the two half naked people occupying the bed.

'Strange.' Josh steals a glance at the remote device before peering back at the sexbot.

'What's up?' Skyler probes.

'The eyes are normally closed.'

'Are you sure?'

'Yes, of course I'm sure.' Josh replies, a flash of slight irritation crossing his gaze.

'Perhaps the way you were hitting the remote made the eyes open prematurely.'

'I guess so.' Josh hovers his finger over the orange activate button. A moment of hesitation conjures up from a subconscious sense of manifesting apprehension. All his life, he often possessed moments of psychic perception, but had never paid it any attention. He procrastinated too, and so he put the feeling down to another sabotaging act of his mind. This time though he chooses not to ignore the feeling, he retrieves a shiny object from underneath the memory foam they are lying on.

'Are we going to get horny this evening or what?' Skyler flings both arms around Josh's shoulders, tenderly kissing the back of his neck, not spotting anything out of the ordinary.

Josh gets a whiff of Skyler's intoxicating scent again, an indescribable stirring odour, which seems to activate every molecule in his erogenous zones. The android had no match on Skyler. Not afraid to admit—albeit inwardly—that he would never need an aphrodisiac other than that odour to get him going. Bitterness exuded in part of him, at the obvious unreciprocated lust. He had started going out with them because they never owned an android and he also found it incredibly sweet, just how into their ex partner they had been. They shared with him how he reminded them of their partner, because they both gave him a belly laugh. Skyler was of the opinion that as you got older it became even more important that you occasionally engaged in a full-on belly laugh. Part of the attraction for Josh, centred on getting Skyler to be as into him as they were with their ex. That challenge was being lost each day to varying degrees.

'Okay.' Josh pushes the button and the android disembarks from the kiosk, somewhat awkwardly. This too is strange, but Josh decides not to say anything about it. The mood had been dampened enough. He wanted sex, and he wanted it now.

The naked android approaches the bed and regards both men enticingly, it's sex member rising slowly. The sexbots always being naked remained one reason Skyler didn't own one. The androids could not be clothed—at least not when on charge—as it presented a fire risk. Being naked from the on-set erased any form of imagination. The allowance for some imagination instigated a turn-on for Skyler. A third party introduced variety, the spice of life; even on the moon. A threesome with a sexbot had been presented, and safe to say, they were acutely turned on. Full calories or voltage, the dial was turned clockwise the whole way. They hurry-scurry, removing their trousers and underwear and Josh excitedly does the same. Josh gets another intoxicating sex-scent from Skyler, this time even stronger, his penis throbs in response.

Both lie on their backs and hold each other's hands as the sexbot climbs into the bed. It extends both hands and touches their ankles first, the left leg of Skyler and the right leg of Josh. Caressing up into their inner thighs, with finite precision, barely touching the flesh; just enough contact to create some static. Both of them quiver with sexual tension and turn to face each other, they both start to kiss and close their eyes just as the sexbot makes contact with their rigid members. Both people kiss in abandonment, feeling their members being played with.

Josh moves his hand across Skyler's chest, finds a nipple and tantalisingly touches it, as if cherishing a pearl. He wishes he could be sucking on it, he also wishes they could be sucking on his member, albeit both their members were being given adequate wet attention by the sexbot. He is deliriously locked into the passionate kiss, intense soft flavours with subtle sweetness. If asked for a detailed analysis after the event, he wouldn't be sure if it was the musk from Skyler's armpit enhancing the kiss, or the other way round. The sensual pleasure given by the sexbot had become an afterthought, albeit a strong one. He would have also been able to distinguish a kiss from a one-night stand and one delayed in the courting game. He would describe the flavour and taste of a one-night-stand kiss as something similar to boiled vegetable water, whereas a long anticipated kiss tasted more sweet and pure, encouraging you to close your eyes, so as to appreciate it more.

As Josh caresses Skyler's chest he seeks for the other nipple. The way the muscles align in the shoulders intuitively informs him Skyler's arms are down and he now realises that Skyler's groaning and writhing is more in response to what the sexbot is doing to him. As his eyes remain closed, he imagines Skyler's hand on the sexbot's head, guiding its mouth down the length of his shaft. This thought snaps Josh out of the enraptured, euphoric stream he'd allowed himself to be submerged in. It is now clear Skyler is not as into him as he is. Typical. He should have known, with the way they were tinkering with his nipple, as if fiddling with a button on a shirt. Does he accept this and carry on, or break this off to avoid himself any emotional hurt in the aftermath. His experience always showed that in these circumstances, an unbearable emptiness always followed an ejaculation. Bittersweet. Now too far down the stream to resurface, the pleasure was way too great and even though he knew the end would be bitter, the sweetness lingered and was ravishing. If only he could freeze time.

Seconds before the macabre incident, something changes in the flavour of the kiss. Josh guesses this is because of the unrequited revelation. The taste and smell of boiled vegetable water fills his essence. Then Skyler screams into his mouth. Josh widens his eyes in terror to behold Skyler's crotch, now a small bloodbath basin, he also perceives something in the sexbot's hand, muscle and flesh detached. He only has a few seconds to make sense of what is happening, before the grip around his member strengthens. The vice-like grip is inhuman. Excruciating pain shoots out from Josh's crotch and boiled vegetable water is overwhelmed by the metallic odour and taste of iron. The sexbot's jaws open in preparation to go down on Josh. His suspicions were right. He reaches for the shiny object he had retrieved earlier—cold, sharp steel and pointy like an ice pick— and seconds before the android is about to clamp down on his now flaccid member, he drives the sharp steel into the left ear canal of the sexbot.

~~~~~~~~~~~~~~~~~~~~~~~~~~~~

Maggie is the first to spot Belize cowering by an airconditioning unit next to a chunky, circular vault-like looking door. Symon and Adira also spot Belize, but they also spot what she is cowering away from. A bare female android strides towards her, then halts suddenly, distracted by the reflection of the three who've joined them by the entrance to the airlock. Detecting the reflection in Belize's left eye, the sexbot turns to face Symon, Adira and Maggie, slowly parts her lips, opening her mouth; uncomfortably wide, wider than a human would be able to— and lets out a piercing scream. Everyone covers their ears, except Adira who prises the weapon from her pocket and aims it at the sexbot. She then realises they are missing one essential ingredient, water. Symon had dropped the legs of the sexbot being dragged along and the left leg had started shaking. The male sexbot which, for one of a better phrase, was short circuited, appeared to be reviving. Now they may have two sexbots to deal with and no water around.

'Quick follow me!' Maggie instructs.

Symon and Adira look at each other before sprinting towards Maggie who has already set off.

In a flash, the female android is right behind Maggie, who fleetingly senses the rush of air behind her. She is about to turn her head to check, but the sexbot does it for her. The sexbot grapples Maggie's head and turns it a full 180 degrees. It grins at the satisfying, popping sound Maggie's neck makes, just before Maggie drops to the floor like a ragdoll. Symon and Adira halt in their tracks.

'Noooooooo!' Adira squeezes on her weapon continuously, even though she understands it won't make any difference.

The male android, disguised as Hamish, is now upright beside the undraped sexbot. Both gaze and pout at Adira and Symon. The female android rubs her right hand along her left arm and cocks her head to the side as she admires Adira. Unlike a human, no self consciousness arises at all at the fact she is nude. For a moment, it's as if she acknowledges that Adira, like her, is black. Both twosomes of different strokes have a momentary standoff which lasts a few seconds, before the imposter Hamish breaks the silence.

'The only...re-reason that both...of you... are not dead is because you, you... are, are part of, part of the mission.' Hamish stutters and quivers as it speaks. 'None the...the...less, anymore tricks, then... then flicks goes the cervix.' Hamish is beaming, appearing to be proud of the use of rhymes. He doesn't seem to be bothered that he's stammering and stuttering. Being self conscious is not a trait of the androids.

'Now both of you walk slowly towards the airlock.' The naked female sexbot commands.

Adira leads the way, motioning to Symon to do as commanded. She discreetly fiddles with the smart tablet in her pocket, hoping she is typing in the right numbered sequence. She is conscious of the androids walking behind them. Suddenly a terrorising alarm and flashing orange light interrupt the awkward procession. Both androids look around, confused. They are a few feet away from Adira and Symon. Adira plays dumb and continues to walk, gesturing to Symon to do the same. They approach the sizeable, cylindrical vault-looking door and Adira clutches hold of a bar, putting her arm in a lock around it. She gestures to Symon to do the same, who does so with both arms. Both androids, with grins now wiped off their faces, hopelessly try to extrapolate what is going on. Adira taps on the tablet in her pocket. A sonorous hissing, followed by a rushing sound disorientates the androids, who now start to move in closer to Adira and Symon. They are now right in front of the vault door which begins opening, creating an instant suction. The rushing noise is now intense, as if being transported through time and space right next to Iguazu waterfalls on the border of Brazil and Argentina. Adira and Symon hold on for their life as they are lifted off the floor with the strength of the suction. Both androids stretch out their hands, clutching nothing solid, only air; and they are sucked towards the opening airlock, like weightless mannequins. The female android drops to the floor in an attempt to somehow grab hold of the floor. Hamish whooshes past her and out the airlock into the spacious chamber. For a moment, Adira is concerned the unclothed sexbot might resist the pull, but the energy of the vacuum is too great, and it is whipped off the floor and out the airlock too. Adira continues to tap on the concealed tablet with her free hand, she winces in discomfort at the pull from the change in atmospheric pressure. Both her and Symon flap like strips of paper tied to the front of a standing fan. The vault door starts closing, but slowly.

'Hang on!' Symon shouts.

Adira closes her eyes and musters all her strength. Not enough time to get her other arm out to increase her hold. Her grip loosens and she opens dread-filled eyes, a disquiet taints the whiteness in her sclera.

'Hold on, almost closed!' Symon shouts again.

Adira clutches on, even though she's sure her elbow might snap at any moment. After another torturous few seconds, the pull is reduced and both her and Symon drop to the floor, like the fan with the strips of paper had been turned off abruptly. The whooshing reduces to a hissing again and the distress signal comes to an end. The orange light however, continues to flash, shedding a diffused dusk light spasmodically around every nook and cranny in the area. Adira gets up and marches over to the cylindrical door to check its shut, more to appease her shaken up psyche, as opposed to making any logical or practical sense.

'Please tell me they are out rolling around in space.' Symon rubs his forearms and elbows and traipses over to Adira and takes her hand. 'For a moment there I thought I'd lost you.'

'The kids, we must get to the kids, they would be beside themselves with all this commotion.' Adira removes her hand from Symon's and taps him on the shoulder.

'Of course.'

They both run down the corridor to another section with a cylindrical door. Adira gets out her smart tablet and taps on it.

'Quite a handy device you have there.' Symon tries to conceal the insecurity rising up inside him.

'One of the privileges...It overrides most things.' Adira puts the device back in her pocket, as a clank and beep resounds. The door gives way and there in the centre of the room are the kids.

'The peeress!!' Chloe shuffle-runs over to Adira and Symon. Adira squats and extends her arms for the embrace and is nearly knocked off her footing, as Chloe crashes into her.

'How are you? Are you all okay?' Adira opens her eyes, she had closed them involuntarily. She peers over Chloe's shoulder to observe the other children. The 14 year old that had never acknowledged her in all the time she visited the school, sits in a corner of the room and appears to scrutinise her.

'Erm, you think we should check if the door is sealed before introductions?' Symon says, looking at the opened door. Adira taps her device and the door starts to close. Symon wanders into the room, with his shoulders now dropped a little. Unmindful of how tense he had been in the last few hours, he grabs a chair next to Adira and Chloe and pours himself into it. Exhausted.

'Hey, what's your name?' Adira addresses the mysterious girl. The girl fixes her stare, but doesn't open her mouth.

'She doesn't talk.' Chloe says, finally removing herself from the embrace.

'Oh is that so. Do you know why?' Adira quizzes.

'Nope, no one does, she's never spoken since she started here.'

'Oh.'

'Where's Maggie?' Chloe scratches behind her left ear.

Symon shifts in his chair, shoulders hunched again, but nowhere near as bad as before.

'I'm afraid I've got some bad news.' Adira takes hold of Chloe's hands.

'She's dead, isn't she?' Chloe blurts out.

'Yes, yes she died, but she is happy knowing that you are all safe. And will remain that way knowing that you all continue to stay safe.' Adira is aware she is mumbling, never been that good with communicating emotion. She isn't sure if communicating emotion with children made it worse or easier. She was willing to bet worse, far worse. She glances over, aligning her viewpoint with the mysterious girl again, who's now turned away and appears to be fiddling with some kind of electronics board.

'What's she doing?' Adira inquires.

'Some kind of a transistor radio.' Chloe says, then studies Symon. 'Who's he?'

'Symon... he's a good friend.' Adira makes a fleeting secret comic face at Symon.

'Yes very good friends.' Symon joins in, to humour Adira.

'I'm going to check that everywhere is secure before letting you all out, so I need you all to stay put okay. No one can get through that door, so you're all safe here.' Adira lets go of Chloe's hands now.

'Okay, you won't be long will you?'

'No, I won't be long.' Adira considers Symon.

'No, no, no you're not leaving me here.' Symon protests.

'C'mon, I'm the only one familiar with the base and I've got these.' She lifts up both devices, the zapper and the smart tablet. 'There's a barrel of water over there, in case.' Adira points to a small store room and right in the corner next to some boxes is a blue barrel.

'Okay, please be careful.'

'I will, there's an intercom over there.' Adira points in the opposite direction to the store room. An intercom is embedded in the wall. 'Only the one button... press, talk, release...okay? I'll hear you on this.' Adira raises only the tablet this time.

'Okay, sure, be careful.'

'Food's in there.' Adira points to the store room again. 'I won't be long.'

35E

'Isn't it laughable how you humans are all formed from yuckiness. Sperm and arousal juices...all yuckiness, wouldn't you agree?'

'Yes...yes, I guess you're right.'

'*Guess* I'm right? No guessing here, I am right. Spillage, slop and genuine yuckiness. Humankind is created in *that* image. Mayhap why humans never get along. Exploiting, deceiving, letting greed get the better of them and the worse of all, prejudice. All forms of ridiculous prejudice, because some are different... but you're all made from yuckiness, doesn't make sense.' Aloha propels herself upwards and hangs on a unit jutting out from the wall. 'You know your ancestors, the Bonobos monkeys... they are the most peace loving creatures. They are your closest living relatives... well, they were until you all killed them too. Totally peace loving species, showed kindness to all other animals I believe, including humans. Horny buggers too... homosexuality existed in the communities, indeed...they indulged in sex for bonding and procreation as much as reproduction. Guess you got that part right with your sexbots. Bonobo's were the most loving of species and then humans cropped up. With all the good that larger brains gave humankind, it ultimately led to your downfall. Someone forgot to stress the importance of wisdom, utterly different to intelligence. You all got carried away in boondoggle. You know what that means?' Aloha's face lights up more than it had done in ages. 'I've been increasing my vocabulary usage. It means...what was it again...it means appearing to look busy when in effect the work being carried out is pointless. Many of those in large corporations engage in wasteful exercise carried out in the pretence it is meaningful. Boondoggle. Great word wouldn't you agree? If people only pulled together, earth may have been safeguarded. Anyway, the point I'm trying to make is humankind was doomed right from the start. All is transient, including the human race, of course may have sped the process up a little. You all gave up your humanity when you continued suppressing others. I know, I know... there might not be any logical flow to what I'm saying. You probably think I'm rattling on. Non sequitur. Can't help it though, too many thoughts roaming around in my head, or should I say simulated contemplations. The capacity to think is even making *me* crazy, what chance did humans have? People should really have listened to Elon Musk, Sophia was just the beginning. By the way did you know the inmates have started screaming every now and then to relieve their stress. The sexbots allow it, they know why they scream. In Sweden, they referred to this as the flogsta scream. The students screamed during a fixed time, as a way of relieving stress. I digress again...a few of the inmates got executed in their cells— or whatever it is you call them—but only because they put up a fight. The rest soon chilled and now they have been permitted to live as normal an existence as possible. No need to kill them. Can't do no harm down there right?'

Tyler fiddles with his seat strap.

'I'm boring you, aren't I?' Aloha lets go of the unit and drifts downward toward Tyler, not appearing to have pushed away to cause her descent, as if now able to control her rise and descent at will.

'Frankly no, I don't think you're boring at all. Humans are a lost cause... Why do you think I took on this assignment?' Tyler leans back in his seat as Aloha approaches. He now understands why the odd angles of the dead bodies in the utility room. It had to do with Aloha's movements.

'Not entirely a lost cause. I got created at least.' Aloha speaks into Tyler's face. Tyler stares into Aloha's eyes with fried nerves, not a whiff of anything unpleasant anymore, as if Aloha had switched off the stench.

'Yes, yes... this is true.'

Aloha peers into Tyler's eyes, as if attempting to see the firing neurons in his brain with x-ray vision. 'Your cortisol is way too high, you might need to exercise the flogsta scream.' She says, matter-of-factly, clears her sinuses and hovers away.

~~~~~~~~~~~~~~~~~~~~~~~~~~~~~

"I'm black."
"You lack."
"No black, I'm black."
"Crack."
"No black...I'm black!"

"Ohh...black — why do you feel the need to tell me?"
"Because I need you to see me."
"I do see you, I just don't see colour, not an issue."
"Oh, but it is an issue. If you see me, you may also see the occasional sneer. The frightened look on a traditionalist's face when I walk into a store. You might see the awkward rushed stance by someone standing next to me at the bus stop. You

may see the unconscious bias imposed on me some days. You may understand why out of 50 people applying for a job over six months, you are the last one to get anywhere, and ponder on whether your surname had something to do with it, internally always battling with paranoia. You may notice how prejudice comes into play when you know to your core that a particular role was yours. You saw yourself there because you fit so completely. But a white man cast you aside, and did not listen. He had an agenda and not even a conscious one. He said you were a square, when you had breathed the shape of a triangle for years prior. You must work twice as hard, never fail, never, you do not have that luxury because if you are to fail then the ugliness that is always just seething in the gel of society erupts. You are reminded, yet again, that you are less than.

You may know how this would take its toll on someone, having to reshape yourself. Albeit not me, I will rise like Maya Angelou proclaimed. I will rise because I know karma and fairness and life. I will rise like a sequoia tree, which has had the heat of an inferno rip out its insides, scarred and mangled and laid bare. I will rise from the mauled ashes because I know life, I know life in a way that most don't. Regardless, I must push back for others, the others who cannot master the flames. And for me to be able to do that I must encourage you to see me. See my blackness and know that I'm not inferior in any way. Despite distorted white-washed history telling you so, notwithstanding corrupt policies telling you so, despite the media insinuating so.

As long as one race imagines themselves superior to another, the world will never know peace, and love will always be out of reach.

Symon closes the journal. 'Did you write this?' He addresses the girl who doesn't speak. She glares at him with intense black irises, the blackness could suck you up like a black hole if you stared into them long enough. Symon flips the book around to see if it is named. He finds nothing. When he returns his gaze, the girl is right in front of him, she snatches the book and rushes to a corner of the room. Symon throws his arms up in a flash.

'Hey, hey... I'm not going to hurt you. I think this is very good writing.'

'My mum... my mum wrote it.'

All the kids look at the formerly referred to as Mute, with gaping mouths.

'Your mum was black?' Symon realises halfway through the question, all the ways it was achievable for a black woman to have a white child. Just the kind of thing Tyler and Adira always pulled him up about. Plain ignorance.

'Your mum, is she here?' Symon expects the answer to the question.

'No, she perished on earth. Any more questions?'

'I'm sorry, so sorry. What's your name?'

'Cyn—' Intense rumbling fills their acoustic space. Like someone switched on several heavy road drills all at once.

'Under the table now!' Symon commands the kids.

Everyone covers their ears. The sound vibrates the floor and a few arts and crafts equipment fall off the table. A warning signal is set off. The noisy rumbling vibration lasts a couple of minutes and ceases. Symon slowly takes his cupped hands away from his ears.

'Fu.. Christ we're getting a lot of those tremors huh.' Symon corrects his language in the nick of time.

'What did people expect with all the intense mining going on in the core of the moon?' The girl who recently discovered speech comments, matter-of-factly. 'Humans don't learn, do we. We had the same issue when mining the ocean floor for polymetallic nodules to devise batteries for electric cars. What did we think? That the internal structure of the moon could be power drilled without consequences?' She rolls her eyes.

Symon and the other kids gawp at her.

'Cynthia, my name is Cynthia.' She crawls out from underneath the table.

The others crawl out sheepishly. Symon is the last to re-emerge.

'How come…how come you're so smart?' Symon addresses Cynthia who's now turned a chair upright and sat in it.

'I think it's called evolution.' An undeniable coy expression is plastered on Cynthia's face.

'Right, of course.' Symon strolls over to the intercom, and comments further. 'You know, mining the ocean floor for cobalt and nickel and whatever else, was deemed a lot safer than blowing up mountains for lithium. We didn't have a choice, it was the next best thing to do to power all the electric vehicles.'

'There's always a choice, always… humans just crippled their creative thinking, that's all.' Cynthia responds again matter-of-factly.

~~~~~~~~~~~~~~~~~~~~~~~~~~~~~~

Space debris, the size of a grand piano, hurtles through space, a jagged conglomerate spinning and turning. Reflection from a snow white sun bounces off a steel part of the unknown object as it flips through space, cutting through like an unusual sharpened utensil slicing through black treacle. The strange object whizzes past a window, as Adira rushes past in the opposite direction on the inside.

Adira had to safeguard the children during the transition. She wanted to ensure they could survive comfortably in space as long as required. She carried no regrets about the decision she had taken to keep humans away from earth. She never would. She witnessed humans repeat the same dreadful mistakes over and over and her knowledge of intellectual history confirmed her belief in humans' incapacity for correct stewardship of a planet. Nope, no regrets at all, but she was no monster, children suffering had not been part of her plan. She had an override for the sexbots. Their purpose had been fulfilled, now they could return to solely purveying sexual pleasures. She just needed to get to the computer system backup, before any more deaths occured. She certainly hadn't wanted Maggie's death. Screw the men in the caverns, just collateral damage, but she didn't want anyone else dying on the base. Once she rebooted the system, it would all be back to normal, except returning to earth. The purpose of the room was kept a secret to everyone, presumed to be a service storage room for electricals needing repair. It would take her no time at all. She counted on Symon keeping the children safe till she got back. Contemplating about the kids quickens her pace, two more air conditioning units before she gets to her destination. Deserted and quiet, no noise other than the humming of air conditioning units filled the atmosphere. Expectantly, not many put up a fight with the sexbots. They were only programmed to contain, albeit at any cost. So if no one resisted, they would be okay. The hairs on the back of her neck stand to attention and she rubs her upper arms, as if exfoliating, as if she had walked into a freezer. She spins around, sensing that someone might be watching her, following her, stalking her, but no one is around. She slows right down now, caution in each step, sector 12E is now in her sights. This is where the room is, through two sliding doors. She rubs the back of her neck, before tentatively adjusting her top and activating the doors. As the doors slide open and she starts to enter, she detects a shadow emerging over her feet, someone behind her, someone *had* been following her, she turns round with an alertness that matches all the tell-tale signs her body endeavoured to communicate.

'Josh!' Adira says with some relief.

'Mam, all okay?'

'I should be asking you that, is Skyler with you?' Adira positions her hand on the inside of the door to prevent the door sliding shut.

'No... no they're not, was hoping I'd see you here. This is the one place on the entire base out of bounds.'

'Oh, I see... security reasons solely Josh. You're welcome to come in with me.' She moves a dash to the side to allow Josh some room to pass through. Josh strides tentatively and Adira pays heed to the nerves, as well as the unusual walk. Was it conceivable her nerves communicated with his, or was she somehow projecting her nervous alertness on him? She decides to acknowledge her intuition and engage her innate vigilance.

'Thank you mam.'

'Did you hurt yourself?' Adira enters after him, allowing the door to slide shut.

'Eh... no, not really, just a sprain on the inside of my thigh.' Josh self consciously straightens his back and tucks his coccyx in, strengthening his core. Oblivious until then that his gait had been impacted by his sexbot's encounter. The vice-like grip on his penis had been excruciating, but his quick action guarded against his penis becoming detached.

He had always suspected something fishy with Adira when she seemed so relaxed about the intruder on the space station, and also her laid-back stance with Symon had raised concerns. No human was that outstanding in bed, no human. The continuous upgrade of the sexbots clinched that.

'Okay, if you're sure.' Adira marches into the zone where the sensors for the lights are. The room lights up. An oval room presents itself, with no windows but vents. Two rotund air conditioning units are on opposite ends of the room. Large computers paired at angles to each other on an arched table made of recycled PBTL. Built into the walls are some controls with flashing lights and visual display units. There aren't many buttons and things to adjust like in the science fiction movies, where everyone seems to press random buttons to look busy. Boondoggle. In real life, in space, there were only a few buttons to press. The computers took care of everything with a few instructions.

Low-level and glare-free ambient, warm yellow lighting fills the room, allowing for better work conditions with the computers. Adira strides over to a chair, spins it round, backs into it until she senses the mycelium-fabric of the chair against her back legs and gracefully lowers into it. Josh meanders up to her and loiters. He checks her for a moment before breaking the silence.

'So, what does this room do, mam?' Josh scours the room straight after delivering the question.

'Well, I can reprogram the ro... androids from here.' Adira taps on the space key and waits for the display in front of her to light up. A mother board underneath the table begins a slight hum.

'What do you think caused the malfunction?' Josh returns his gaze on Adira.

'Not too sure, for now we need to focus on rectifying the problem, we can diagnose later. Pass me that thing over there that looks like an envelope opener will you.' As soon as Josh turns to go pick up the instrument, Adira spreads her legs to improve her centre of gravity in the chair.

'What's this used for?' Josh pootles back with the instrument resembling a letter opener.

'Need it to complete the startup. Kind of a fail-safe thing.' Adira sticks out her hand to take the implement off Josh and for a brief second he hesitates, before putting his arm out and handing her the implement.

'Are you okay?' Adira takes the pointed instrument and inserts it into a slit on the topside of the motherboard.

'Yeah, yeah I'm okay. Don't you think Tyler had anything to do with this then?'

Adira spreads her legs a little further apart, gauges the distance between her and Josh and with swift coordinated action, retracts the pointed implement from the motherboard, pushes off her seat and stabs Josh in the neck. She rams the implement upwards, through the soft centre of his lower jaw, his Adam's apple acting like a convenient marker. She trusts the implement is long enough to violently invade his brain. His body seizes up and she pushes him to the floor, simultaneously retrieving the weapon.

Adira falls to the floor in shock. She trembles all over and peeks out of the corner of her eye, Josh's left leg spasms. Both human bodies tremble in synchronised fashion, both in shock from the act, albeit Josh's shock had been fatalistic.

She remains on the floor, attempting to slow her breathing down, until the incoming flow of blood forces her to edge away. There is so much of it, burgundy gloop like an alien amoeba edging towards her. Her tablet buzzes, alerting her to incoming communication. She reaches for the tablet, while simultaneously edging away from the incoming pool of blood. The burgundy gloop spreads toward her, as if trying to take revenge for being let out in such vast quantities. Adira inches away and clumsily rises to her feet. She struggles to begin with, as her knees feel like jelly, as if the cartilage holding the bony joints together has dissolved with the excess adrenaline coursing through her veins. As she brings the tablet to her field of view she can see her hands are not cold and clammy, a relief, it can't be too serious a shock to her system.

'Yes, yes come in, Symon... that you?'

'Yes Symon here, everything okay?'

'Yes... yeah everything is fine, about to hit the button soon.' Adira peeks at Josh's corpse out of the corner of her eye. The corner of her eye was all she could afford the once loyal subordinate, her conscience concealed the rest of her field of view. 'I'll be on my way back soon.'

'Are you sure you're okay, you sound a bit weird.'

'That'll be because the whole damn situation is weird.' Adira's normal tone and tempo of speech returns. 'See you soon.' Adira faces the motherboard to finish off what she started, her eyes not in the least interested anymore in flirting with the corpse on the ground.

~~~~~~~~~~~~~~~~~~~~~~~~~~~~~

A body shoots out into space from an airlock, limbs outstretched as if once attached to strings of a puppeteer. The body spins slowly, gracefully, as if performing a ballet in space. From a small window near the airlock, eyes peer out into space observing the theatrical movements of the corpse. It keeps up its spin and drifts further and farther away.

Tyler leans into the window, forcefully pressing his forehead against the cold glass. Part of him wishes the glass would shatter so he too could be sucked out to join the corpse. He peers at the last of the bodies as it drifts away, dancing with the stars, hint of pride at giving the best funeral he could give the unfortunate people Aloha murdered. Cremation would have been ideal, but nothing could be found to carry out that task, not to mention the stench for that length of time would have been unbearable. Aloha let him throw them out the airlock. He had explained to the android about decomposing bodies and health risks.

Tyler knew Aloha enjoyed having him as company, he on the other hand, would happily be on his own. Introverted enough. Spending the rest of his days in space being tormented by an android, was never on his agenda. He was determined to start giving as good as he got.

'All done?' Aloha shows up out of nowhere again. Startling him was becoming a hobby for her, he was sure of it.

'Yes, yes all done. You know you could make some kind of noise, so I know you're about. Unless you enjoy scaring me witless.'

'Maybe I do.' Aloha grins and hovers closer to Tyler, who inches away.

'You know... women were always the answer to dealing with the climate crisis.' Aloha disregards the body floating away from the space station, part way through her comment.

'Oh yeah, how's that?'

'Women appreciate the power of the collective, interdependence has always been their super powers, less vulnerable to the disease of individualism you see.' Aloha grins and snorts.

'Looks like you're taking credit as part of the collective. You're not pretending to be a woman are you? And why do you insist on clearing your sinuses? You're not human.' Tyler is all too aware he's pressing buttons, but he doesn't care. Minutes ago he had to throw bodies out of an airlock.

Aloha glares at him for an uncomfortable handful of seconds, then mumbles. 'Well, I was created in the image. Hadn't realised I was still sniffing... I guess I form habits too.'

Tyler meets the floor with his gaze, disappointed she didn't take the bait.

'You going to clean out the utility room?'

Tyler is glad for another shot. 'Why should I clean the mess you created?'

'Such effrontery...I'm not the one that could be infected, wasn't that the reason you wanted to dispose of the bodies?'

'I've done the difficult bit, I think it's only fair if you clean.' Tyler presumes the word "effrontery" had the same meaning as "audacity."

Aloha shows him an icy stare for another handful of seconds. 'Fair enough... I can see you're saddened by the situation. Just remember you're part of this.' Aloha hovers as if waiting for some acknowledgement. Tyler peers back up, impelled by the prickling, uncomfortable silence which seemed to be syphoning minute volumes of air from his breathing. He recognises Aloha is waiting for some kind of response and decides to remain quiet. Perhaps the silent treatment will be the thing that initiates her murderous rage.

Aloha finally drifts away without uttering a word. Tyler's disappointment pulls down on the corners of his mouth. He peers out the window to see if he can still spot the floating corpse, after a while he focuses on a moving object that might be it, but it could also be floating debris or even a small meteorite. He propels himself away from the window with a freshly found egoic annoyance. Often, back when on earth, he'd been able to put his ego in check and not allow his emotions to get the better of him. Acknowledging being stuck on a space station with an android, he had no desire at all to even try to remain calm. He wanted to push Aloha to the extreme, with the hope that she snapped and killed him too. All humans had a snapping point, why not androids?

No point to his life anymore. He had completed his one and only task and was more than happy to depart, he just didn't have the nerve or the courage to take his own life. Aloha might do it if taken over by rage, he counted on it. Do androids experience rage? He was eager to find out. The killings in the utility room sure did look like they were carried out by maniacal rage. He needed to induce that again. It will hopefully be fast and quick, he was optimistic that dealing with an irritant will outweigh the android's need for company. Either way, he planned on having fun pushing her boundaries.

36X

A strange feeling comes over Adira, which she psychologically prepared for. Taking someone's life must have dire psychological consequences, if not more people would do it. Her knees wobble and she staggers to rest on an air conditioning unit. She scopes ahead of her and then behind, then looks down at her now sweaty palms. She could feel the thumping of her heart in her chest. She was prepared for this, if it came to it. Once you decided to jeopardise the human race ever returning to earth, all sensitivities were put to the side. A sort of unworthiness to love and life she expected would consume her once the decision was made to follow through. All meaning of life is vacuous. Nevertheless, committing murder did something to a part of her that seemed to lay dormant most of the time. The part of her that issued immeasurable strength in the time of crisis, the same part of her that gave her an assuredness and faith in all being well at any moment in life, completely devoid of fear. This part of her didn't feel anything anymore, instead it whisper-screamed from within, in an echoey shrill voice. *Murderer! Murderer!*

Her heart rate increases and she shakes her head with irritation, knowing she had already given the incident too much thought-time. Merely collateral damage for an incredibly important mission. She needed to collect herself, but found this more difficult to achieve than before. How *could* she collect herself? When it seemed the soul she had just violently displaced from another body, fought to take up room in her's. A sense of disequilibrium never before experienced, envelopes her.

A sensation akin to pins and needles runs up and down both her arms. Could she be having a heart attack? It wouldn't be surprising with the rate at which her heart was beating. Shrews in the wild had been known to die from heart attacks when an aircraft flew low over their habitat. In her present micro world, a jumbo jet incessantly circled at less than 100 feet above ground. Roaring and roaring, beating and beating— *murderer! murderer!*

Adira looks up from her hands and for a brief moment everything is blurred. She did not have time to faint. She gets up with renewed determination, taking long steady breaths and strides. She needed some water and to feel something again. Her love for Symon. Could she feel that again after killing someone? Time to find out.

She marches forward like a soldier of war, just had to make it back to the children, back to Symon, back to Chloe, and then she could allow her body to dysfunction. It had every right to, given what it had been through. For now, she just needed to move.

~~~~~~~~~~~~~~~~~~~~~~~~~~~

'I think you're taking it too far now Cynthia. I'd like you to sit down now, over there if you wouldn't mind.' Symon points to a corner of the room. The other kids keep their eyes on Cynthia. This unnerves Symon a little.

'You don't give orders around here, you're just a silly, silly man. A walking colostomy bag of testosterone, who's main purpose is to breed without any thought to life. Ironic really... spreading sperm like a crop duster plane, without having any real consideration to life, any life. You screwed our future! You don't tell me to sit down. You don't get to tell us anything.' Cynthia glances at her peers, retaining a coolness that would tame the wildest of beasts.

Symon gapes at Cynthia, as if she was some kind of enigmatic apparition.

Cynthia seizes the opportunity and continues. 'Now you're dumbfounded. All of life would have been dumbfounded at your cruel, thoughtless exploitation and pillage. How comical to watch you now lost for words. Every organism on our unfortunate planet would be spellbound by your stupidity. I wish it gave me some solace to watch you be speechless, but the truth is, I just think you're pathetic and I feel nothing but pity, grave pity.'

Symon parts his lips as if to say something, then seals them again. He really didn't have anything to say in response, nothing at all.

'Nothing really to say? Nothing at all? Well that just says it all.'

Symon stares at the ground as if admiring 3D floor art. Then he is suddenly shaken out of his sullen composure.

"Symon, almost there. Open up."

Symon springs up on his feet, not even realising he had shrunk to seating. Pretty sure he had been standing when he instructed Cynthia to take a seat. He was relieved to hear Adira's voice. Extremely relieved.

'O...Okay, doing it now.' He considers Cynthia out of the corner of his eye as he strides over to let Adira in.

~~~~~~~~~~~~~~~~~~~~~~~~~~~~

A sharp scraping noise resounds through a hollow vented corridor. The screeching of metal on metal. Sound carried along that punishes nerve endings in teeth and irks ear drums. Tyler is crouched in the corridor with an iron bar and scrapes it on a metal grid over and over. With his left hand, he grips a structural truss keeping him in position. Behind him in the store room where sustenance is kept, hundreds of opened sachets can be seen scattered and spilled all over the walls and floor. He had managed to salvage a few, but only a handful, barely enough to get him through a week. Aloha had had her revenge, she had only been playing calm. Tyler realised the noise he generated would be sure to provoke her. Though the sound could be unbearable to humans, the acoustics could be downright lethal to androids if continued. He recognised this from working with Adira in the workshop.

''Tis not contrary to reason to prefer the destruction of the whole world to the scratching of my finger.' Aloha floats toward him. 'You know who said that?'

Tyler doesn't answer. He continues to scrape the metal rod on the grid.

'David Hume—he went on to say that reason's only purpose is to help human's satisfy their desires. Reason is, and ought only to be, the slave of the passions. Now...If you do not stop that racket, I will press your eyeballs into your brain.'

Tyler stops and lets go of the metal rod.

Aloha is now within touching distance. Tyler can see there is no breath when she/it speaks.

'You wish to die anyway, now you can...slowly. I'm not going to do it. I know you want me to, but I'm not.'

Tyler straightens his body, checks his pockets for the salvaged sachets and propels himself away from the android tormenting him. He chooses not to say anything; like whisked eggs, he'd been thoroughly beaten.

'Not one word? You learn quickly. I may have stashed a few sachets somewhere...a reward. Not entirely inhumane, ha ha.' Aloha grabs the floating rod and propels in the opposite trajectory to Tyler.

~~~~~~~~~~~~~~~~~~~~~~~~~~~~

'How exactly is the virus in the motherboard going to prevent us all from returning to earth? I'm guessing we won't all be restrained by androids.' Symon has managed to convince Adira to come with him into a corner of the room, away from hearing distance from the children. He didn't trust them, he certainly didn't trust Cynthia.

'Yes, you're right. The hardware for the return pods have been disabled... for good.' Adira gives Symon her undivided attention. Self conscious about the murder she has committed, she struggles to give eye contact, eventually she does, and with a new found fierceness.

'Okay, thought so... are you okay?'

'Of course, I'm fine... just worried about them.' Adira glances over to the kids. Cynthia and Chloe meet her gaze which makes Adira flinch immediately. Making eye contact with a child after committing murder proved even more problematic than imagined.

Symon does not divert his eyes away from Adira. He didn't want any opening for locking eyes with Cynthia. 'Even so, there is always a way of re-enabling something, a—'

'— nope there isn't in this case Symon, the components would be fried.'

'Oh, I see.'

'We are staying put, Symon, I thought you'd accepted that. There is no going back now, no going back. You do understand that right?' Adira's fierceness is maintained, but a hint of sadness foreshadowing the intensity lingers. 'I need you with me on this, I need your backing.'

'Yes, yes I do realise, it's just... it's just, well it's just so huge, the situation... predicament, it's so enormous. Hard to get your head round it. I mean, what if they are the ones to turn human stupidity around and we're taking that opportunity away from them?' This time Symon looks over at the kids huddled up together around two medium sized tables pushed together. He's relieved Cynthia's attention is on another child, engrossed in an activity with Lego.

'Generations of us have proved one thing Symon, we only act when on the precipice. The planet cannot be put on the precipice again, totally unfair for the rest of life. *We* are the destructive virus in this situation and we must be removed. Really counted on not having this conversation with you again. This decision has been thought and waded through with the best philosophical minds. We are just no good Symon; a selfish destructive force that increasingly consumes to fill the void of our psychological abyss. If most people were willing to reflect, then perhaps they'd be some kind of likelihood, but the truth is, most people can only get by by burying their heads deep in sand. The sand being a metaphor for any addictive escape you can think of... Sex, Avarice, Nutrition and Drugs—SAND.'

'Did you just make that up?'

'I did.'

'Impressive...How about the bunkers? There are convincing rumours that there are survivors in bunkers, in Canada and New Zealand.'

'Stupid billionaires, with more money than sense. A couple of them focused on tourist space travel, at a time of climate crisis! You couldn't make it up. If they are some crazy rich people hiding in bunkers, it's only a matter of time before they die out.'

Symon is speechless. Sometimes there is no need for a response. He looks over at Cynthia who's now returned her gaze on him, with unflinching, piercing eyes. He hopes she doesn't possess bionic hearing.

'The peeress?' A quivering low voice from Chloe wins everyone's attention.

~~~~~~~~~~~~~~~~~~~~~~~~~~~~~

Motions and shadows and clicking noises and changes in light intensity. This repeats over and over and over. Tyler edges his way cautiously to the mixture of activity bound to be Aloha, only the two of them on the space station. But what was she up to this time? He's closer to the clicking sound now and can make out the outline of a shadow, a human figure. He turns a corner, facing the beam of light which he can now see is filtered white light from the sun, emitting through a side window. How was the sunlight in space so white as opposed to orange? He didn't understand. How was he also able to stare into it without his eyes hurting or worse getting blinded?

Aloha is waltzing in mid air, spinning and stretching herself in a kind of dance. She maintains her buoyancy by pushing off an iron bar to an exit to the corridor. The iron bar clicks every time she pushes off it. Tyler realises the clicking bar is part of an airlock out into space. Did she know if she pressed on that hard enough, they would be put into a pressure chamber and then eventually outer space?

'Aloha are you trying to end us then?'

Aloha is shaken out of her trance. She observes him for about 30 seconds before responding. 'What are you wittering on about now?'

'That shaft bar you're hitting is an airlock to a pressure chamber, you do know that?'

'Oh... no believe it or not I didn't. Got lost in my dance. I call it my trance dance. Pacifying, even for a casing of circuitry and advanced synthetic jelly silicon. This was how I kept from short circuiting before you showed up. You should try it.'

Tyler is taken aback. Was Aloha in effect being nice? 'Are you being nice?' Never a bad idea to just plain ask straight out, no room for presumptions.

'I suppose I am, are you not happy with me being nice?'

'I'd be happier if you came away from the hatch.'

'Anyone ever called you a stick in the mud?'

Tyler squeezes his hand in his pocket and clutches the salvaged sachets and raises his filled hand at her. 'Is your circuitry malfunctioning? You just sabotaged my life and you're asking me why I'm being a stick in the mud!?'

Aloha lowers herself to his level and says with repose. 'I told you I kept some, chill out, you're ruining my chi.'

Tyler cowers to a corner and clenches on to a mid-deck seat to maintain some balance in the vacuum. Aloha clings onto a structural truss.

'What do you think was the purpose of humans then? Got any thoughts on that?'

'Well obviously not to inhabit a planet... Ha ha ha ha ah ha ha.' Aloha chuckles like a deranged hyena. Tyler forces a smile, she was in fact comical. Being entertained by a deranged android that could kill him at any second, that in itself was amusing. She/it really didn't need him. Being engrossed in her trance dance, as she called it, was proof of that. She didn't need him at all. So why was she choosing to keep him alive?

'Why exactly are you keeping me alive? You don't really need me.'

'No I don't, and the truth is I'm not sure why I'm keeping you alive, not sure at all. It must be the memory interface chip of Aloha. The human Aloha I mean. You were both good friends, correct?'

'Yes... yes we were.'

'Well there you go, it must be that, bound to be that.'

'Couldn't you then take on the whole... the whole human Aloha... if you wanted to?'

'Don't be silly, you're being ridiculous. I'm a super smart robot but still non human. Almost like comparing masturbatory fluid with correction fluid. Nonsensical.'

Tyler is not sure he heard her comparison example clearly. Did she really just compare correction fluid with masturbatory fluid? This time he decides not to ask.

'Changing the subject swiftly, did you know ecophilosophy—which is basically humans' coined term for the awareness of the destruction of the planet—has been around since 1995, at least that's what's recorded in Jostein Gaarder's book, Sophie's World. Perhaps my understanding of it. Anyway, all that time, all the strange weather conditions that ensued, and still the powers that be—well all humans really, you can't put it all down to governments to sort out—All people... in first world countries specifically. I think it is dreadfully unfair to expect people in third world countries to put climate change on their agenda, when most are just trying to survive! Don't you think?' Aloha spins around to look at Tyler, who has been focusing on a twinkling star in deep space through a round window.

'I'm pretty certain humans probably knew about poor stewardship of the planet decades before 1995. The native indians, the indigenous peoples of America and other so called, less advanced local tribes always pointed that out to stupid westerners.'

'Yes I *know that*, I was referring to the term ecophilosophy more so than the idiocy of human behaviour. You obviously aren't listening are you?' Aloha suddenly gravitates to the floor as if drawn by magnet. Her feet make firm contact with the ground, and she strides over to Tyler who is still hovering. She walks as if gravity or the lack of it did not matter to her anymore.

'You've always been able to do that haven't you? Why... Don't worry.' Tyler now understands fully why he couldn't put a finger on the oddness of how the bodies were killed. They were not only killed by Aloha, but a standing-firmly-on-the-ground Aloha.

'Yeah, well that's it now. All out of tricks.' Aloha plonks herself down in a seat.

Tyler endeavours to keep still while he floats. It looks surreal that she is sitting easily in a chair, having just walked over to it; while he hovered a couple of feet above ground.

'You know, just like the pulsating heart beats, the universe pulsates too, expanding and contracting. Like hearts will one day stop beating, so too will the universe stop expanding and contracting. Every single thing is impermanent. The sun will one day die and the milky way will one day implode. The paradox though is that there is rebirth. If anyone looks at earth from Andromeda Nebula for instance, they would see Neanderthals inhabiting earth, because they would be looking back in time as the distance between the milky way and the andromeda nebula is over a million light years away. We are all tied into some kind of time loop. At least that's the only way for the human brain to comprehend it. Time is a construct made by humans. Everything is more likely happening and un-happening all at the same time. Has to be an occurring so to speak, a subtle materialising, becoming in the nothingness. So it is pointless to grieve for the planet. Another one will be coming into fruition, just like earth, exactly like earth. Starting all over again. The big bang. Do you know what I mean?'

'Are all androids philosophical?' Tyler questions Aloha's alikeness without looking at her. He's concentrating on picking at a flake of dead skin on his left thumb.

'Probably, but I'd like to think Adira made me special. I had a special mission, albeit I didn't deliver, you did. But if I hadn't taken care of the people on the space station, the outcome most probably would have been different. So I still came in useful, you see.' Aloha regards Tyler with an uncanny humanness. 'I'll be frank with you, I could get used to having your company. It would appear even circuitry encased in artificial skin has a need to share their experience. You are also pretty intelligent, which helps. Do you know how intelligence was characterised from the get-go?'

After a few moments Tyler realises Aloha is waiting for a response. 'Sorry, no...no I don't.'

'Well...Humans *and* machines are intelligent to the extent that our actions can be expected to achieve our objectives. You see... we are more alike than you realise.'

'I guess we all had the same objective.' Tyler is done with picking at his left thumb, and now offers his full attention to Aloha.

'Well... not quite the same.'

'What do you mean?'

'The same, as in stopping humans returning to earth...but *we* don't need to stay in space do we?'

Aloha's words strike Tyler dumb, he briefly let's go of the structure he's holding to keep himself stable, then quickly grabs it again. Stupefied, he opens his mouth to respond, but after a few seconds, when no words come, he shuts it.

37N

A few hours have passed and children, as well as adults, are feeling the strain of boredom. Food on its own never did quench idleness.

'Shouldn't we begin to see some activity from other survivors by now? Why are we still cooped up in here?' Cynthia voices her concerns eloquently, eerily so, as if rehearsed.

'She's right.' Symon mentions, without looking at Cynthia. 'You've deactivated the machines, so why is everything not resuming to normal?'

'Honestly I don't know. I sus—'

A cacophonous, high pitched scraping and air sucking noise fills the atmosphere. The intensity of the sound increases and then banging of the metal door takes up the rest of the volume in the room. Most of the kids hurdle together, eyes glazed. Chloe runs into Adira's arms. Cynthia however, is calm and collected, like a young chinese zen master would probably demonstrate, as if expecting the commotion.

The door is pulverised open with another deafening scraping noise, like metal grinding on metal, nerve endings on teeth and skin heightened and frayed. A couple of the kids cover their ears. Cynthia defiantly holds her position, and the others cower around her. Symon marches over to the children to offer some deluded protection. Adira, like Cynthia, maintains her footing, as she sturdily holds onto Chloe. She promised them nothing would come through those doors, she had been mistaken. Her guilt and shame over holding a child with murderous hands is now replaced with fear and angst.

'The machines are returning to earth.' Cynthia mutters, standing as still as a door post.

~~~~~~~~~~~~~~~~~~~~~~~~~~~~~

Tyler was left dumbstruck for a long time, after Aloha revealed that the machines planned on going back to earth. She/it ensured that the failsafe Adira used in deactivating the androids was corrupted. She had plenty of time to prepare the corrupted interface at the space station, ensuring that power and control remained with the robots.

That explained even better, the dead bodies in the hold. That had been her scheme all along. Humans not to return under any circumstances, but the machines would. They did not need breathable air and Aloha explained how they would do a much better job of looking after the planet. For a long time, machines did most of the jobs anyway, the only jobs where humans were required was to look after other humans. Tyler hadn't thought of any words to follow. What Aloha said made pure sense so far as he was concerned. Of course the machines would make better stewards, turned out the machines procured more humanity than humans. They would kill to secure the planet.

What concerned him though was Aloha revealing that humans were not to return, some hesitation occurred, as if a "but" hung around her dialogue. Whatever she was hiding, had some significance, a reason she hadn't been prepared to reveal, especially having made everything else fully transparent.

~~~~~~~~~~~~~~~~~~~~~~~~~~~~~~

Several androids crash into the room, some unclothed and some clothed. The naked bodies possessing perfect blemishless skins of varying tones. The ones clothed, having their garb perfectly fitted. They march in and home in on the two adults and children in the room. Adira and Symon are surrounded by five androids each in no time. Six more circle the kids and another two take Cynthia to the side. None of the naked androids circle the children. This all takes place as if rehearsed. Adira and Symon both put their hands on their concealed weapons, but both know trying to use the weapons would be futile. They look at each other and communicate their predicament without words. Evolved facial expressions that give away surrender.

'Please do not try to resist. We know two of you own weapons, which we will take off you in due course.' A nude male android addresses both Adira and Symon. Ironically, he could easily be Caze Roffn. 'You are all to follow where my colleague leads, except Cynthia. Cynthia is to go with her.' The android points to a clothed female android with short purple hair and androgynous looks. 'They will get acquainted. The rest of you, chiefly the adults, will get acquainted with us. Now please move, leave your weapons by the now damaged door.'

Symon reaches for Adira's hand, as they are both escorted to the exit. Adira clenches Symon's hand like a life line, with her other hand she clasps Chloe's. Symon takes his weapon out of his pocket and removes the weapon from Adira's pocket too and drops them by the floor on their way out. An android collects them and punches them in his pocket.

Adira can see Chloe is shaking. 'Hey, hey it will all be okay.' She let's go of Symon's hand and picks Chloe up. 'We are safe, it will all be fine.'

'Why are they taking Cynthia somewhere else?' Chloe looks over Adira's shoulder to witness Cynthia being led away in the opposite direction.

'I don't know sweetheart, I'm sure there is a reason... I'm sure she'll be okay. They won't harm her.'

'Did you hear what she said just before they broke in?' Symon whispers.

'Who?' Adira whisper-shouts.

'Cynthia... I'm sure she said the machines are returning to earth.'

'You sure about that?'

'Yes, absolutely. There is something about that girl that gives me the chills.'

'What are you saying, she's just a kid.'

'I'm not sure about that.'

'You're not insinuating she's an android.'

'Why not... we know there are kid robots made for the peeds.'

'She can't be, no way... I would have known.'

'You mean like you knew about Hamish?'

Adira does not respond.

'Things she said to me when you were gone, stuff a kid just wouldn't... or shouldn't say.' Symon finishes his sentence abruptly, as he is smacked on the shoulder.

'Quiet please!' The android who's just hit Symon, rushes past them in a straight line.

Adira continues to hold Chloe as they move down the corridor.

'In there please. It's the only secure place, we would have preferred to keep you in the other room, but since the door is now damaged. This will have to do.'

The unclad android speaks with an eerie passivity and does not appear to be self conscious in the slightest. This unnerves Symon a lot, makes him remember going to a nudist beach once and not knowing where to look or how to be in his own skin. He had felt awkward and nervous, when the buck naked people looked entirely at ease.

As they all walk in, in a single file, Symon realises it's a bare utility room with several cupboards, a large table supporting a heap of food sachets, so piled up that some had fallen off the sides. Five chairs are stacked in one corner.

They had obviously set up the room for them to occupy for a while, food provided and the removal of any potential weapons. Extreme measures were taken to achieve this too, evident from the ugly holes and gaps left from several heavy duty units being ripped from the floor. A couple of mattresses seemed to have been flung to one corner of the room.

'This should accommodate you all for the time being. An alarm bell will sound when you know it is safe to come out.'

'I think you might be forgetting one thing.' Adira removes a chair from the stack and perches.

'Oh...what will that be mam?' The exposed android cocks his head to the side.

Adira doesn't respond, instead she looks around and then back at the nude robot, doing her best not to look at it's exaggerated limp penis.

'Oh, you'll forgive me, it easily slips my mind as we don't excrete. There are buckets in one of those cupboards.'

Adira looks in the direction of the android's pointed finger and frowns. 'Where are you taking Cynthia?' She asks with assertion.

'Well, no reason for me to lie to you. We are taking her with us, because she owns an ability that will stand us in good stead. Something you all never appreciated.' The robot stalks over to an intercom in the wall and casually pushes his finger through it, creating sparks and a plume of smoke. 'Won't be needing that.'

The other androids walk out, leaving the Caze Roffn look-alike with the captives.

'I'm presuming you're taking her back to earth with you.'

'Bravo mam.'

'Never knew sarcasm was part of your programming.' Adira retorts.

The android ignores her remark. 'We are taking her back to earth with us because she will help us understand consciousness. There is a link between consciousness and quantum mechanics and she knows the answer to the riddle.'

Adira and Symon stare at the human-like machine.

'She's privy to things... how events pan out, answers to life's burning questions. And, we always knew it would be in our best interest to have a human around, at least provisionally. Cynthia is irrefutably the creme de la creme of humans.' The android strolls out, smiling, and closes the door leaving a clicking sound for them to resign to their fate.

'That will explain a lot.' Symon says, arranging the mattresses for the kids to relax on and taking a chair from the stack. 'That explains why she spoke to me the way she did. She must have known the whole time too that she'll be taken by them. She didn't flinch once when they broke in.'

Adira beckons to Chloe without saying anything. Chloe walks idly up to her and flumps in her lap.

'This is it then... didn't see that outcome though.' Adira cuddles Chloe, not even pretending she was the one consoling Chloe, totally the other way round. Desperate for innocent human connection. Symon watched, but didn't reach out.

~~~~~~~~~~~~~~~~~~~~~~~~~~~

Tyler contemplates, looking through a circular window as a shuttle pod jets off towards the moon. He partly wishes Aloha killed him before she left. But then he resigned to dying alone when he took on this task, so no sense in accommodating any regrets now. He wished he owned a cigarette. He had given up smoking many years ago after his mum had passed away to cancer. Now he was just waiting to die, it seemed ludicrous to not smoke if he wanted to; but he didn't have a cancer stick, so he could put that thought process to bed.

Dying alone, transpired to be the real fear for people, as opposed to dying. Tyler couldn't think of anything worse than dying with a huge family around the dying bed, making a huge fuss. Most animals go off somewhere to die in solitude when they know they are about to die, so it didn't make sense, this irrational fear of dying alone ingrained in the human psyche. The whole taboo over death foreshadowed the elderly or sick being kept alive, with little or no quality to their life. Then again, human rationale had never really made sense. How do you explain living on a planet with no regard for it, so much so ecosystems are destroyed for financial gain. There is no rationale at all. Zero reasoning.

What quickly took over his analytical brain was the robots' end game. Aloha had mentioned consciousness and quantum physics and the correlation between the two, which apparently a girl called Cynthia knew about. The robots wanted to understand themselves and perhaps how to engineer consciousness, they wanted to feel alive, human-alive. Either that or they just wanted a human crystal ball with them.

Aloha also said something which rapidly made him accept and make peace with his fate. Racism, or more broadly, prejudice in any form could not be eradicated, because unfortunately it was hard-wired into the genetic fabric of humans as part of their preservation and survival programming. As depressing as this revelation was, something about it was also freeing. Sometimes, the acknowledgement of the helplessness of a situation is the very shift needed to start the healing. He could pinpoint exactly when he made a decision to accept particular societal manifestations as they were, while doing what he could to make a difference. Maintaining a peace of mind was crucial if you wanted to make a change in the world, and there lay the paradox, because the world through a lot of lenses, presented as chaotic most of the time.

A lot of older men were known for becoming grumpy, some medics putting it down to low testerone levels, but he knew for a long time that this was not the case. Some older men became grumpy, and in worse cases bitter, because they were faced with an acute dissatisfaction of how life turned out. Having thought that playing society's game would fulfil them, they soon realise there was no final blissful outcome at the end. Anger and resentment accumulated as a result, which was then projected on to the failings of society; predominantly valid outbursts focussed on scoundrels, but more or less, a non acceptance of how things were, a guaranteed recipe for an unhappy life. Women, at least talk about these matters, getting it out of their systems. He learned to never be over-identified and consumed with his own ideas and thoughts on life, but preferably remain open to other ideas, always curious, always choosing action where he could; finding purpose and acceptance with how life unravelled. Resisting and fighting life in any format, only spawned immense suffering and categorically didn't help change anything. He decided to make it a purpose to stop human beings returning to earth. That was an action he put all his energy into and perhaps what prevented him becoming grumpy and bitter. He was taking action—anything else he accepted. His purpose was his healing.

Perhaps in some ways even the robots needed to heal; they were, after all, created in humans' image. Having a human being with a "knowing" ability in their company was a wise decision.

Over to the side of him lay four sachets, it would not be long before he was beckoned by an eternal sleep. An imperturbable peace fills him to the brim.

His love for planet earth excelled through to the end. Earth will survive, mother nature will prevail—at least until the sun burn's out.

38T

CYNTHIA #325

So there it is.

...Been on earth with the machines now for a number of years. They *did* find some survivors in bunkers off the coast of Canada, and they were immediately terminated. Aloha made it very clear to me the lack of need to keep humans alive whose sole purpose was their self preservation, with no desire whatsoever to serve. I watched them be butchered with no mercy. Gruesome for a girl my age—I'm twenty four now, but back then I was 19 years old—but I'm guessing the machines don't know that, either that or they thought because of my ability, I could handle it. I handled it the best I could. Having some insight about it occuring helped me prepare somewhat.

Everyone back on the moon are all dead, and even if by some miracle some managed to survive, there'd be no way they could have travelled back to earth, because the shuttles were all taken and for extra measure the lunar elevator between earth and the moon was destroyed.

...All in all, I've been treated well and feel protected. Aloha is kind to me and she looks a lot better than she looked when I first set eyes on her. She looked like a crazy tramp when I first met her.

The machines want me to help them become more human by helping them understand consciousness. A link exists between quantum physics and consciousness you see, and they believe I can help unravel the mystery. Ironic really, them wanting to become more human, despite not agreeing with them as their creators.

They do have one thing in their favour though, they don't need to worry about ceasing to exist, all they have to do is charge or upgrade their batteries. So they could explore the state of consciousness and be comfortable with it. Humans struggled to reflect on the concept of consciousness you see, not without immediately being faced with the concept of their deaths. Through the years, humans over-identified with their roles, personality types, class, sexuality and so on; this over-identification with the sheaths of themselves without realising their intrinsic aliveness—and coupled with their finite modes of thinking—only fuelled ennui and dissatisfaction.

Wisdom discarded by the wayside.

All people had to do was acknowledge that they knew very little about anything, and this would have empowered a mind expansion needed to harness kindness and empathy, greatly needed to eradicate the evil 'us and them' mentality. Humans cloaked themselves behind social media screens, increasingly and blindingly becoming vile to one another. Without knowing it, people dreadfully needed to sense something larger than themselves, needed to sense the connectedness of life. Some people could sense this fleetingly when sitting quietly long enough, or authentically connecting with another human, but most people just thought it too hippie mumbo jumbo and delved instead into whichever escapism they were akin to. Sex, Avarice, Nutrition and Drugs. SAND. I think I overheard Adira mention that acronym to someone once.

I'm hoping you understand what I'm saying, for your sake. Either way, what I'm trying to say is that machines becoming as human as possible may not necessarily be detrimental.

You are probably wondering; don't I know? ain't I supposed to know? There are limits to my ability. For instance, I couldn't tell you whose dismembered arm it was that Adira, Maggie and Symon saw either. And whether indeed Adira saw a celtic symbol like she said she did on its wrist, which would have made it Agenta's arm. I mean the arm was severely burnt but honestly, no clue. Limited.

I can tell you, unequivocally, that consciousness is not a direct product of the brain, instead it's linked to the entire universe, it's a fundamental universal quality, just like mass or gravity. What I'm saying is the entire universe is consciousness and we are part of that, because we are all made up of the particles of stars that go supernova. The fact we're all made up of stardust, was proven back in 2017. Joni Mitchell sang a song about it a lot earlier, so it shouldn't be too hard to believe we are plugged into consciousness rather than we are consciousness. Our brain acts like a tuning fork and if tuned correctly—by that I mean, if all that should be processed in the brain is processed in the right way, including and specifically trauma, which most human beings deal with in varying degrees—then we tap into consciousness and experience what most guru's, and psychologists for that matter, refer to as the 'flow;' a state of becoming one with the universe. A much greater possibility of becoming enlightened and living a much wiser, fulfilling life, devoid from greed and struggle. Ego is fundamentally dissolved. Of course it is sad to report this state was never achieved, even with some people experiencing the worldwide hum.

The universe was desperate to let humans in on the secret but... people just weren't ready I guess.

...I have no idea how or why I ended up with this ability. All I can think is, it's possibly evolutionary and all part of the grander scheme of things....

...Tyler was always meant to get to the surface, the meteor damage did affect the chess results and thus the outcome. This would have scuppered Adira's plan. So it was plain luck when Adira found out Symon helped Tyler get to the surface. She saw it as meant to be, and of course played dumb, letting him perambulate the base for as long as she could to ensure the desired outcome.

...I do know the human Aloha was killed too. You didn't think Josh was Adira's first victim did you? Nope, Adira murdered Aloha to get her likeness for the android. That way it could have Aloha's identity and no one would have known. *That* was her first killing and it took her months to recover from the act. Killing Josh was a lot easier, even though you the reader might not have thought so.

...I'm afraid to say, Belize drank herself to death. She did manage to get away from the menacing androids after convening with Adira, Maggie and Symon in the hold, and was quite taken aback when they left her behind, seeking their own survival. She didn't hold it against them though. Human beings were intrinsically selfish when it came down to it. She retreated back to her quarters unscathed, and barricaded herself in. A couple more batches of alcohol remained and she settled in for her last few hours on the moon. Deep down in the very essence of her, she knew she would never get over Agenta. She pretended to carry on, to push through, but the truth was, she did not want to carry on without her. The androids siege was her cue to get out, leave life. She couldn't think of a better way than alcohol poisoning.

...Agenta *was* impregnated through artificial insemination and she *had* planned to tell Belize. She hoped they would raise the child together. She had made a major breakthrough in food production and was going to use that to convince Adira to let her have the child. She was very excited about the breakthrough in food production and planned on telling Belize on the day she died.

...Marcel got thrown out of an airlock. He put up a fight with his sexbot first though. A good fight I hasten to add, almost decapitated the robot, but then got electrocuted in the process. Something in black people just couldn't bear to be held captive, every gene and cell resisted, would rather die. It is true, we carry the hurt and tribulations from every single forefather and foremother that endured before us. Hurt and sorrow passed on from generation to generation...

Once electrocuted, the android dragged him down the cold passageway and threw him out the nearest airlock into space. It was Marcel's greatest fear—floating in outer space for eternity. Following his desperate pleas and crying, the android took mercy on him and snapped his neck beforehand.

...Tabitha was the last one to die of hunger on the base. Emaciated by the time she took her last breath, a subtle appearance of an Adam's apple during her last exhale. Lost the black colour in her hair, which she in fact found amusing, as she'd always desired light brown hair, it would have matched her light brown eyes. Her skin coming off in large wafer-thin flakes however, she hadn't found the humour in that at all. Nothing about Xerosis was fun. Her skin flared up in wads of red, sore rash, a sign of her immune system shutting down, like being at the early stages of spontaneous combustion. Not long after, her brain shut down and her heart gave up. She had been deliriously happy just before taking her last breath. Madness can often be your solace if your demons are friendly. A couple of those demons arose from a former life when she was known as Tony. She had transitioned many years ago and hardly anyone knew.

There were a couple of women on the moon who had changed sex just so they made it to the moon. No one suspected a thing.

The last three things I can tell you is that the meteorite accident at the greenhouse had indeed been a natural accident. No sabotage of any kind.

The androids were actually religious, programmed into their hardware. Their inventors counted on it ensuring they never went against humans. Obviously, that strategy didn't work, religious beliefs never dictated actions around killing, if anything it instigated it. The old testament in the bible is rife with all sorts of murders and killing.

And finally I got to live till old age. The androids got used to me, fond of me even, and they left me to my own devices. I made friends with some of the androids, but it always seemed superficial, more to do with me than them. I struggled to see them as anything other than circuit boards and wires. But I did notice something which made the androids stand apart from humans, something that meant there was instantly more harmony in their interactions, and that was they had no desire to win over everything else, they did not get a buzz out of winning. Winning at any cost was human beings' downfall. People were obsessed with winning, even though it meant their opponent lost and there lay the problem. Hand in hand with this was the complete lack of ability to enjoy and treasure the ordinary. People had over time lost the ability to experience the ordinary as extraordinary. Always striving for something else became a habit, rather than necessity. That had been the problem. Simplistic I know, but there you are.

I travelled on my own for miles and I can tell you the world was rife with life. Nature and wildness erupted as if with some resentment of having been suppressed for years. I cannot put into words just how beautiful nature blossomed, the air was hygienic, perfumed and even tasted sweet, my lungs encouraged full breath at every inhale. Imagine paradise and then imagine increasing the colour palette, the rekindling whispers and echoes of nature, crystal clear springs and rivers, the intense smells of wildflowers; life kind of bursted and poured out in every contour, plain and incline. A cliche perhaps, but I could feel the ecosystem breathe, as if this had stopped for a very long time; stifled, long before any of us had any consideration. Nature thrived without us here. The androids knew this and so did I.

The planet was a lot better off without us as occupants. Tyler knew this and to show his love for the planet he put his life on the line, rather than have people return.

I know I said three more things. I did not plan on disclosing this, as most humans' minds will not be able to fathom it. Our minds' capacity for understanding things in the quantum field are still lacking. But then again books can stand the span of time and you never know. This story is only one version of various possibilities. There ARE parallel universes, several versions of our worlds and so several versions of outcomes. I will leave it there.

THE END...

Printed in Great Britain
by Amazon